Cagaster

Kachou Hashimoto

Book 3

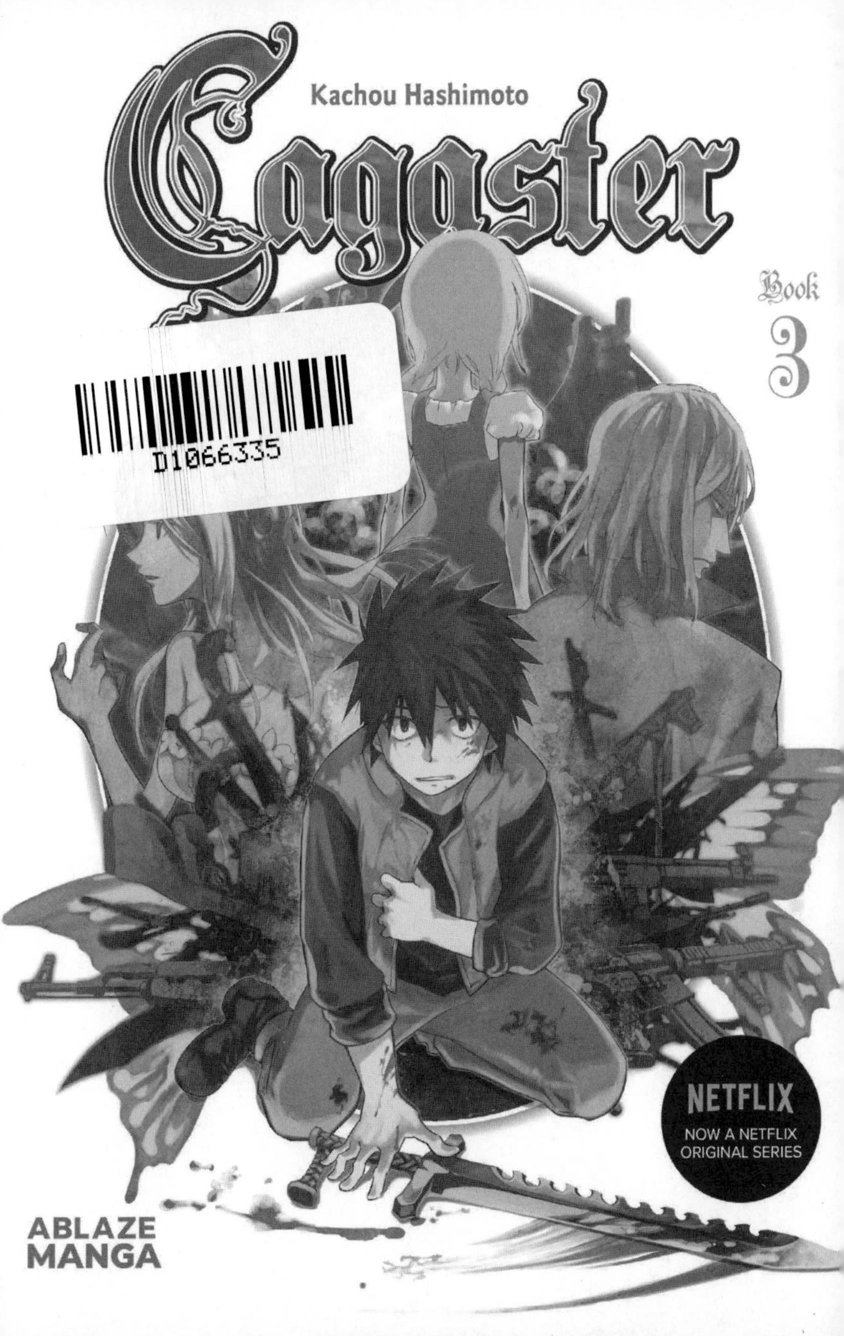

NETFLIX

NOW A NETFLIX ORIGINAL SERIES

ABLAZE MANGA

[CHAPTER 11]

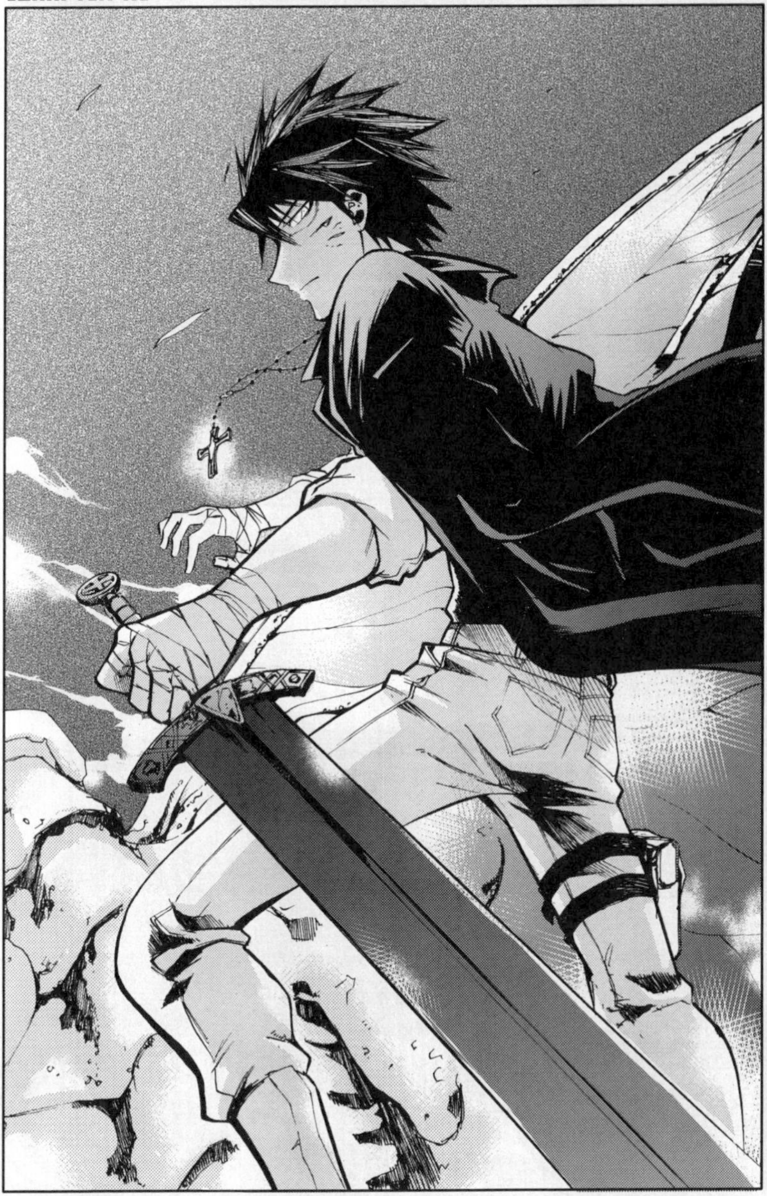

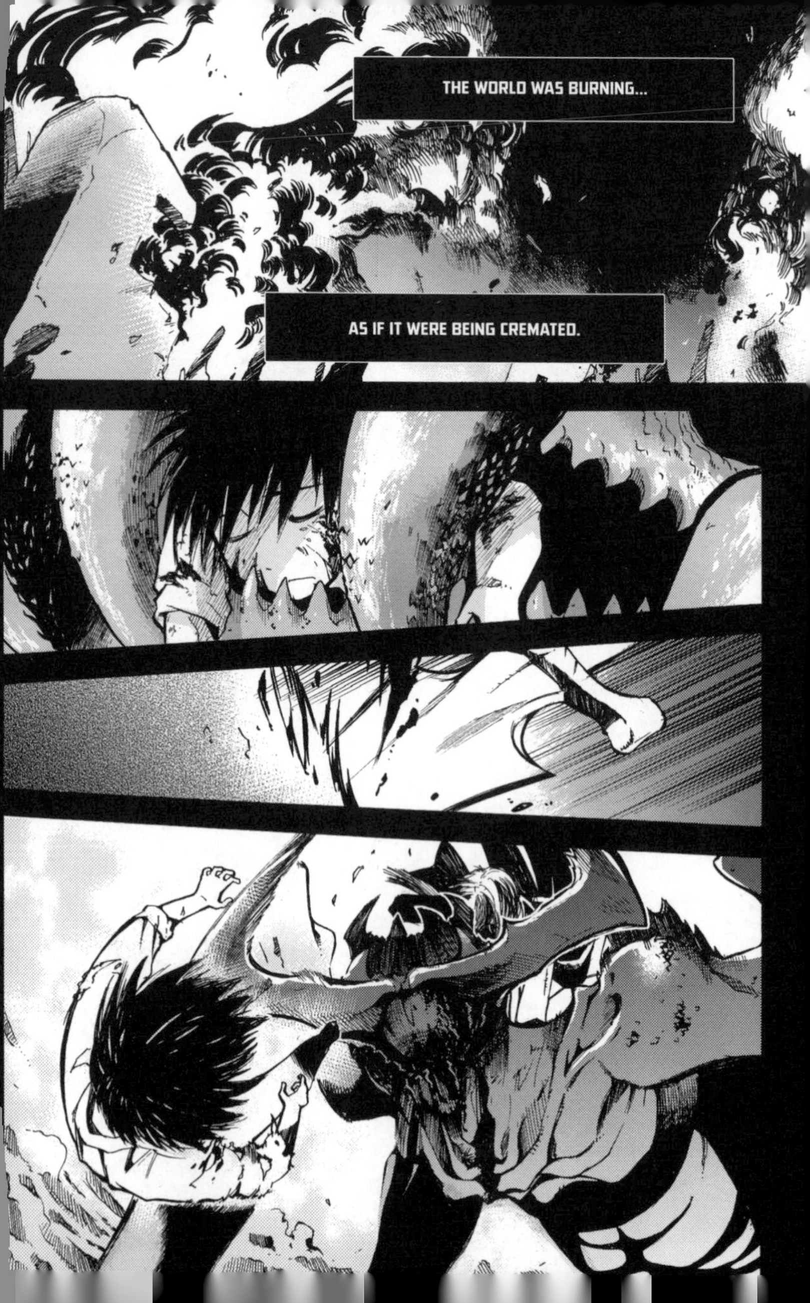
THE WORLD WAS BURNING...
AS IF IT WERE BEING CREMATED.

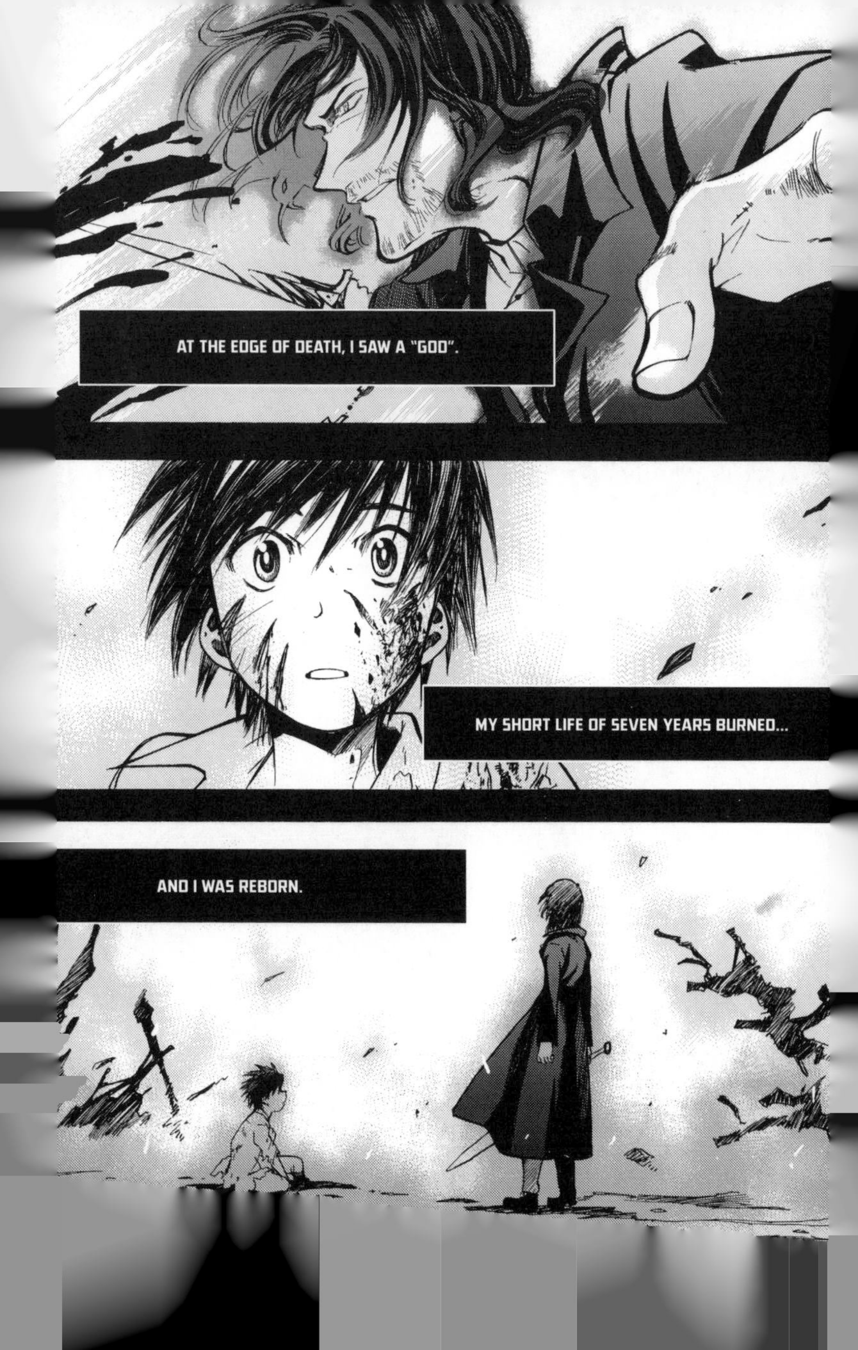
AT THE EDGE OF DEATH, I SAW A "GOD".
MY SHORT LIFE OF SEVEN YEARS BURNED...
AND I WAS REBORN.

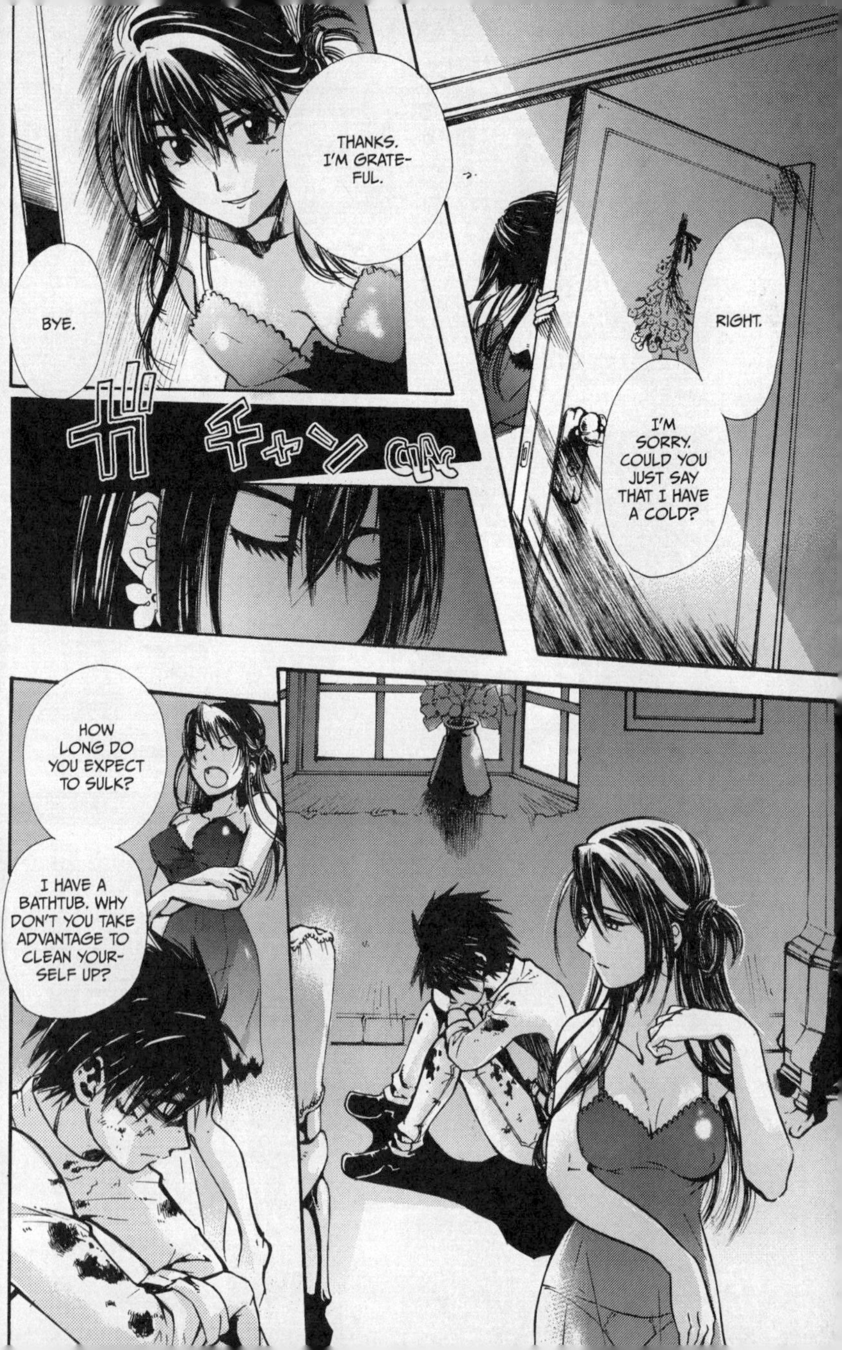
RIGHT.
I'M SORRY. COULD YOU JUST SAY THAT I HAVE A COLD?
THANKS. I'M GRATE-FUL.
BYE.
ガチャン CLAC
HOW LONG DO YOU EXPECT TO SULK?
I HAVE A BATHTUB. WHY DON'T YOU TAKE ADVANTAGE TO CLEAN YOUR-SELF UP?

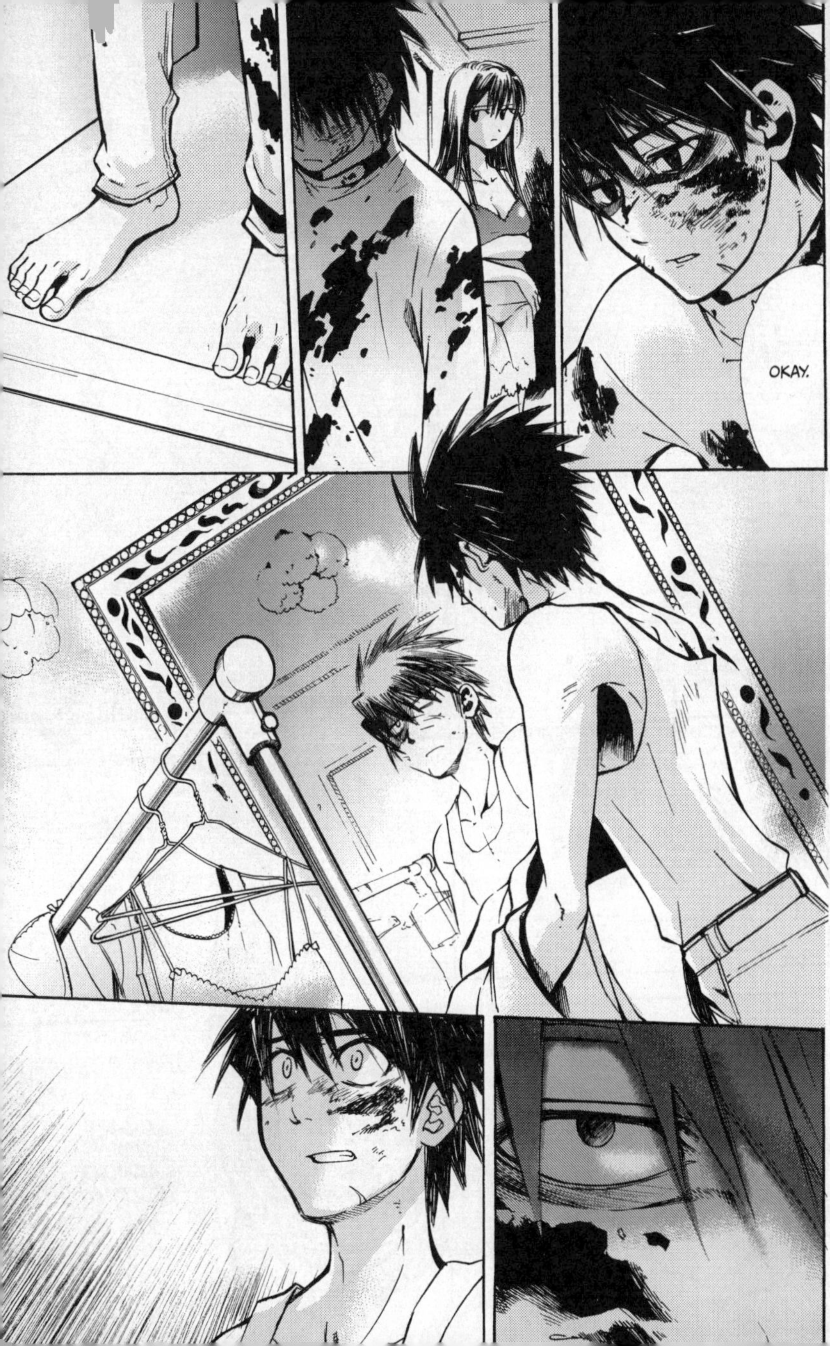
OKAY.

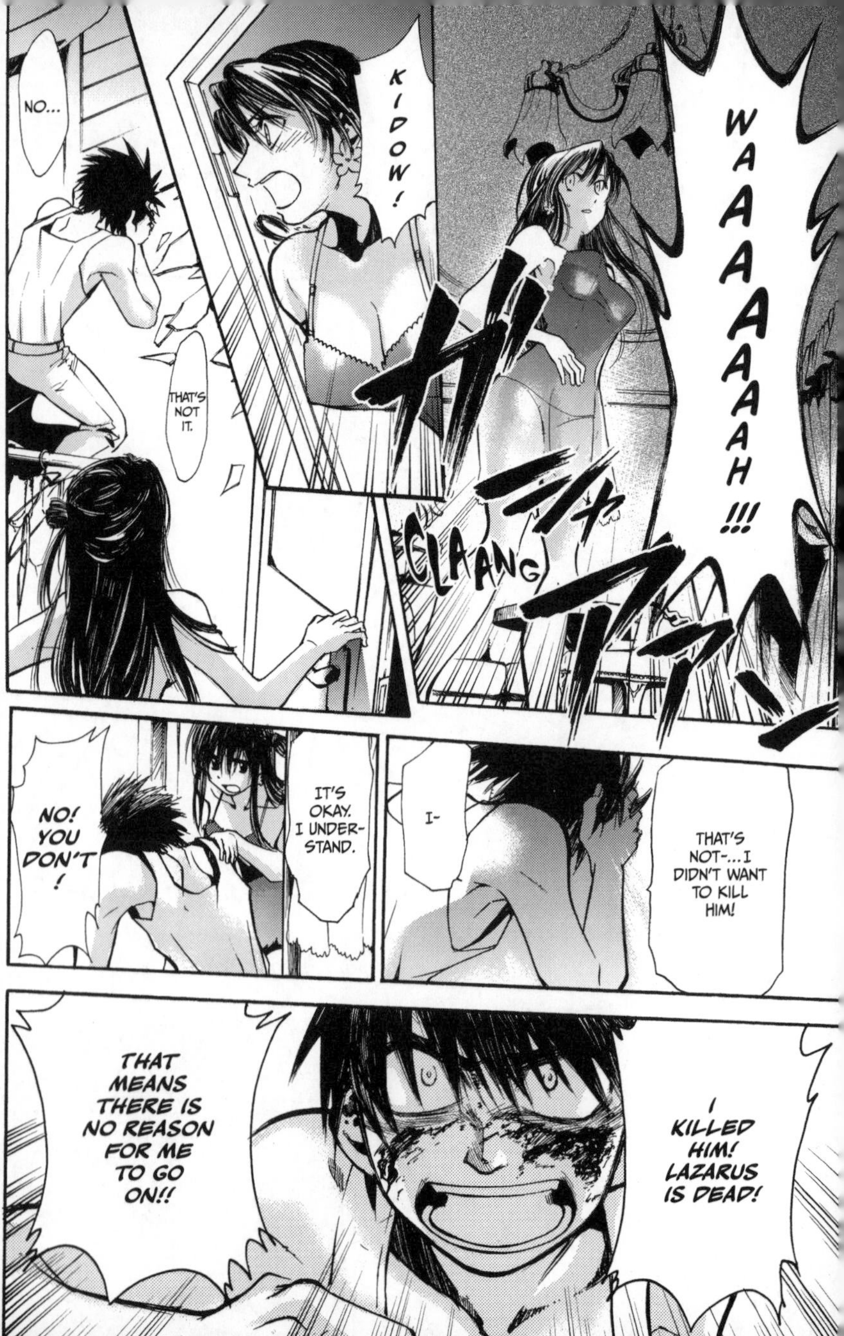
WAAAAAAAH!!!
CLAANG
KIDOW!
NO...
THAT'S NOT IT.
THAT'S NOT-... I DIDN'T WANT TO KILL HIM!
I-
IT'S OKAY. I UNDERSTAND.
NO! YOU DON'T!
I KILLED HIM! LAZARUS IS DEAD!
THAT MEANS THERE IS NO REASON FOR ME TO GO ON!!

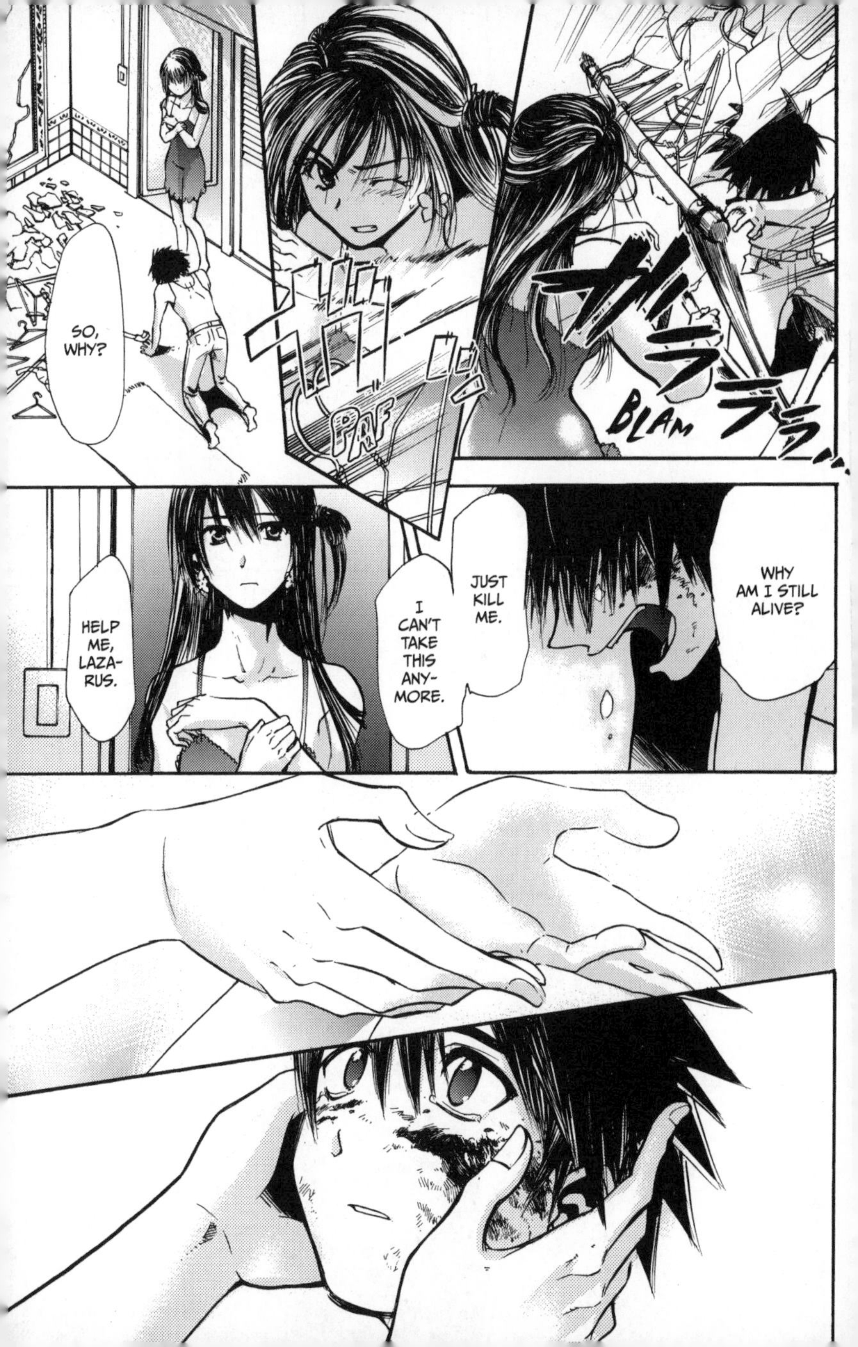
BLAM
PAF
SO, WHY?
WHY AM I STILL ALIVE?
JUST KILL ME.
I CAN'T TAKE THIS ANYMORE.
HELP ME, LAZARUS.

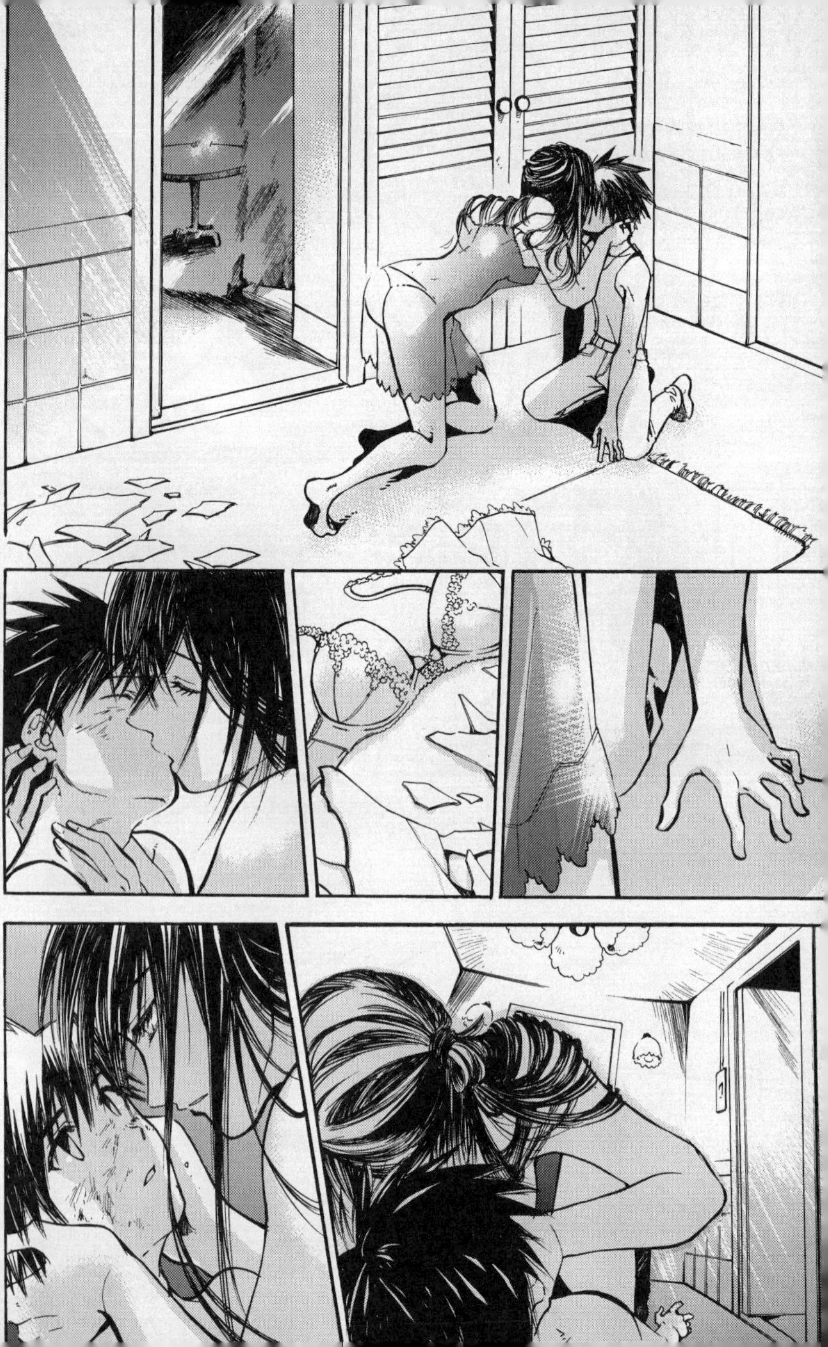

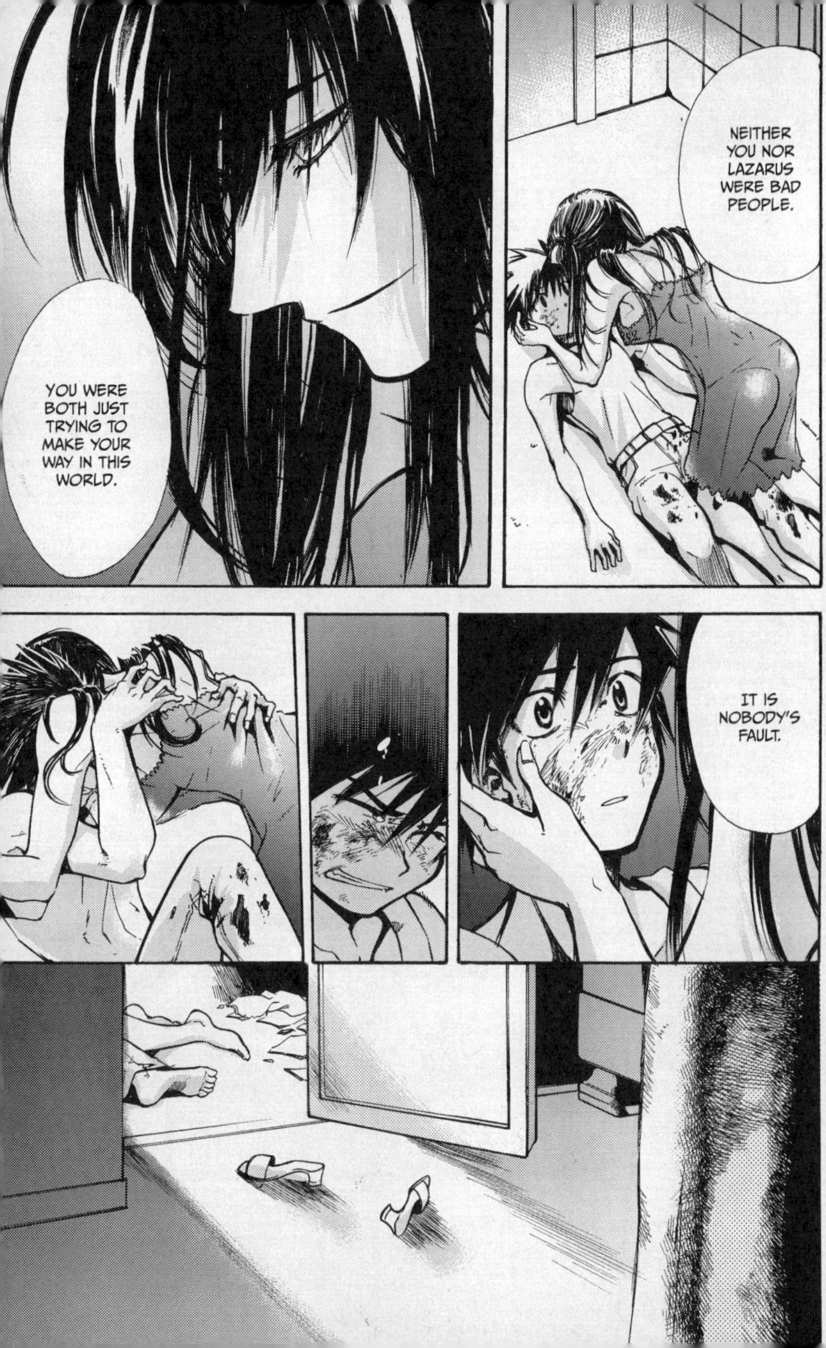
NEITHER YOU NOR LAZARUS WERE BAD PEOPLE.
YOU WERE BOTH JUST TRYING TO MAKE YOUR WAY IN THIS WORLD.
IT IS NOBODY'S FAULT.

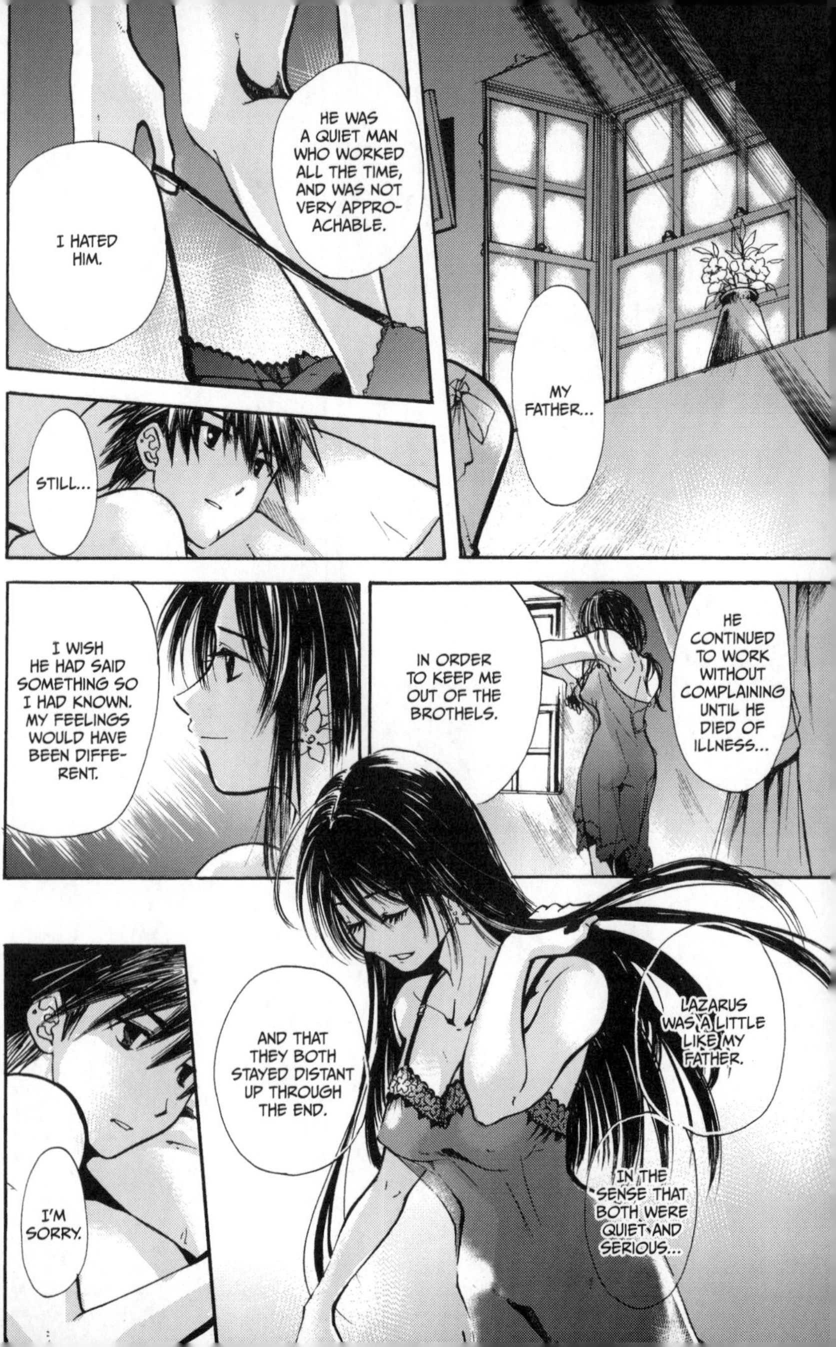
MY FATHER...
HE WAS A QUIET MAN WHO WORKED ALL THE TIME, AND WAS NOT VERY APPRO-ACHABLE.
I HATED HIM.
STILL...
HE CONTINUED TO WORK WITHOUT COMPLAINING UNTIL HE DIED OF ILLNESS...
IN ORDER TO KEEP ME OUT OF THE BROTHELS.
I WISH HE HAD SAID SOMETHING SO I HAD KNOWN. MY FEELINGS WOULD HAVE BEEN DIFFE-RENT.
LAZARUS WAS A LITTLE LIKE MY FATHER.
IN THE SENSE THAT BOTH WERE QUIET AND SERIOUS...
AND THAT THEY BOTH STAYED DISTANT UP THROUGH THE END.
I'M SORRY.

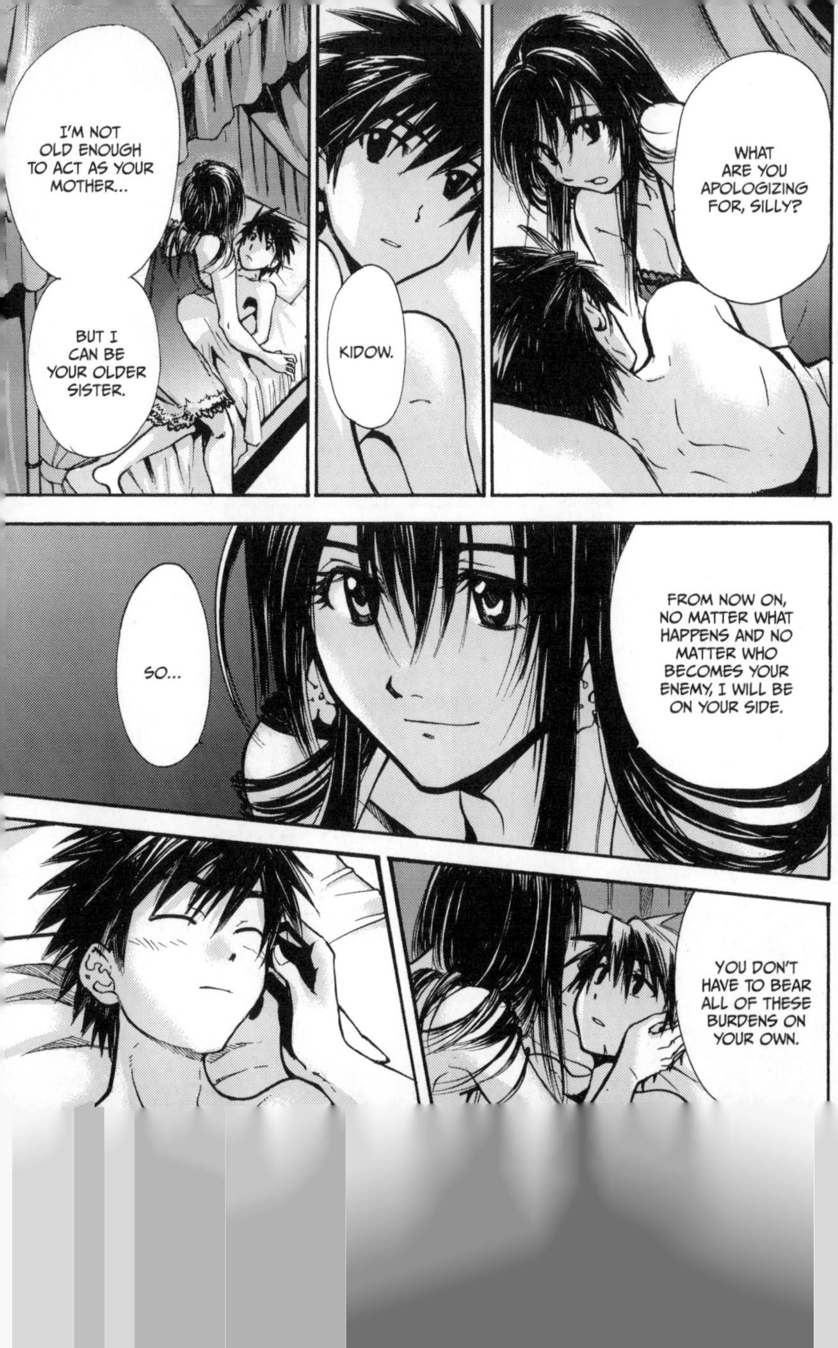
WHAT ARE YOU APOLOGIZING FOR, SILLY?
KIDOW.
I'M NOT OLD ENOUGH TO ACT AS YOUR MOTHER...
BUT I CAN BE YOUR OLDER SISTER.
FROM NOW ON, NO MATTER WHAT HAPPENS AND NO MATTER WHO BECOMES YOUR ENEMY, I WILL BE ON YOUR SIDE.
SO...
YOU DON'T HAVE TO BEAR ALL OF THESE BURDENS ON YOUR OWN.

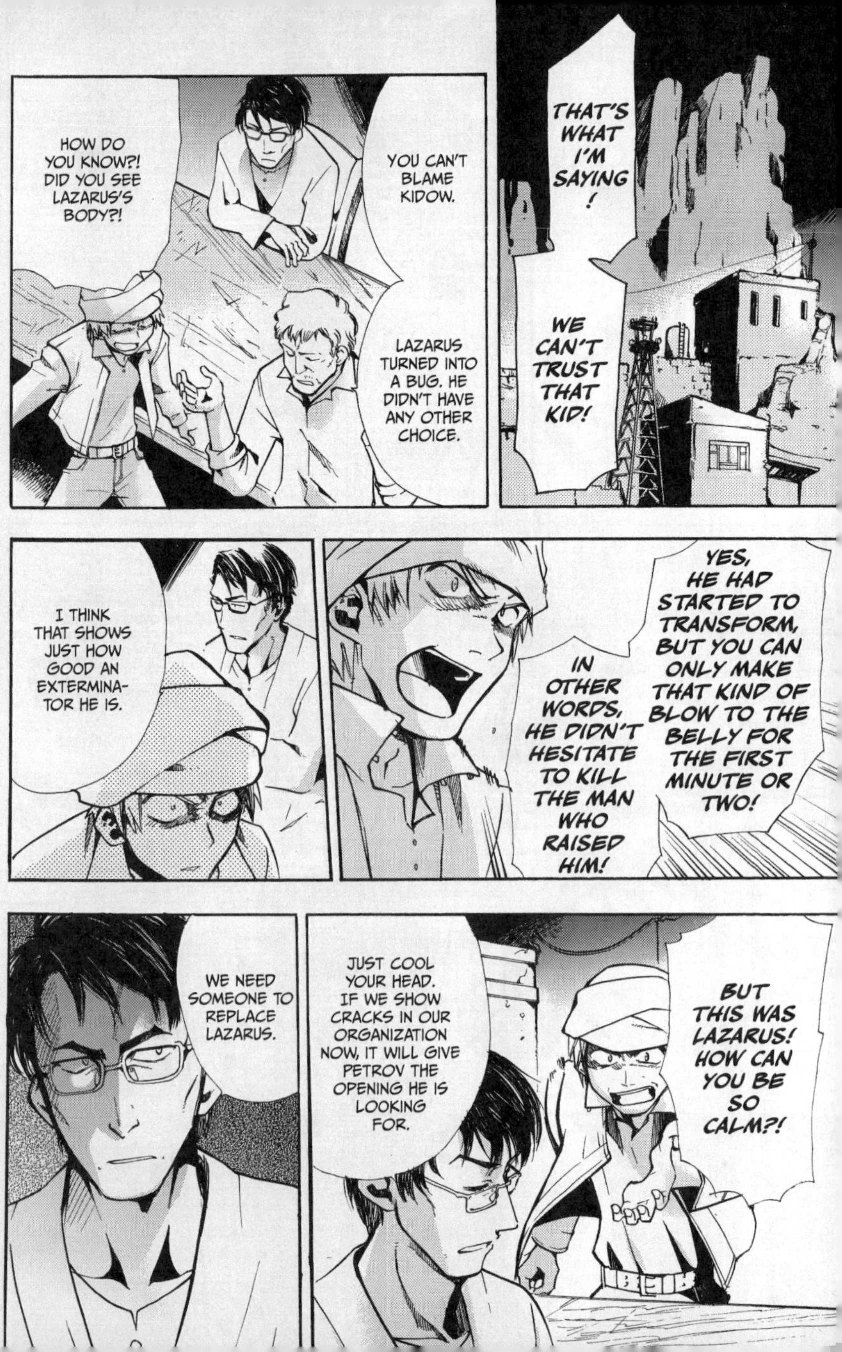
THAT'S WHAT I'M SAYING!
WE CAN'T TRUST THAT KID!
YOU CAN'T BLAME KIDOW.
LAZARUS TURNED INTO A BUG. HE DIDN'T HAVE ANY OTHER CHOICE.
HOW DO YOU KNOW?! DID YOU SEE LAZARUS'S BODY?!
YES, HE HAD STARTED TO TRANSFORM, BUT YOU CAN ONLY MAKE THAT KIND OF BLOW TO THE BELLY FOR THE FIRST MINUTE OR TWO!
IN OTHER WORDS, HE DIDN'T HESITATE TO KILL THE MAN WHO RAISED HIM!
I THINK THAT SHOWS JUST HOW GOOD AN EXTERMINATOR HE IS.
BUT THIS WAS LAZARUS! HOW CAN YOU BE SO CALM?!
JUST COOL YOUR HEAD. IF WE SHOW CRACKS IN OUR ORGANIZATION NOW, IT WILL GIVE PETROV THE OPENING HE IS LOOKING FOR.
WE NEED SOMEONE TO REPLACE LAZARUS.

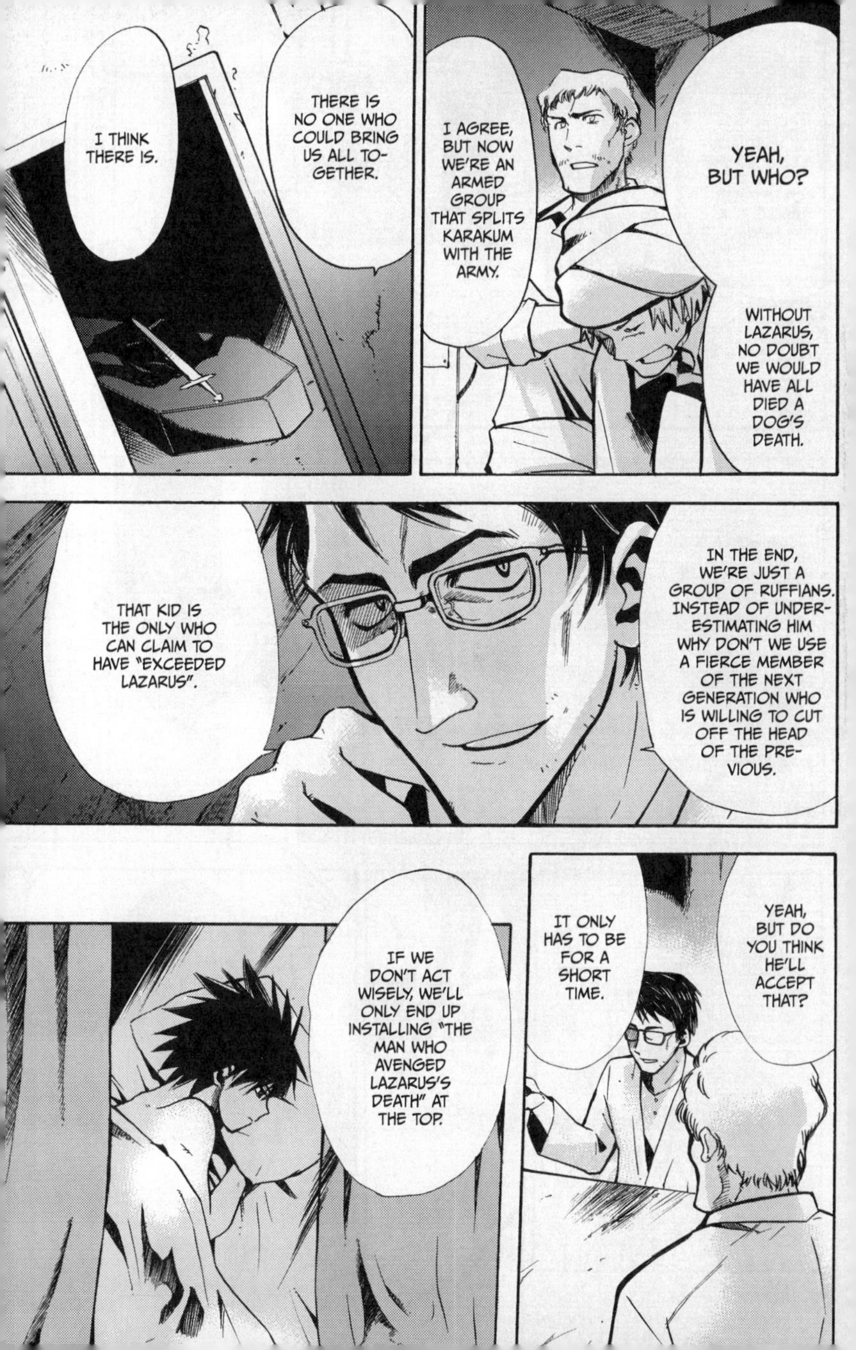
YEAH, BUT WHO?
I AGREE, BUT NOW WE'RE AN ARMED GROUP THAT SPLITS KARAKUM WITH THE ARMY.
WITHOUT LAZARUS, NO DOUBT WE WOULD HAVE ALL DIED A DOG'S DEATH.
THERE IS NO ONE WHO COULD BRING US ALL TO-GETHER.
I THINK THERE IS.
IN THE END, WE'RE JUST A GROUP OF RUFFIANS. INSTEAD OF UNDER-ESTIMATING HIM WHY DON'T WE USE A FIERCE MEMBER OF THE NEXT GENERATION WHO IS WILLING TO CUT OFF THE HEAD OF THE PRE-VIOUS.
THAT KID IS THE ONLY WHO CAN CLAIM TO HAVE "EXCEEDED LAZARUS".
YEAH, BUT DO YOU THINK HE'LL ACCEPT THAT?
IT ONLY HAS TO BE FOR A SHORT TIME.
IF WE DON'T ACT WISELY, WE'LL ONLY END UP INSTALLING "THE MAN WHO AVENGED LAZARUS'S DEATH" AT THE TOP.

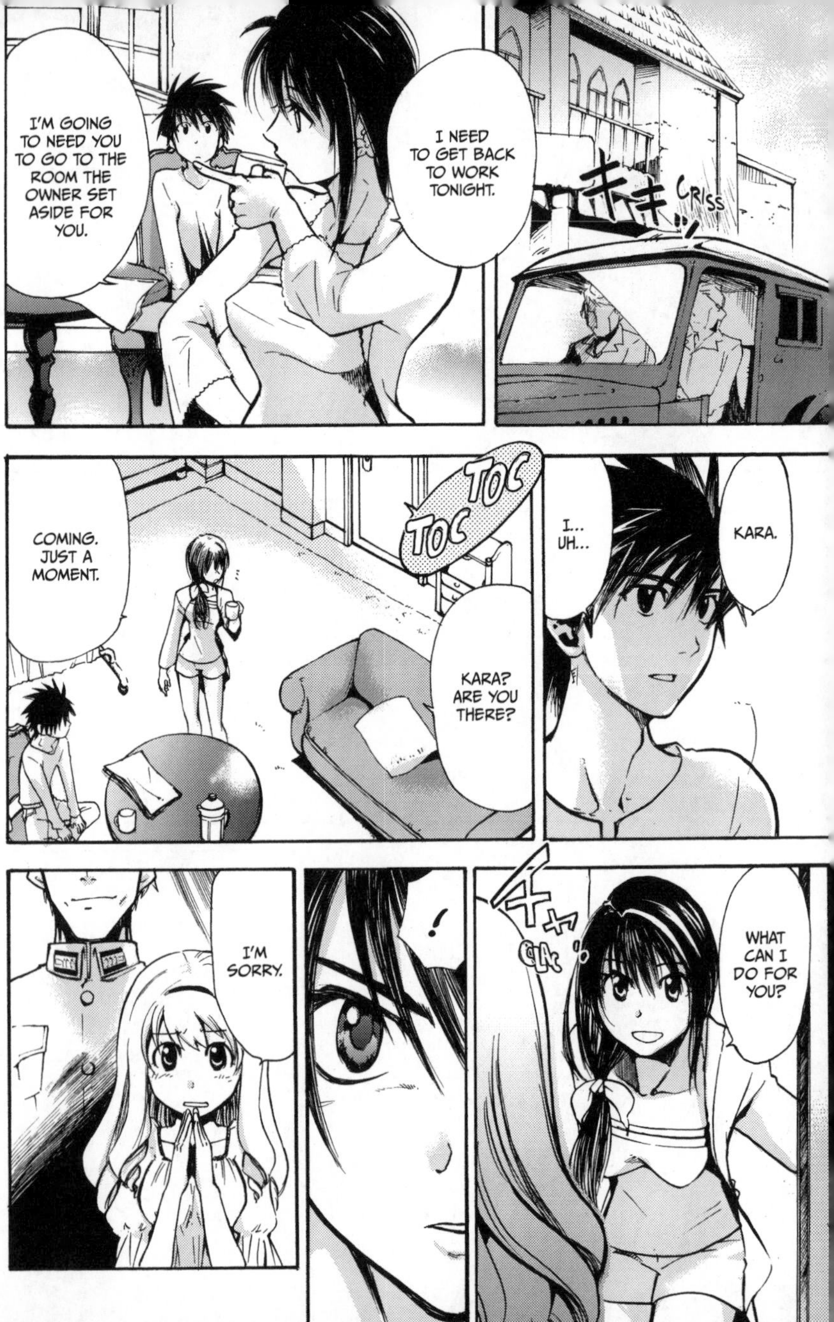
キキ
CRISS
I NEED TO GET BACK TO WORK TONIGHT.
I'M GOING TO NEED YOU TO GO TO THE ROOM THE OWNER SET ASIDE FOR YOU.
KARA.
I... UH...
TOC TOC
KARA? ARE YOU THERE?
COMING. JUST A MOMENT.
CLAC
WHAT CAN I DO FOR YOU?
!
I'M SORRY.

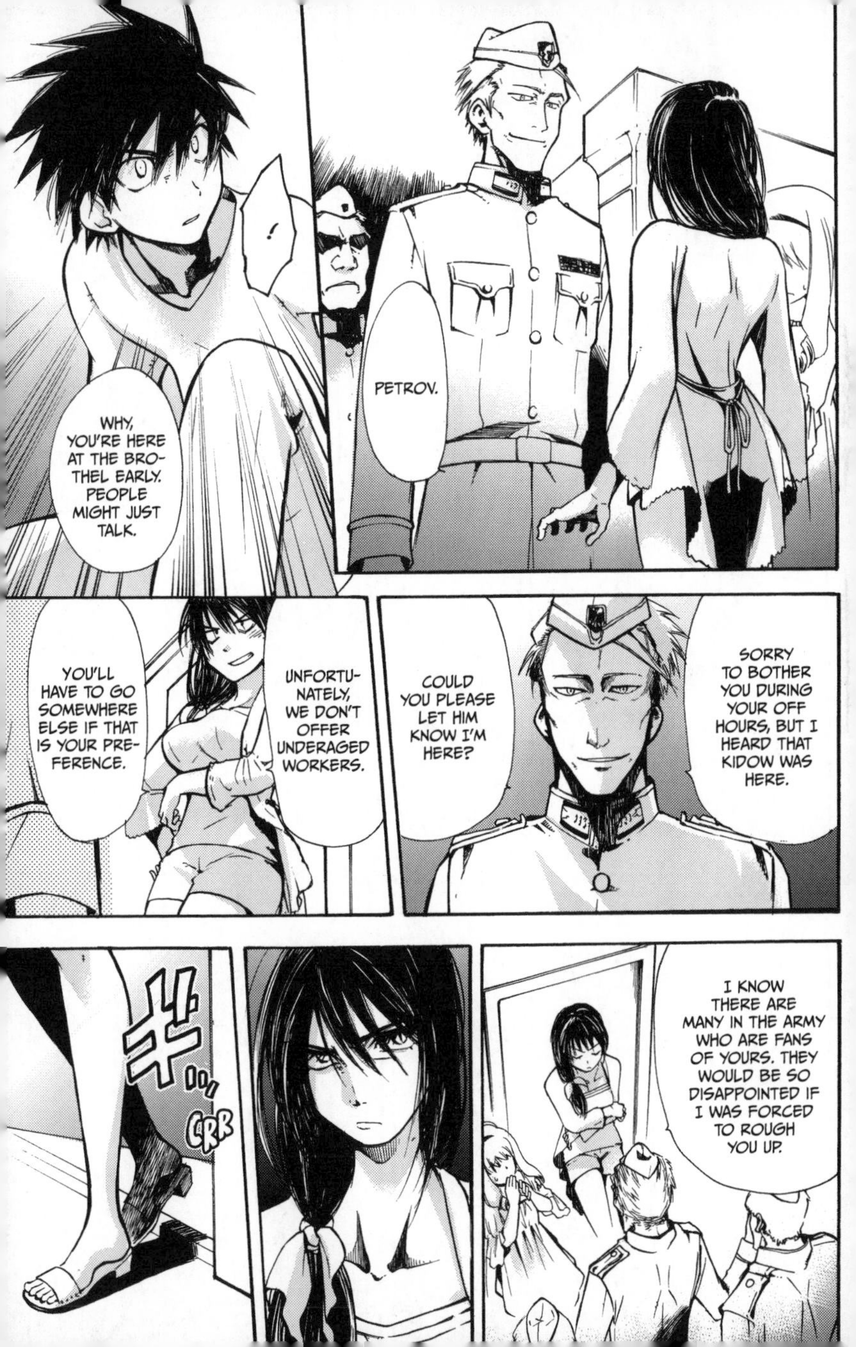
PETROV.
!
WHY, YOU'RE HERE AT THE BRO-THEL EARLY. PEOPLE MIGHT JUST TALK.
SORRY TO BOTHER YOU DURING YOUR OFF HOURS, BUT I HEARD THAT KIDOW WAS HERE.
COULD YOU PLEASE LET HIM KNOW I'M HERE?
UNFORTU-NATELY, WE DON'T OFFER UNDERAGED WORKERS.
YOU'LL HAVE TO GO SOMEWHERE ELSE IF THAT IS YOUR PRE-FERENCE.
I KNOW THERE ARE MANY IN THE ARMY WHO ARE FANS OF YOURS. THEY WOULD BE SO DISAPPOINTED IF I WAS FORCED TO ROUGH YOU UP.
CRR

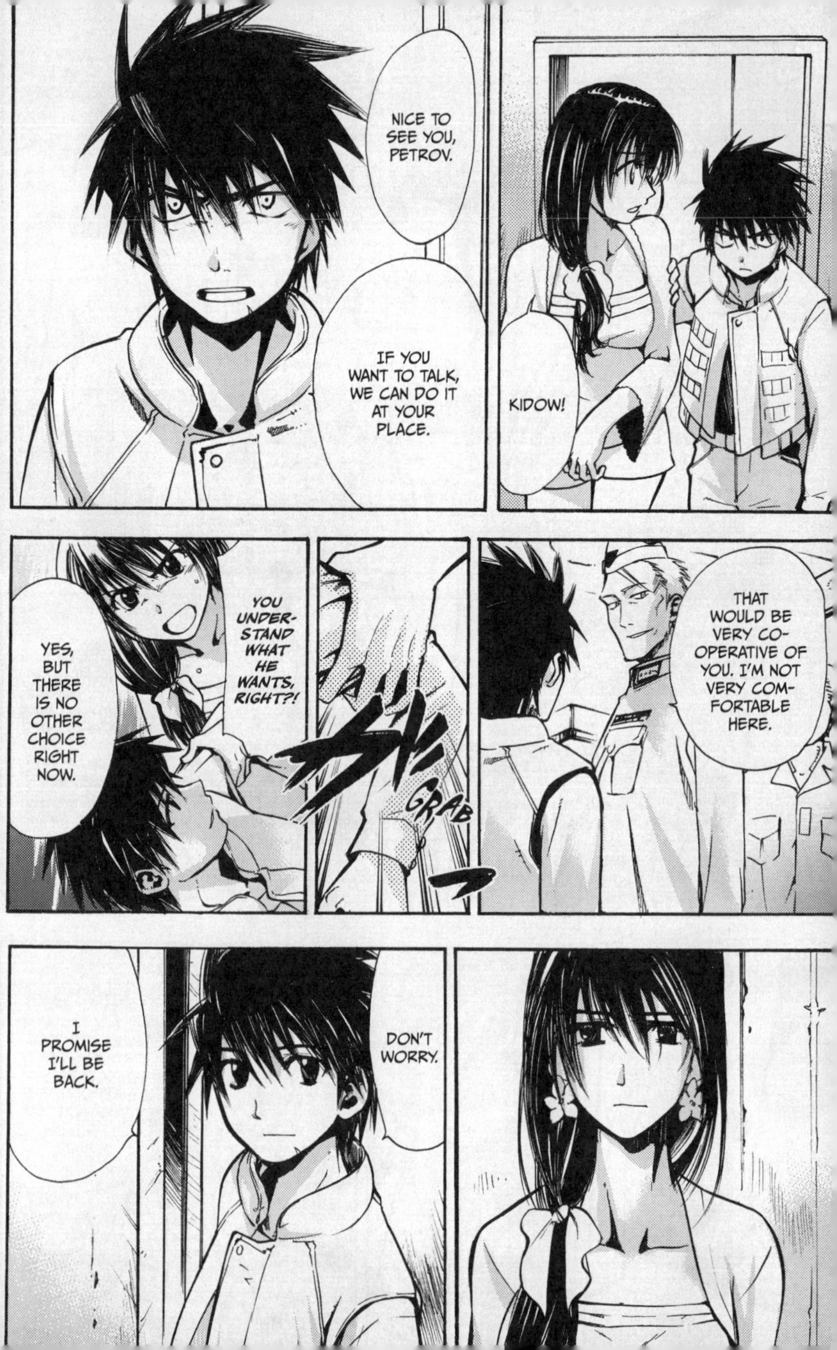
KIDOW!
NICE TO SEE YOU, PETROV.
IF YOU WANT TO TALK, WE CAN DO IT AT YOUR PLACE.
THAT WOULD BE VERY CO-OPERATIVE OF YOU. I'M NOT VERY COMFORTABLE HERE.
GRAB
YOU UNDERSTAND WHAT HE WANTS, RIGHT?!
YES, BUT THERE IS NO OTHER CHOICE RIGHT NOW.
DON'T WORRY.
I PROMISE I'LL BE BACK.

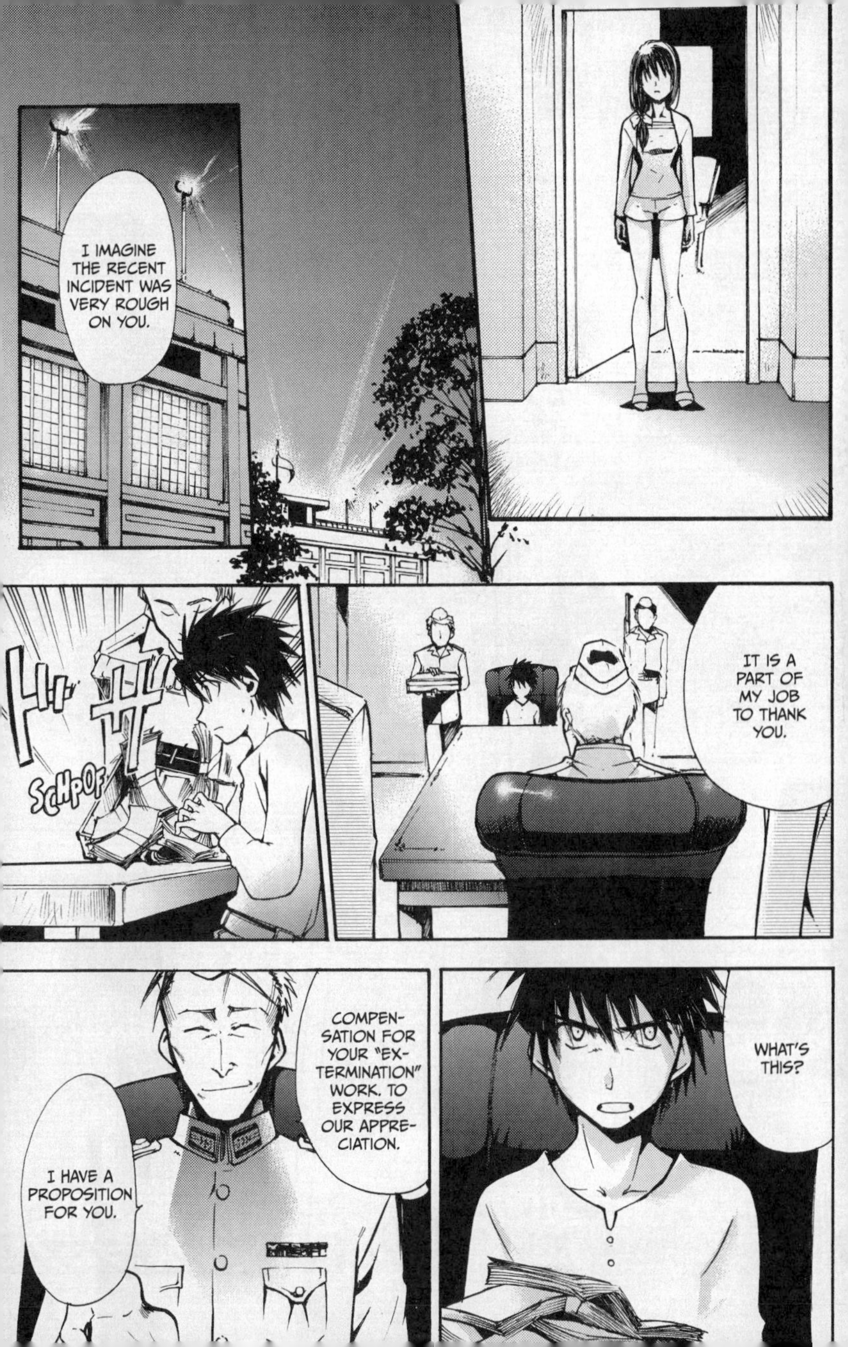
I IMAGINE THE RECENT INCIDENT WAS VERY ROUGH ON YOU.
IT IS A PART OF MY JOB TO THANK YOU.
SCHPOF
WHAT'S THIS?
COMPEN-SATION FOR YOUR "EX-TERMINATION" WORK. TO EXPRESS OUR APPRE-CIATION.
I HAVE A PROPOSITION FOR YOU.

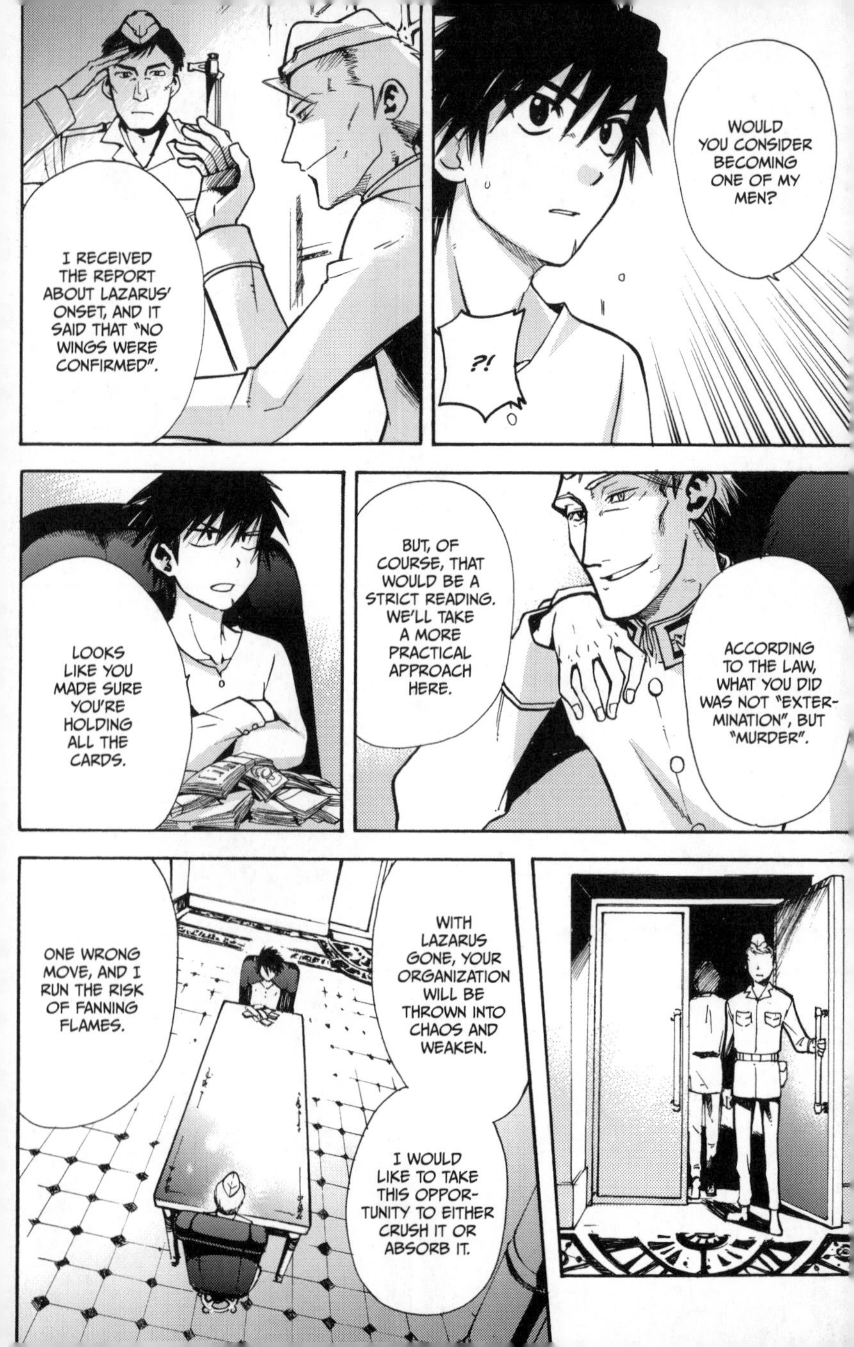
WOULD YOU CONSIDER BECOMING ONE OF MY MEN?
?!
I RECEIVED THE REPORT ABOUT LAZARUS' ONSET, AND IT SAID THAT "NO WINGS WERE CONFIRMED".
ACCORDING TO THE LAW, WHAT YOU DID WAS NOT "EXTER-MINATION", BUT "MURDER".
BUT, OF COURSE, THAT WOULD BE A STRICT READING. WE'LL TAKE A MORE PRACTICAL APPROACH HERE.
LOOKS LIKE YOU MADE SURE YOU'RE HOLDING ALL THE CARDS.
WITH LAZARUS GONE, YOUR ORGANIZATION WILL BE THROWN INTO CHAOS AND WEAKEN.
I WOULD LIKE TO TAKE THIS OPPOR-TUNITY TO EITHER CRUSH IT OR ABSORB IT.
ONE WRONG MOVE, AND I RUN THE RISK OF FANNING FLAMES.

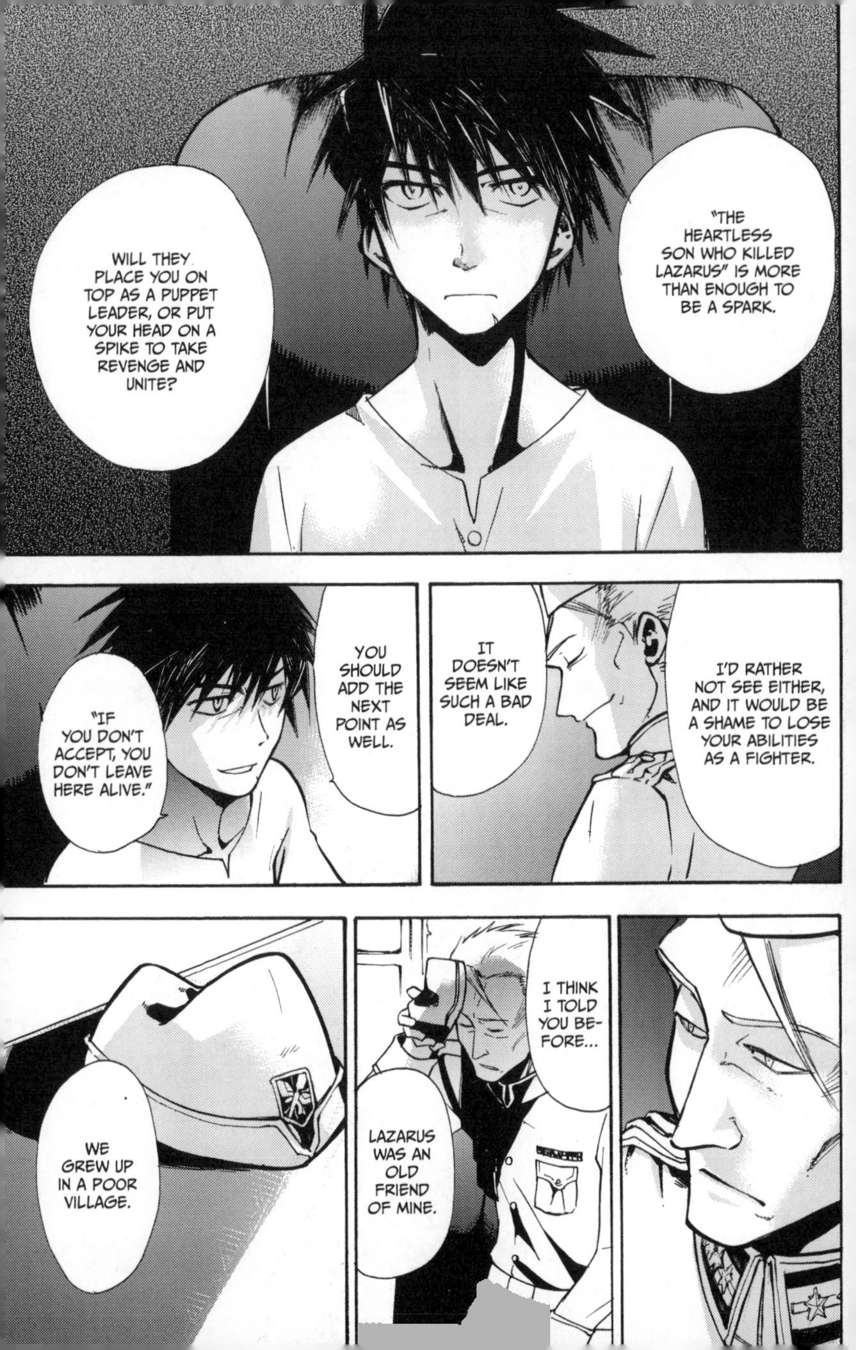
"THE HEARTLESS SON WHO KILLED LAZARUS" IS MORE THAN ENOUGH TO BE A SPARK.
WILL THEY PLACE YOU ON TOP AS A PUPPET LEADER, OR PUT YOUR HEAD ON A SPIKE TO TAKE REVENGE AND UNITE?
I'D RATHER NOT SEE EITHER, AND IT WOULD BE A SHAME TO LOSE YOUR ABILITIES AS A FIGHTER.
IT DOESN'T SEEM LIKE SUCH A BAD DEAL.
YOU SHOULD ADD THE NEXT POINT AS WELL.
"IF YOU DON'T ACCEPT, YOU DON'T LEAVE HERE ALIVE."
I THINK I TOLD YOU BE-FORE...
LAZARUS WAS AN OLD FRIEND OF MINE.
WE GREW UP IN A POOR VILLAGE.

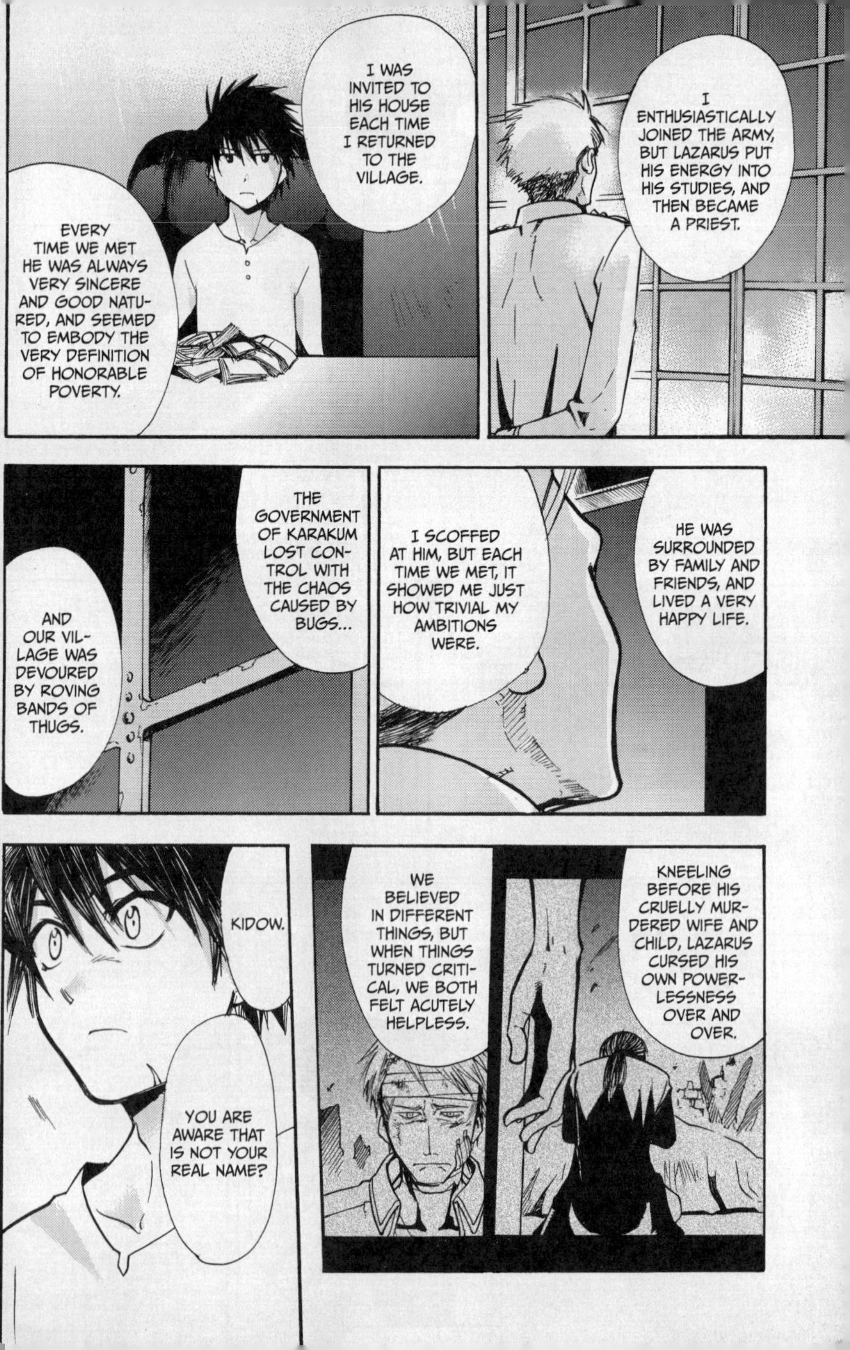
I ENTHUSIASTICALLY JOINED THE ARMY, BUT LAZARUS PUT HIS ENERGY INTO HIS STUDIES, AND THEN BECAME A PRIEST.
I WAS INVITED TO HIS HOUSE EACH TIME I RETURNED TO THE VILLAGE.
EVERY TIME WE MET HE WAS ALWAYS VERY SINCERE AND GOOD NATU-RED, AND SEEMED TO EMBODY THE VERY DEFINITION OF HONORABLE POVERTY.
HE WAS SURROUNDED BY FAMILY AND FRIENDS, AND LIVED A VERY HAPPY LIFE.
I SCOFFED AT HIM, BUT EACH TIME WE MET, IT SHOWED ME JUST HOW TRIVIAL MY AMBITIONS WERE.
THE GOVERNMENT OF KARAKUM LOST CON-TROL WITH THE CHAOS CAUSED BY BUGS...
AND OUR VIL-LAGE WAS DEVOURED BY ROVING BANDS OF THUGS.
KNEELING BEFORE HIS CRUELLY MUR-DERED WIFE AND CHILD, LAZARUS CURSED HIS OWN POWER-LESSNESS OVER AND OVER.
WE BELIEVED IN DIFFERENT THINGS, BUT WHEN THINGS TURNED CRITI-CAL, WE BOTH FELT ACUTELY HELPLESS.
KIDOW.
YOU ARE AWARE THAT IS NOT YOUR REAL NAME?

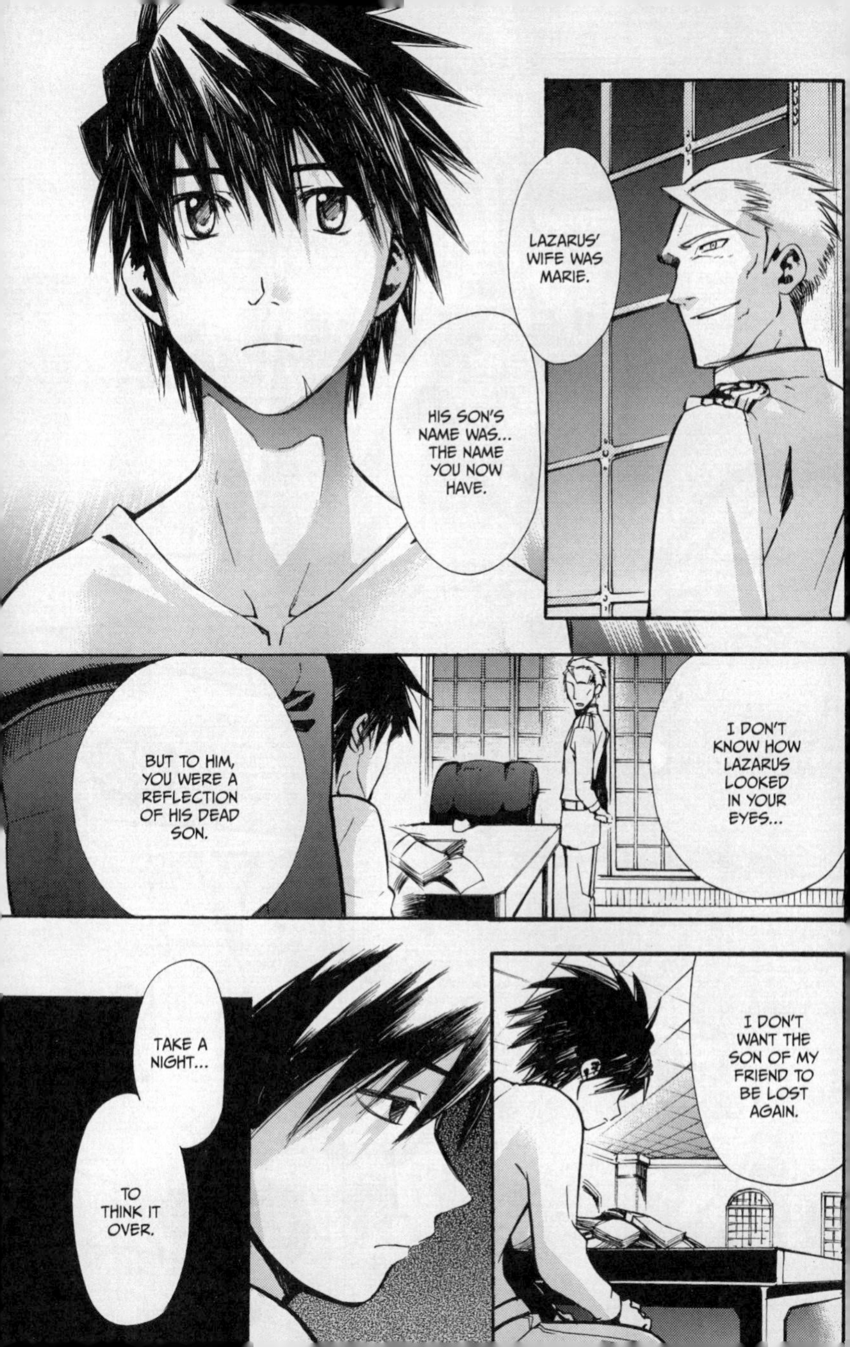
LAZARUS' WIFE WAS MARIE.
HIS SON'S NAME WAS... THE NAME YOU NOW HAVE.
I DON'T KNOW HOW LAZARUS LOOKED IN YOUR EYES...
BUT TO HIM, YOU WERE A REFLECTION OF HIS DEAD SON.
I DON'T WANT THE SON OF MY FRIEND TO BE LOST AGAIN.
TAKE A NIGHT...
TO THINK IT OVER.

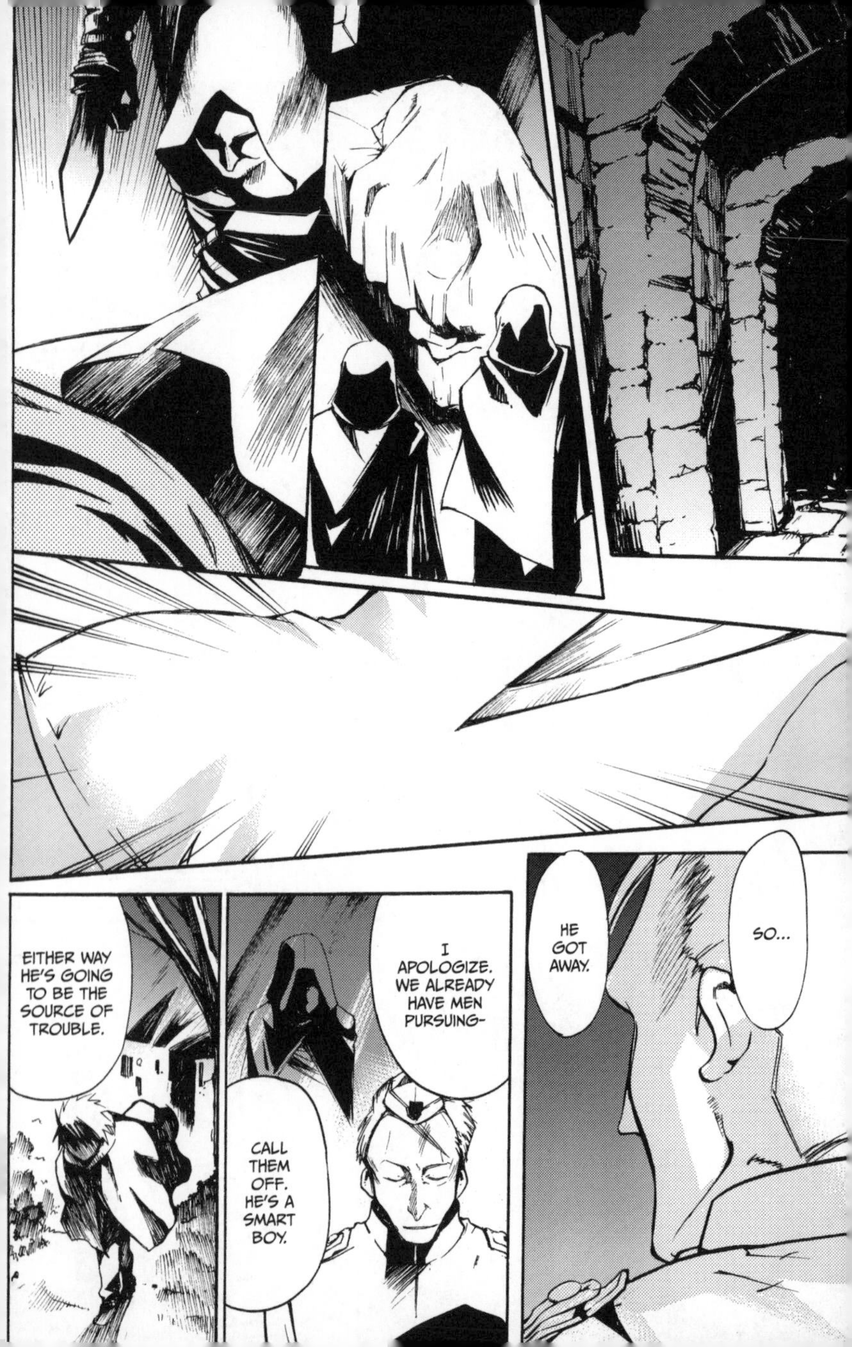
SO...
HE GOT AWAY.
I APOLOGIZE. WE ALREADY HAVE MEN PURSUING-
CALL THEM OFF. HE'S A SMART BOY.
EITHER WAY HE'S GOING TO BE THE SOURCE OF TROUBLE.

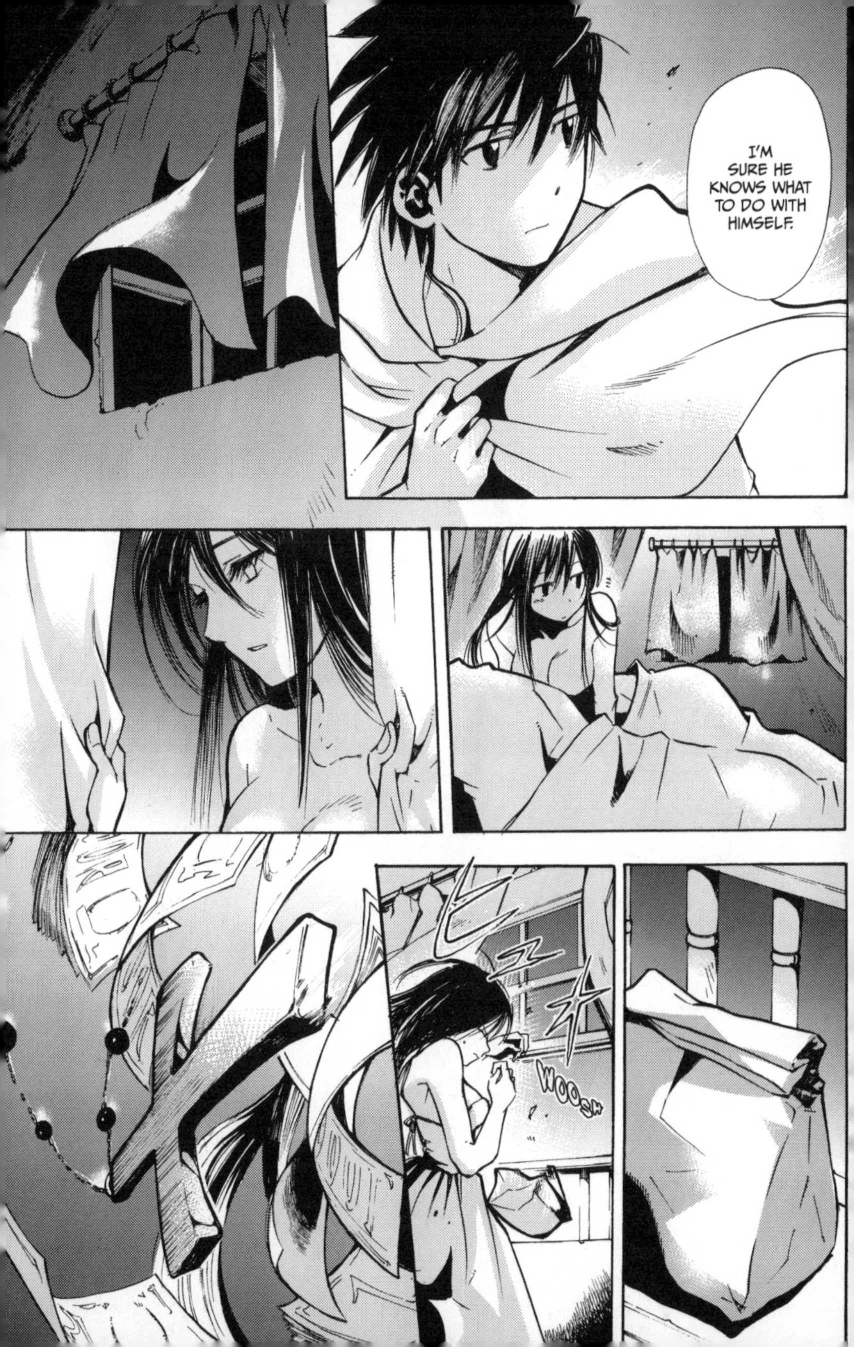
I'M SURE HE KNOWS WHAT TO DO WITH HIMSELF.
WOOSH

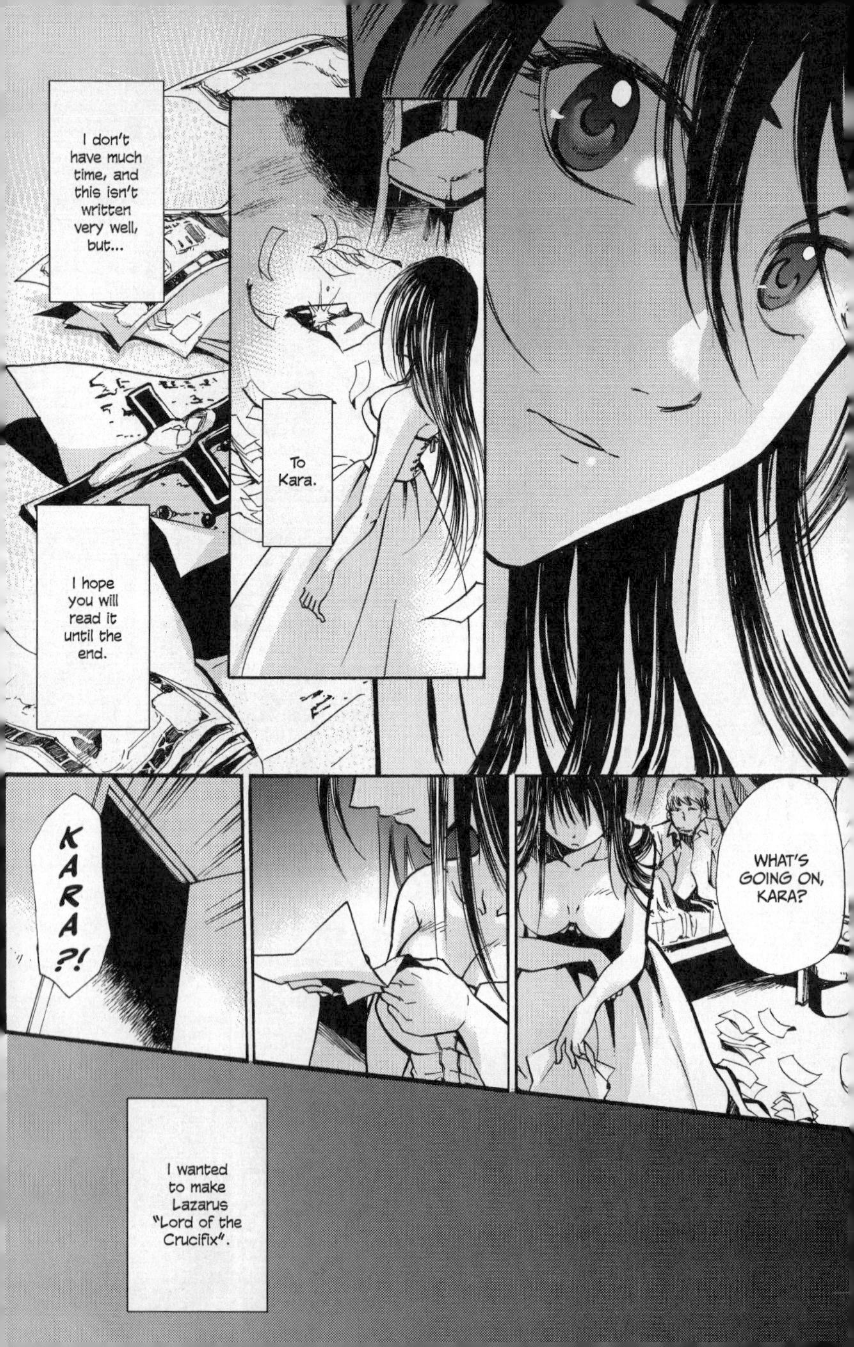
To Kara.
I don't have much time, and this isn't written very well, but...
I hope you will read it until the end.
WHAT'S GOING ON, KARA?
KARA?!
I wanted to make Lazarus "Lord of the Crucifix".

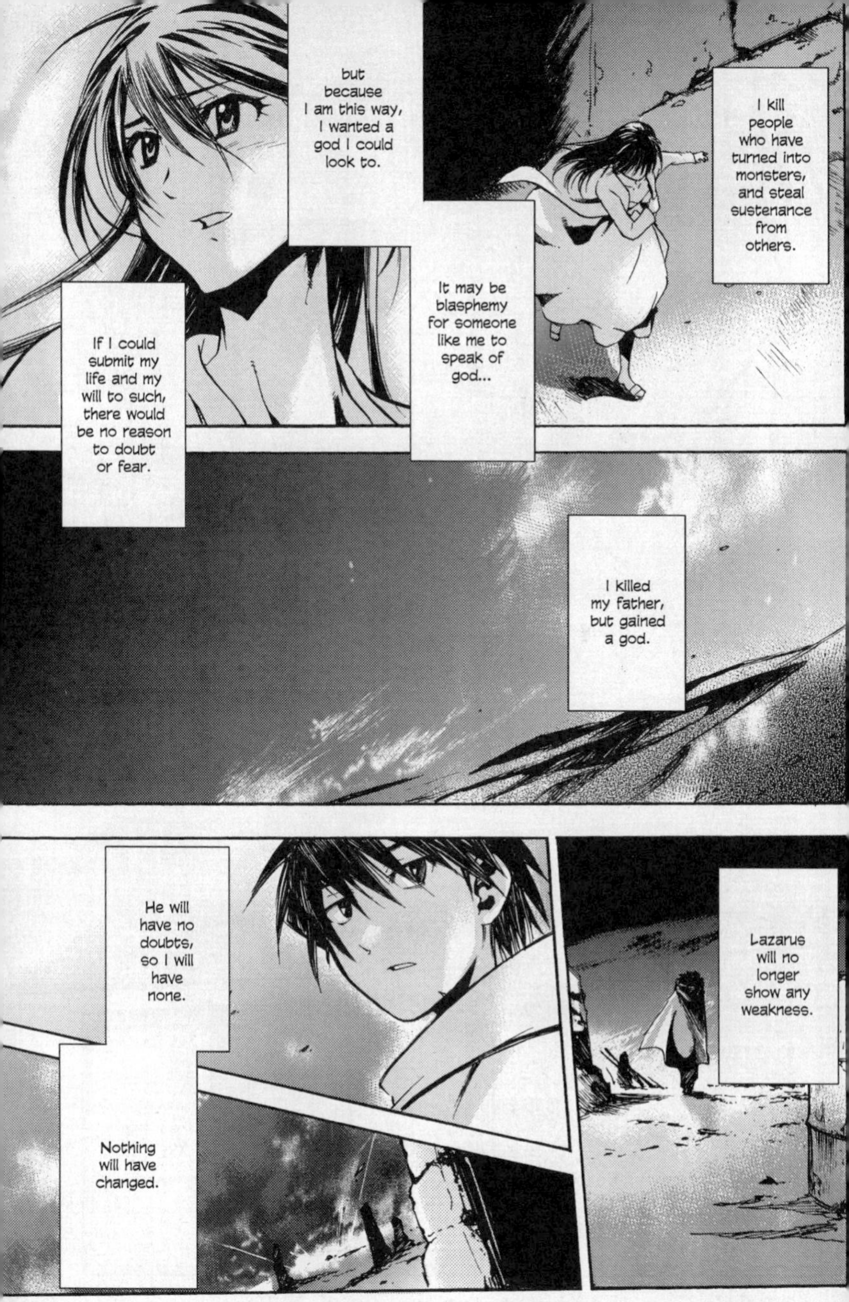
I kill people who have turned into monsters, and steal sustenance from others.
It may be blasphemy for someone like me to speak of god...
but because I am this way, I wanted a god I could look to.
If I could submit my life and my will to such, there would be no reason to doubt or fear.
I killed my father, but gained a god.
Lazarus will no longer show any weakness.
He will have no doubts, so I will have none.
Nothing will have changed.

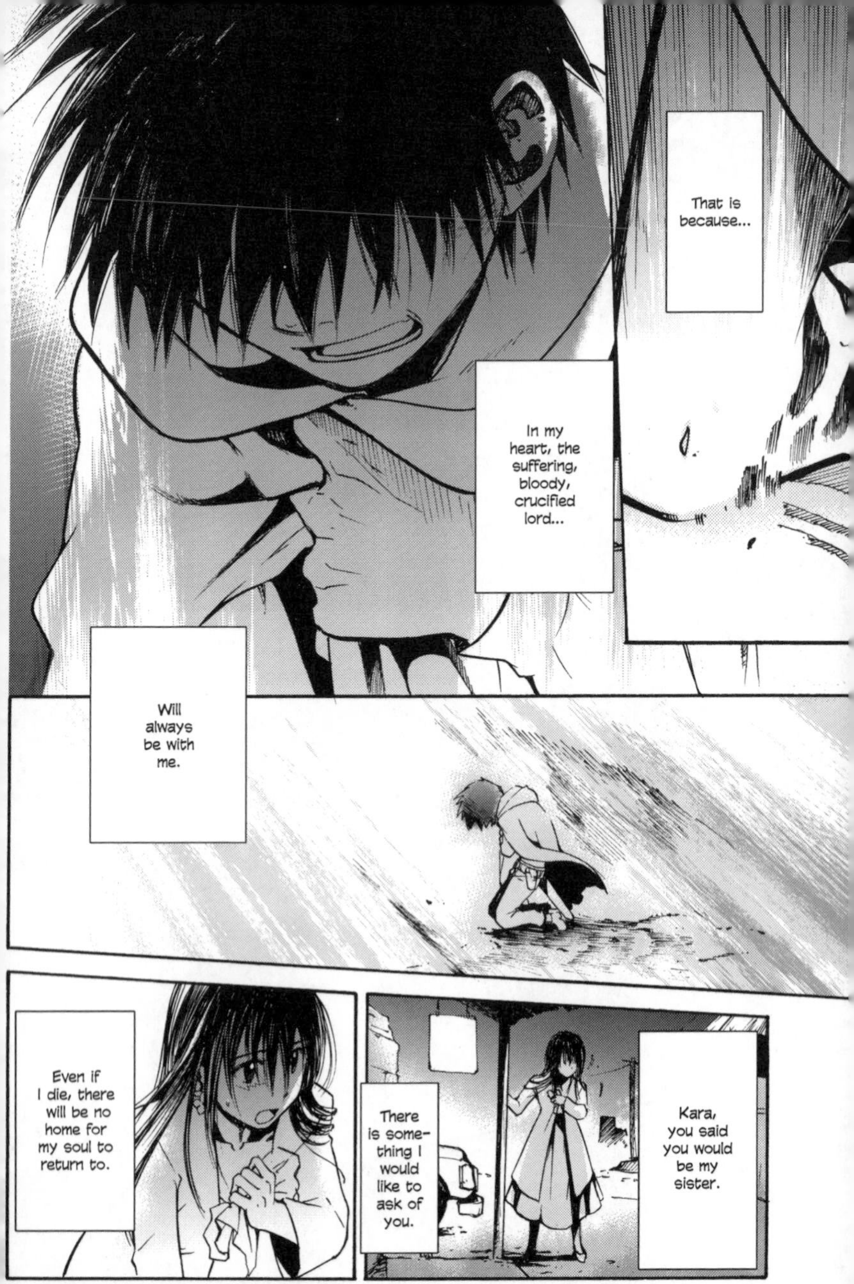
That is because...
In my heart, the suffering, bloody, crucified lord...
Will always be with me.
Kara, you said you would be my sister.
There is something I would like to ask of you.
Even if I die, there will be no home for my soul to return to.

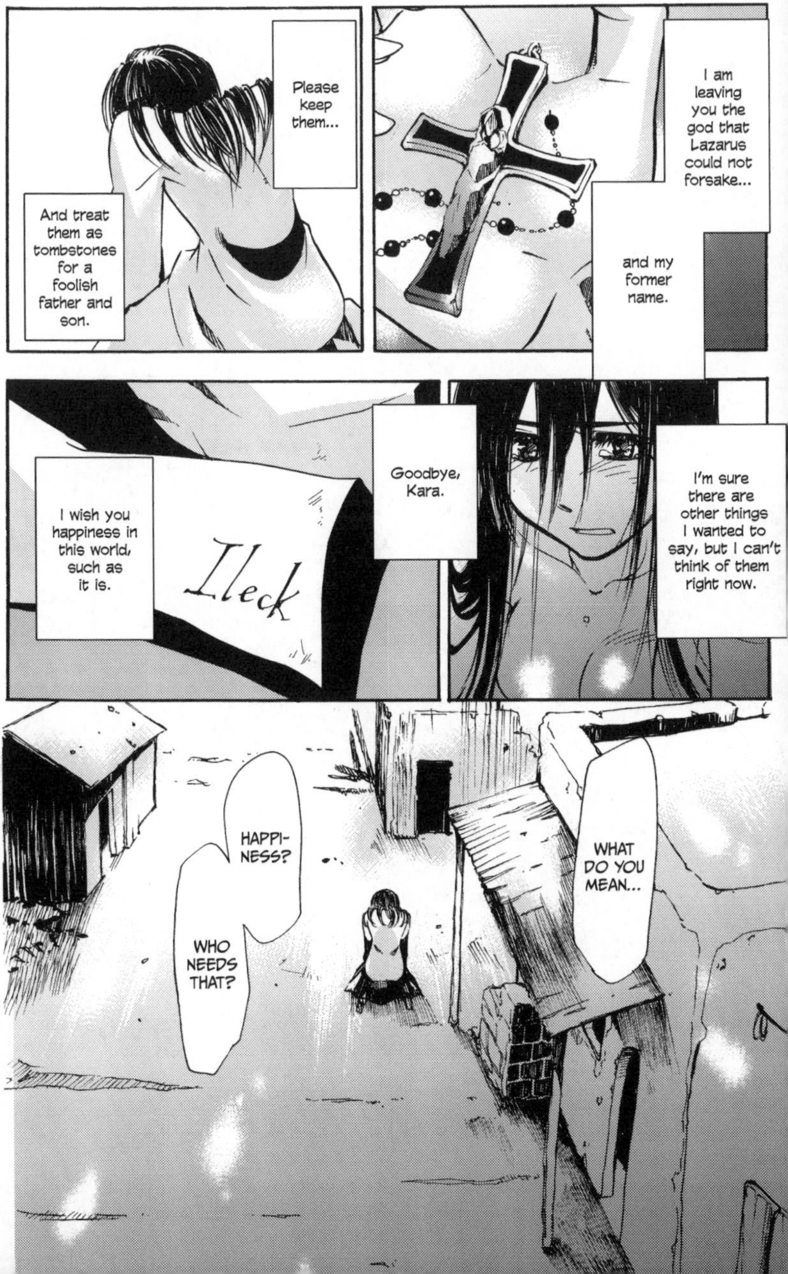
I am leaving you the god that Lazarus could not forsake...
and my former name.
Please keep them...
And treat them as tombstones for a foolish father and son.
I'm sure there are other things I wanted to say, but I can't think of them right now.
Goodbye, Kara.
I wish you happiness in this world, such as it is.
Ileck
WHAT DO YOU MEAN...
HAPPI-NESS?
WHO NEEDS THAT?

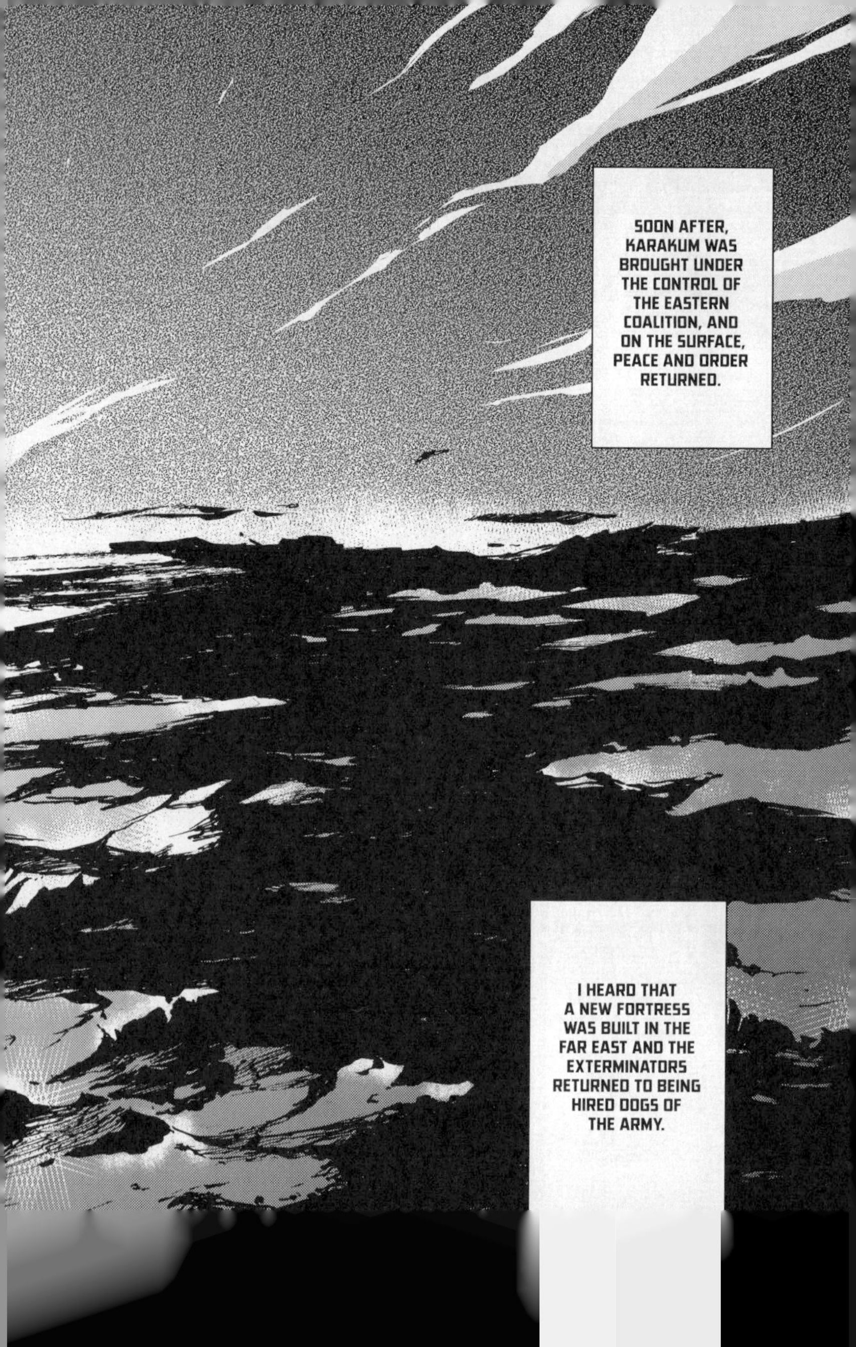
SOON AFTER, KARAKUM WAS BROUGHT UNDER THE CONTROL OF THE EASTERN COALITION, AND ON THE SURFACE, PEACE AND ORDER RETURNED.
I HEARD THAT A NEW FORTRESS WAS BUILT IN THE FAR EAST AND THE EXTERMINATORS RETURNED TO BEING HIRED DOGS OF THE ARMY.

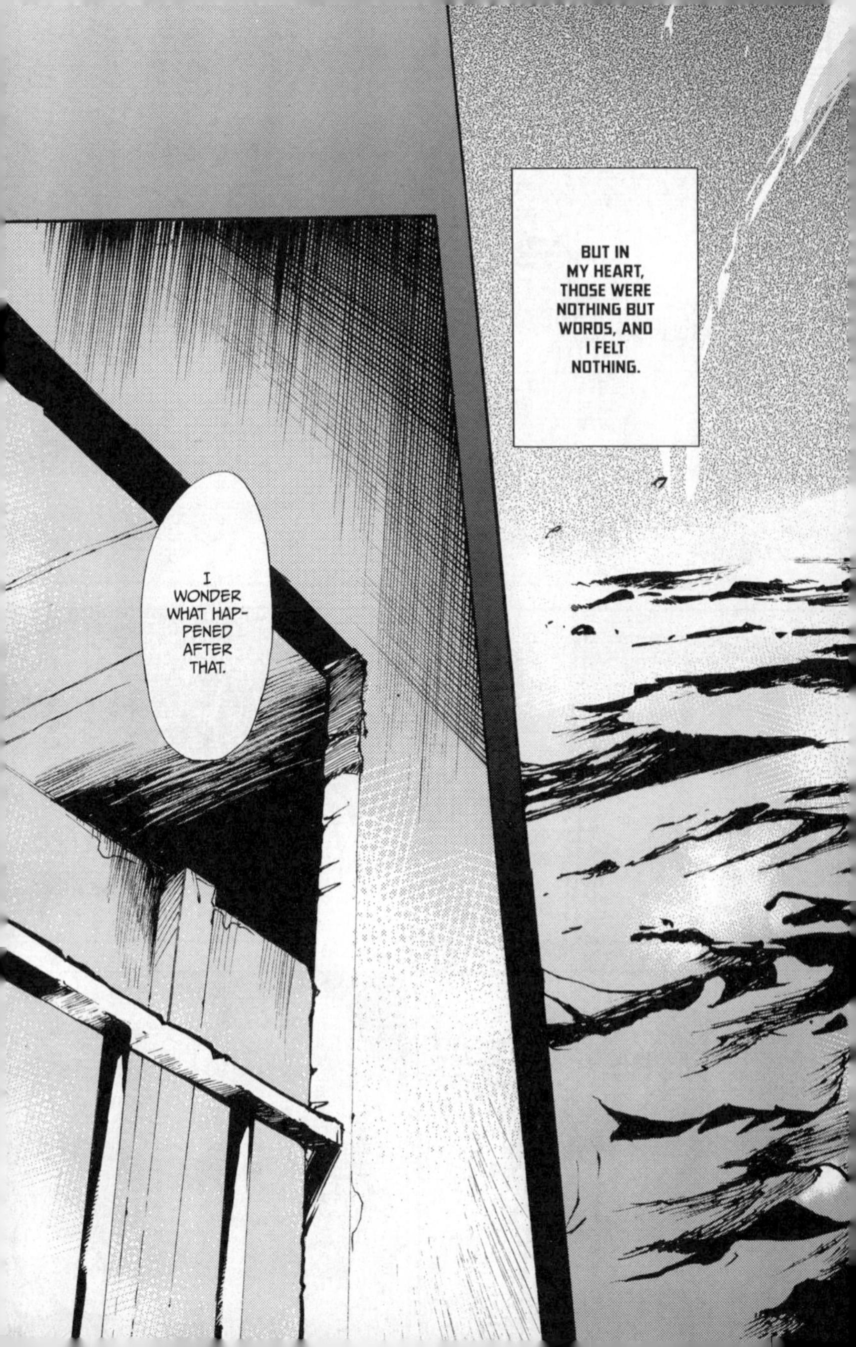
BUT IN MY HEART, THOSE WERE NOTHING BUT WORDS, AND I FELT NOTHING.
I WONDER WHAT HAP-PENED AFTER THAT.

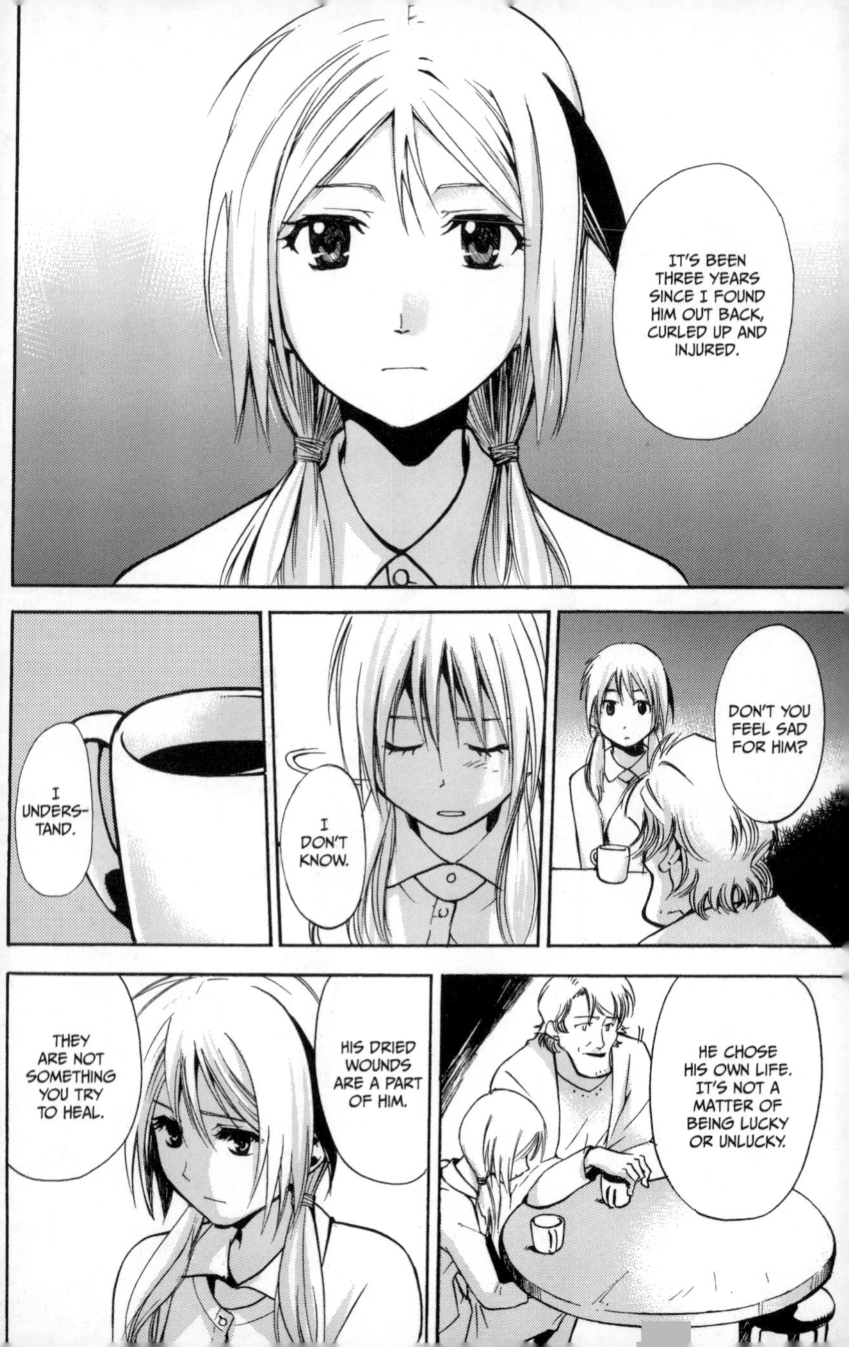
IT'S BEEN THREE YEARS SINCE I FOUND HIM OUT BACK, CURLED UP AND INJURED.
DON'T YOU FEEL SAD FOR HIM?
I DON'T KNOW.
I UNDERS-TAND.
HE CHOSE HIS OWN LIFE. IT'S NOT A MATTER OF BEING LUCKY OR UNLUCKY.
HIS DRIED WOUNDS ARE A PART OF HIM.
THEY ARE NOT SOMETHING YOU TRY TO HEAL.

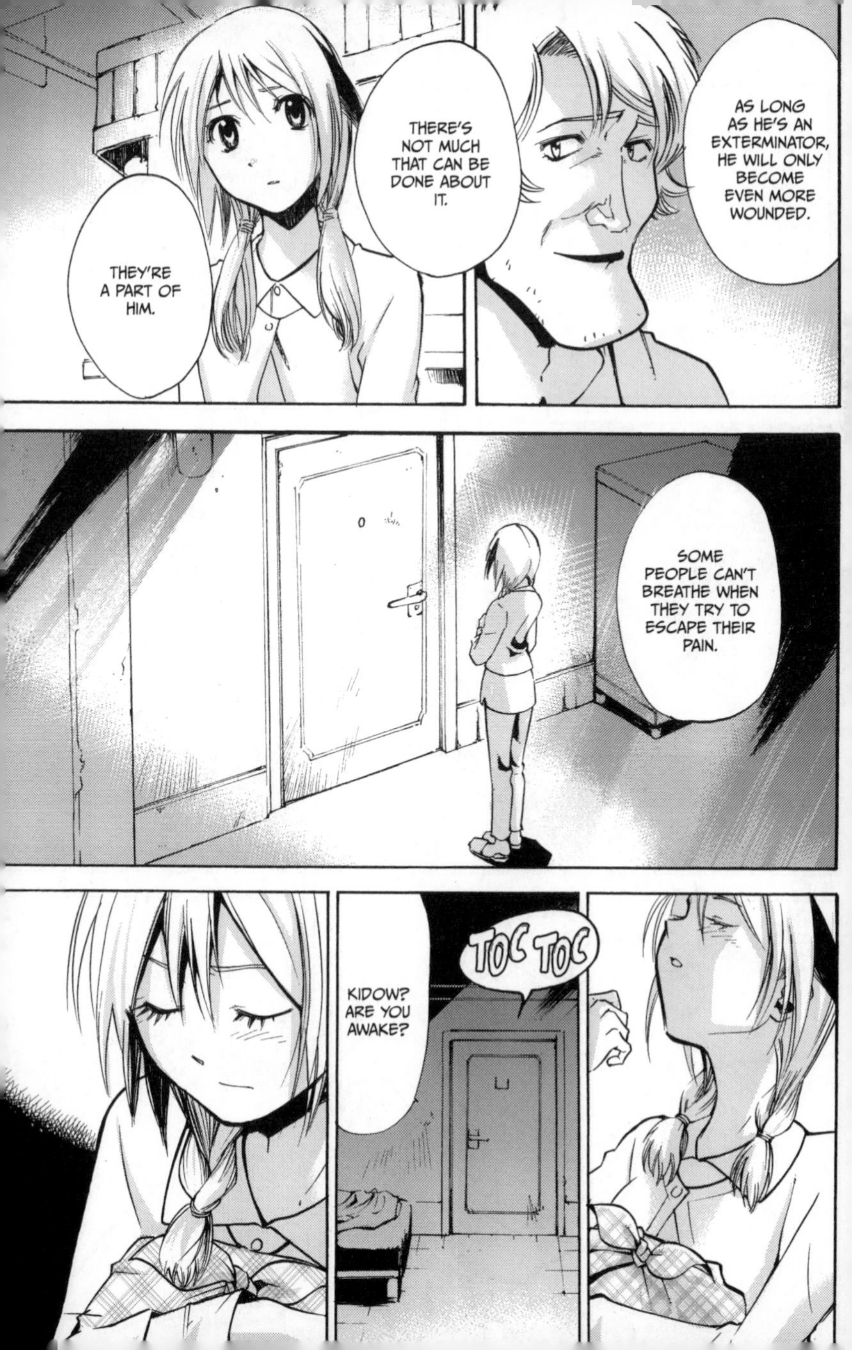
AS LONG AS HE'S AN EXTERMINATOR, HE WILL ONLY BECOME EVEN MORE WOUNDED.
THERE'S NOT MUCH THAT CAN BE DONE ABOUT IT.
THEY'RE A PART OF HIM.
SOME PEOPLE CAN'T BREATHE WHEN THEY TRY TO ESCAPE THEIR PAIN.
TOC TOC
KIDOW? ARE YOU AWAKE?

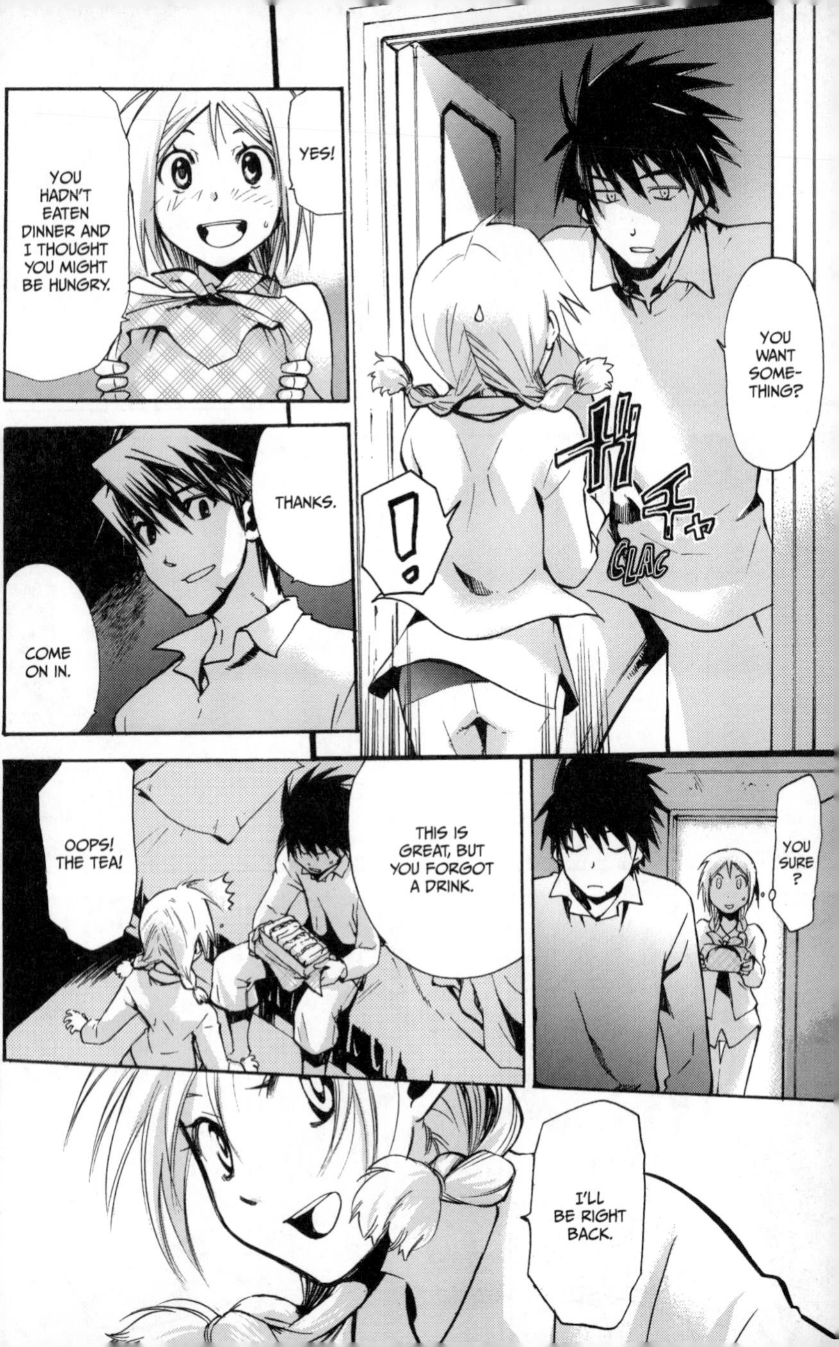
YOU WANT SOMETHING?
CLAC
!
YES!
YOU HADN'T EATEN DINNER AND I THOUGHT YOU MIGHT BE HUNGRY.
THANKS.
COME ON IN.
YOU SURE?
THIS IS GREAT, BUT YOU FORGOT A DRINK.
OOPS! THE TEA!
I'LL BE RIGHT BACK.

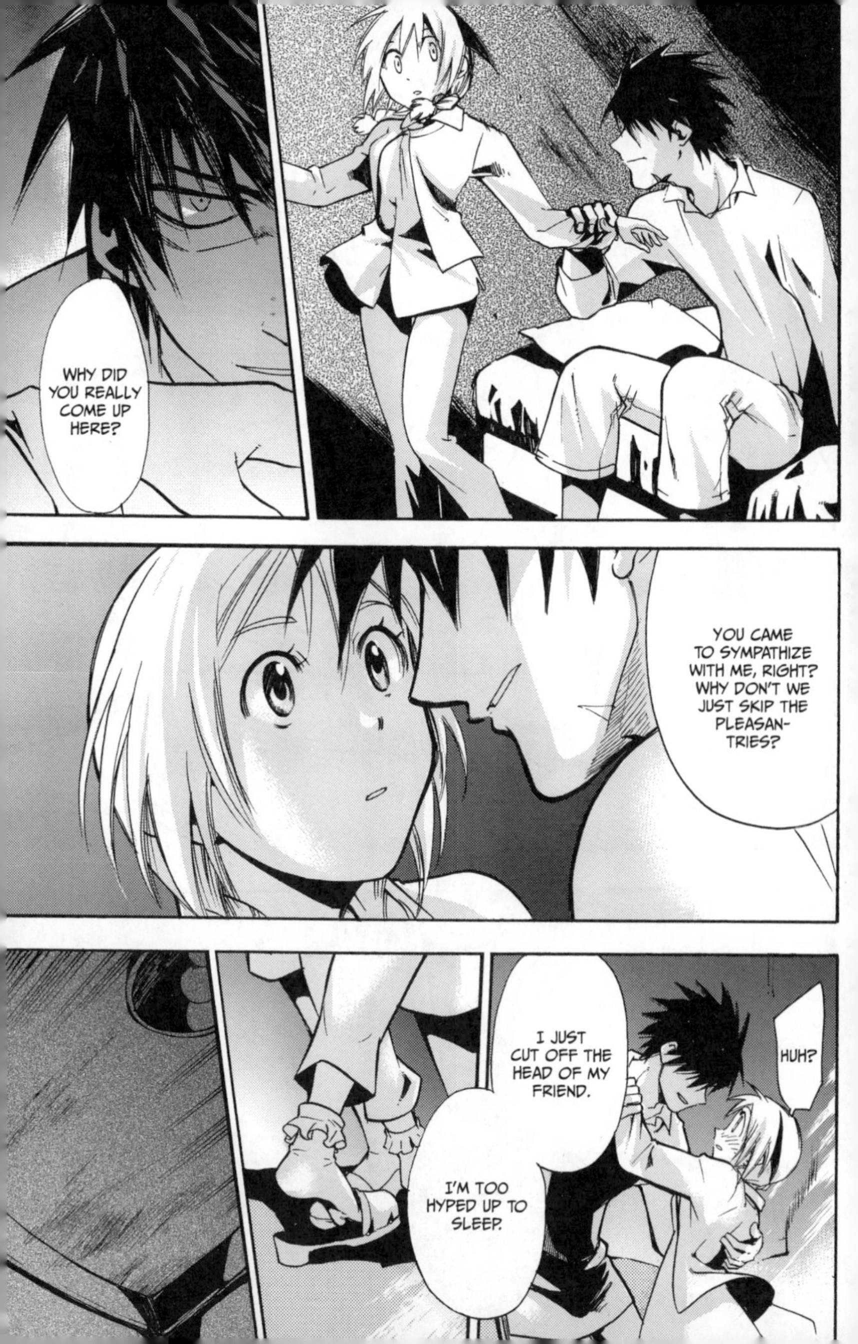
WHY DID YOU REALLY COME UP HERE?
YOU CAME TO SYMPATHIZE WITH ME, RIGHT? WHY DON'T WE JUST SKIP THE PLEASAN-TRIES?
HUH?
I JUST CUT OFF THE HEAD OF MY FRIEND.
I'M TOO HYPED UP TO SLEEP.

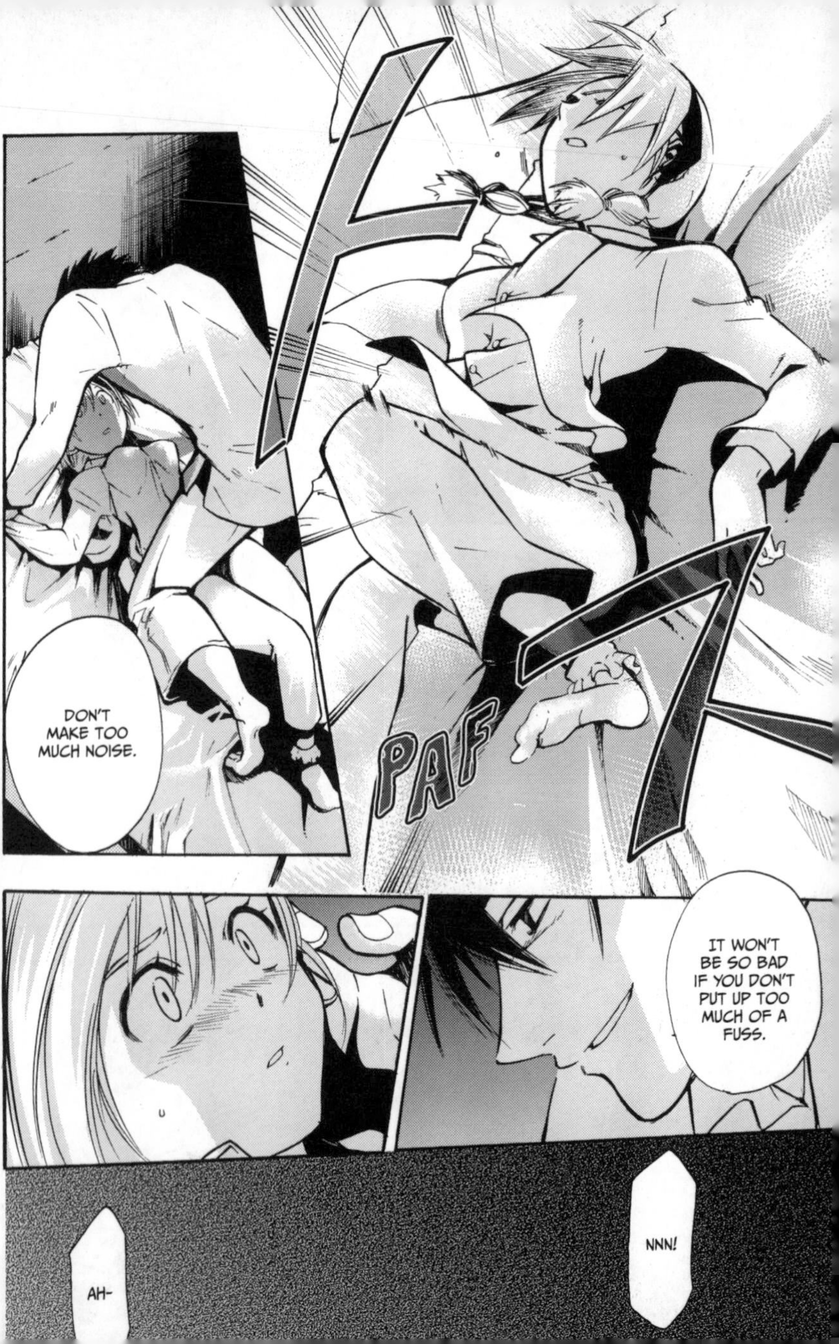
PAF
DON'T MAKE TOO MUCH NOISE.
IT WON'T BE SO BAD IF YOU DON'T PUT UP TOO MUCH OF A FUSS.
NNN!
AH-

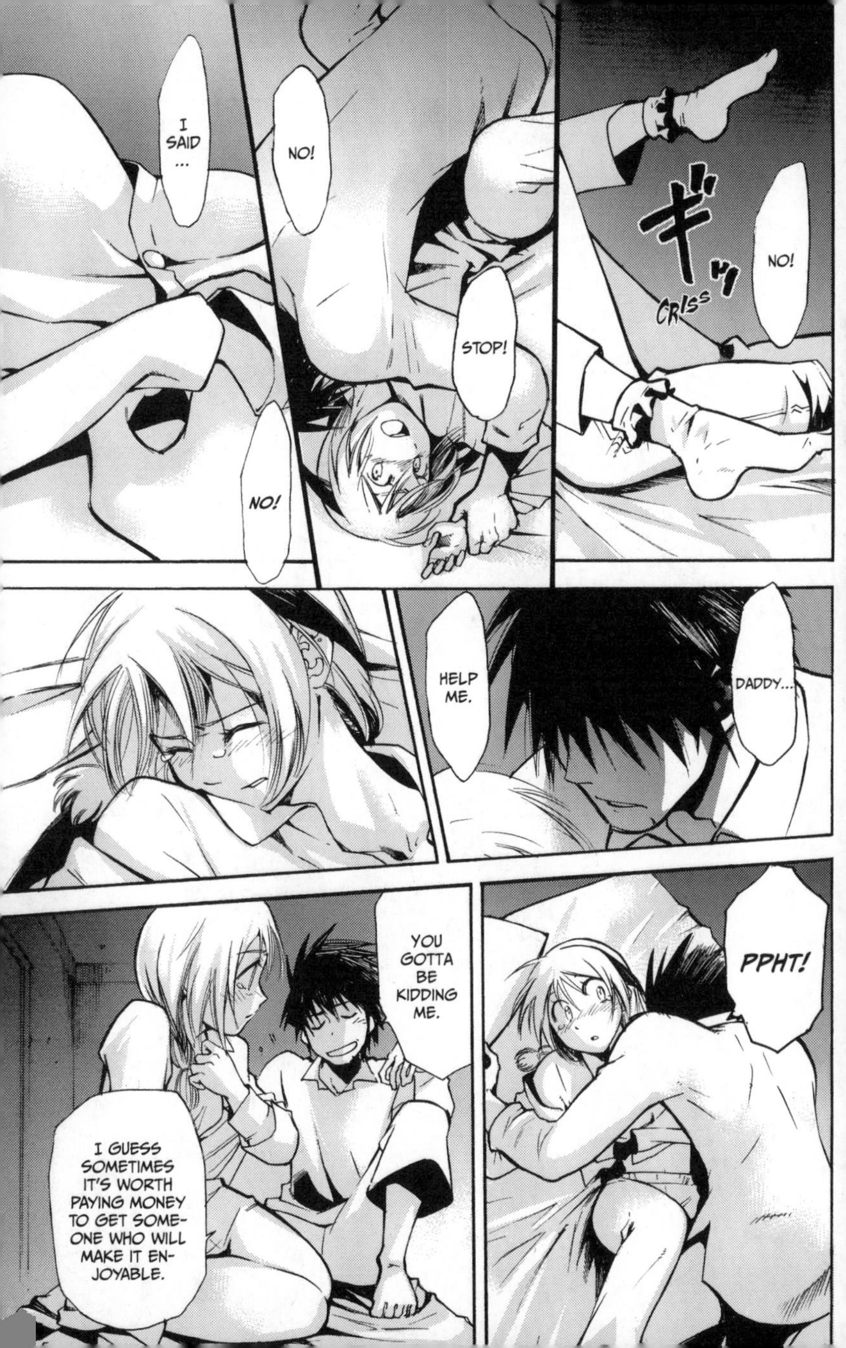
NO!
ギリ
CRISS
NO!
STOP!
I SAID ...
NO!
DADDY...
HELP ME.
PPHT!
YOU GOTTA BE KIDDING ME.
I GUESS SOMETIMES IT'S WORTH PAYING MONEY TO GET SOME-ONE WHO WILL MAKE IT EN-JOYABLE.

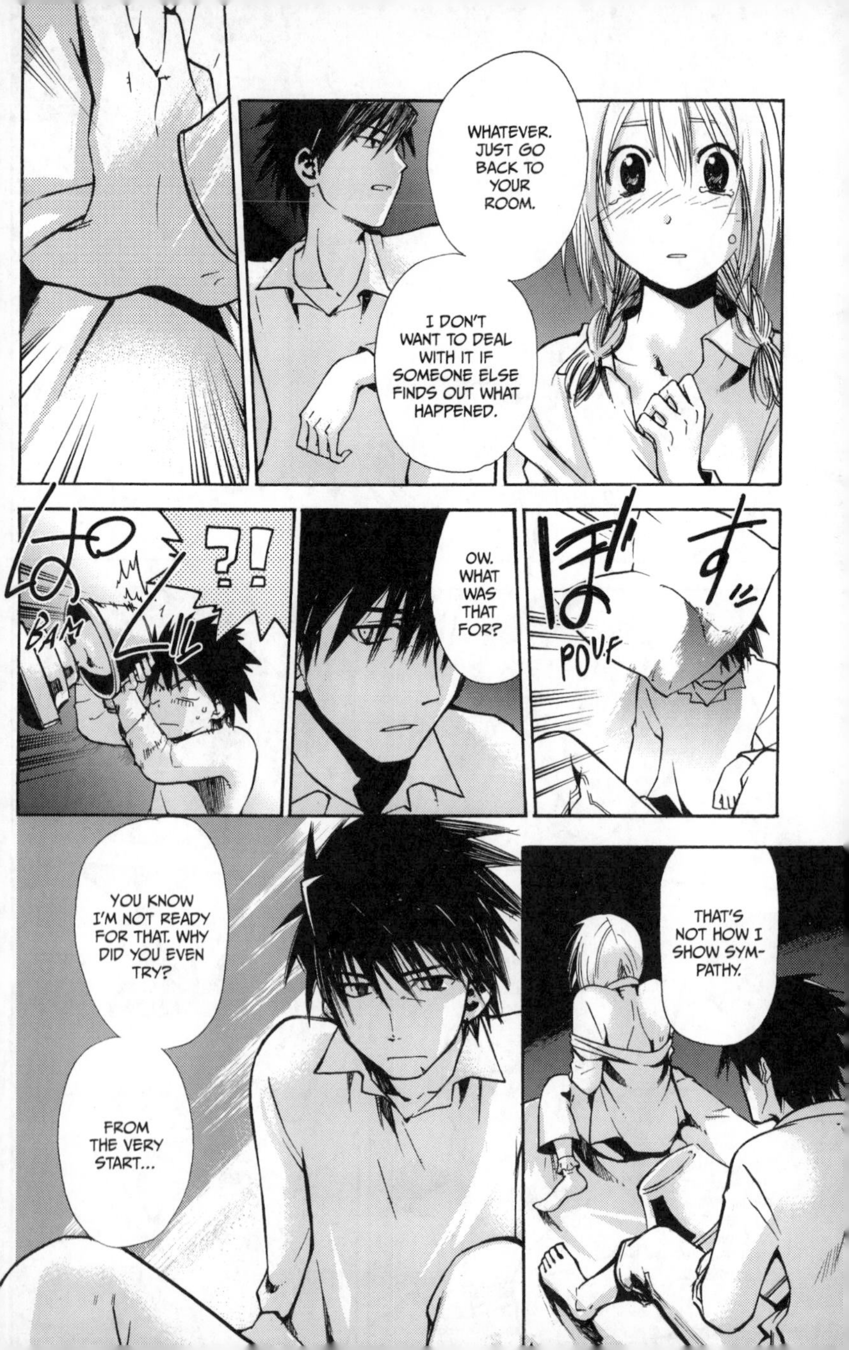
WHATEVER. JUST GO BACK TO YOUR ROOM.
I DON'T WANT TO DEAL WITH IT IF SOMEONE ELSE FINDS OUT WHAT HAPPENED.
POUF
OW. WHAT WAS THAT FOR?
?!
BAM
THAT'S NOT HOW I SHOW SYM-PATHY.
YOU KNOW I'M NOT READY FOR THAT. WHY DID YOU EVEN TRY?
FROM THE VERY START...

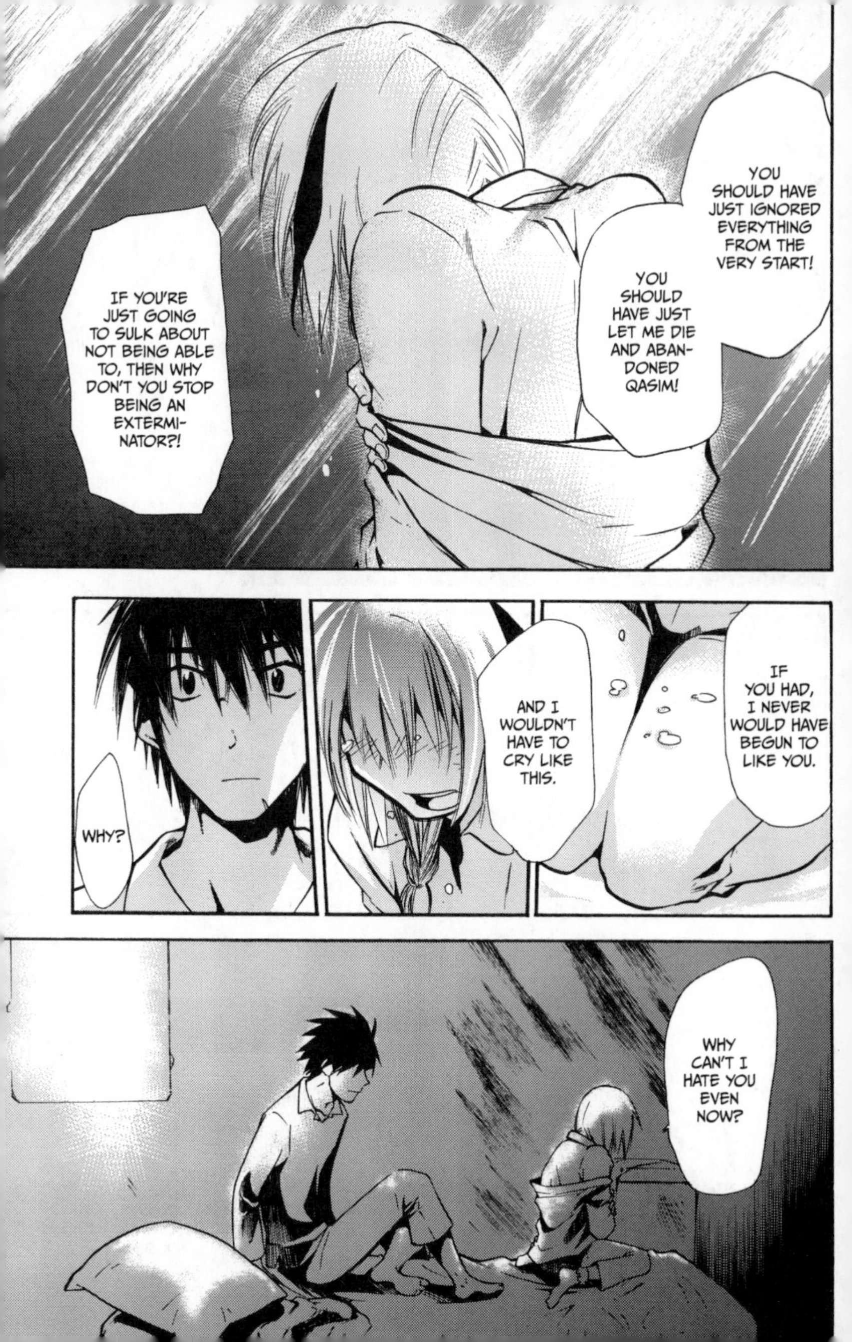
YOU SHOULD HAVE JUST IGNORED EVERYTHING FROM THE VERY START!
YOU SHOULD HAVE JUST LET ME DIE AND ABAN-DONED QASIM!
IF YOU'RE JUST GOING TO SULK ABOUT NOT BEING ABLE TO, THEN WHY DON'T YOU STOP BEING AN EXTERMI-NATOR?!
IF YOU HAD, I NEVER WOULD HAVE BEGUN TO LIKE YOU.
AND I WOULDN'T HAVE TO CRY LIKE THIS.
WHY?
WHY CAN'T I HATE YOU EVEN NOW?

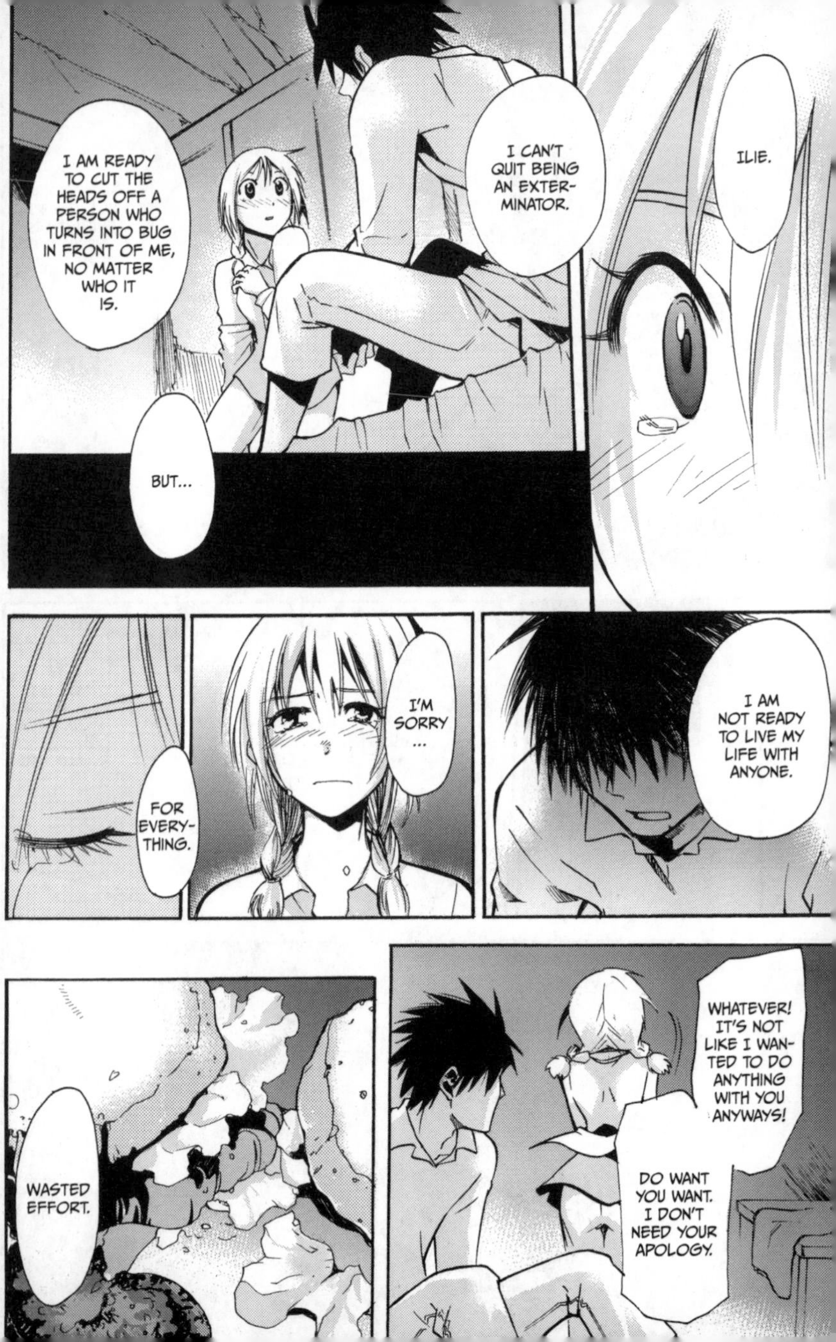
ILIE.
I CAN'T QUIT BEING AN EXTER-MINATOR.
I AM READY TO CUT THE HEADS OFF A PERSON WHO TURNS INTO BUG IN FRONT OF ME, NO MATTER WHO IT IS.
BUT...
I AM NOT READY TO LIVE MY LIFE WITH ANYONE.
I'M SORRY ...
FOR EVERY-THING.
WHATEVER! IT'S NOT LIKE I WAN-TED TO DO ANYTHING WITH YOU ANYWAYS!
DO WANT YOU WANT. I DON'T NEED YOUR APOLOGY.
WASTED EFFORT.

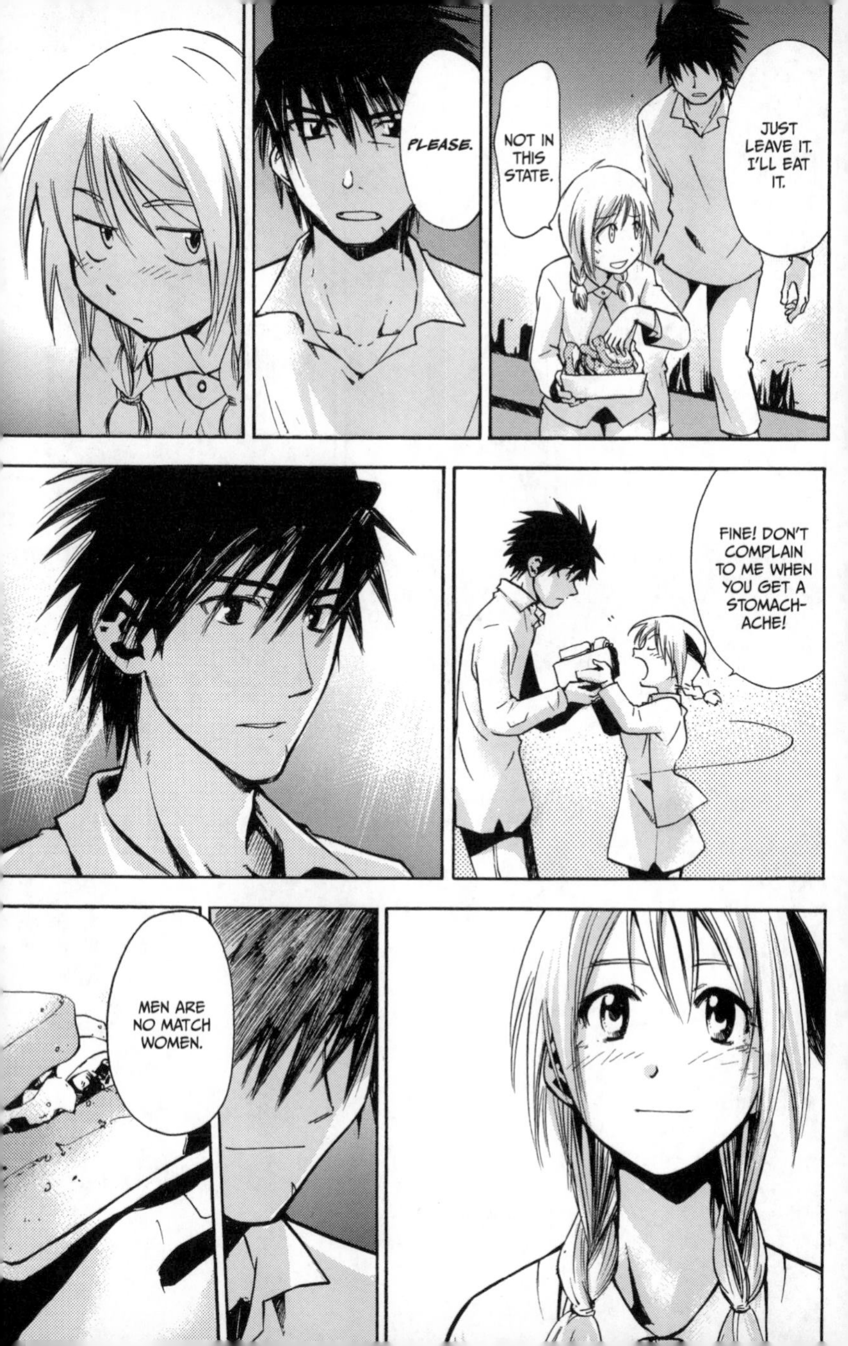
JUST LEAVE IT. I'LL EAT IT.
NOT IN THIS STATE.
PLEASE.
FINE! DON'T COMPLAIN TO ME WHEN YOU GET A STOMACH-ACHE!
MEN ARE NO MATCH WOMEN.

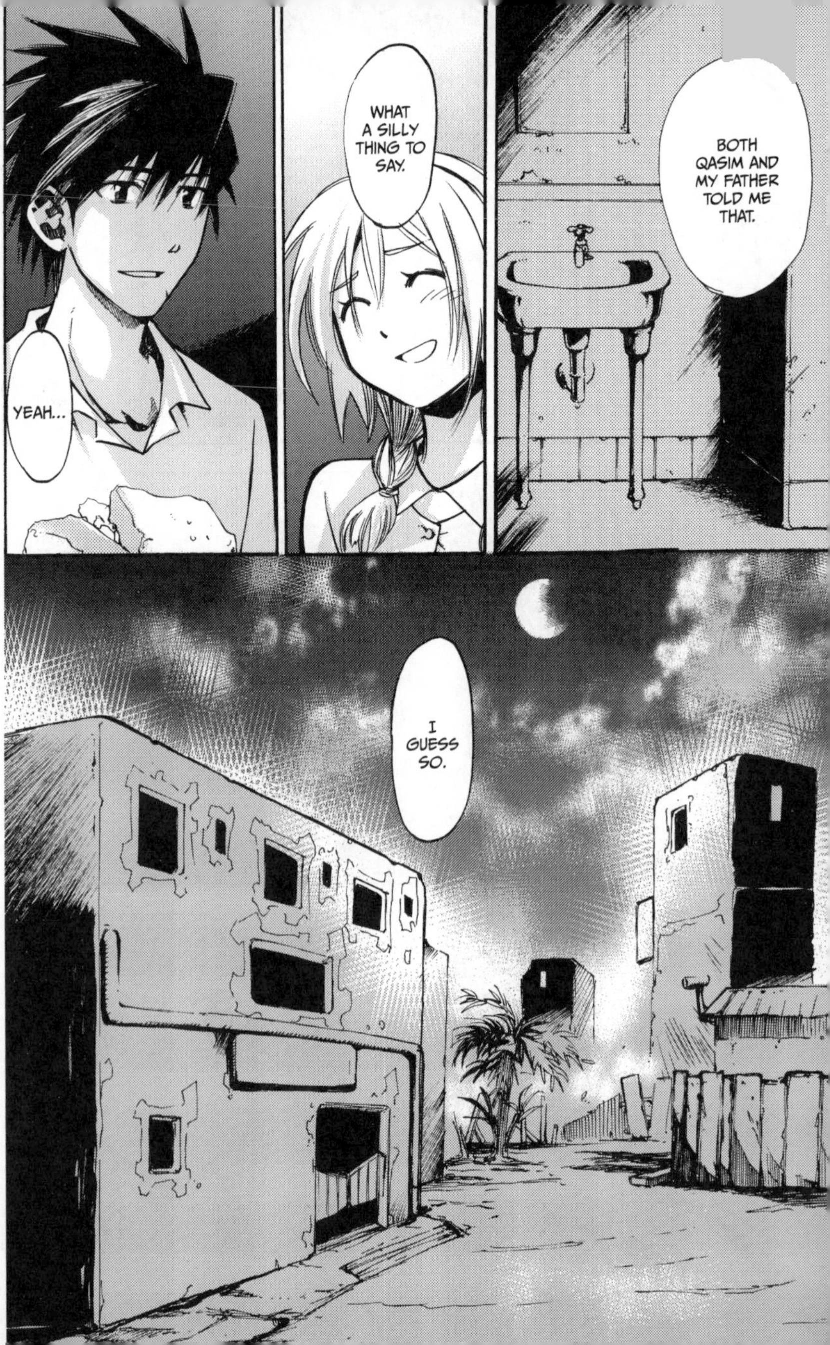
BOTH QASIM AND MY FATHER TOLD ME THAT.
WHAT A SILLY THING TO SAY.
YEAH...
I GUESS SO.

[CHAPTER 12]

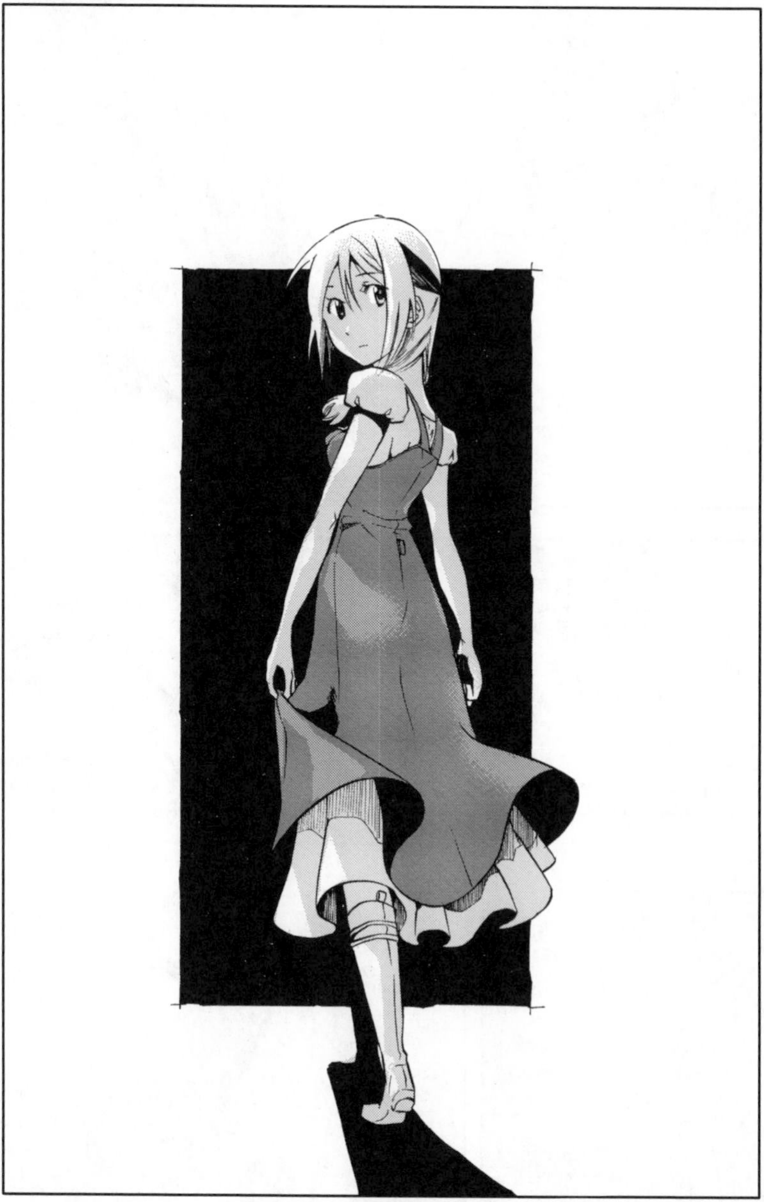

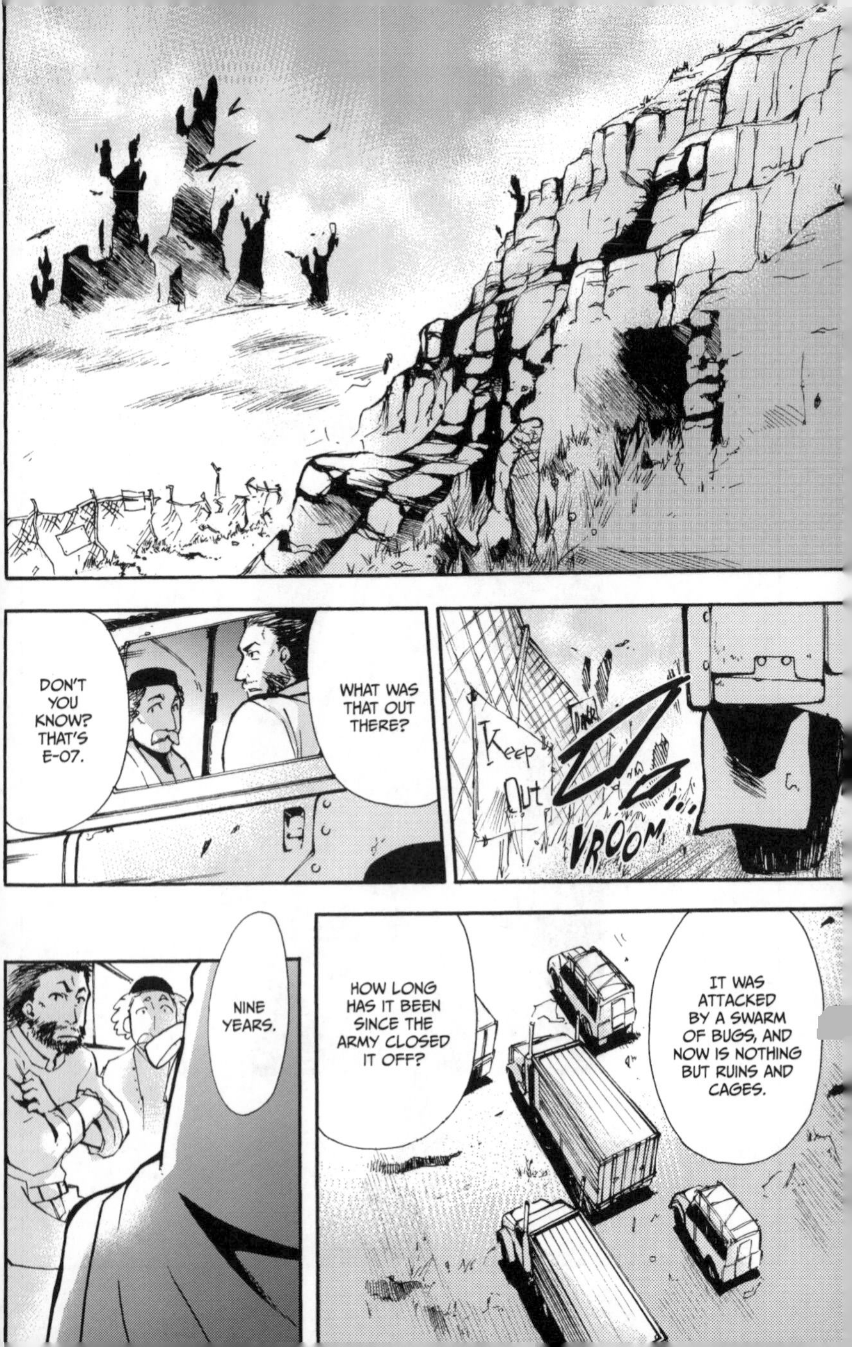
Keep Out
VROOM
WHAT WAS THAT OUT THERE?
DON'T YOU KNOW? THAT'S E-07.
IT WAS ATTACKED BY A SWARM OF BUGS, AND NOW IS NOTHING BUT RUINS AND CAGES.
HOW LONG HAS IT BEEN SINCE THE ARMY CLOSED IT OFF?
NINE YEARS.

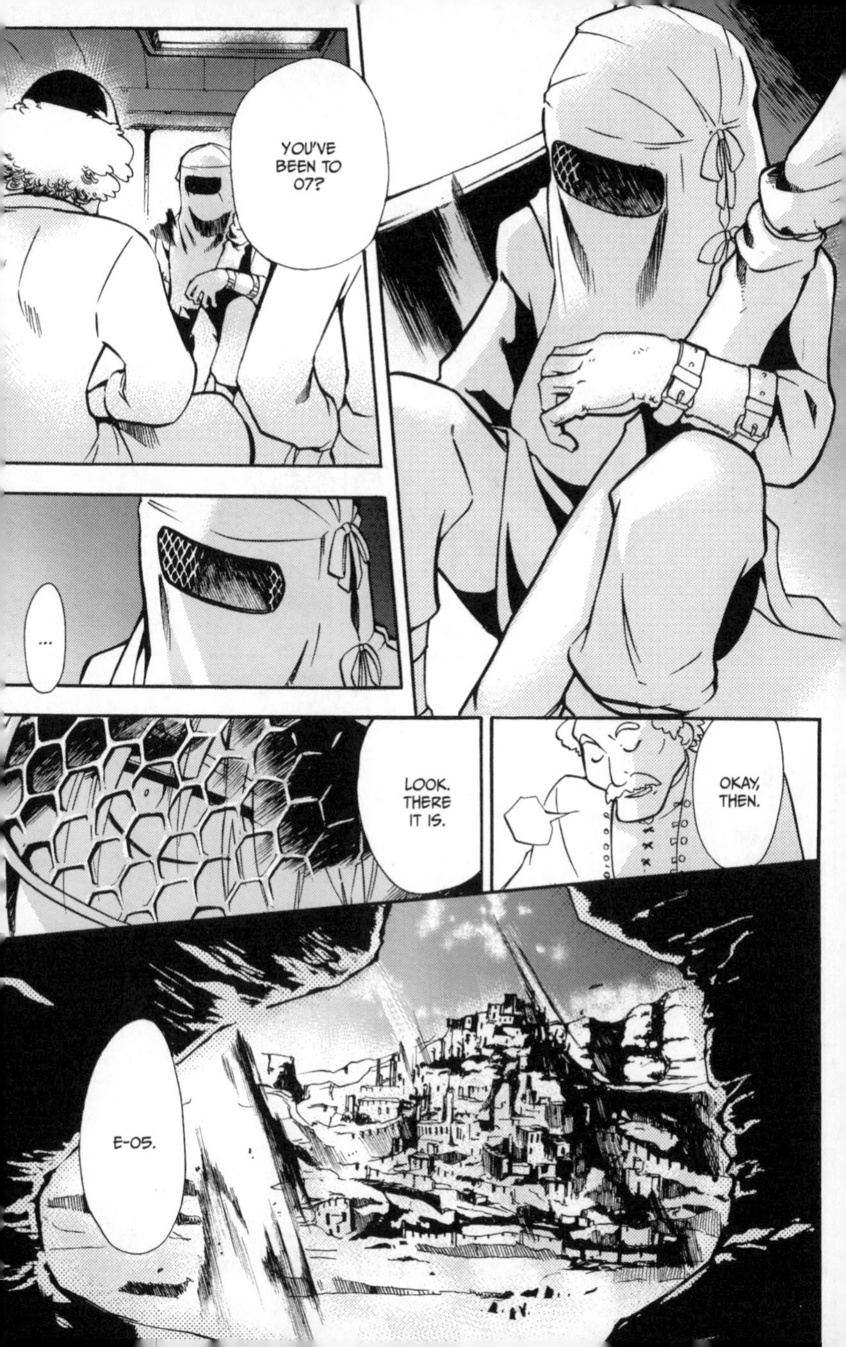
YOU'VE BEEN TO 07?
...
OKAY, THEN.
LOOK. THERE IT IS.
E-05.

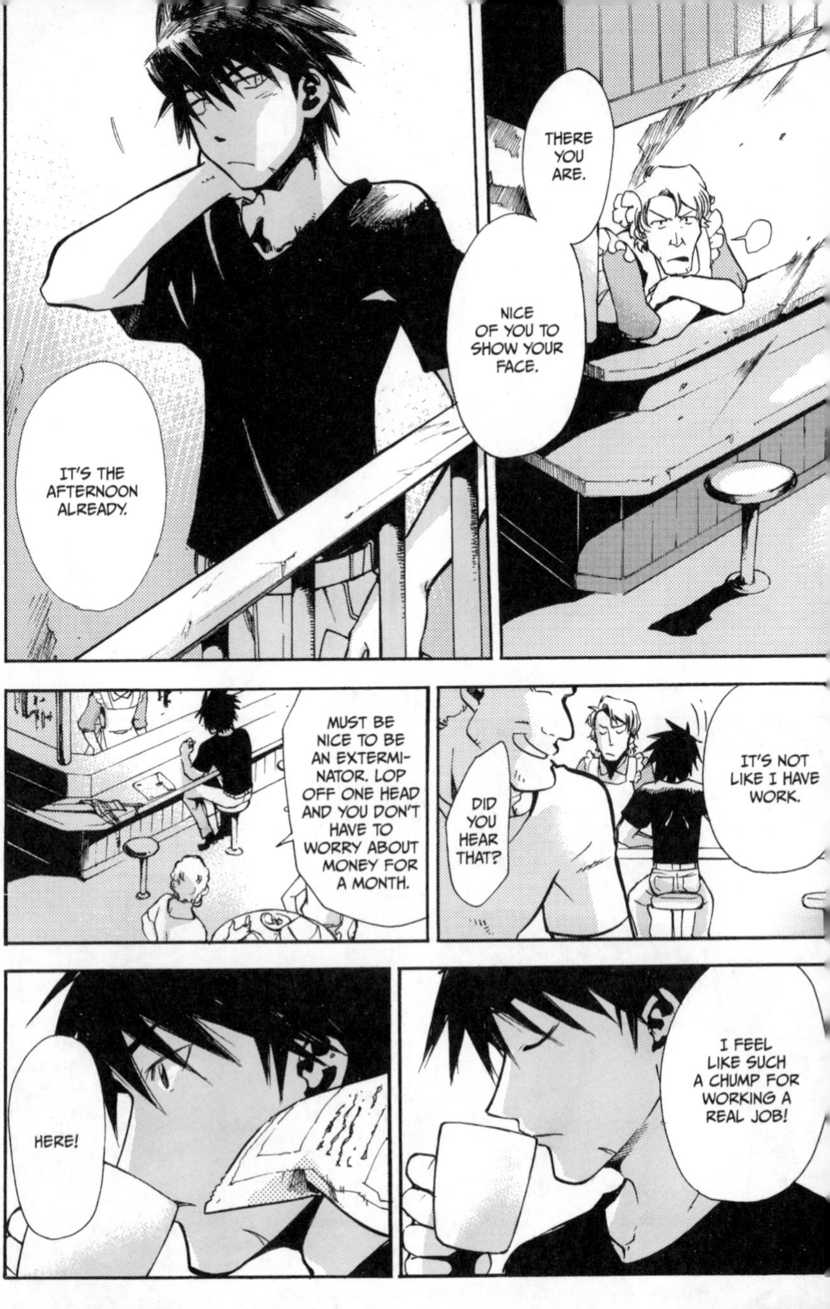
THERE YOU ARE.
NICE OF YOU TO SHOW YOUR FACE.
IT'S THE AFTERNOON ALREADY.
IT'S NOT LIKE I HAVE WORK.
DID YOU HEAR THAT?
MUST BE NICE TO BE AN EXTERMI-NATOR. LOP OFF ONE HEAD AND YOU DON'T HAVE TO WORRY ABOUT MONEY FOR A MONTH.
I FEEL LIKE SUCH A CHUMP FOR WORKING A REAL JOB!
HERE!

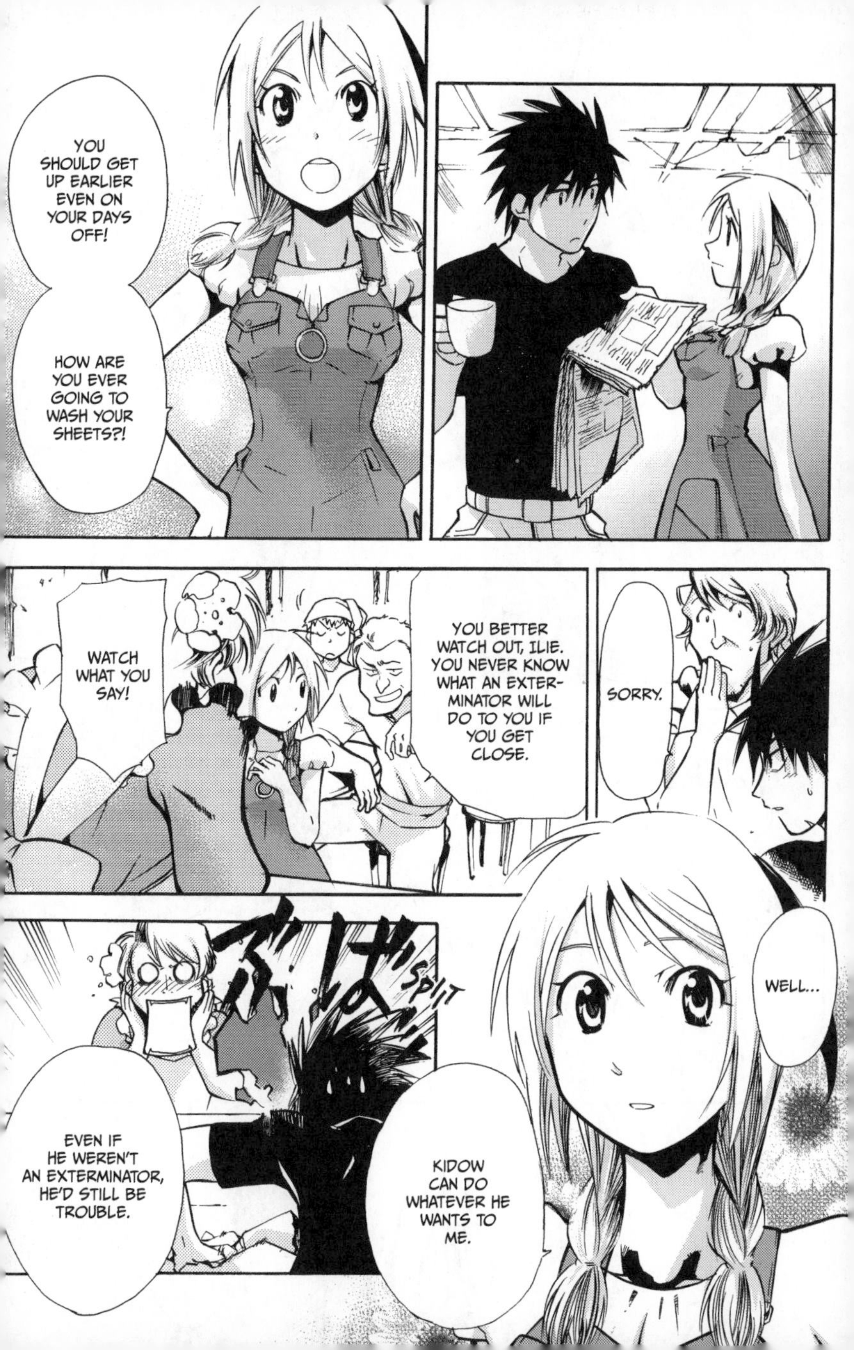
YOU SHOULD GET UP EARLIER EVEN ON YOUR DAYS OFF!
HOW ARE YOU EVER GOING TO WASH YOUR SHEETS?!
SORRY.
YOU BETTER WATCH OUT, ILIE. YOU NEVER KNOW WHAT AN EXTER-MINATOR WILL DO TO YOU IF YOU GET CLOSE.
WATCH WHAT YOU SAY!
WELL...
KIDOW CAN DO WHATEVER HE WANTS TO ME.
SPLIT
EVEN IF HE WEREN'T AN EXTERMINATOR, HE'D STILL BE TROUBLE.

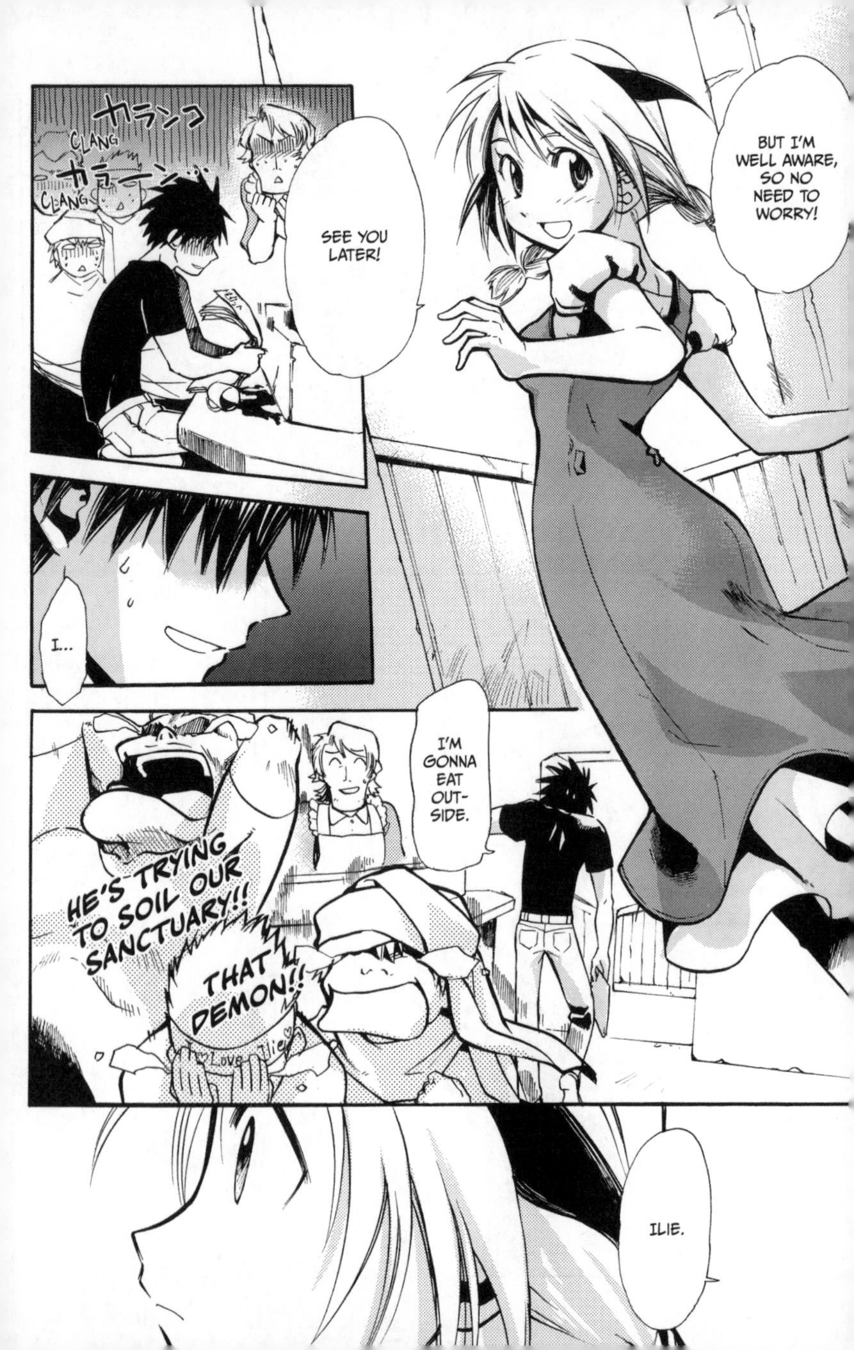
BUT I'M WELL AWARE, SO NO NEED TO WORRY!
SEE YOU LATER!
カランコ
CLANG
カラーン…
CLANG
I...
I'M GONNA EAT OUT-SIDE.
HE'S TRYING TO SOIL OUR SANCTUARY!!
THAT DEMON!!
Love Ilie
ILIE.

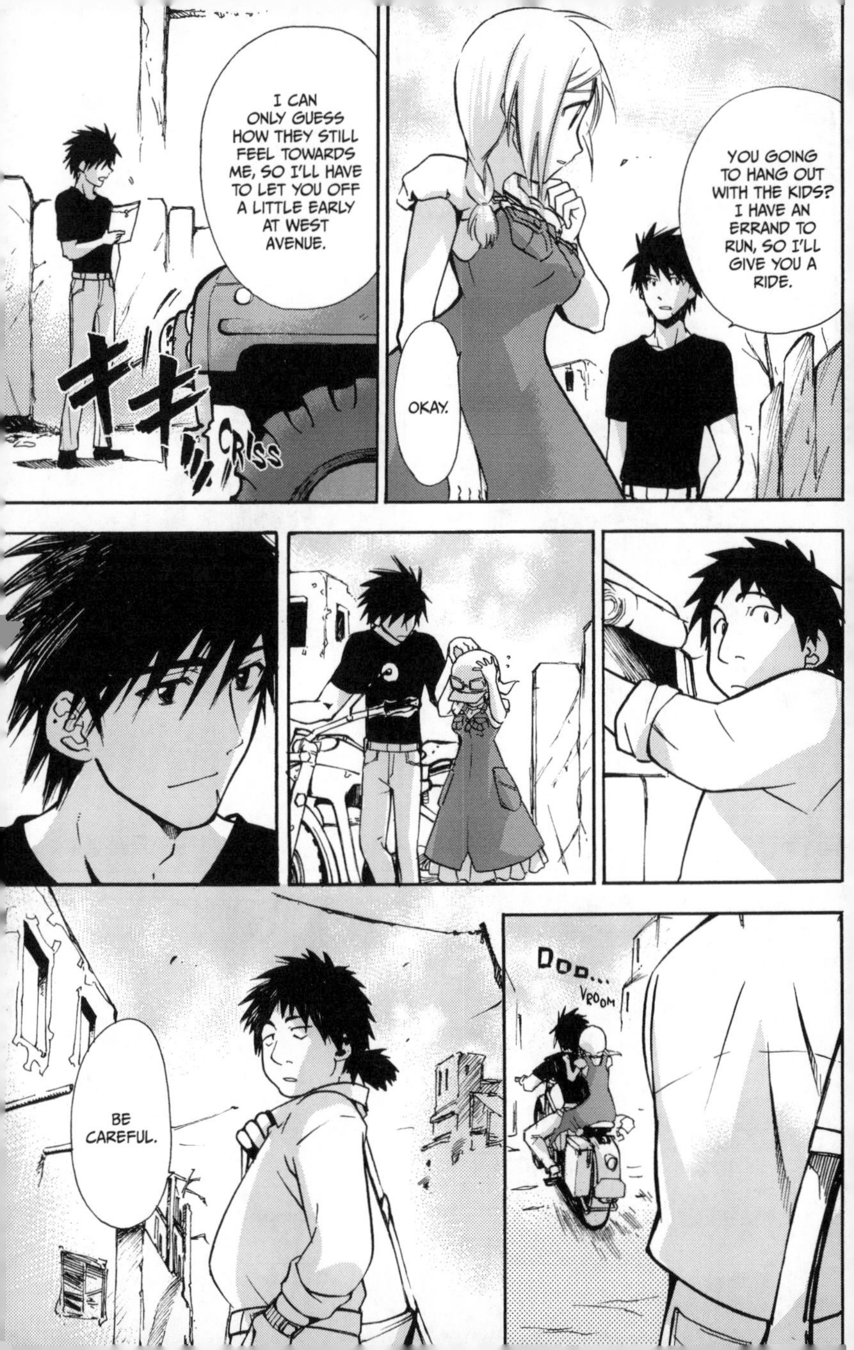
YOU GOING TO HANG OUT WITH THE KIDS? I HAVE AN ERRAND TO RUN, SO I'LL GIVE YOU A RIDE.
OKAY.
I CAN ONLY GUESS HOW THEY STILL FEEL TOWARDS ME, SO I'LL HAVE TO LET YOU OFF A LITTLE EARLY AT WEST AVENUE.
キキ
CRISS
DOD...
VROOM
BE CAREFUL.

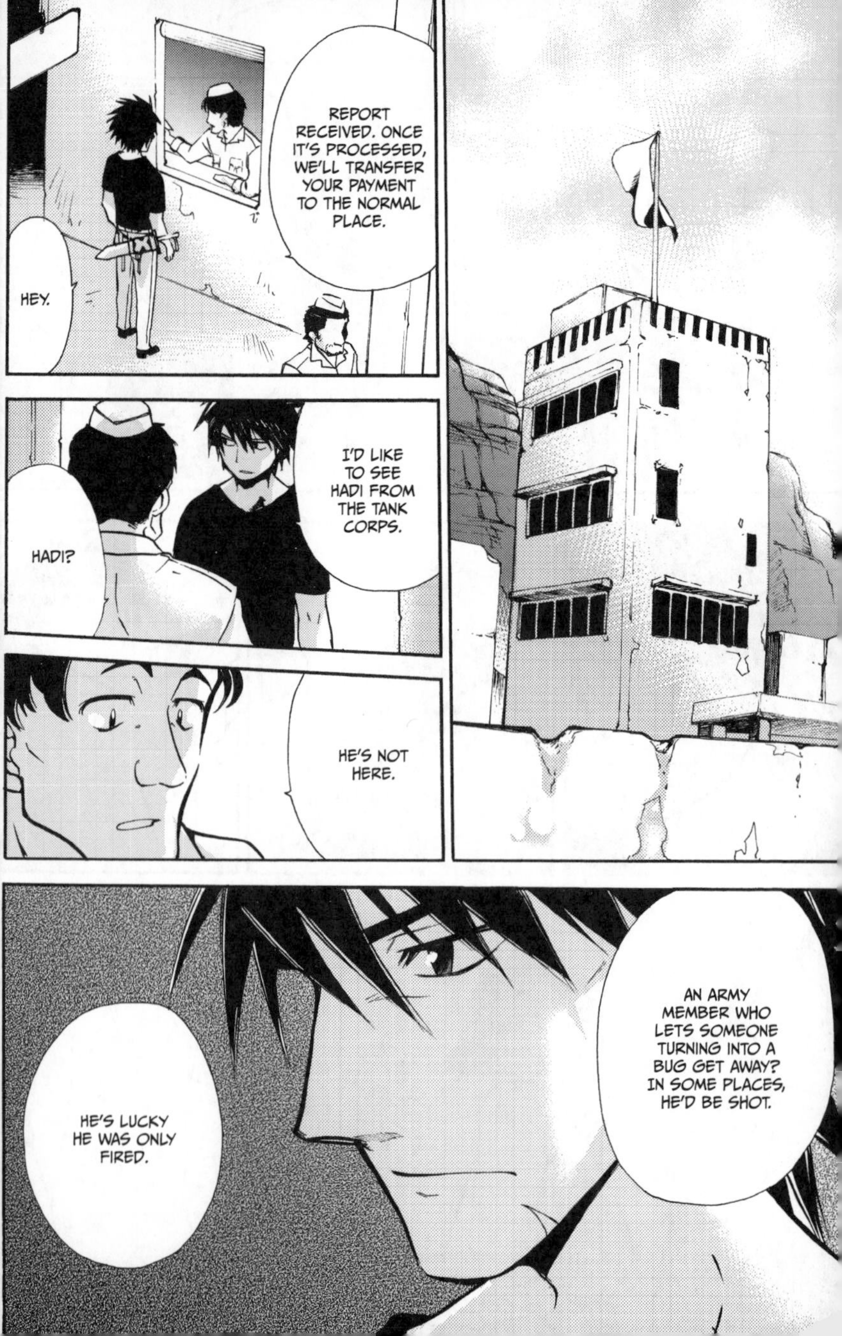
REPORT RECEIVED. ONCE IT'S PROCESSED, WE'LL TRANSFER YOUR PAYMENT TO THE NORMAL PLACE.
HEY.
I'D LIKE TO SEE HADI FROM THE TANK CORPS.
HADI?
HE'S NOT HERE.
AN ARMY MEMBER WHO LETS SOMEONE TURNING INTO A BUG GET AWAY? IN SOME PLACES, HE'D BE SHOT.
HE'S LUCKY HE WAS ONLY FIRED.

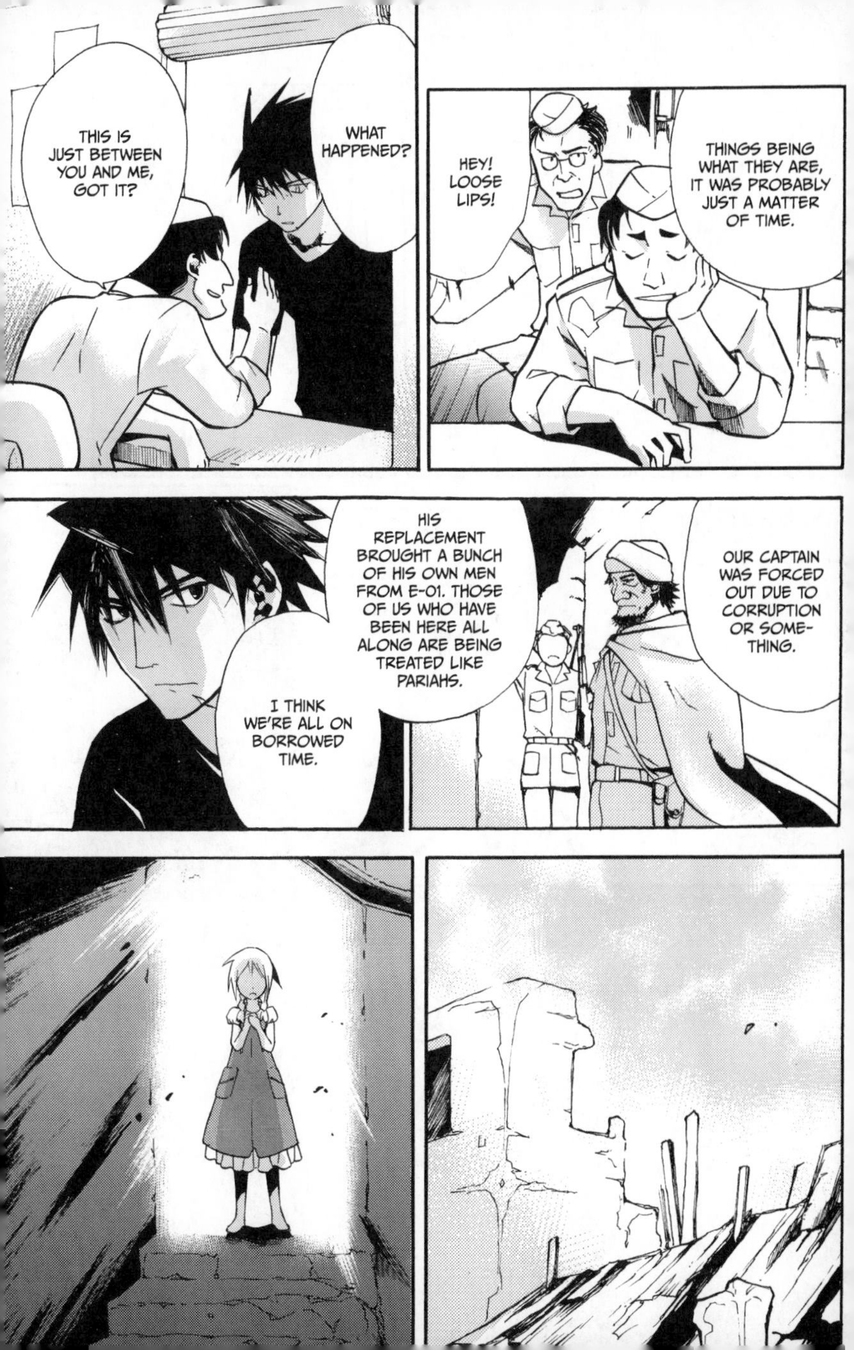
THINGS BEING WHAT THEY ARE, IT WAS PROBABLY JUST A MATTER OF TIME.
HEY! LOOSE LIPS!
WHAT HAPPENED?
THIS IS JUST BETWEEN YOU AND ME, GOT IT?
OUR CAPTAIN WAS FORCED OUT DUE TO CORRUPTION OR SOME-THING.
HIS REPLACEMENT BROUGHT A BUNCH OF HIS OWN MEN FROM E-01. THOSE OF US WHO HAVE BEEN HERE ALL ALONG ARE BEING TREATED LIKE PARIAHS.
I THINK WE'RE ALL ON BORROWED TIME.

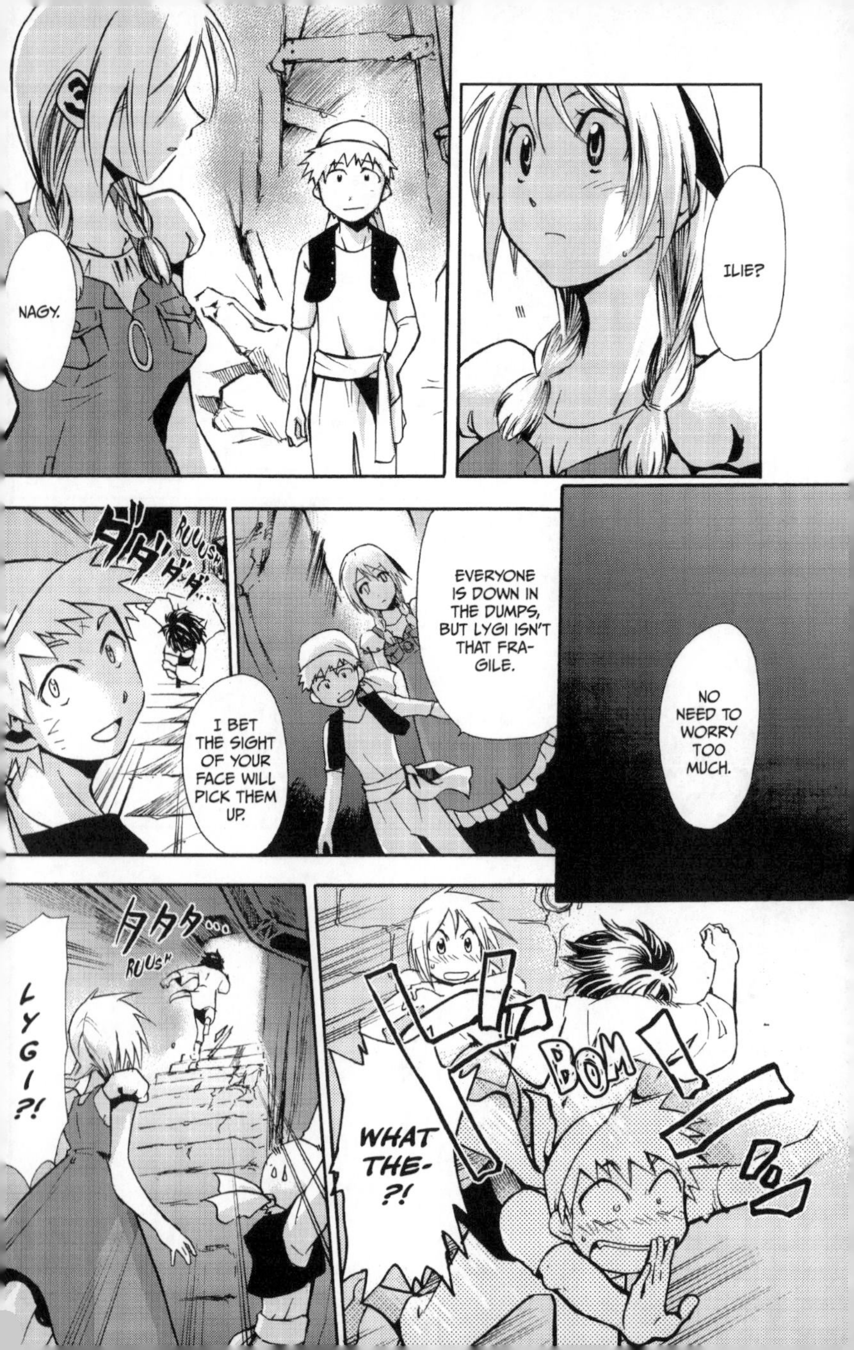
ILIE?
NAGY.
NO NEED TO WORRY TOO MUCH.
EVERYONE IS DOWN IN THE DUMPS, BUT LYGI ISN'T THAT FRA-GILE.
I BET THE SIGHT OF YOUR FACE WILL PICK THEM UP.
ダダダ…
RUUUSH…
BOM!
WHAT THE-?!
タタタ…
RUUSH
LYGI?!

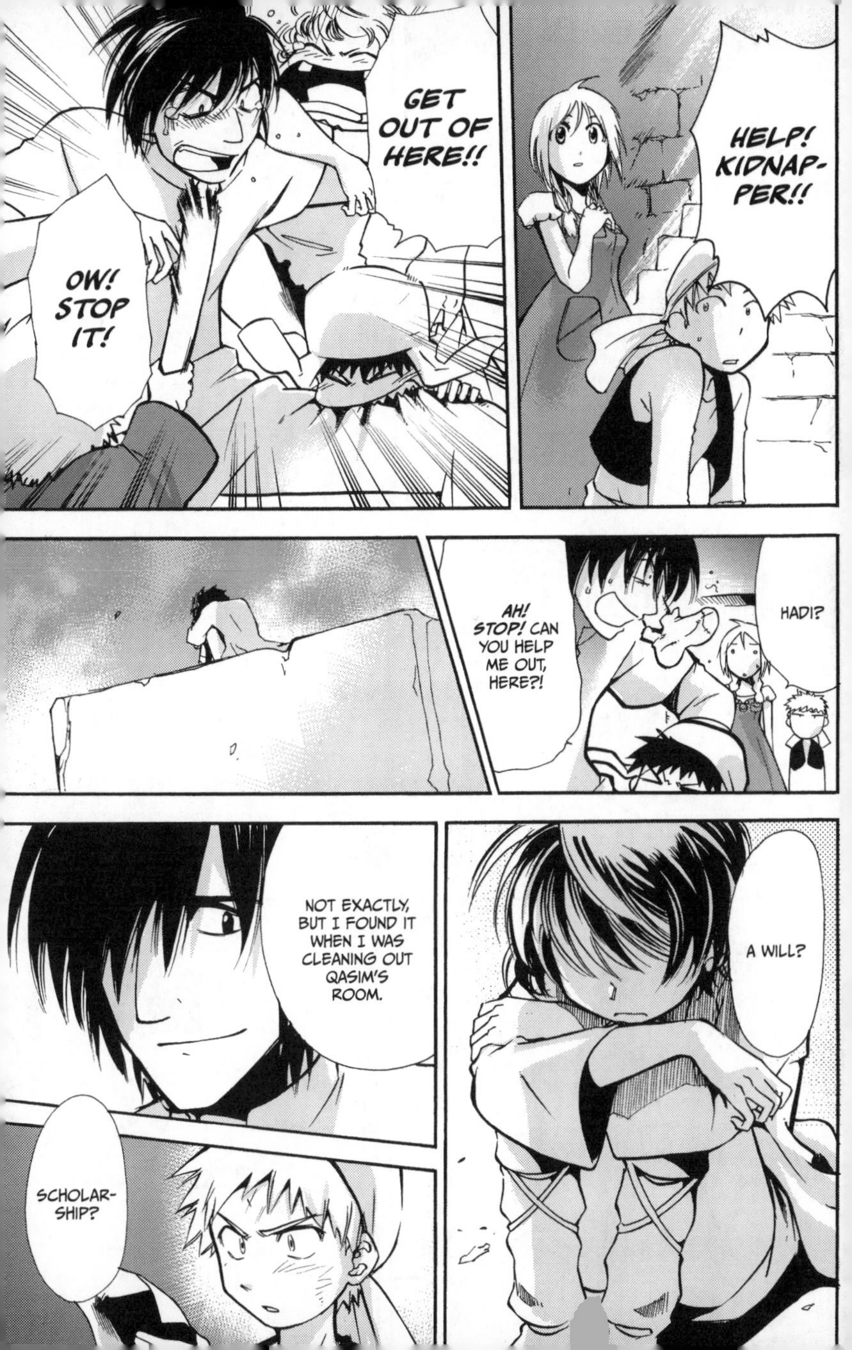
HELP! KIDNAPPER!!
GET OUT OF HERE!!
OW! STOP IT!
HADI?
AH! STOP! CAN YOU HELP ME OUT, HERE?!
A WILL?
NOT EXACTLY, BUT I FOUND IT WHEN I WAS CLEANING OUT QASIM'S ROOM.
SCHOLARSHIP?

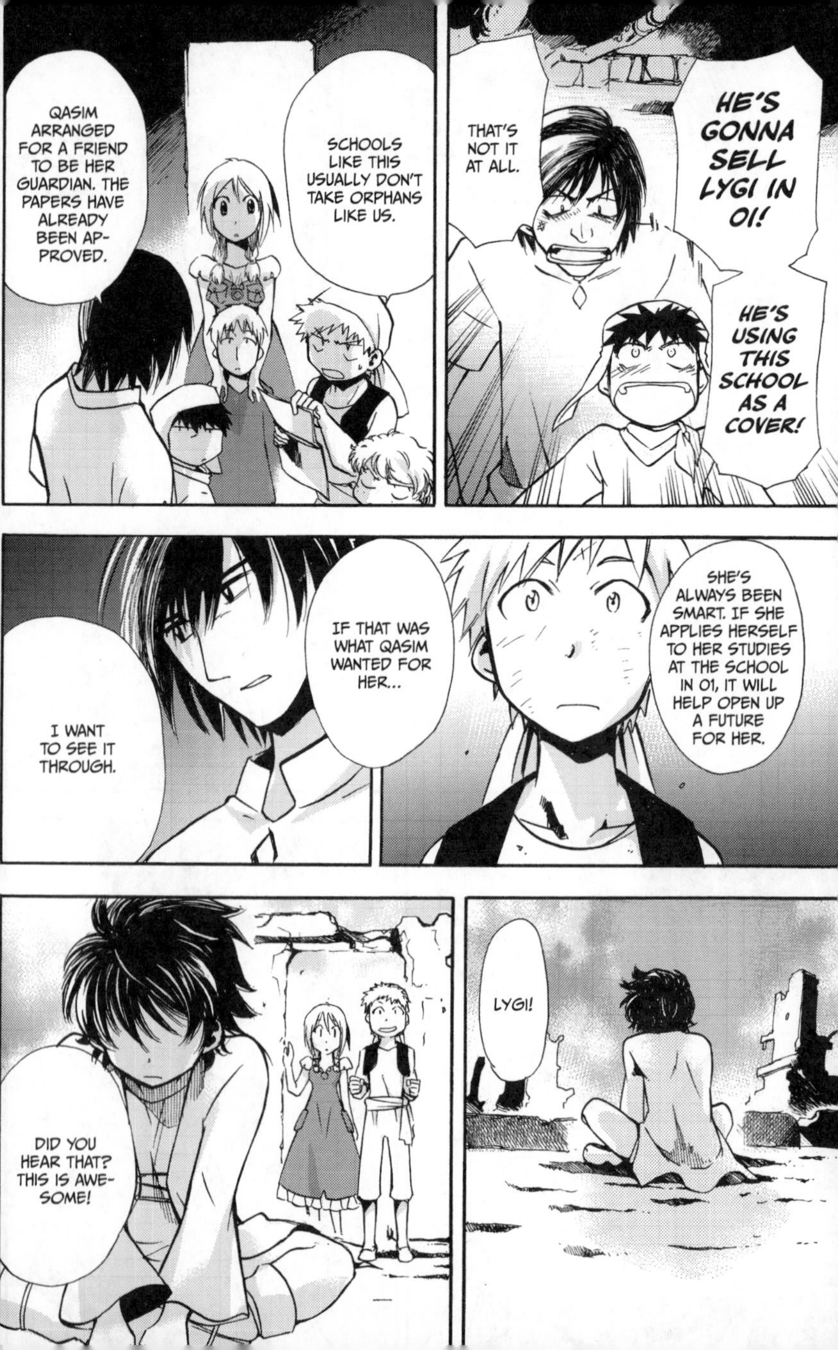
HE'S GONNA SELL LYGI IN OI!
HE'S USING THIS SCHOOL AS A COVER!
THAT'S NOT IT AT ALL.
SCHOOLS LIKE THIS USUALLY DON'T TAKE ORPHANS LIKE US.
QASIM ARRANGED FOR A FRIEND TO BE HER GUARDIAN. THE PAPERS HAVE ALREADY BEEN AP-PROVED.
SHE'S ALWAYS BEEN SMART. IF SHE APPLIES HERSELF TO HER STUDIES AT THE SCHOOL IN 01, IT WILL HELP OPEN UP A FUTURE FOR HER.
IF THAT WAS WHAT QASIM WANTED FOR HER...
I WANT TO SEE IT THROUGH.
LYGI!
DID YOU HEAR THAT? THIS IS AWE-SOME!

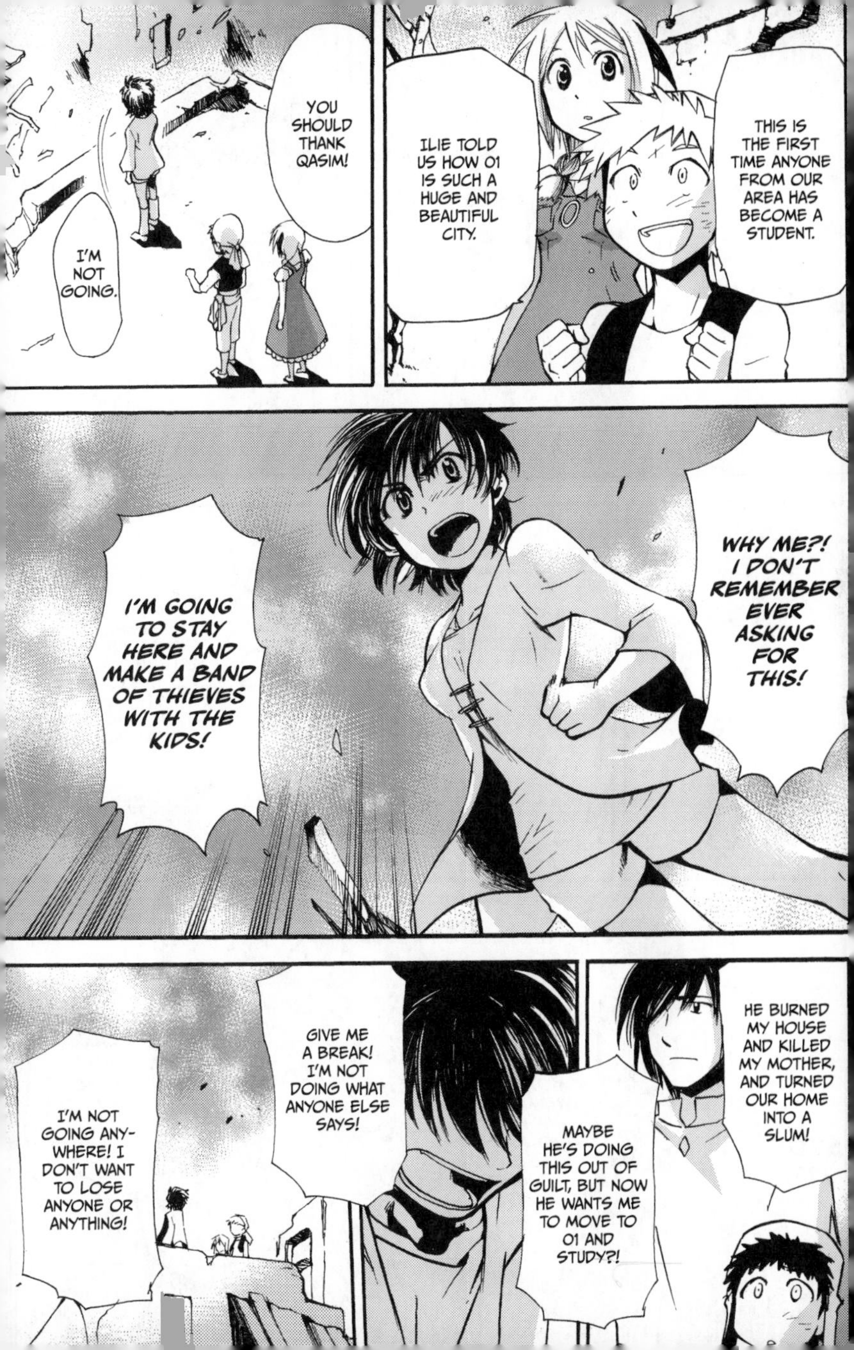
THIS IS THE FIRST TIME ANYONE FROM OUR AREA HAS BECOME A STUDENT.
ILIE TOLD US HOW 01 IS SUCH A HUGE AND BEAUTIFUL CITY.
YOU SHOULD THANK QASIM!
I'M NOT GOING.
WHY ME?! I DON'T REMEMBER EVER ASKING FOR THIS!
I'M GOING TO STAY HERE AND MAKE A BAND OF THIEVES WITH THE KIDS!
HE BURNED MY HOUSE AND KILLED MY MOTHER, AND TURNED OUR HOME INTO A SLUM!
MAYBE HE'S DOING THIS OUT OF GUILT, BUT NOW HE WANTS ME TO MOVE TO 01 AND STUDY?!
GIVE ME A BREAK! I'M NOT DOING WHAT ANYONE ELSE SAYS!
I'M NOT GOING ANYWHERE! I DON'T WANT TO LOSE ANYONE OR ANYTHING!

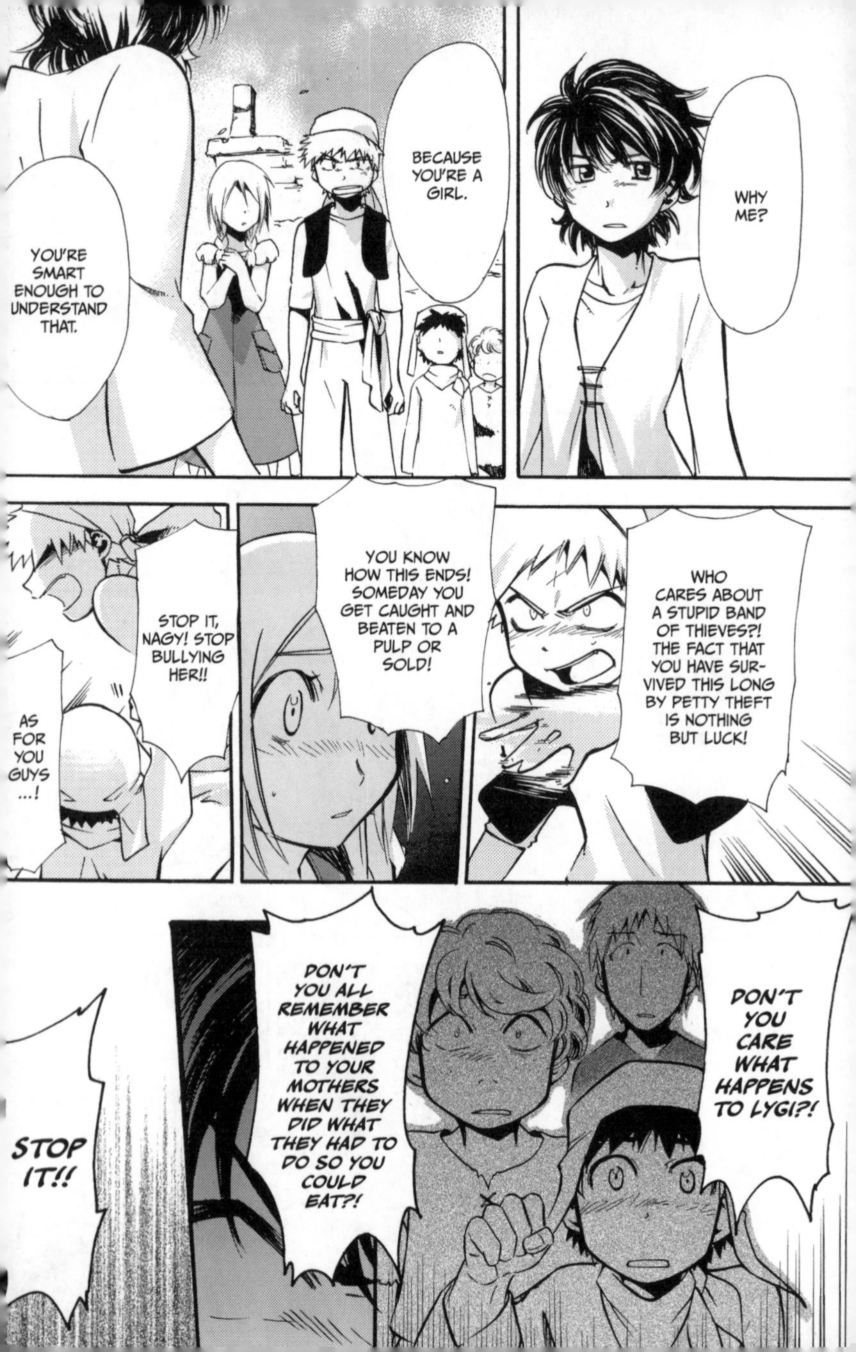
WHY ME?
BECAUSE YOU'RE A GIRL.
YOU'RE SMART ENOUGH TO UNDERSTAND THAT.
WHO CARES ABOUT A STUPID BAND OF THIEVES?! THE FACT THAT YOU HAVE SURVIVED THIS LONG BY PETTY THEFT IS NOTHING BUT LUCK!
YOU KNOW HOW THIS ENDS! SOMEDAY YOU GET CAUGHT AND BEATEN TO A PULP OR SOLD!
STOP IT, NAGY! STOP BULLYING HER!!
AS FOR YOU GUYS ...!
DON'T YOU CARE WHAT HAPPENS TO LYGI?!
DON'T YOU ALL REMEMBER WHAT HAPPENED TO YOUR MOTHERS WHEN THEY DID WHAT THEY HAD TO DO SO YOU COULD EAT?!
STOP IT!!

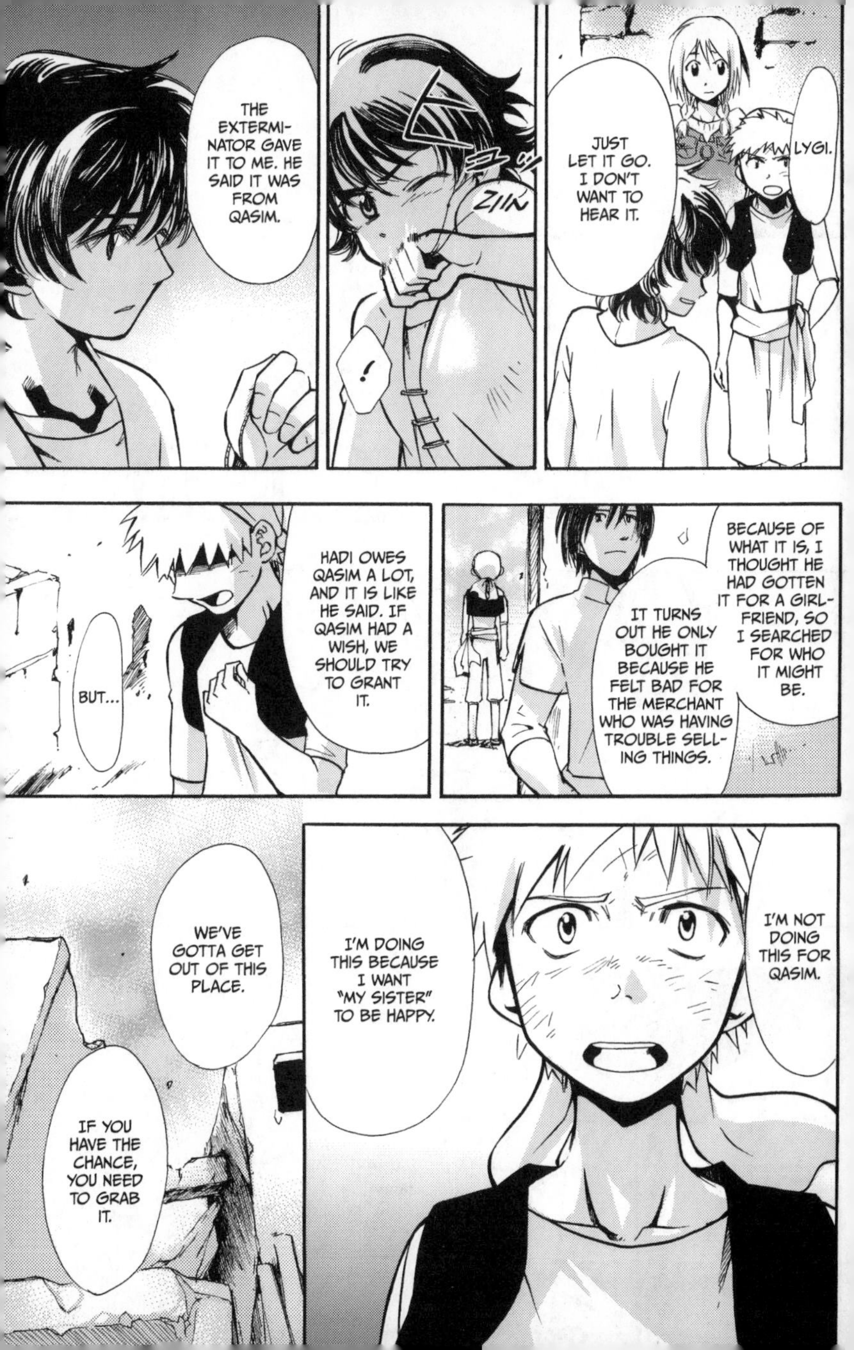
LYGI.
JUST LET IT GO. I DON'T WANT TO HEAR IT.
ZIIN
!
THE EXTERMINATOR GAVE IT TO ME. HE SAID IT WAS FROM QASIM.
BECAUSE OF WHAT IT IS, I THOUGHT HE HAD GOTTEN IT FOR A GIRLFRIEND, SO I SEARCHED FOR WHO IT MIGHT BE.
IT TURNS OUT HE ONLY BOUGHT IT BECAUSE HE FELT BAD FOR THE MERCHANT WHO WAS HAVING TROUBLE SELLING THINGS.
HADI OWES QASIM A LOT, AND IT IS LIKE HE SAID. IF QASIM HAD A WISH, WE SHOULD TRY TO GRANT IT.
BUT...
I'M NOT DOING THIS FOR QASIM.
I'M DOING THIS BECAUSE I WANT "MY SISTER" TO BE HAPPY.
WE'VE GOTTA GET OUT OF THIS PLACE.
IF YOU HAVE THE CHANCE, YOU NEED TO GRAB IT.

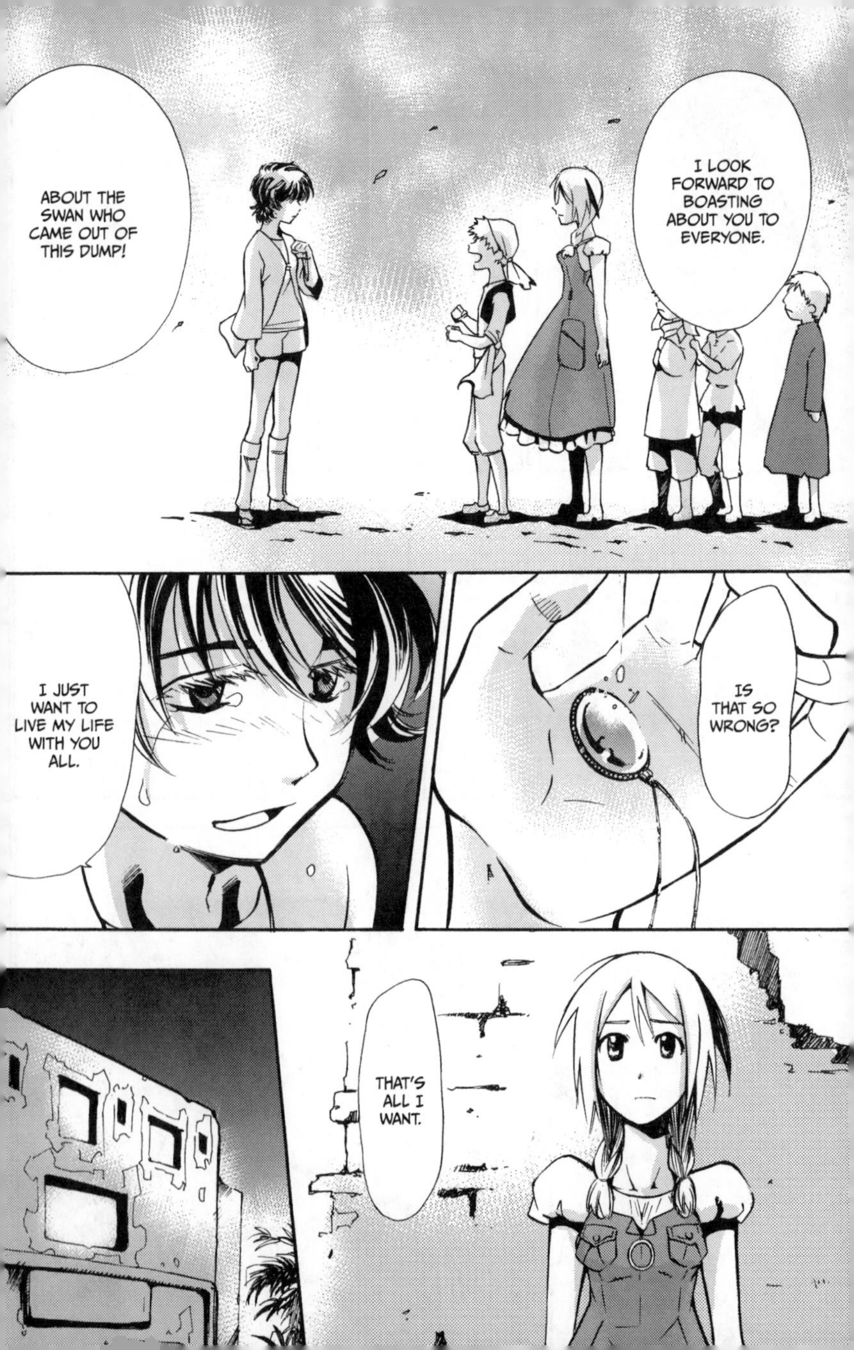
I LOOK FORWARD TO BOASTING ABOUT YOU TO EVERYONE.
ABOUT THE SWAN WHO CAME OUT OF THIS DUMP!
IS THAT SO WRONG?
I JUST WANT TO LIVE MY LIFE WITH YOU ALL.
THAT'S ALL I WANT.

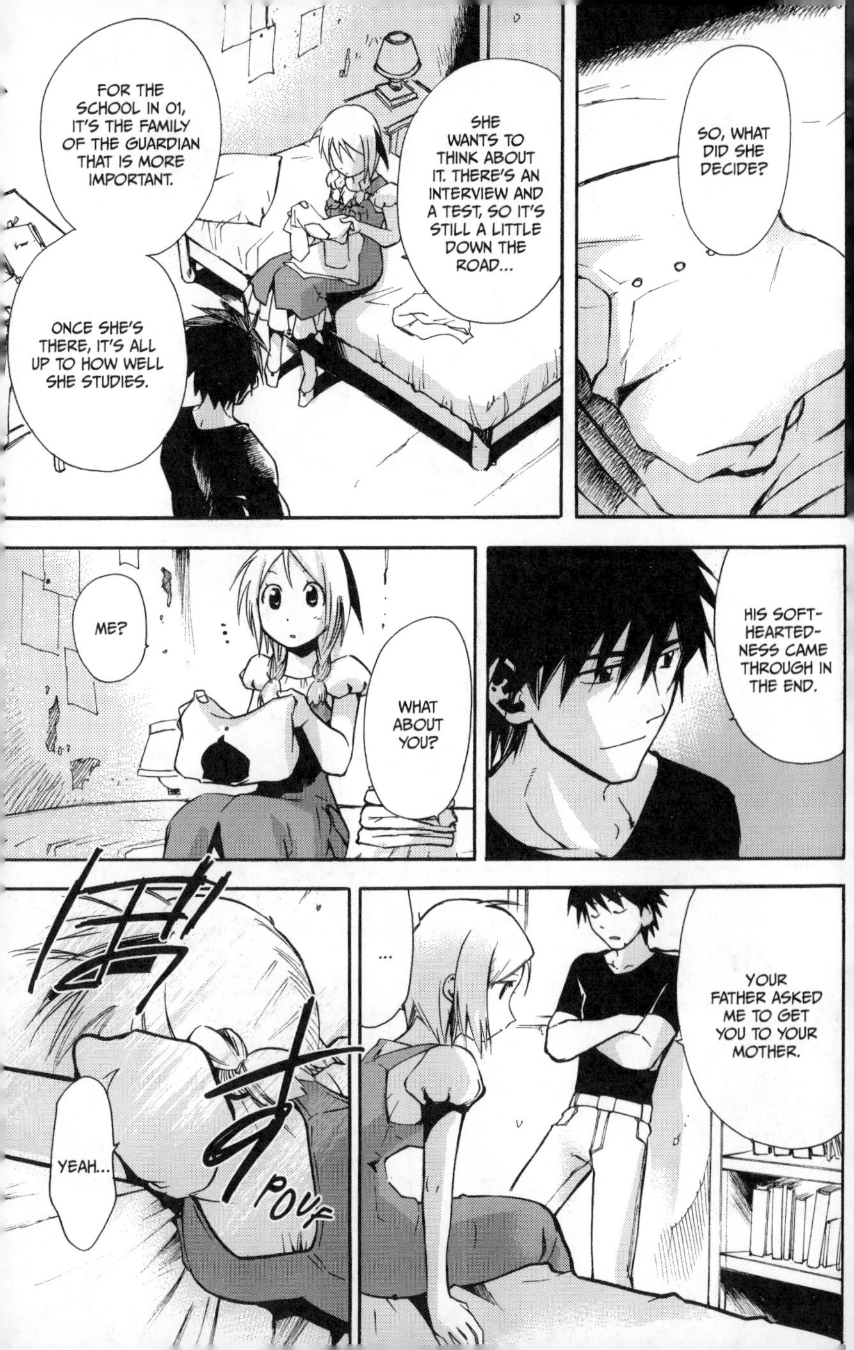
SO, WHAT DID SHE DECIDE?
SHE WANTS TO THINK ABOUT IT. THERE'S AN INTERVIEW AND A TEST, SO IT'S STILL A LITTLE DOWN THE ROAD...
FOR THE SCHOOL IN 01, IT'S THE FAMILY OF THE GUARDIAN THAT IS MORE IMPORTANT.
ONCE SHE'S THERE, IT'S ALL UP TO HOW WELL SHE STUDIES.
HIS SOFT-HEARTED-NESS CAME THROUGH IN THE END.
WHAT ABOUT YOU?
ME?
YOUR FATHER ASKED ME TO GET YOU TO YOUR MOTHER.
...
YEAH...
POUF

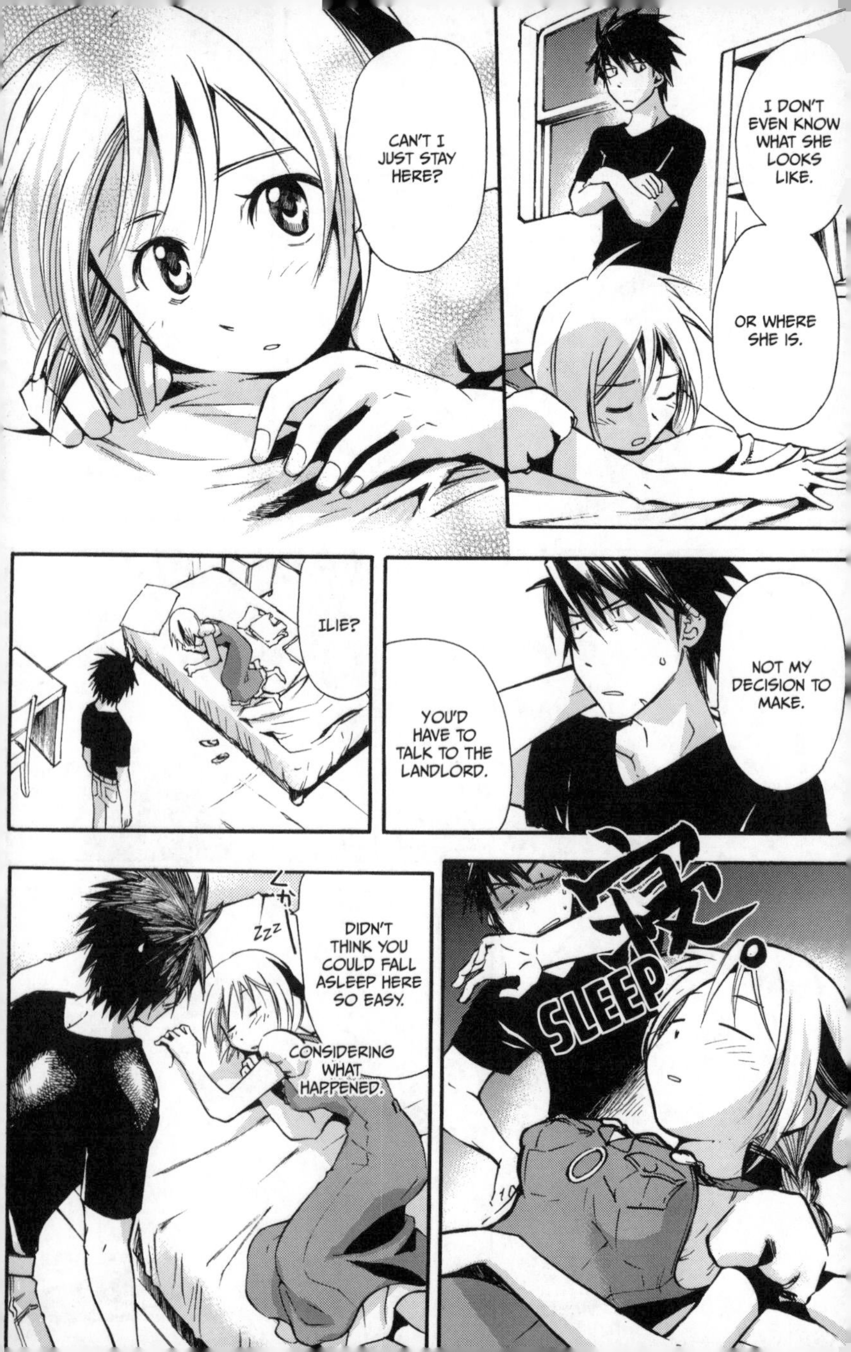
I DON'T EVEN KNOW WHAT SHE LOOKS LIKE.
OR WHERE SHE IS.
CAN'T I JUST STAY HERE?
NOT MY DECISION TO MAKE.
YOU'D HAVE TO TALK TO THE LANDLORD.
ILIE?
SLEEP
DIDN'T THINK YOU COULD FALL ASLEEP HERE SO EASY.
CONSIDERING WHAT HAPPENED.
zzz

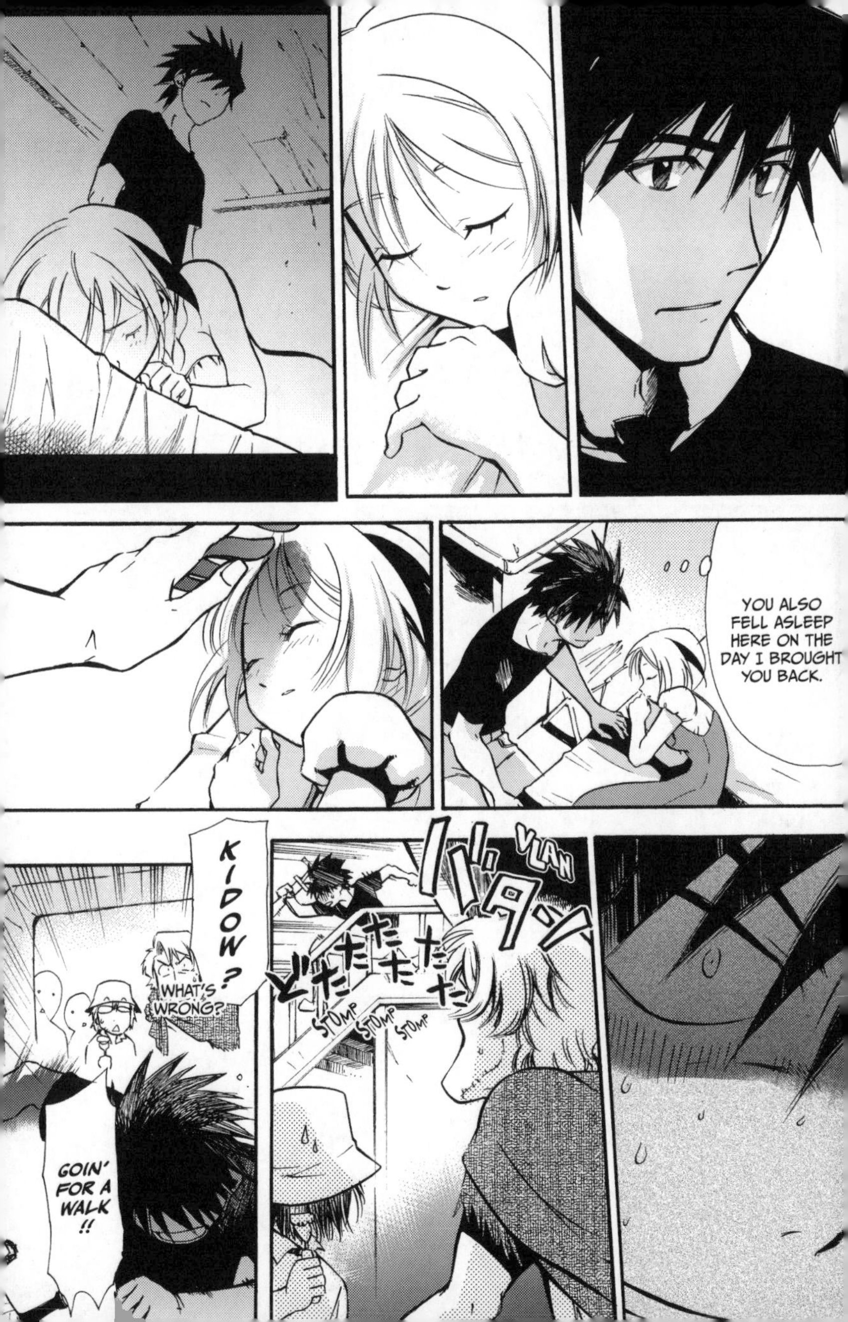
YOU ALSO FELL ASLEEP HERE ON THE DAY I BROUGHT YOU BACK.
VLAN
STOMP STOMP STOMP
KIDOW?
WHAT'S WRONG?
GOIN' FOR A WALK!!

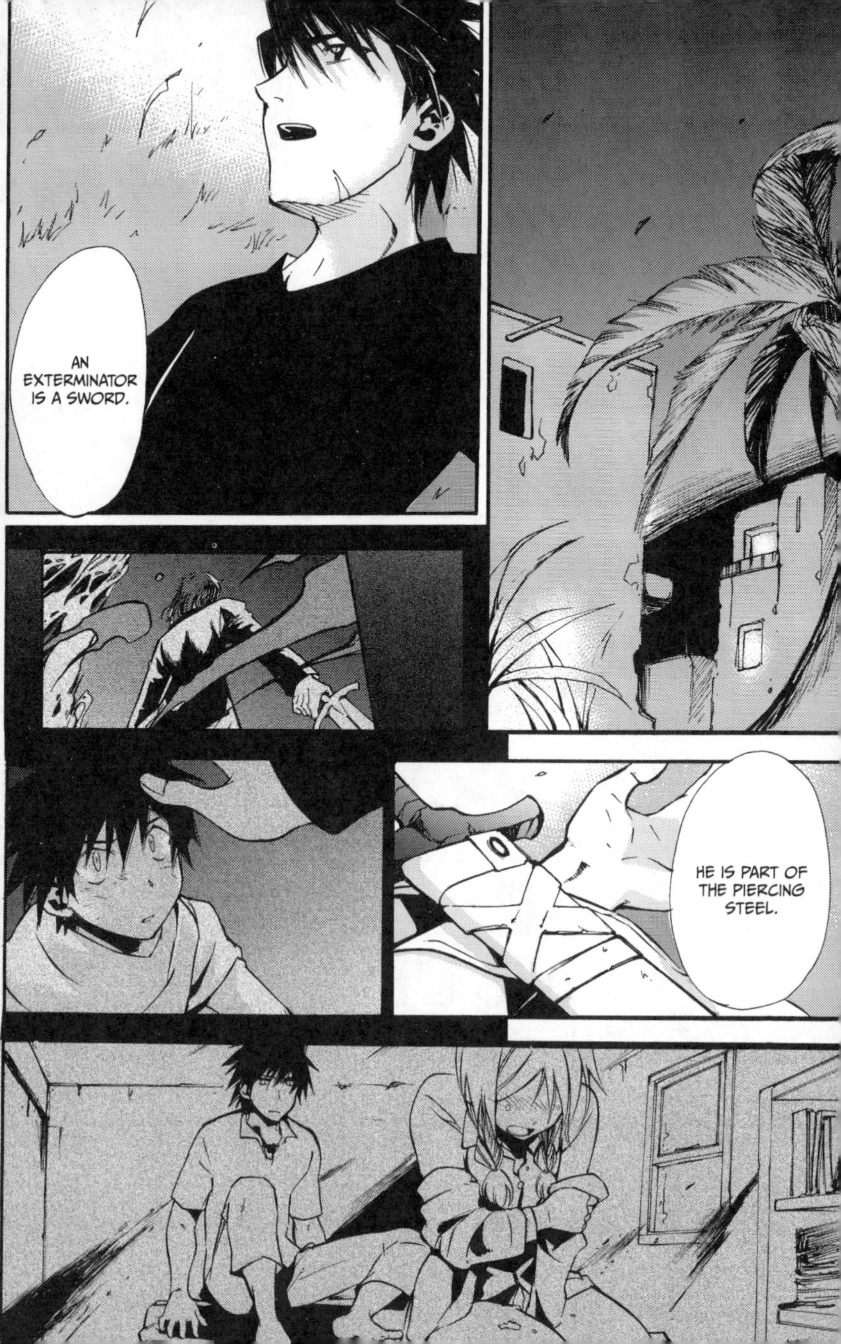
AN EXTERMINATOR IS A SWORD.
HE IS PART OF THE PIERCING STEEL.

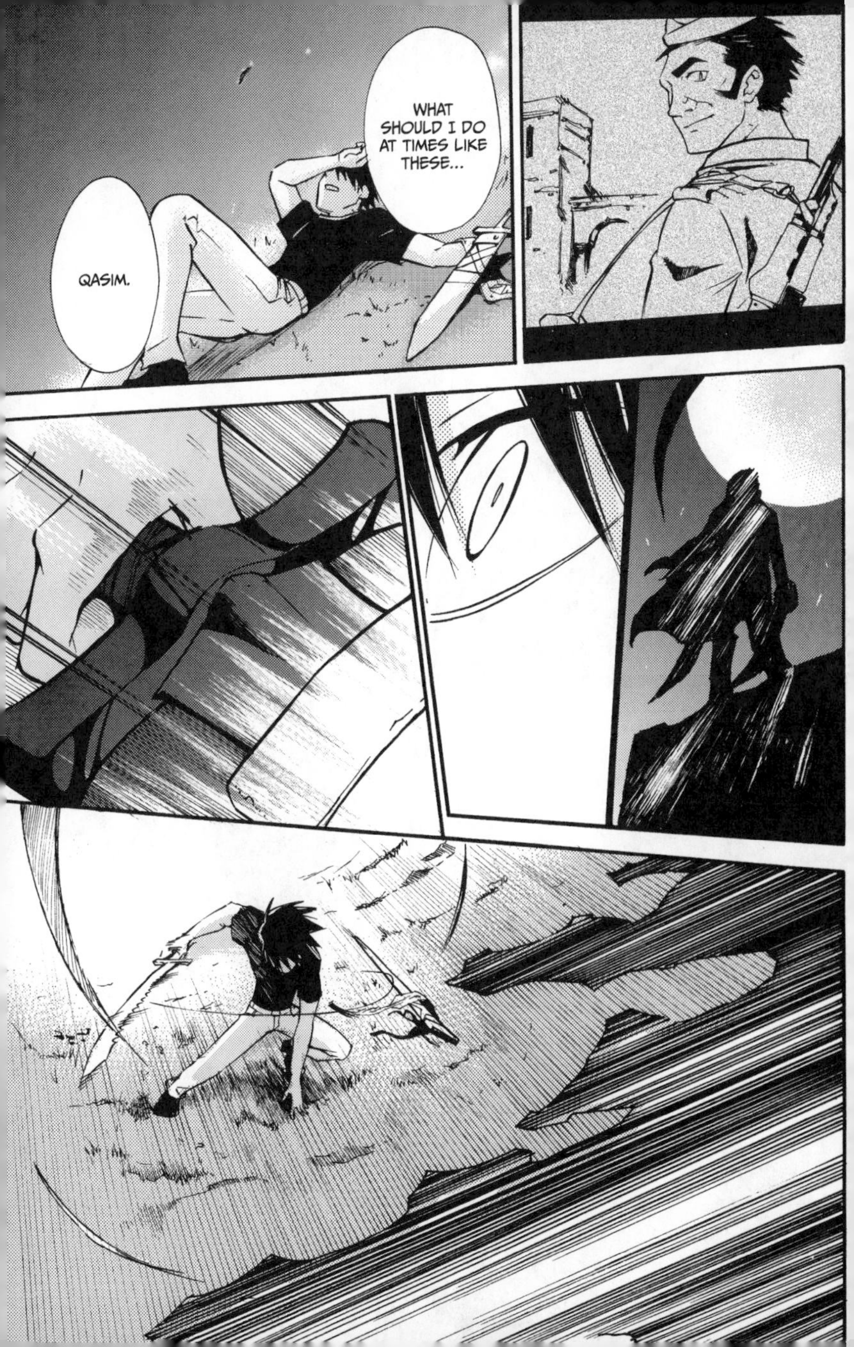
WHAT SHOULD I DO AT TIMES LIKE THESE...
QASIM.

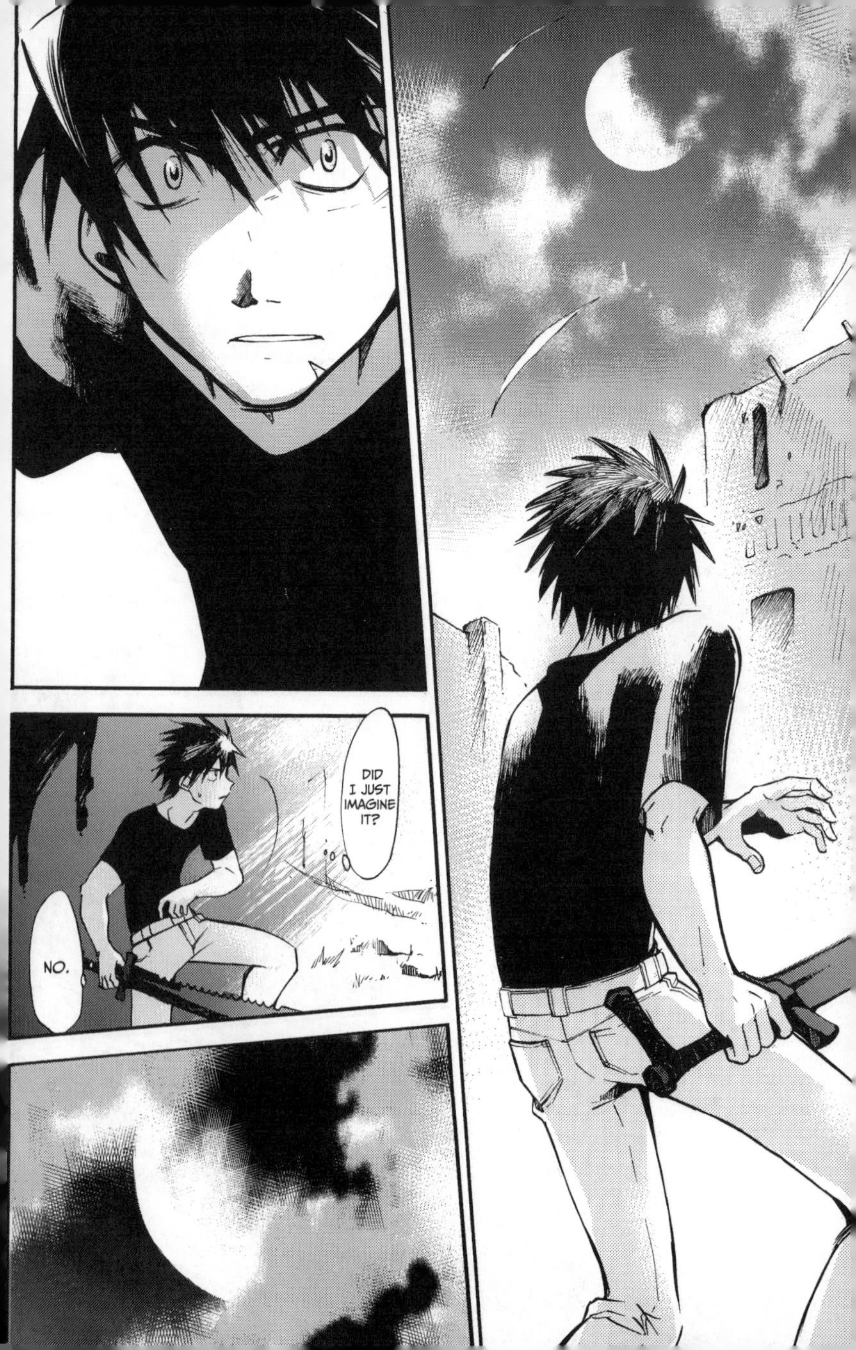
DID I JUST IMAGINE IT?
NO.

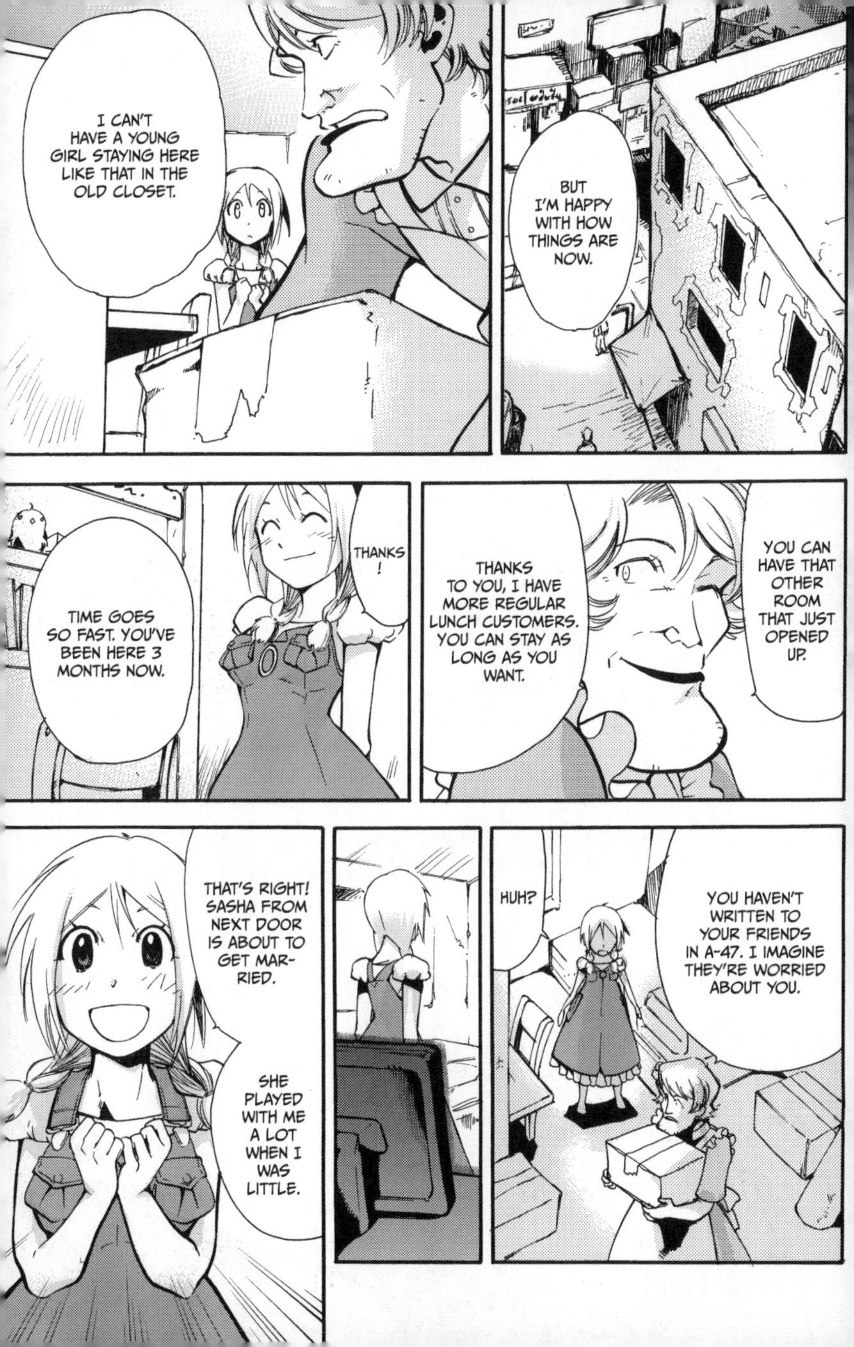
BUT I'M HAPPY WITH HOW THINGS ARE NOW.
I CAN'T HAVE A YOUNG GIRL STAYING HERE LIKE THAT IN THE OLD CLOSET.
YOU CAN HAVE THAT OTHER ROOM THAT JUST OPENED UP.
THANKS TO YOU, I HAVE MORE REGULAR LUNCH CUSTOMERS. YOU CAN STAY AS LONG AS YOU WANT.
THANKS!
TIME GOES SO FAST. YOU'VE BEEN HERE 3 MONTHS NOW.
YOU HAVEN'T WRITTEN TO YOUR FRIENDS IN A-47. I IMAGINE THEY'RE WORRIED ABOUT YOU.
HUH?
THAT'S RIGHT! SASHA FROM NEXT DOOR IS ABOUT TO GET MAR-RIED.
SHE PLAYED WITH ME A LOT WHEN I WAS LITTLE.

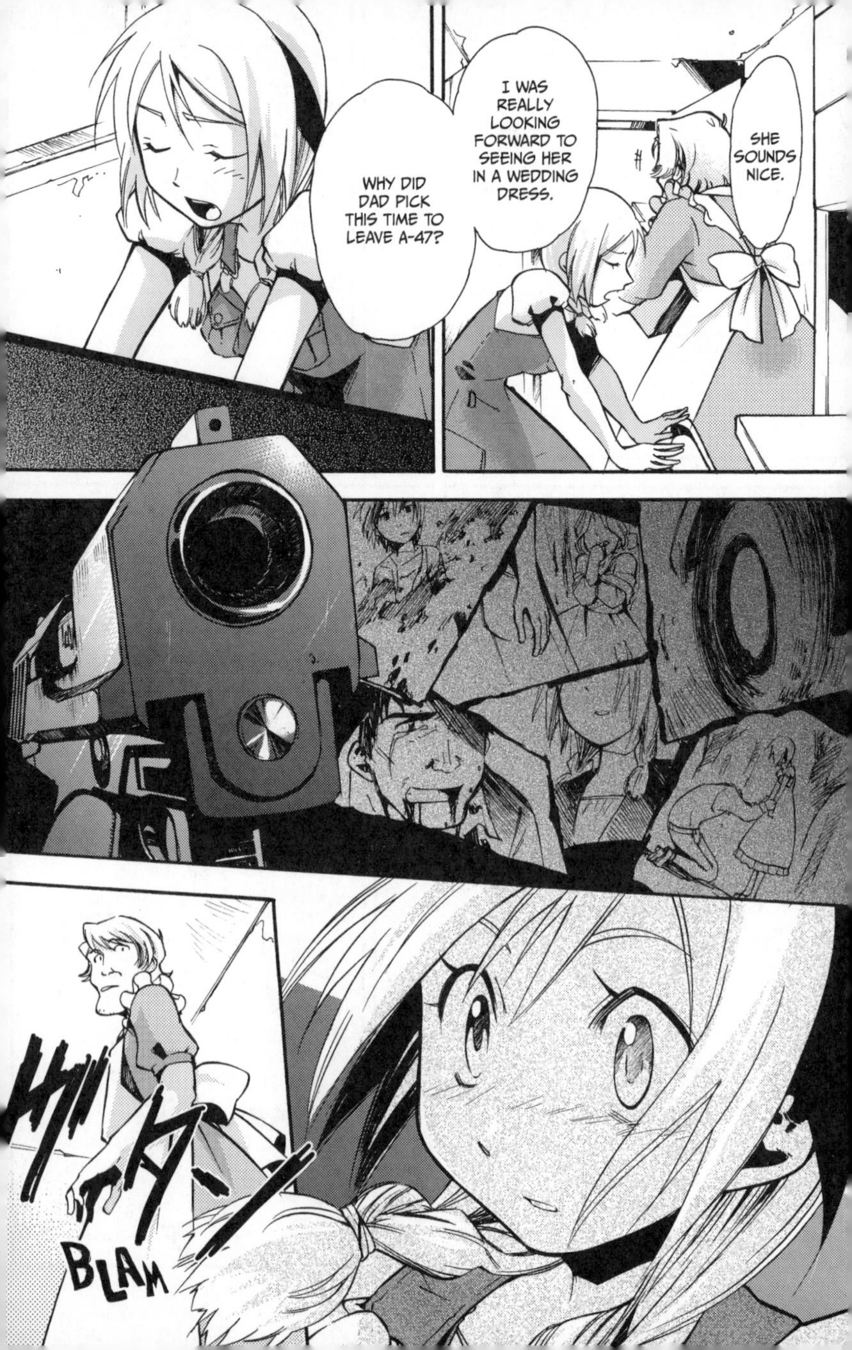
SHE SOUNDS NICE.
I WAS REALLY LOOKING FORWARD TO SEEING HER IN A WEDDING DRESS.
WHY DID DAD PICK THIS TIME TO LEAVE A-47?
BLAM

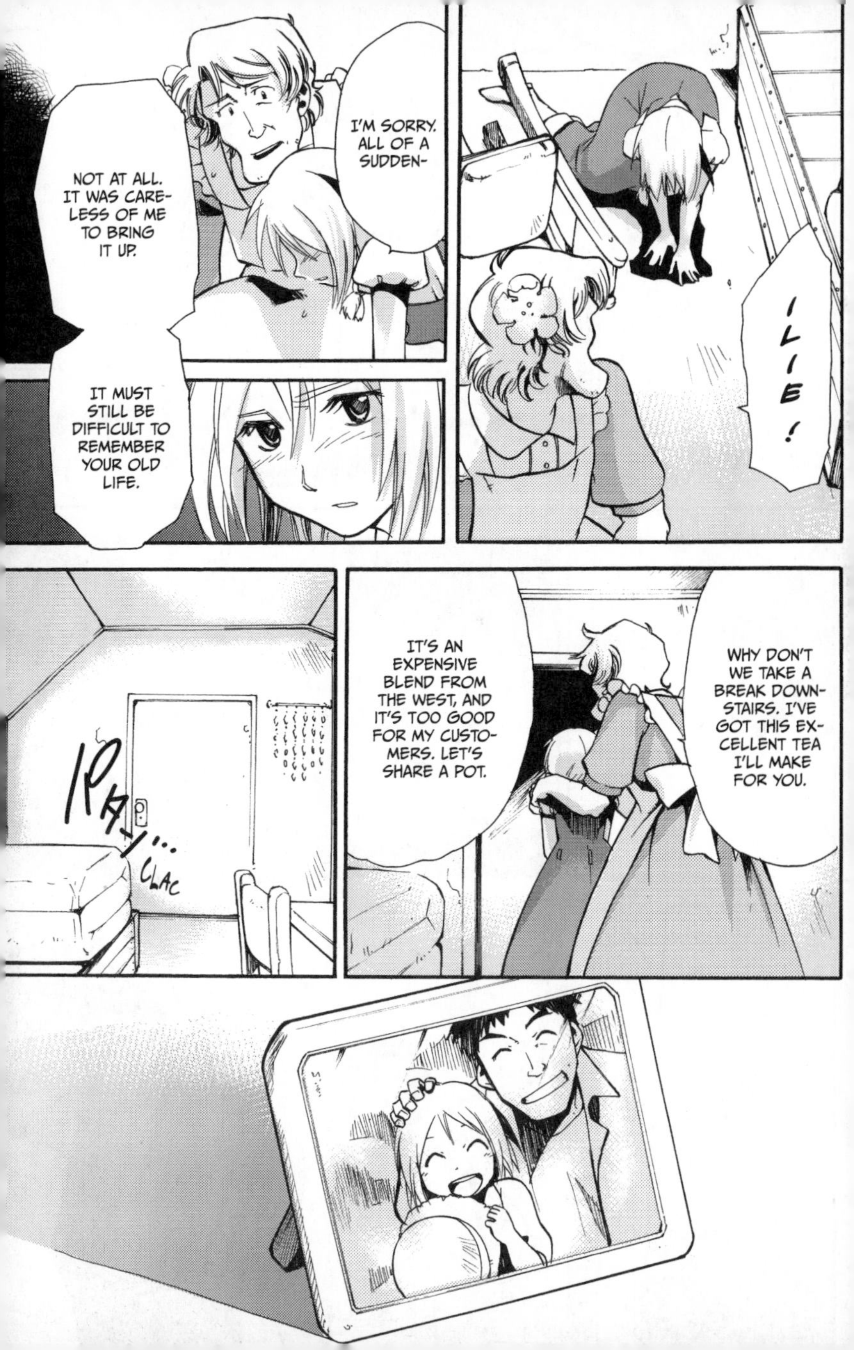
ILIE!
I'M SORRY. ALL OF A SUDDEN-
NOT AT ALL. IT WAS CARELESS OF ME TO BRING IT UP.
IT MUST STILL BE DIFFICULT TO REMEMBER YOUR OLD LIFE.
WHY DON'T WE TAKE A BREAK DOWNSTAIRS. I'VE GOT THIS EXCELLENT TEA I'LL MAKE FOR YOU.
IT'S AN EXPENSIVE BLEND FROM THE WEST, AND IT'S TOO GOOD FOR MY CUSTOMERS. LET'S SHARE A POT.
CLAC

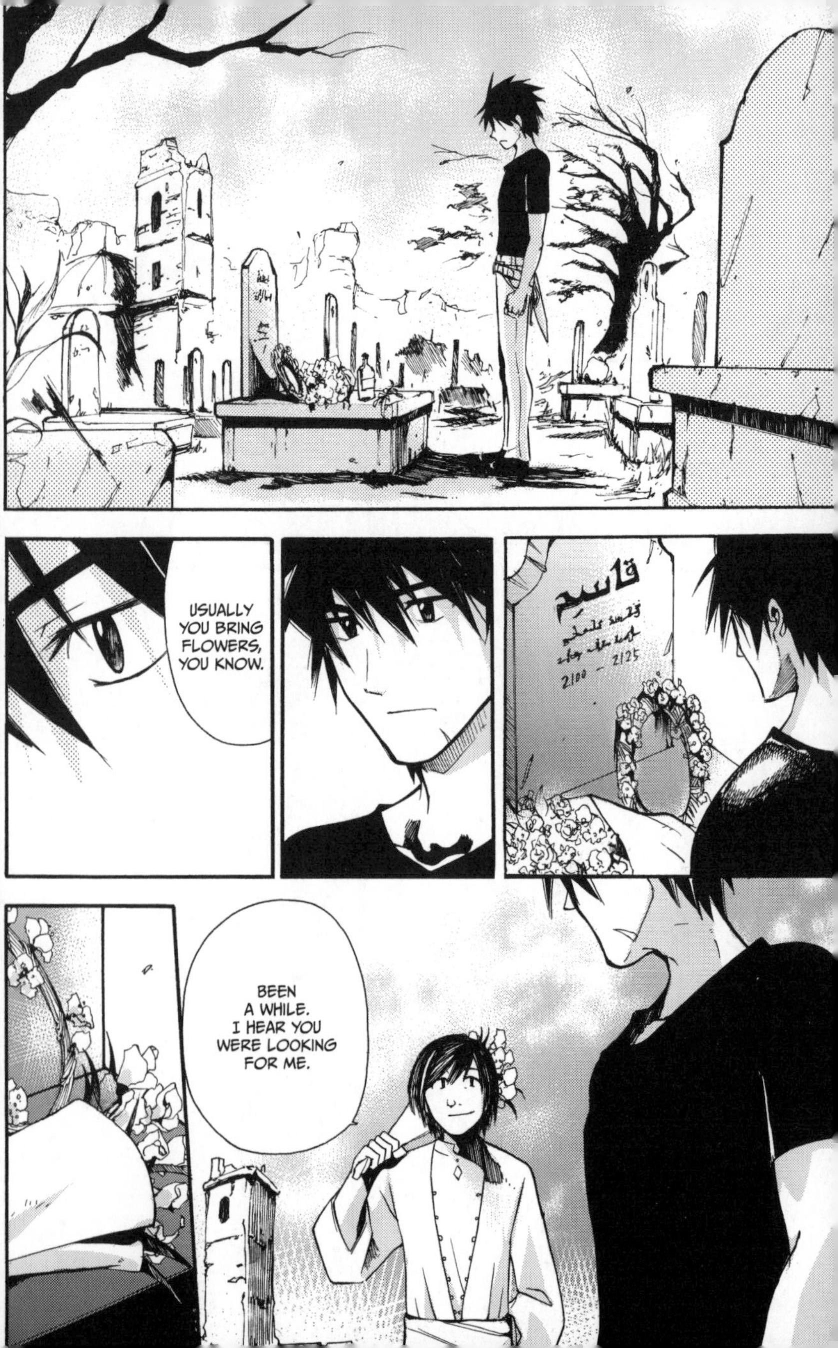
قاسم
2100 - 2125
USUALLY YOU BRING FLOWERS, YOU KNOW.
BEEN A WHILE. I HEAR YOU WERE LOOKING FOR ME.

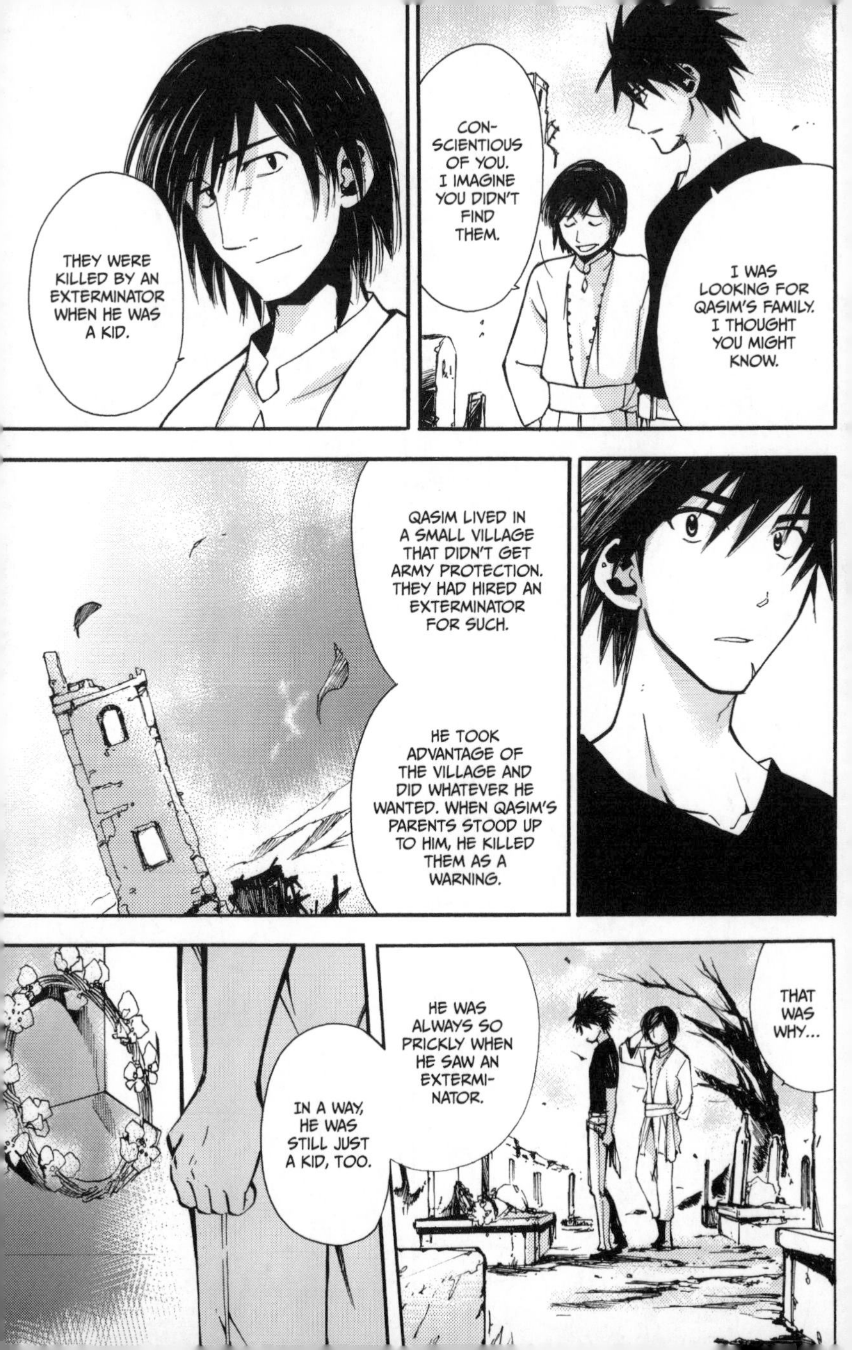
I WAS LOOKING FOR QASIM'S FAMILY. I THOUGHT YOU MIGHT KNOW.
CON-SCIENTIOUS OF YOU. I IMAGINE YOU DIDN'T FIND THEM.
THEY WERE KILLED BY AN EXTERMINATOR WHEN HE WAS A KID.
QASIM LIVED IN A SMALL VILLAGE THAT DIDN'T GET ARMY PROTECTION. THEY HAD HIRED AN EXTERMINATOR FOR SUCH.
HE TOOK ADVANTAGE OF THE VILLAGE AND DID WHATEVER HE WANTED. WHEN QASIM'S PARENTS STOOD UP TO HIM, HE KILLED THEM AS A WARNING.
THAT WAS WHY...
HE WAS ALWAYS SO PRICKLY WHEN HE SAW AN EXTERMI-NATOR.
IN A WAY, HE WAS STILL JUST A KID, TOO.

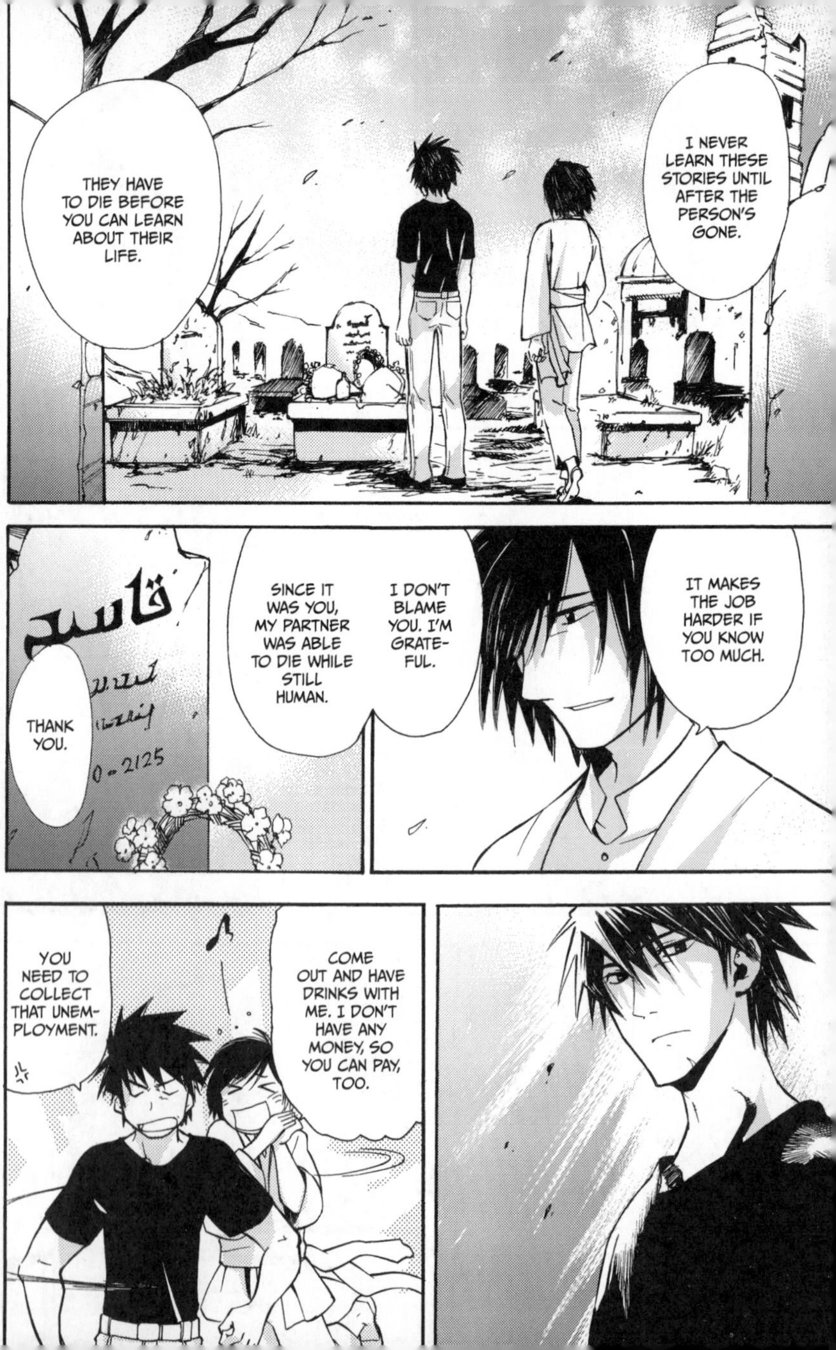
I NEVER LEARN THESE STORIES UNTIL AFTER THE PERSON'S GONE.
THEY HAVE TO DIE BEFORE YOU CAN LEARN ABOUT THEIR LIFE.
IT MAKES THE JOB HARDER IF YOU KNOW TOO MUCH.
I DON'T BLAME YOU. I'M GRATE-FUL.
SINCE IT WAS YOU, MY PARTNER WAS ABLE TO DIE WHILE STILL HUMAN.
قاسم
THANK YOU.
COME OUT AND HAVE DRINKS WITH ME. I DON'T HAVE ANY MONEY, SO YOU CAN PAY, TOO.
YOU NEED TO COLLECT THAT UNEM-PLOYMENT.

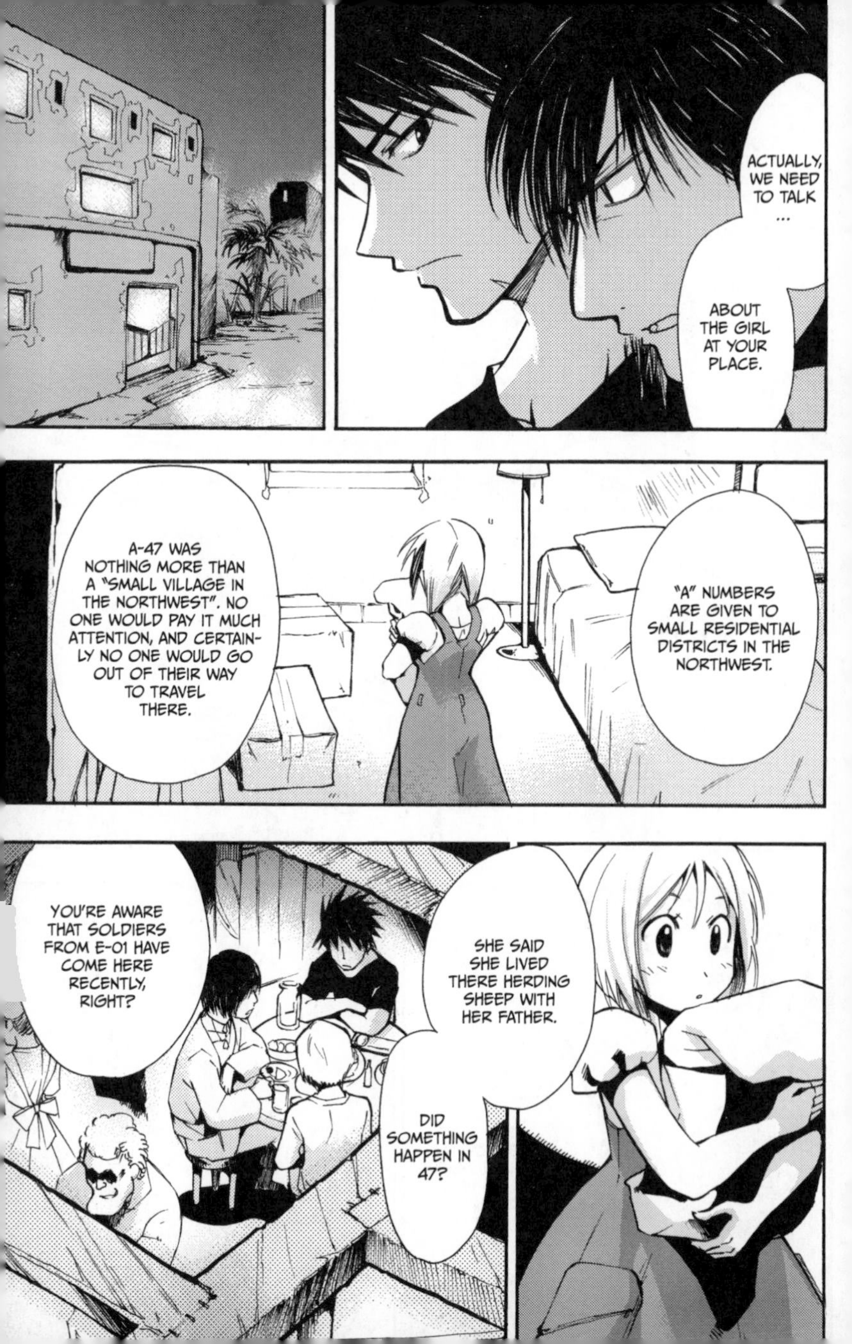
ACTUALLY, WE NEED TO TALK ...
ABOUT THE GIRL AT YOUR PLACE.
"A" NUMBERS ARE GIVEN TO SMALL RESIDENTIAL DISTRICTS IN THE NORTHWEST.
A-47 WAS NOTHING MORE THAN A "SMALL VILLAGE IN THE NORTHWEST". NO ONE WOULD PAY IT MUCH ATTENTION, AND CERTAIN-LY NO ONE WOULD GO OUT OF THEIR WAY TO TRAVEL THERE.
SHE SAID SHE LIVED THERE HERDING SHEEP WITH HER FATHER.
DID SOMETHING HAPPEN IN 47?
YOU'RE AWARE THAT SOLDIERS FROM E-01 HAVE COME HERE RECENTLY, RIGHT?

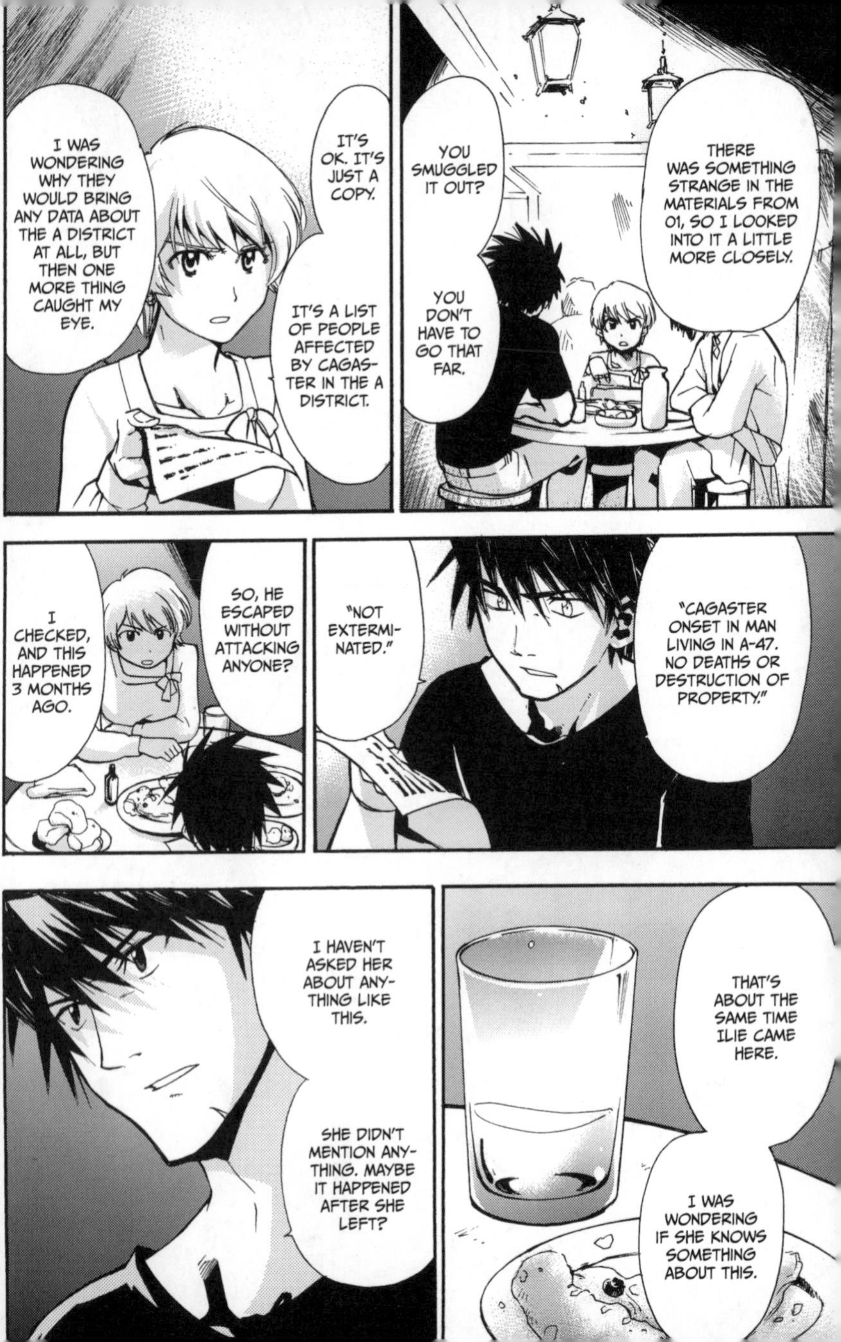
THERE WAS SOMETHING STRANGE IN THE MATERIALS FROM 01, SO I LOOKED INTO IT A LITTLE MORE CLOSELY.
YOU SMUGGLED IT OUT?
YOU DON'T HAVE TO GO THAT FAR.
IT'S OK. IT'S JUST A COPY.
IT'S A LIST OF PEOPLE AFFECTED BY CAGAS-TER IN THE A DISTRICT.
I WAS WONDERING WHY THEY WOULD BRING ANY DATA ABOUT THE A DISTRICT AT ALL, BUT THEN ONE MORE THING CAUGHT MY EYE.
"CAGASTER ONSET IN MAN LIVING IN A-47. NO DEATHS OR DESTRUCTION OF PROPERTY."
"NOT EXTERMI-NATED."
SO, HE ESCAPED WITHOUT ATTACKING ANYONE?
I CHECKED, AND THIS HAPPENED 3 MONTHS AGO.
THAT'S ABOUT THE SAME TIME ILIE CAME HERE.
I WAS WONDERING IF SHE KNOWS SOMETHING ABOUT THIS.
I HAVEN'T ASKED HER ABOUT ANY-THING LIKE THIS.
SHE DIDN'T MENTION ANY-THING. MAYBE IT HAPPENED AFTER SHE LEFT?

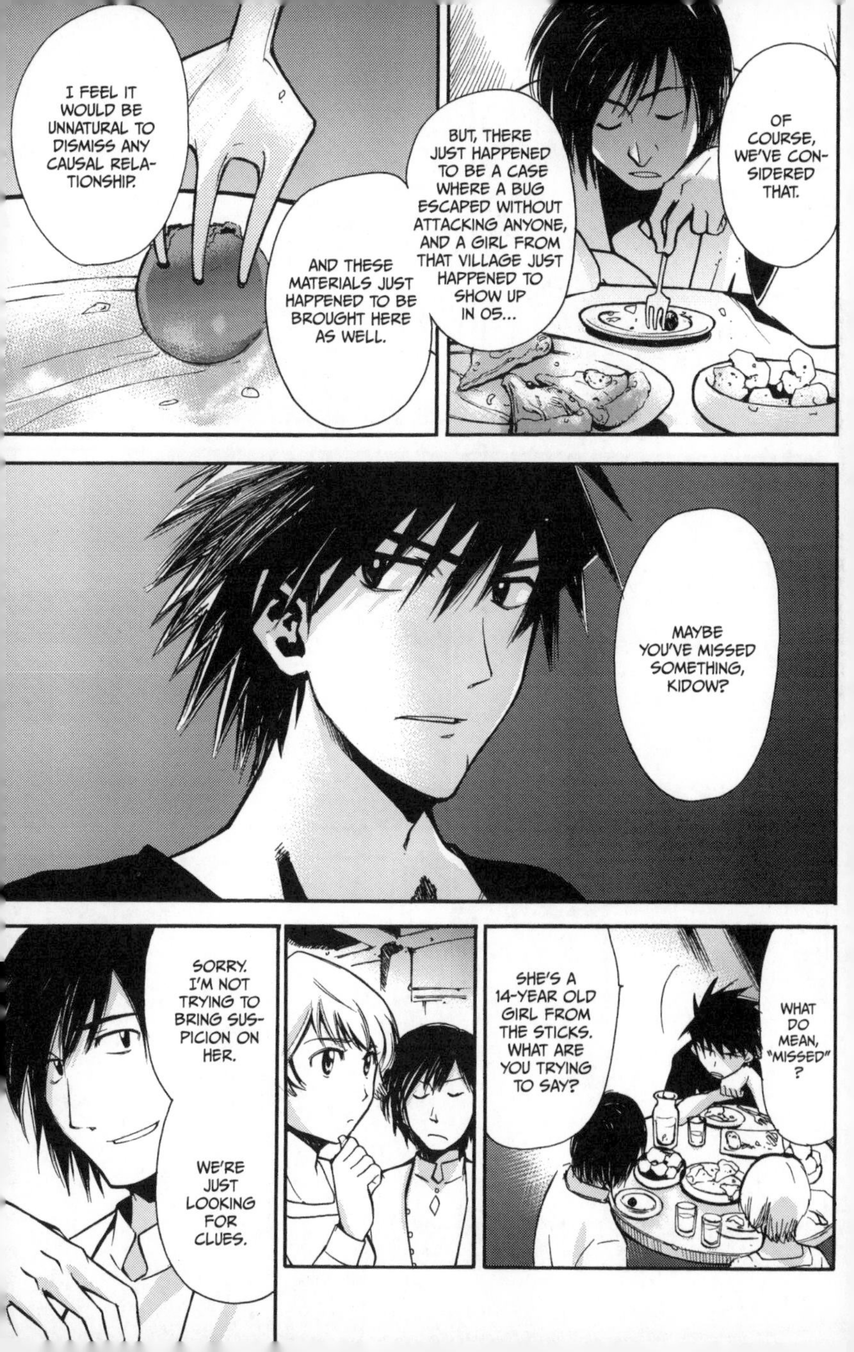
OF COURSE, WE'VE CON-SIDERED THAT.
BUT, THERE JUST HAPPENED TO BE A CASE WHERE A BUG ESCAPED WITHOUT ATTACKING ANYONE, AND A GIRL FROM THAT VILLAGE JUST HAPPENED TO SHOW UP IN 05...
AND THESE MATERIALS JUST HAPPENED TO BE BROUGHT HERE AS WELL.
I FEEL IT WOULD BE UNNATURAL TO DISMISS ANY CAUSAL RELA-TIONSHIP.
MAYBE YOU'VE MISSED SOMETHING, KIDOW?
WHAT DO MEAN, "MISSED"?
SHE'S A 14-YEAR OLD GIRL FROM THE STICKS. WHAT ARE YOU TRYING TO SAY?
SORRY. I'M NOT TRYING TO BRING SUS-PICION ON HER.
WE'RE JUST LOOKING FOR CLUES.

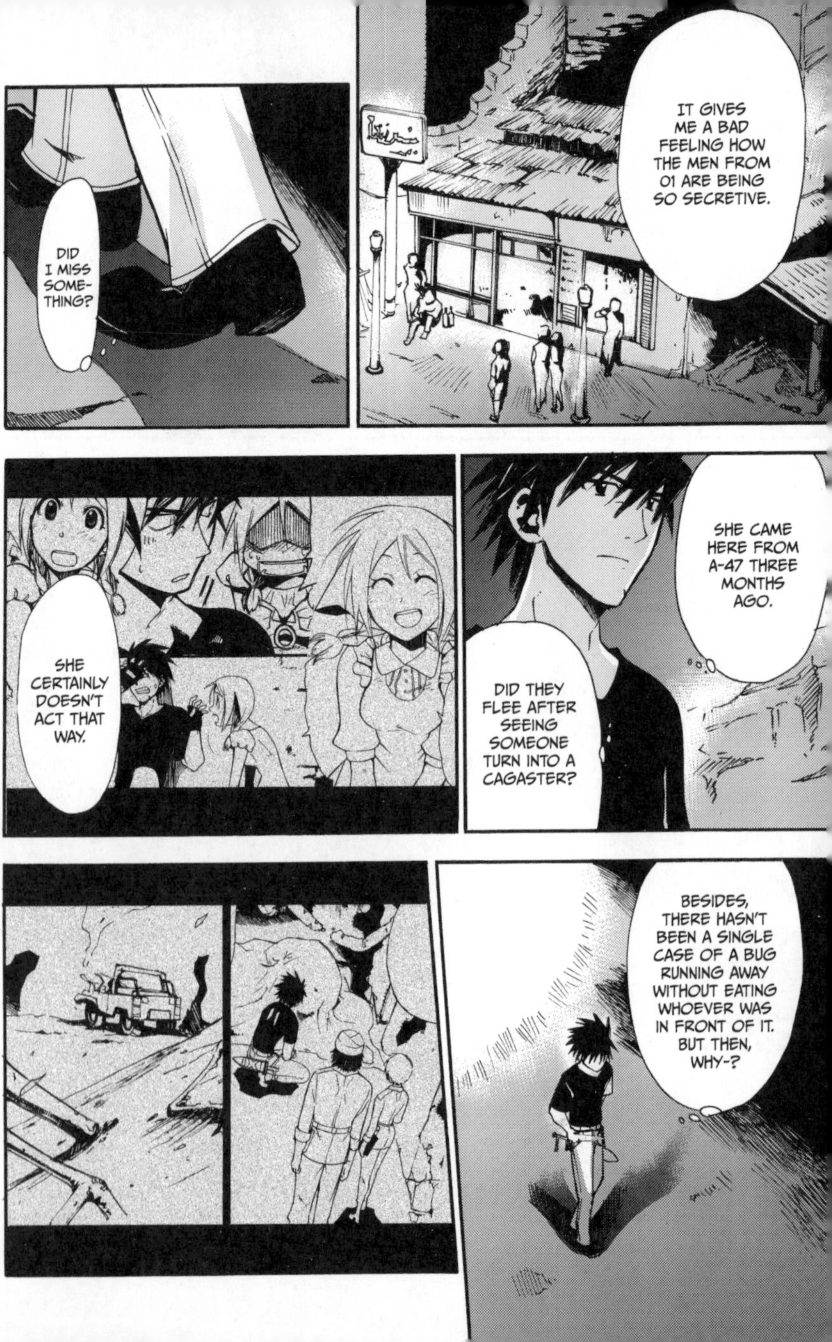
IT GIVES ME A BAD FEELING HOW THE MEN FROM 01 ARE BEING SO SECRETIVE.
DID I MISS SOME-THING?
SHE CAME HERE FROM A-47 THREE MONTHS AGO.
DID THEY FLEE AFTER SEEING SOMEONE TURN INTO A CAGASTER?
SHE CERTAINLY DOESN'T ACT THAT WAY.
BESIDES, THERE HASN'T BEEN A SINGLE CASE OF A BUG RUNNING AWAY WITHOUT EATING WHOEVER WAS IN FRONT OF IT. BUT THEN, WHY-?

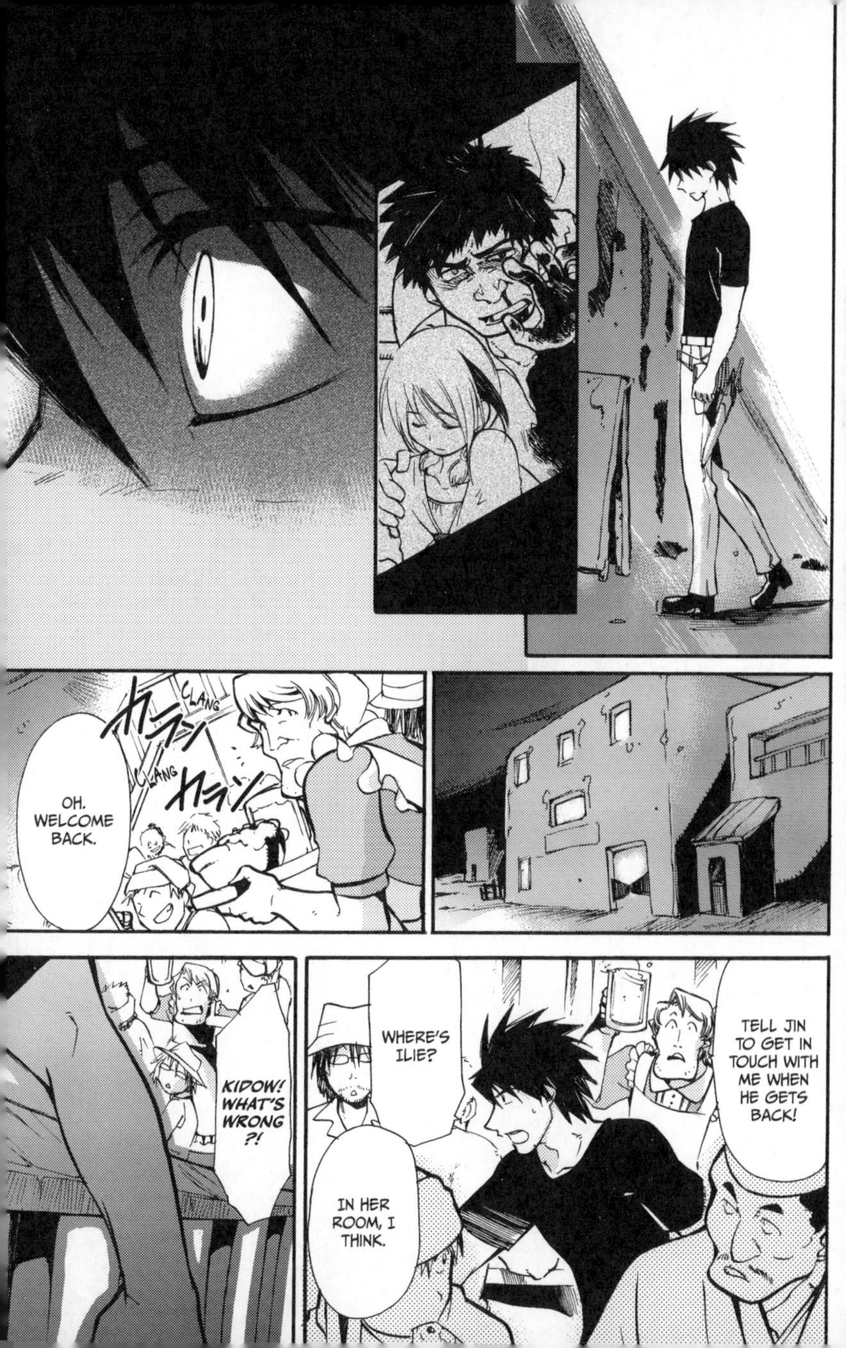

CLANG
カラン
CLANG
カラン
OH. WELCOME BACK.
TELL JIN TO GET IN TOUCH WITH ME WHEN HE GETS BACK!
WHERE'S ILIE?
IN HER ROOM, I THINK.
KIDOW! WHAT'S WRONG ?!

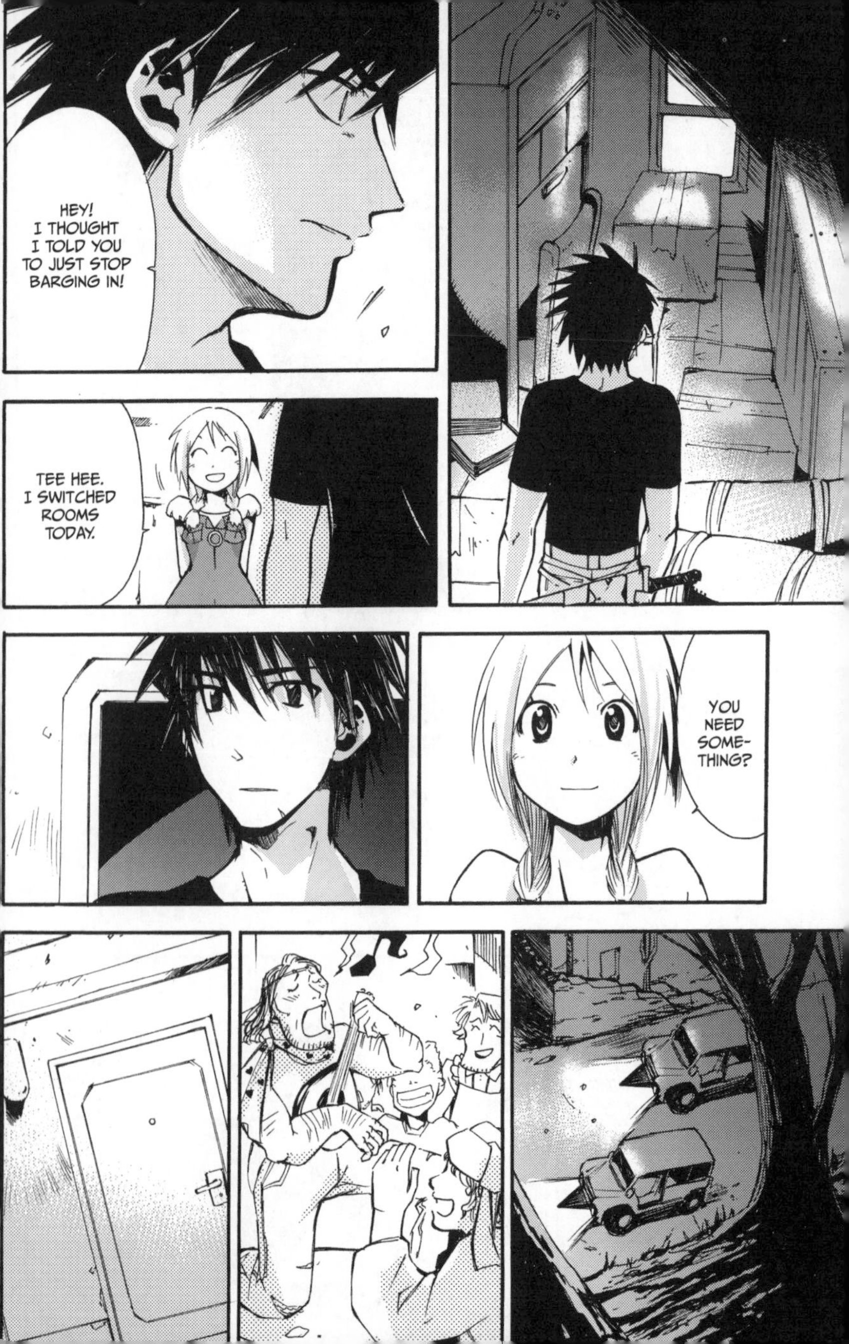
HEY! I THOUGHT I TOLD YOU TO JUST STOP BARGING IN!
TEE HEE. I SWITCHED ROOMS TODAY.
YOU NEED SOME-THING?

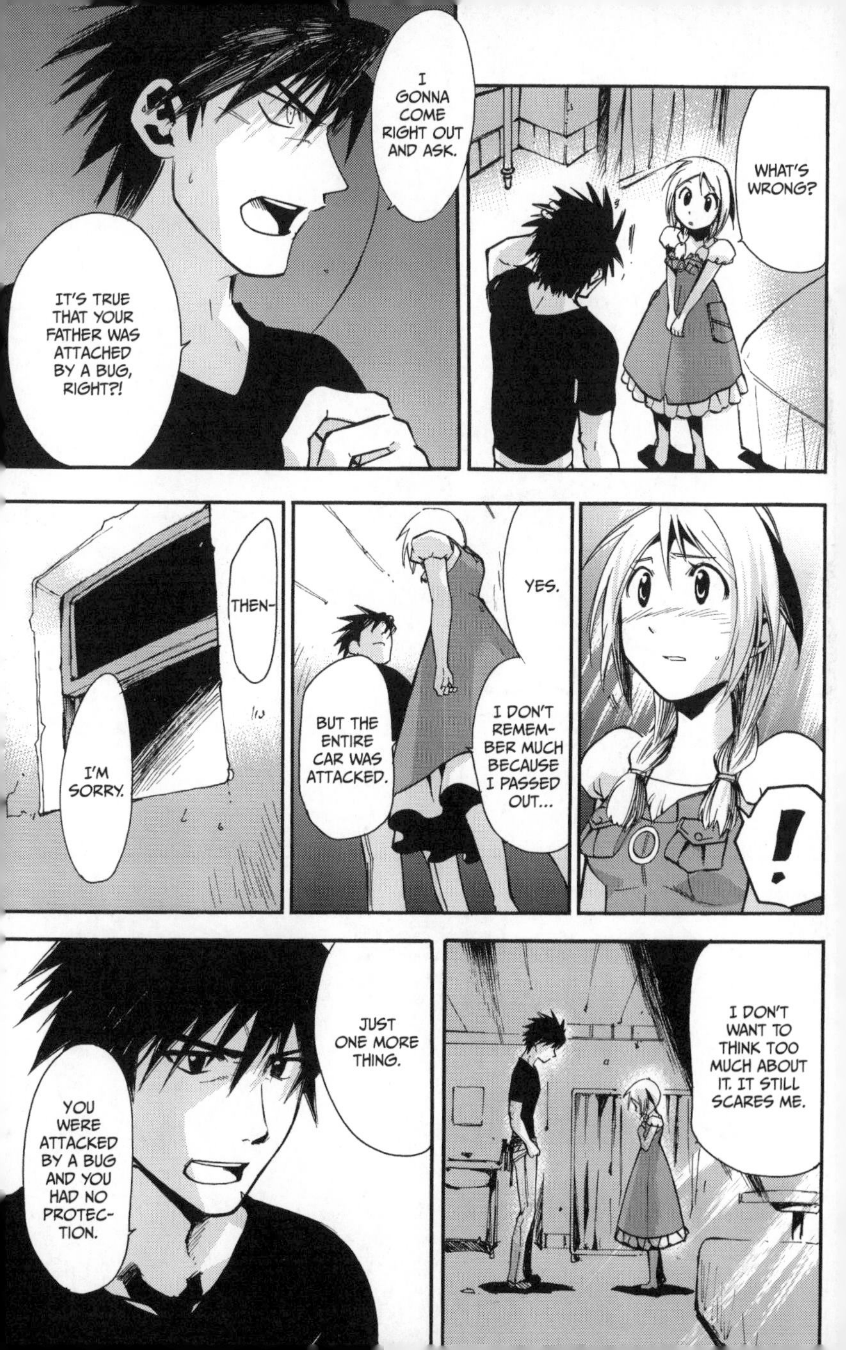
WHAT'S WRONG?
I GONNA COME RIGHT OUT AND ASK.
IT'S TRUE THAT YOUR FATHER WAS ATTACHED BY A BUG, RIGHT?!
!
YES.
I DON'T REMEMBER MUCH BECAUSE I PASSED OUT...
BUT THE ENTIRE CAR WAS ATTACKED.
THEN-
I'M SORRY.
I DON'T WANT TO THINK TOO MUCH ABOUT IT. IT STILL SCARES ME.
JUST ONE MORE THING.
YOU WERE ATTACKED BY A BUG AND YOU HAD NO PROTECTION.

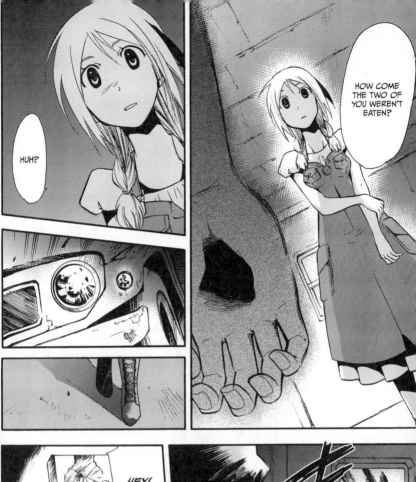

HOW COME THE TWO OF YOU WEREN'T EATEN?

HUH?

HEY! WHAT ARE YOU DOING?!

CRISS

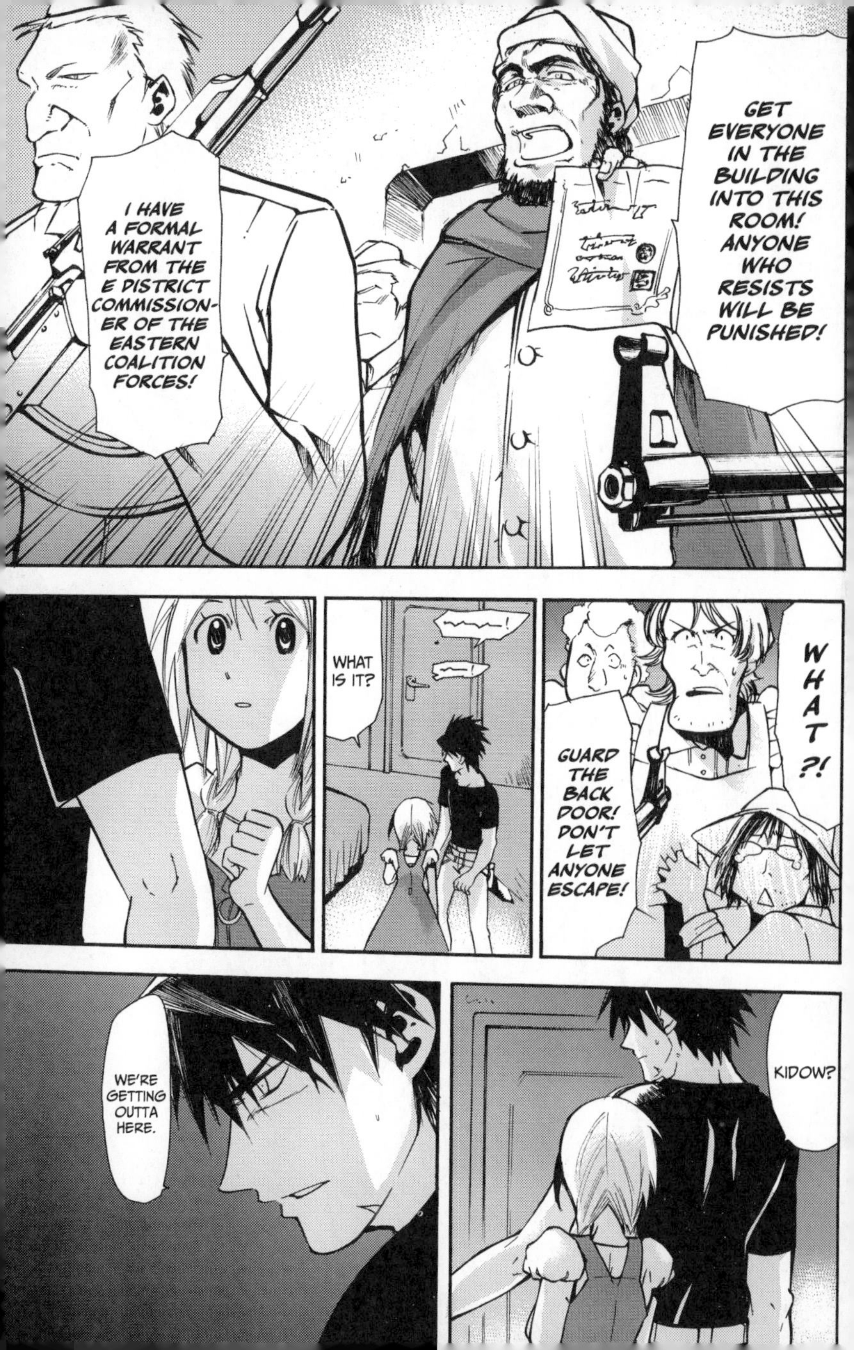
GET EVERYONE IN THE BUILDING INTO THIS ROOM! ANYONE WHO RESISTS WILL BE PUNISHED!
I HAVE A FORMAL WARRANT FROM THE E DISTRICT COMMISSION-ER OF THE EASTERN COALITION FORCES!
WHAT?!
GUARD THE BACK DOOR! DON'T LET ANYONE ESCAPE!
WHAT IS IT?
KIDOW?
WE'RE GETTING OUTTA HERE.

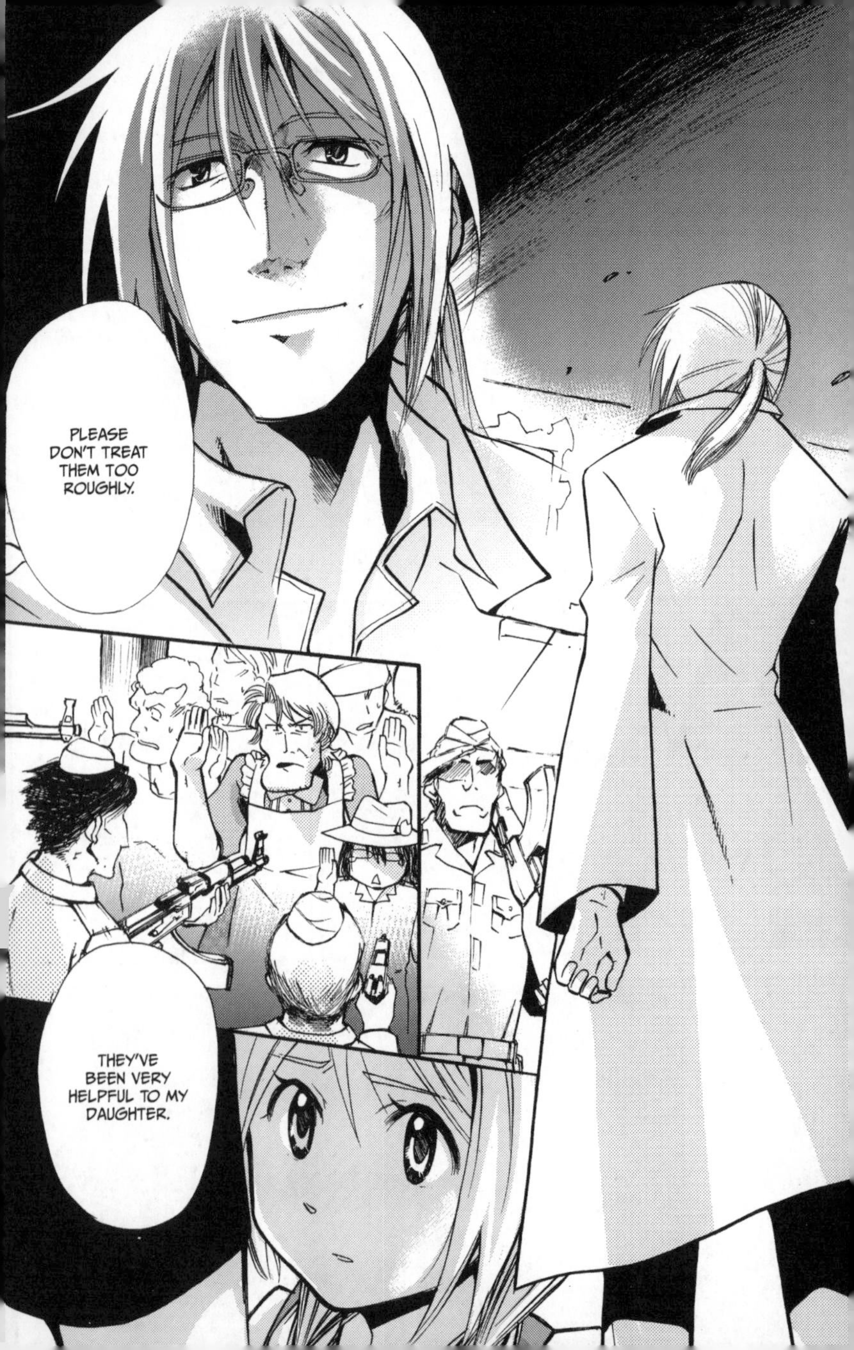
PLEASE DON'T TREAT THEM TOO ROUGHLY.
THEY'VE BEEN VERY HELPFUL TO MY DAUGHTER.

[CHAPTER 13]

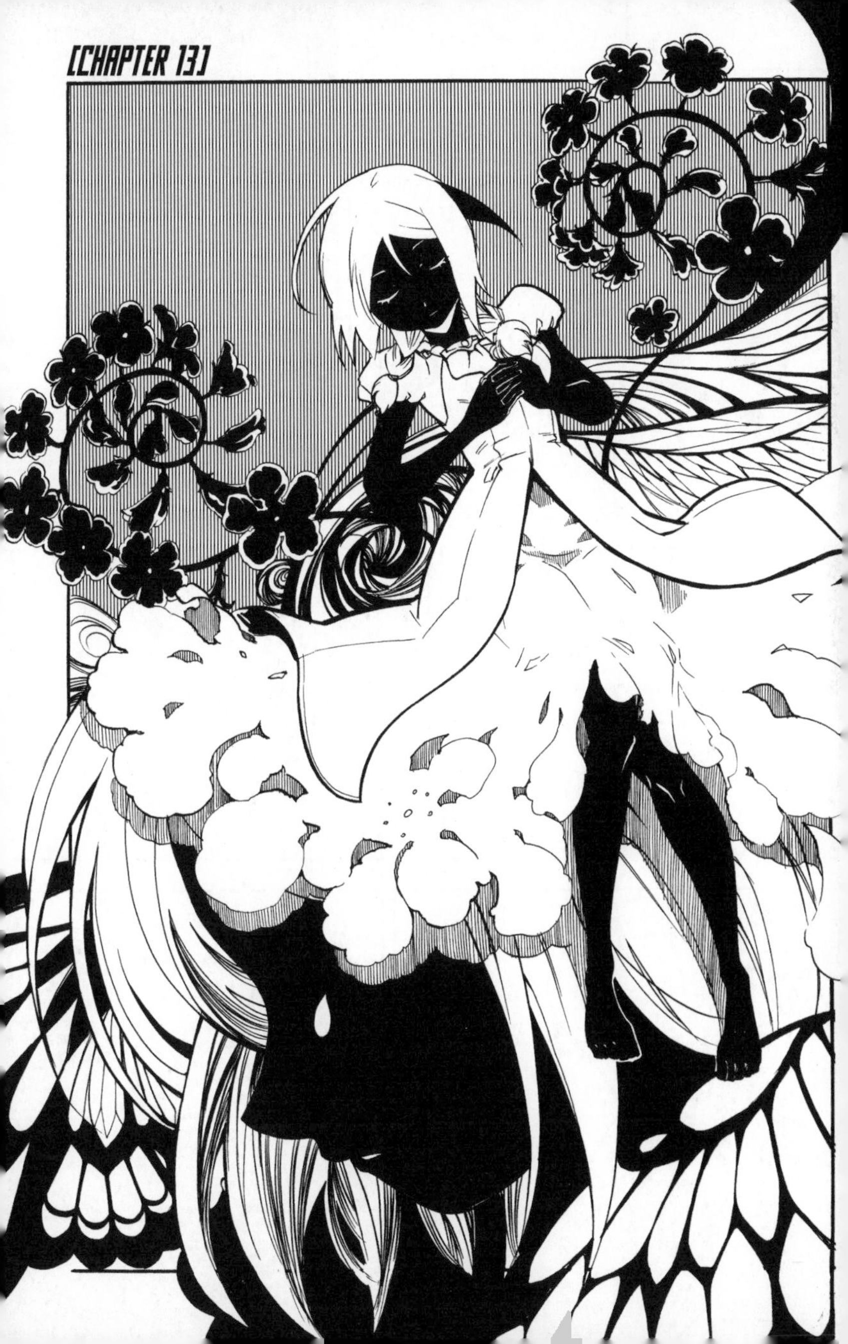

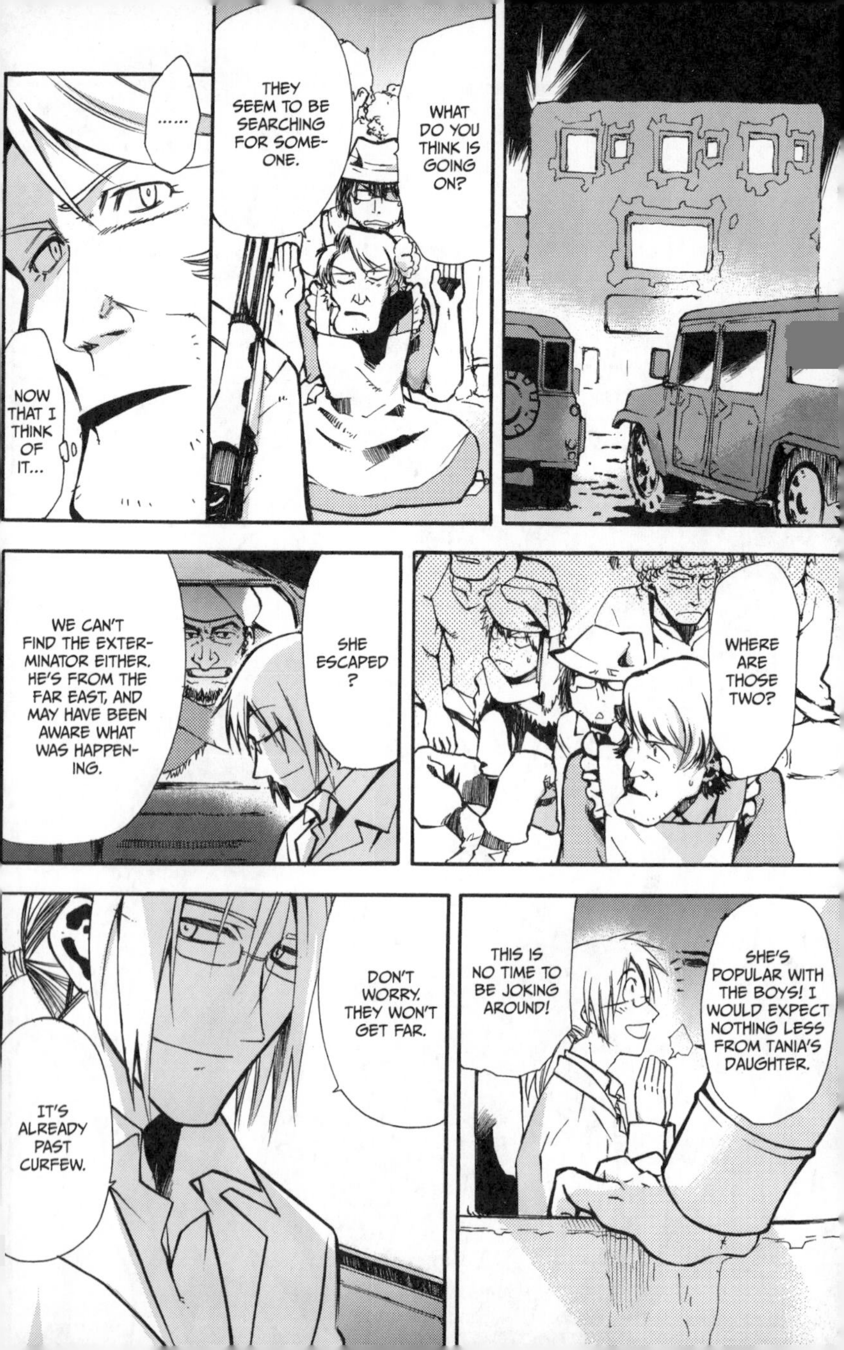
WHAT DO YOU THINK IS GOING ON?
THEY SEEM TO BE SEARCHING FOR SOME-ONE.
......
NOW THAT I THINK OF IT...
WHERE ARE THOSE TWO?
SHE ESCAPED?
WE CAN'T FIND THE EXTER-MINATOR EITHER. HE'S FROM THE FAR EAST, AND MAY HAVE BEEN AWARE WHAT WAS HAPPEN-ING.
SHE'S POPULAR WITH THE BOYS! I WOULD EXPECT NOTHING LESS FROM TANIA'S DAUGHTER.
THIS IS NO TIME TO BE JOKING AROUND!
DON'T WORRY. THEY WON'T GET FAR.
IT'S ALREADY PAST CURFEW.

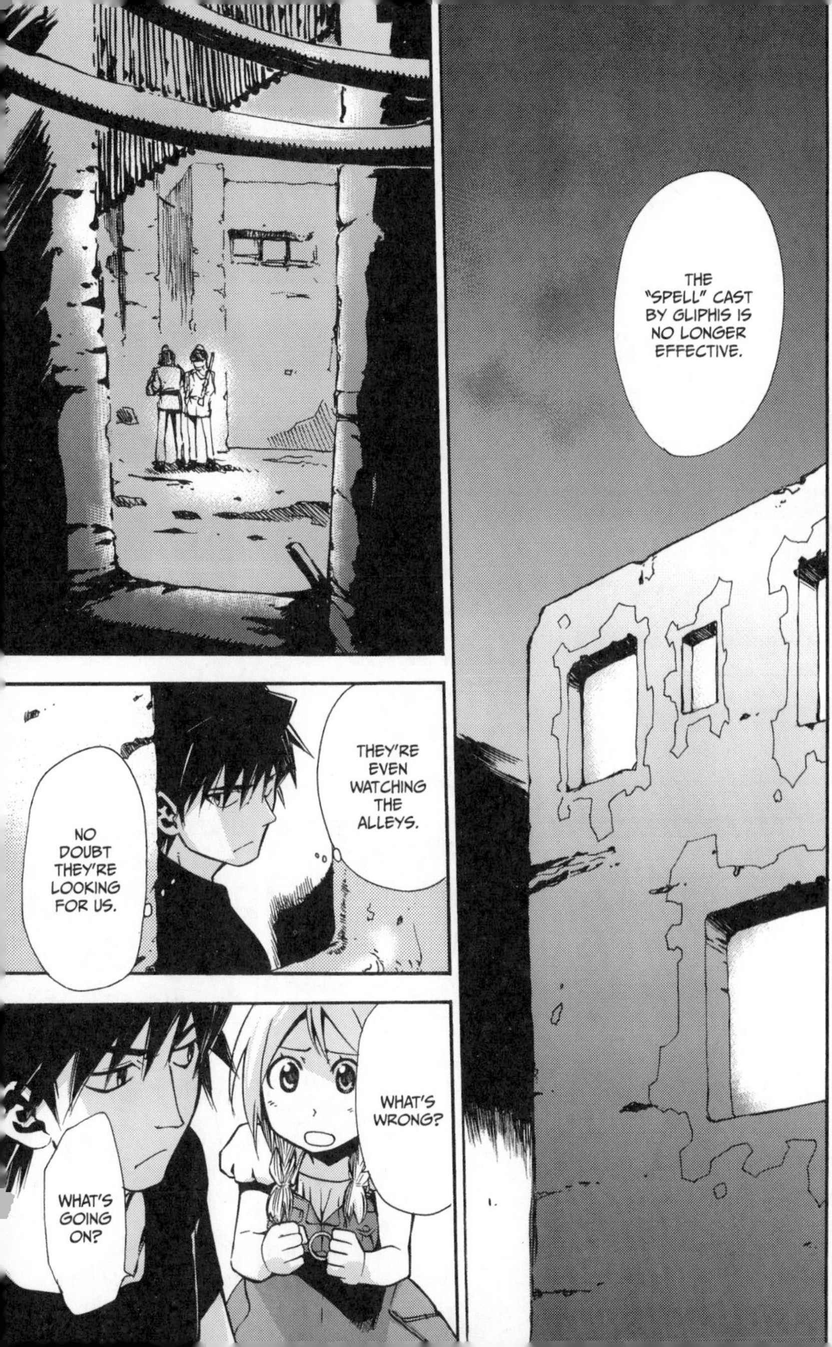
THE "SPELL" CAST BY GLIPHIS IS NO LONGER EFFECTIVE.
THEY'RE EVEN WATCHING THE ALLEYS.
NO DOUBT THEY'RE LOOKING FOR US.
WHAT'S WRONG?
WHAT'S GOING ON?

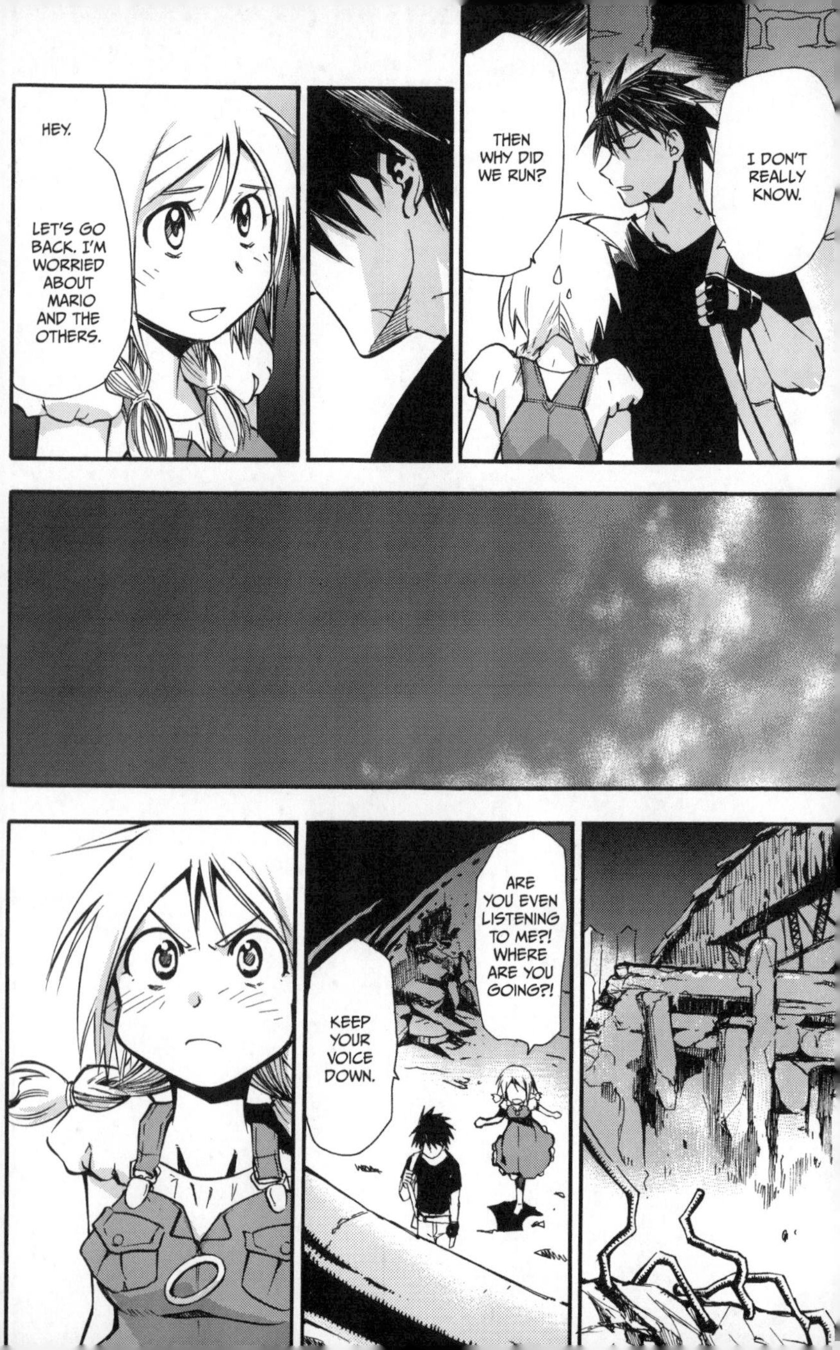
I DON'T REALLY KNOW.
THEN WHY DID WE RUN?
HEY.
LET'S GO BACK. I'M WORRIED ABOUT MARIO AND THE OTHERS.
ARE YOU EVEN LISTENING TO ME?! WHERE ARE YOU GOING?!
KEEP YOUR VOICE DOWN.

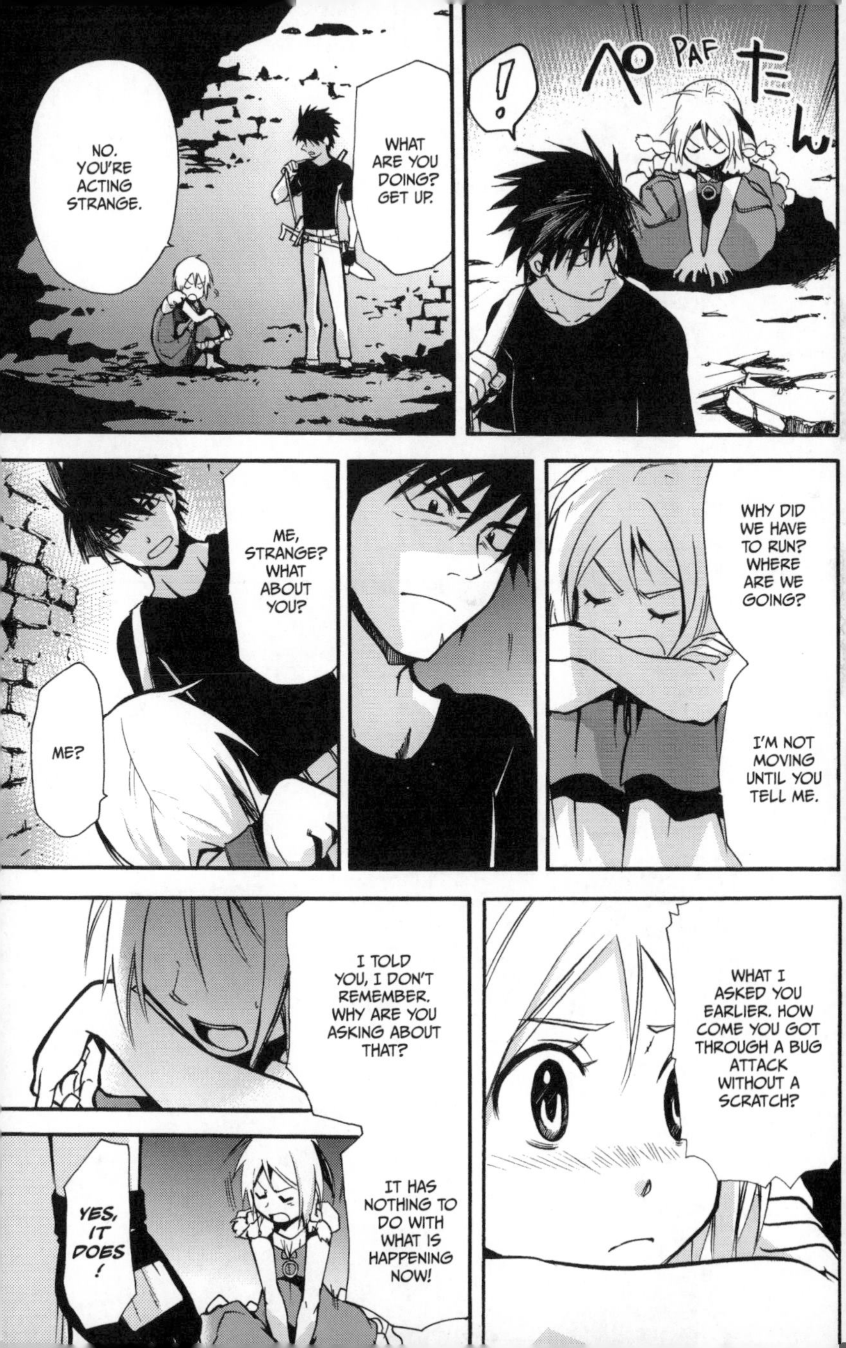
!
ぺ
PAF
たん
WHAT ARE YOU DOING? GET UP.
NO. YOU'RE ACTING STRANGE.
WHY DID WE HAVE TO RUN? WHERE ARE WE GOING?
I'M NOT MOVING UNTIL YOU TELL ME.
ME, STRANGE? WHAT ABOUT YOU?
ME?
WHAT I ASKED YOU EARLIER. HOW COME YOU GOT THROUGH A BUG ATTACK WITHOUT A SCRATCH?
I TOLD YOU, I DON'T REMEMBER. WHY ARE YOU ASKING ABOUT THAT?
IT HAS NOTHING TO DO WITH WHAT IS HAPPENING NOW!
YES, IT DOES!

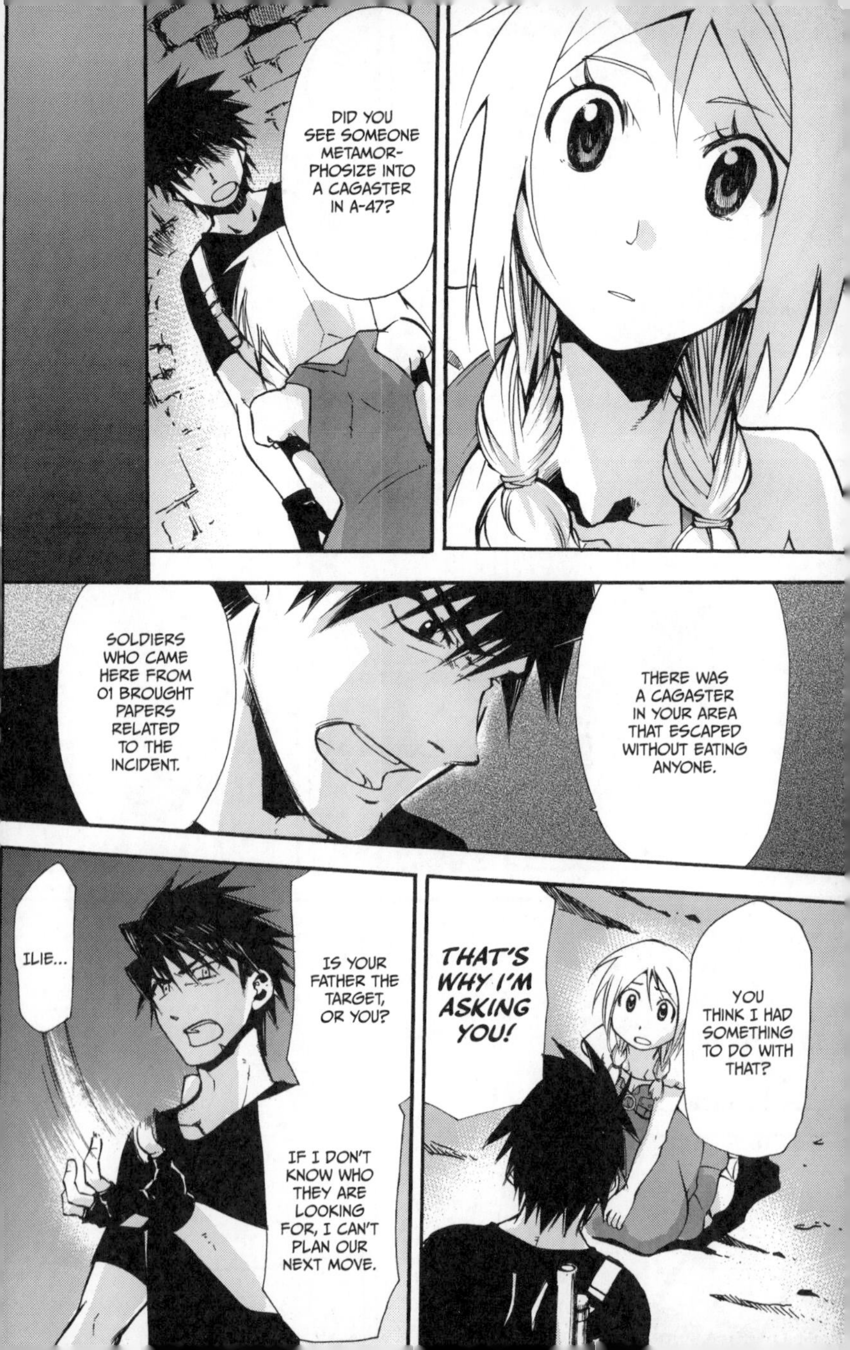
DID YOU SEE SOMEONE METAMORPHOSIZE INTO A CAGASTER IN A-47?
THERE WAS A CAGASTER IN YOUR AREA THAT ESCAPED WITHOUT EATING ANYONE.
SOLDIERS WHO CAME HERE FROM 01 BROUGHT PAPERS RELATED TO THE INCIDENT.
YOU THINK I HAD SOMETHING TO DO WITH THAT?
THAT'S WHY I'M ASKING YOU!
IS YOUR FATHER THE TARGET, OR YOU?
ILIE...
IF I DON'T KNOW WHO THEY ARE LOOKING FOR, I CAN'T PLAN OUR NEXT MOVE.

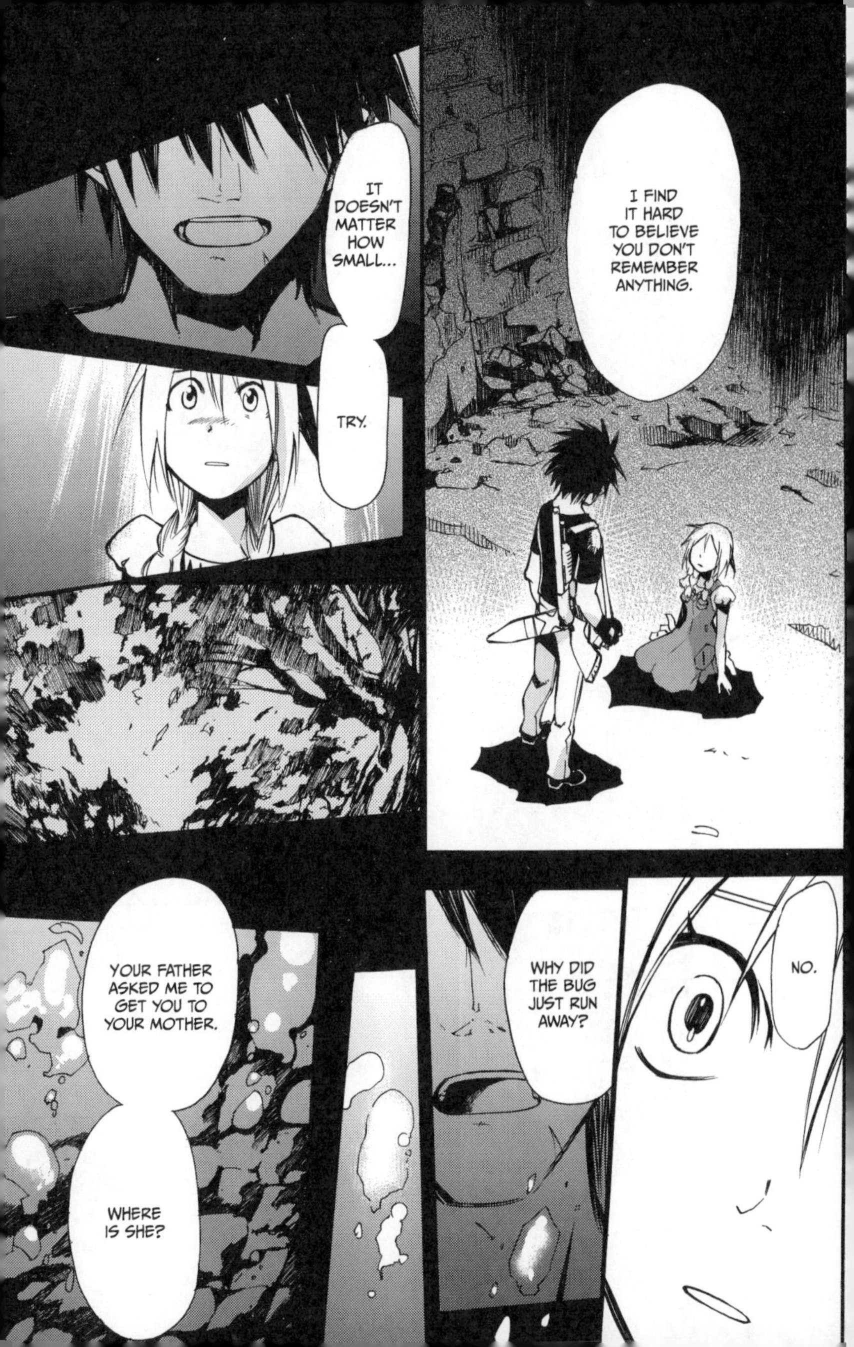
I FIND IT HARD TO BELIEVE YOU DON'T REMEMBER ANYTHING.
IT DOESN'T MATTER HOW SMALL...
TRY.
NO.
WHY DID THE BUG JUST RUN AWAY?
YOUR FATHER ASKED ME TO GET YOU TO YOUR MOTHER.
WHERE IS SHE?

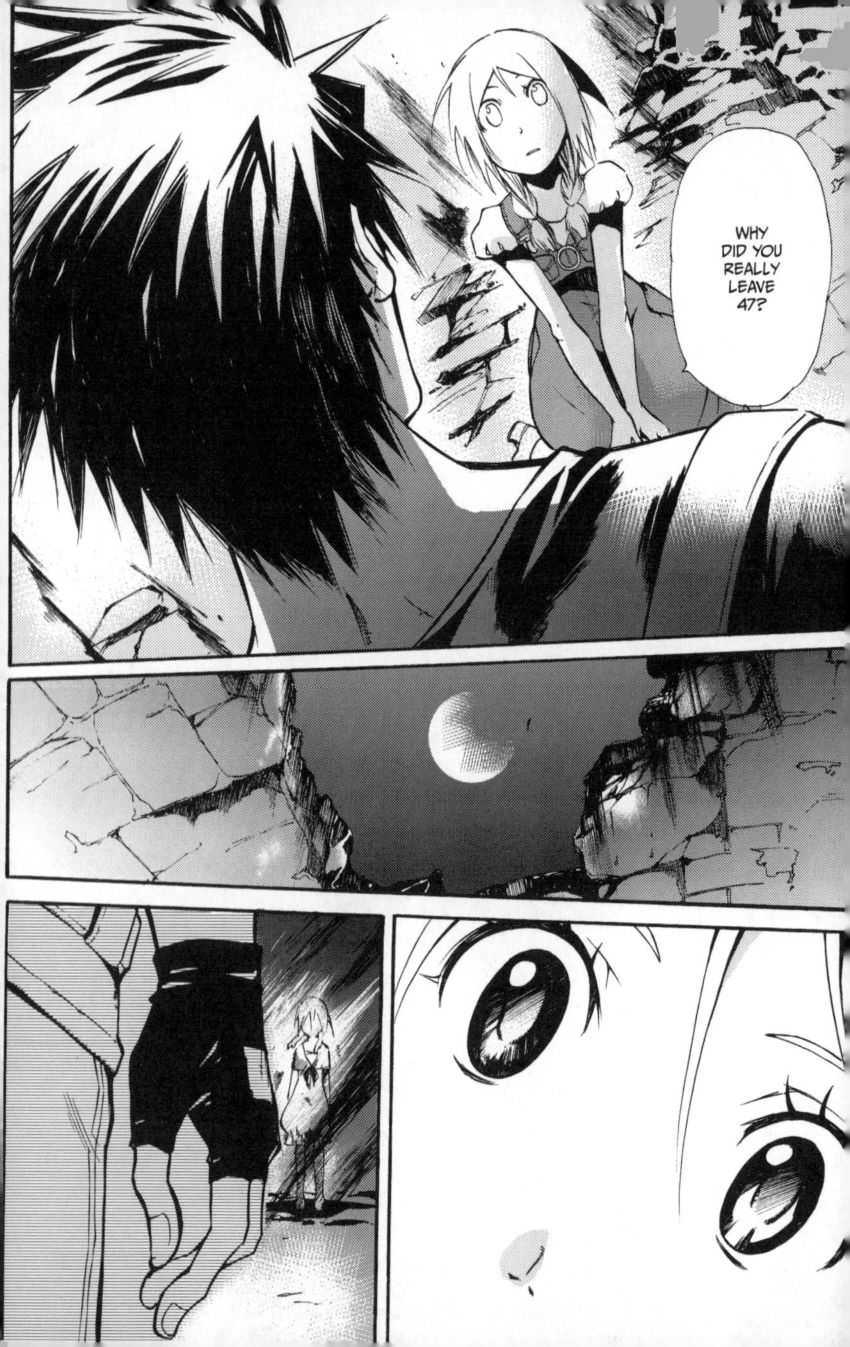
WHY DID YOU REALLY LEAVE 47?

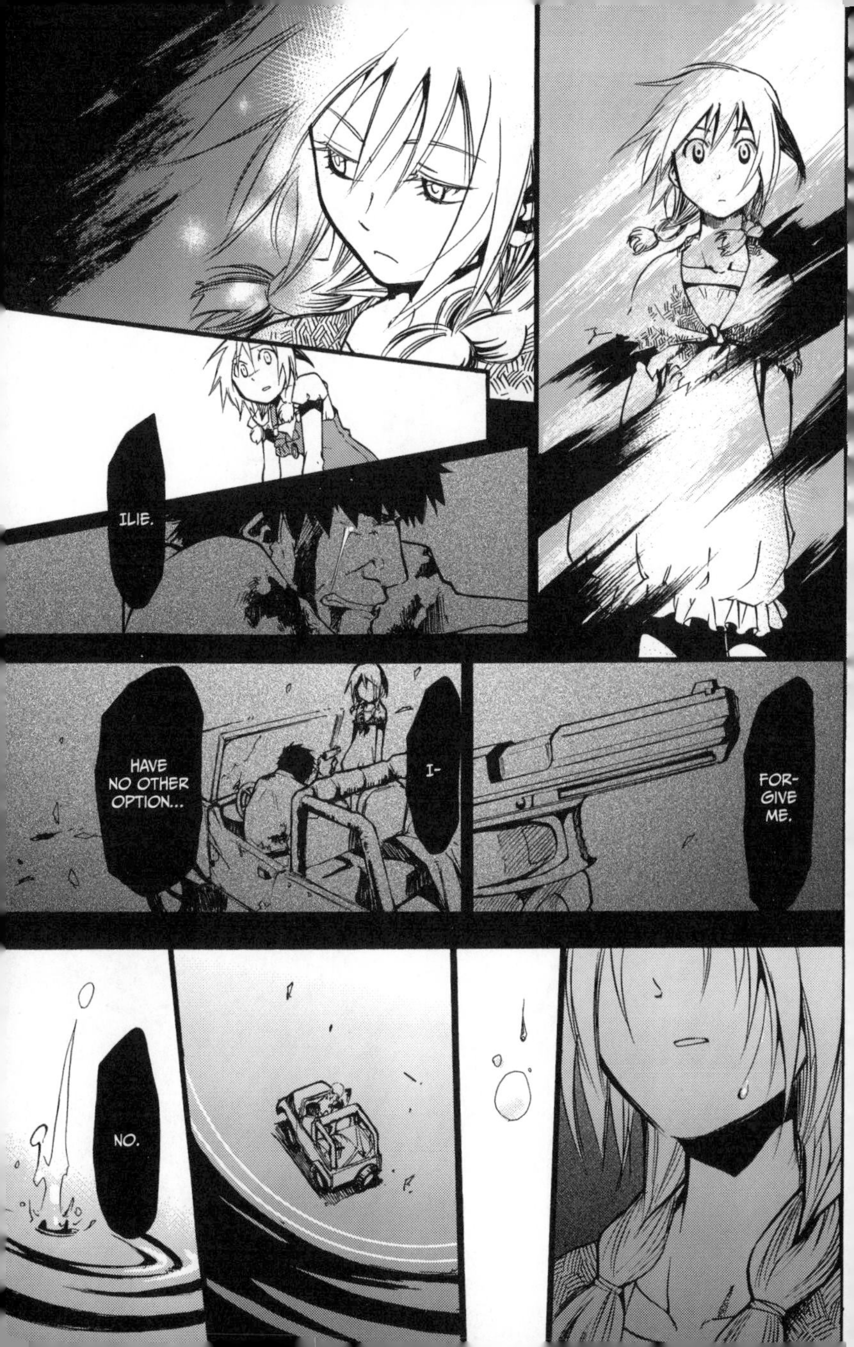
ILIE.
FOR-GIVE ME.
I-
HAVE NO OTHER OPTION...
NO.

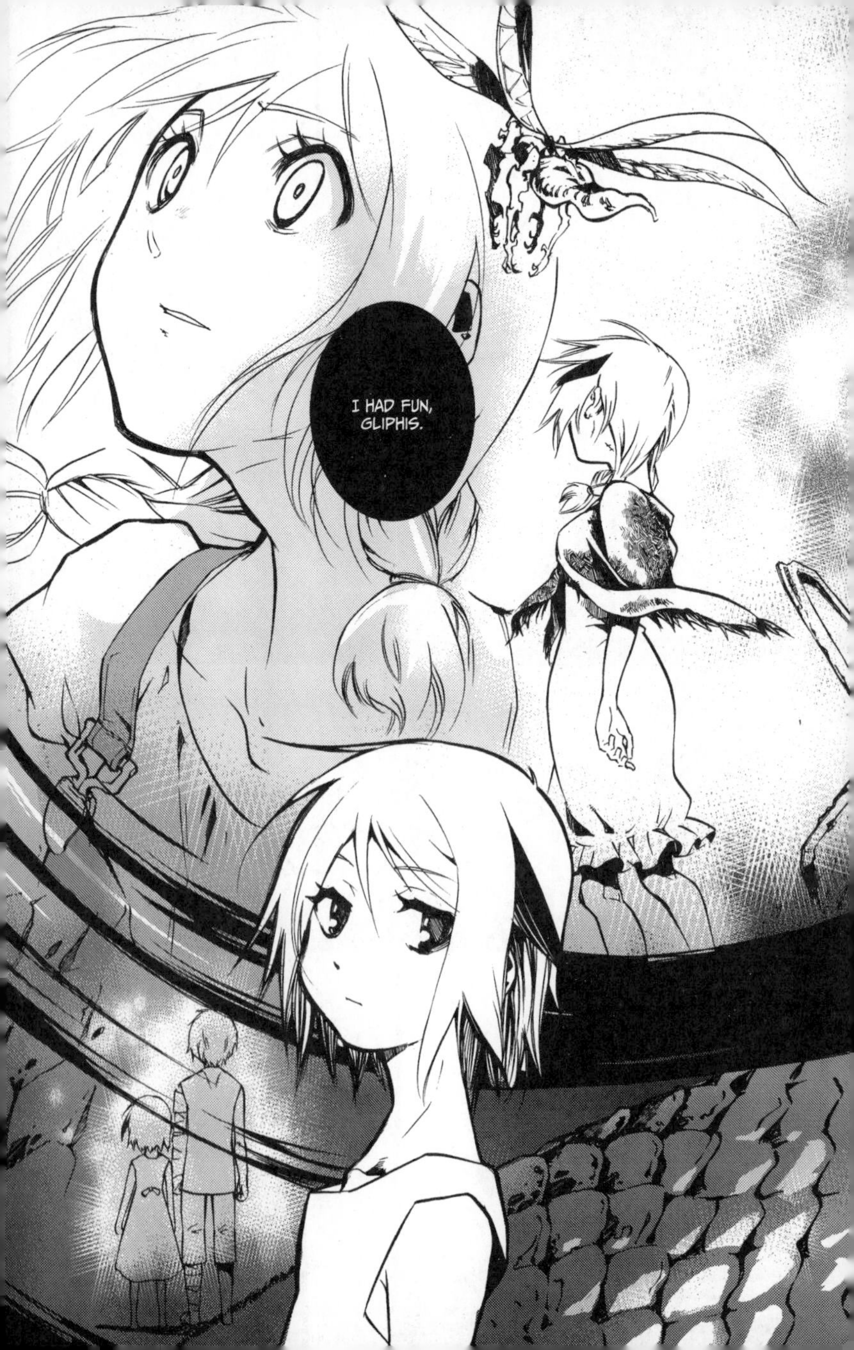
I HAD FUN, GLIPHIS.

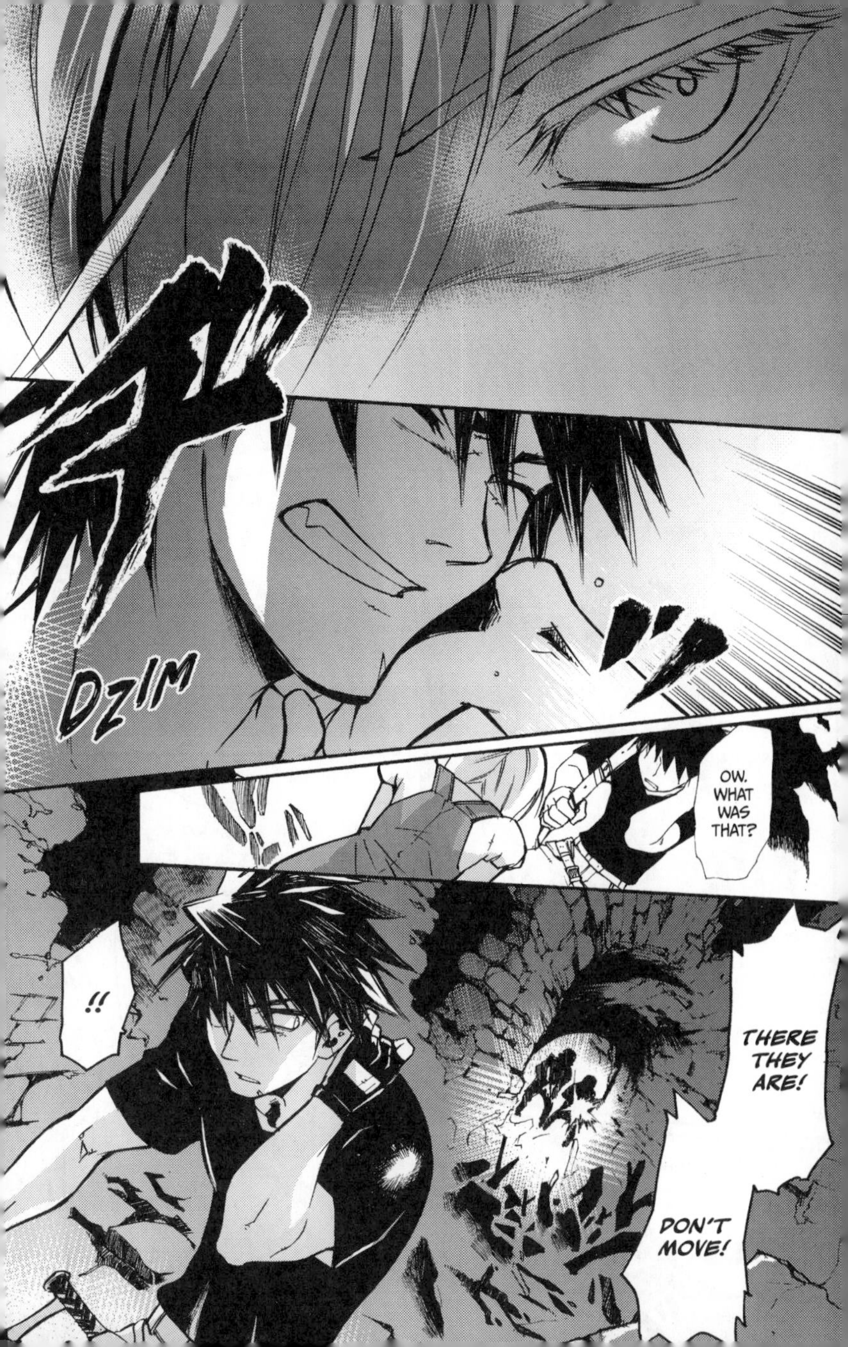
DZIM
OW. WHAT WAS THAT?
THERE THEY ARE!
DON'T MOVE!
!!

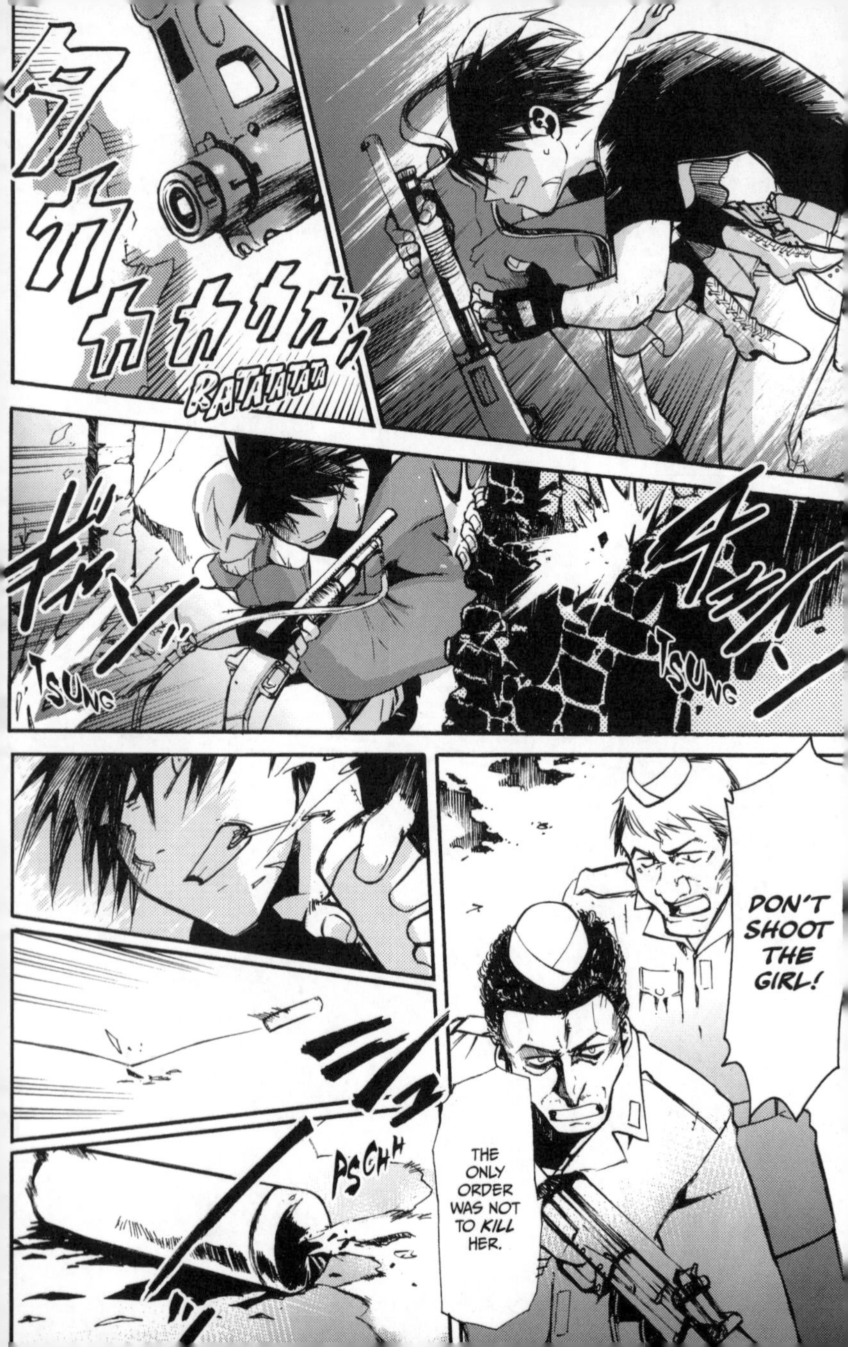
BATATATA
TSUNG
TSUNG
DON'T SHOOT THE GIRL!
THE ONLY ORDER WAS NOT TO *KILL* HER.
PSCHH

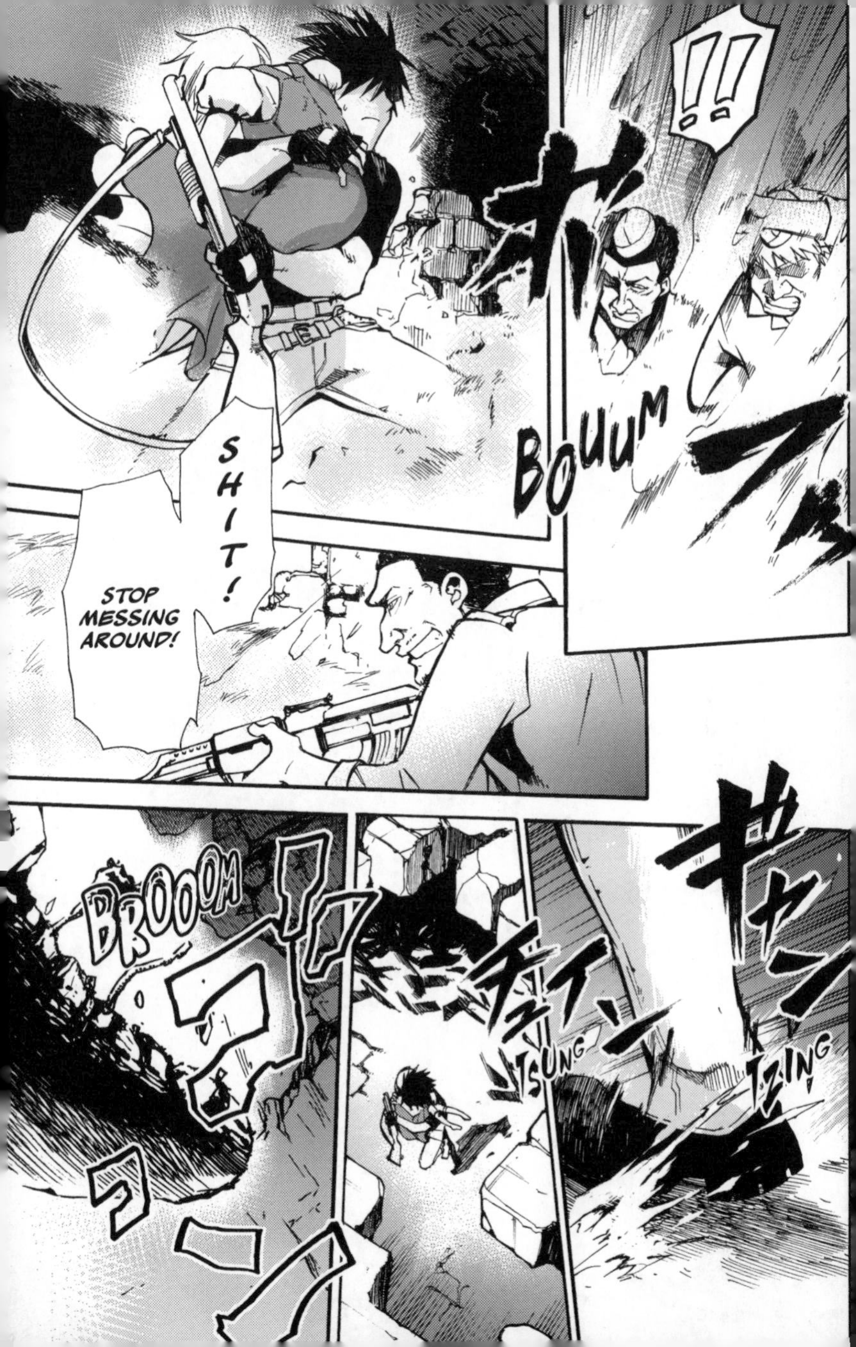
!!
BOUUM
SHIT!
STOP MESSING AROUND!
TZING
TSUNG
BROOOM

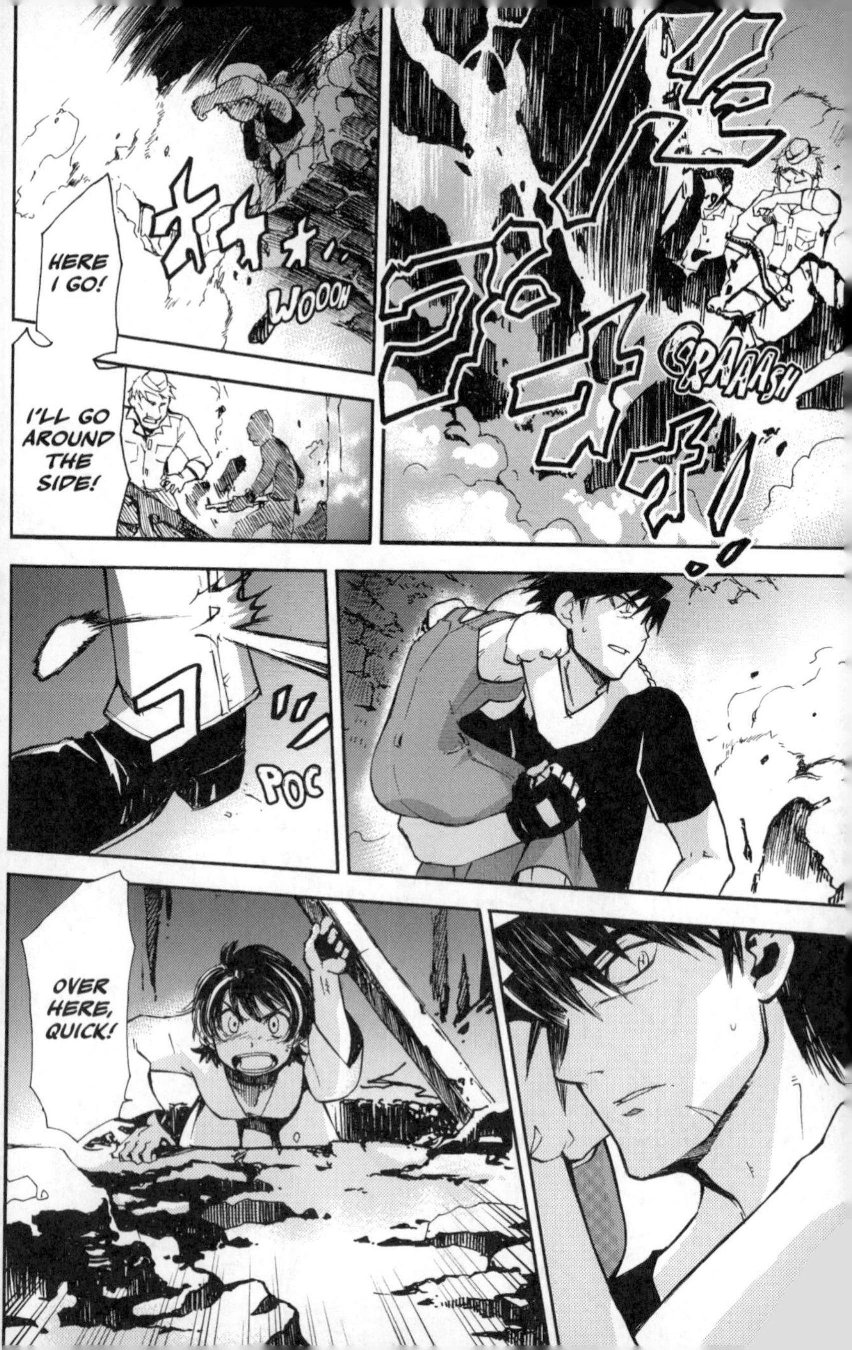
CRAAASH
HERE I GO!
WOOOH
I'LL GO AROUND THE SIDE!
POC
OVER HERE, QUICK!

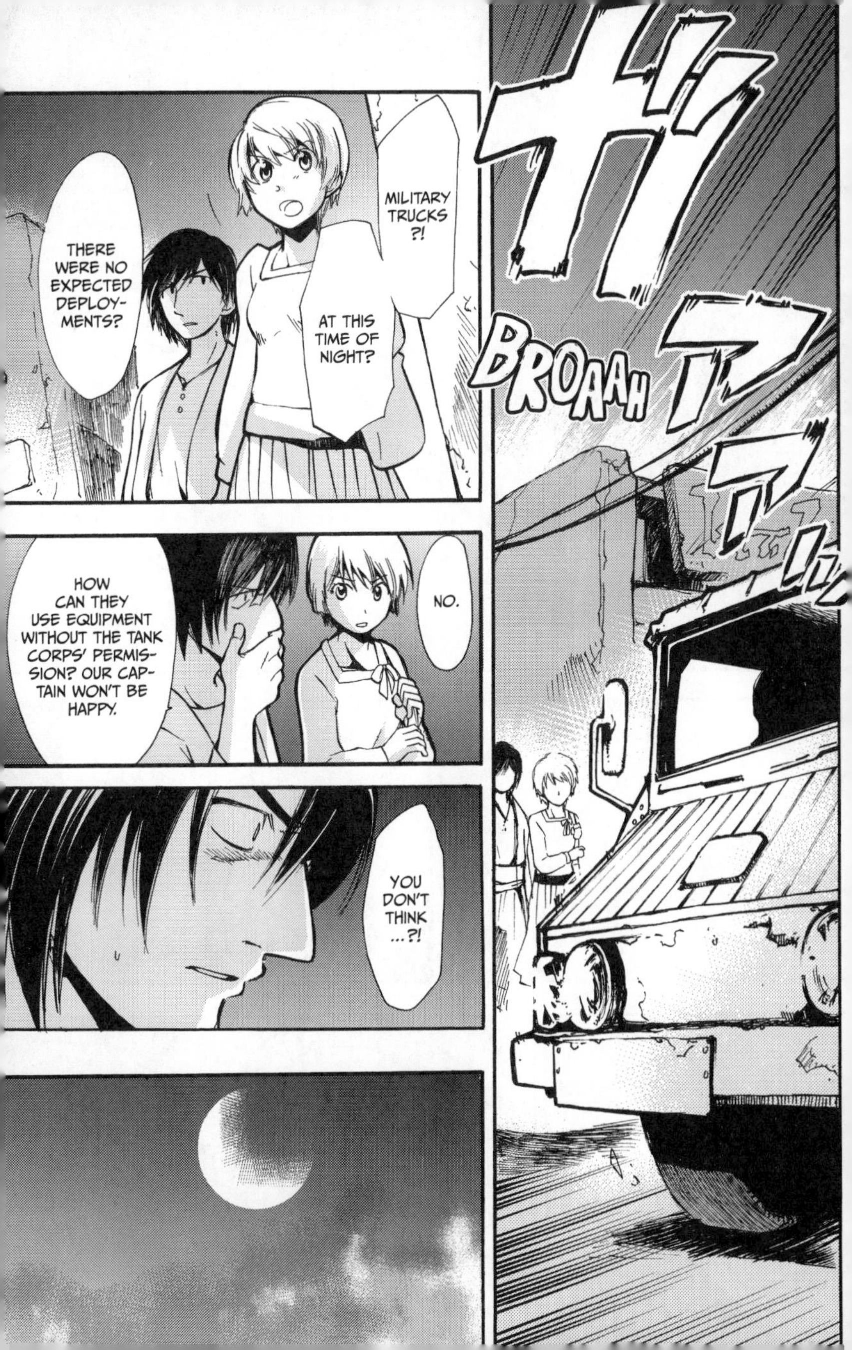
BROAAH
MILITARY TRUCKS ?!
AT THIS TIME OF NIGHT?
THERE WERE NO EXPECTED DEPLOY-MENTS?
NO.
HOW CAN THEY USE EQUIPMENT WITHOUT THE TANK CORPS' PERMIS-SION? OUR CAP-TAIN WON'T BE HAPPY.
YOU DON'T THINK ...?!

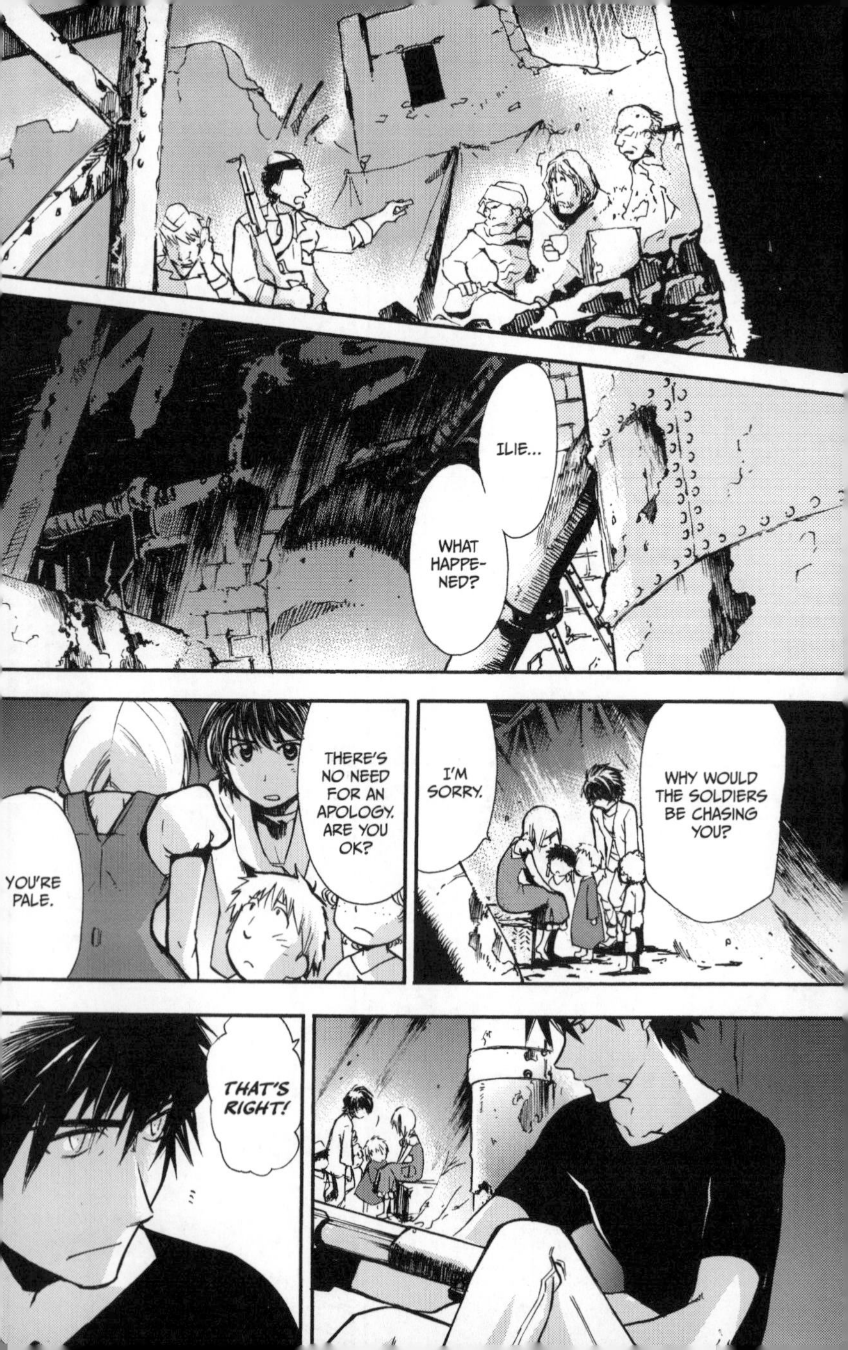
ILIE...
WHAT HAPPE-NED?
WHY WOULD THE SOLDIERS BE CHASING YOU?
I'M SORRY.
THERE'S NO NEED FOR AN APOLOGY. ARE YOU OK?
YOU'RE PALE.
THAT'S RIGHT!

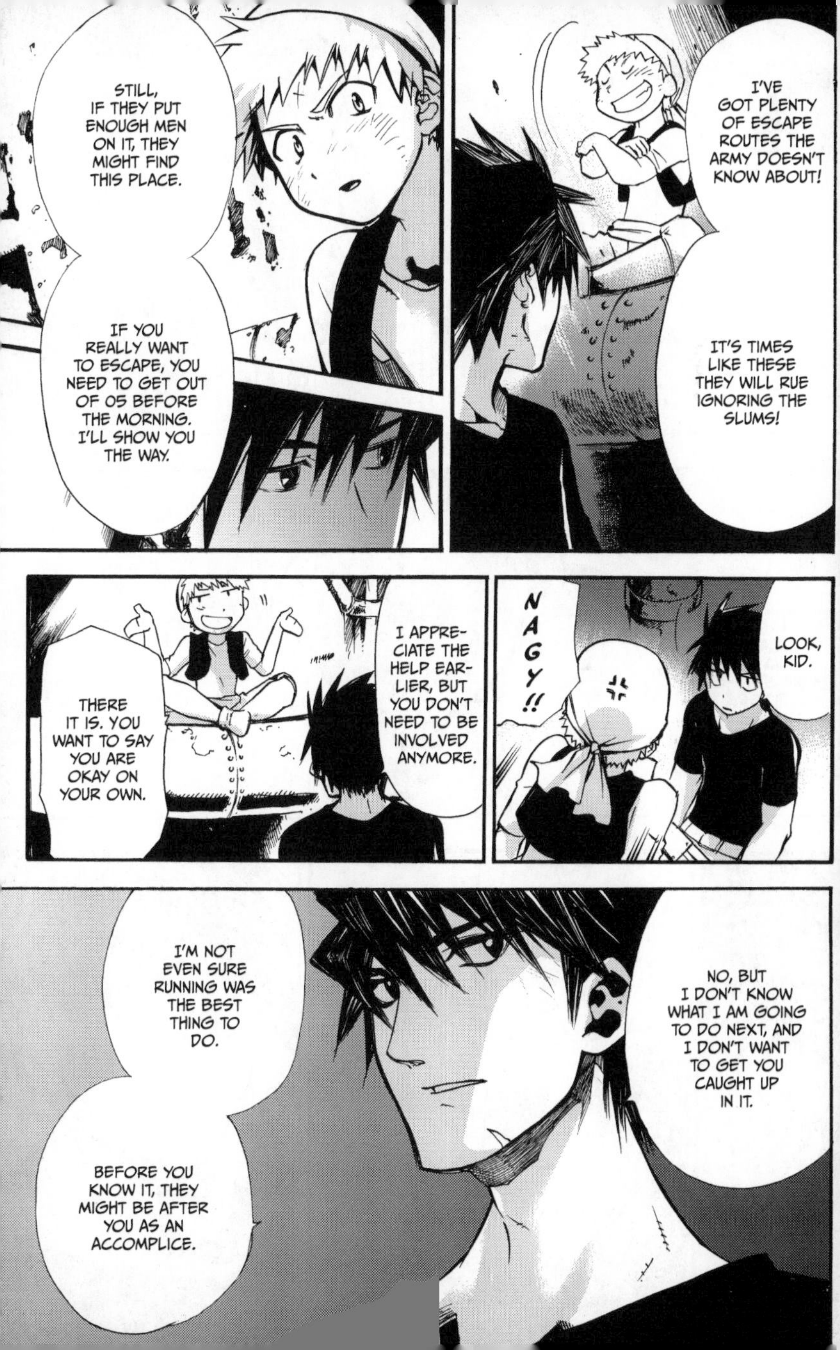
I'VE GOT PLENTY OF ESCAPE ROUTES THE ARMY DOESN'T KNOW ABOUT!
IT'S TIMES LIKE THESE THEY WILL RUE IGNORING THE SLUMS!
STILL, IF THEY PUT ENOUGH MEN ON IT, THEY MIGHT FIND THIS PLACE.
IF YOU REALLY WANT TO ESCAPE, YOU NEED TO GET OUT OF 05 BEFORE THE MORNING. I'LL SHOW YOU THE WAY.
LOOK, KID.
NAGY!!
I APPRE-CIATE THE HELP EAR-LIER, BUT YOU DON'T NEED TO BE INVOLVED ANYMORE.
THERE IT IS. YOU WANT TO SAY YOU ARE OKAY ON YOUR OWN.
NO, BUT I DON'T KNOW WHAT I AM GOING TO DO NEXT, AND I DON'T WANT TO GET YOU CAUGHT UP IN IT.
I'M NOT EVEN SURE RUNNING WAS THE BEST THING TO DO.
BEFORE YOU KNOW IT, THEY MIGHT BE AFTER YOU AS AN ACCOMPLICE.

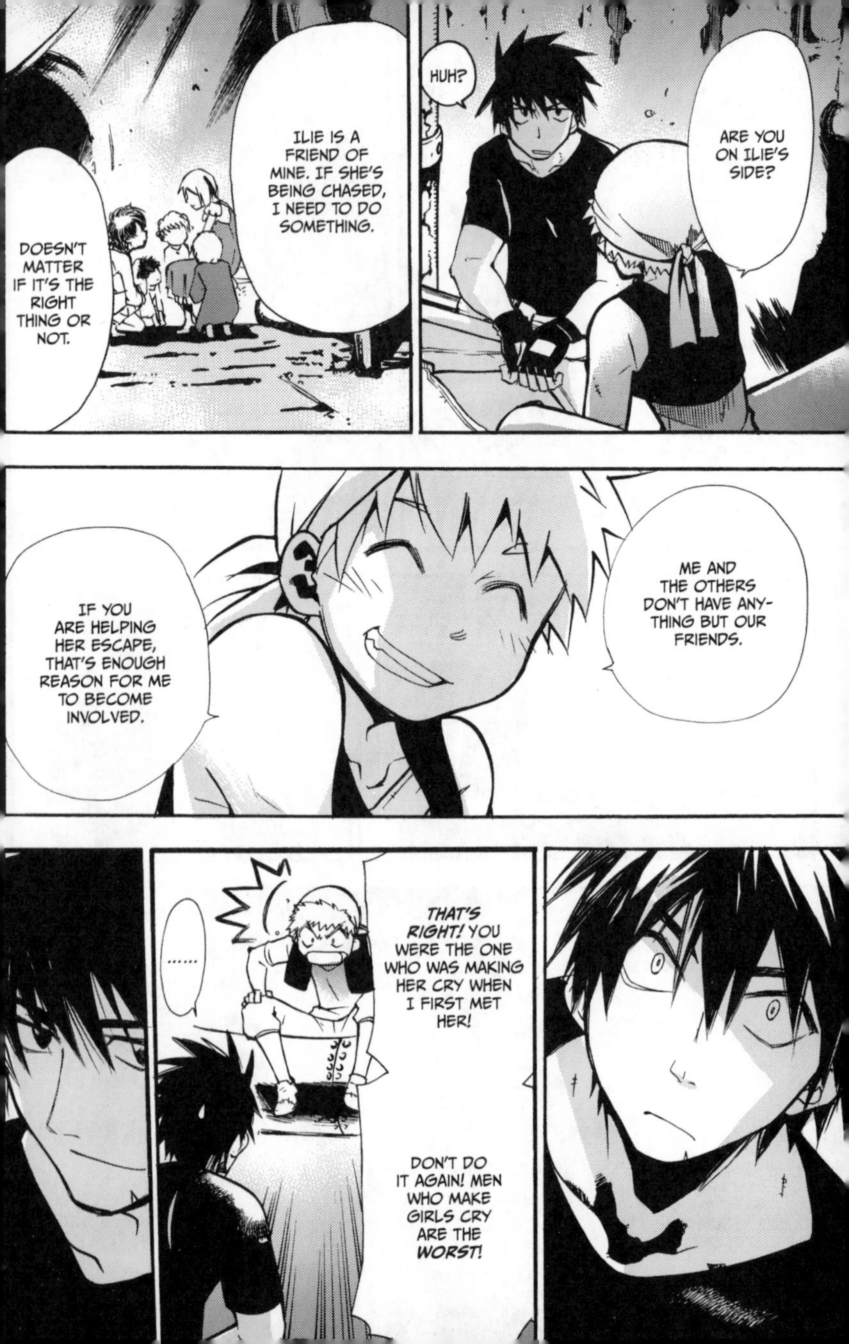
ARE YOU ON ILIE'S SIDE?
HUH?
ILIE IS A FRIEND OF MINE. IF SHE'S BEING CHASED, I NEED TO DO SOMETHING.
DOESN'T MATTER IF IT'S THE RIGHT THING OR NOT.
ME AND THE OTHERS DON'T HAVE ANYTHING BUT OUR FRIENDS.
IF YOU ARE HELPING HER ESCAPE, THAT'S ENOUGH REASON FOR ME TO BECOME INVOLVED.
THAT'S RIGHT! YOU WERE THE ONE WHO WAS MAKING HER CRY WHEN I FIRST MET HER!
DON'T DO IT AGAIN! MEN WHO MAKE GIRLS CRY ARE THE *WORST!*
......

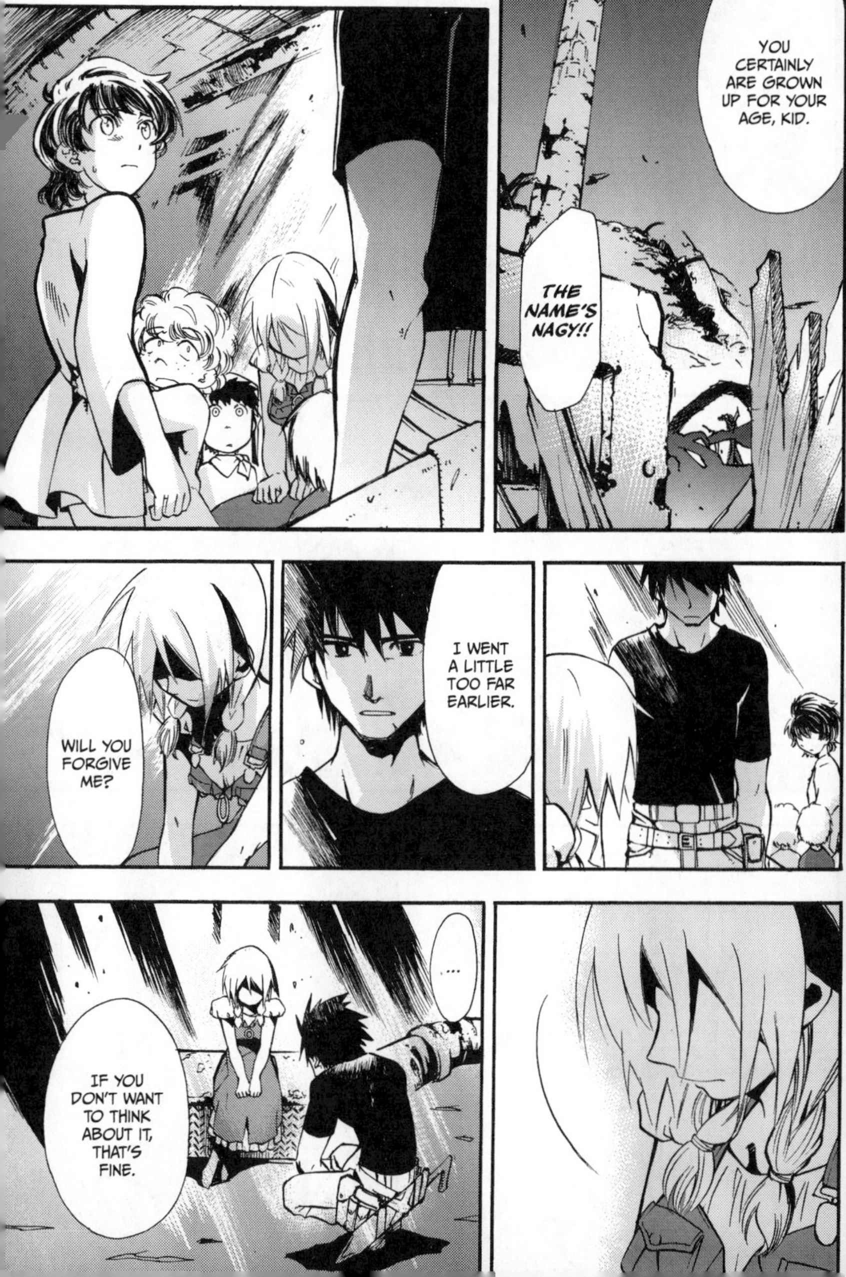
YOU CERTAINLY ARE GROWN UP FOR YOUR AGE, KID.
THE NAME'S NAGY!!
I WENT A LITTLE TOO FAR EARLIER.
WILL YOU FORGIVE ME?
...
IF YOU DON'T WANT TO THINK ABOUT IT, THAT'S FINE.

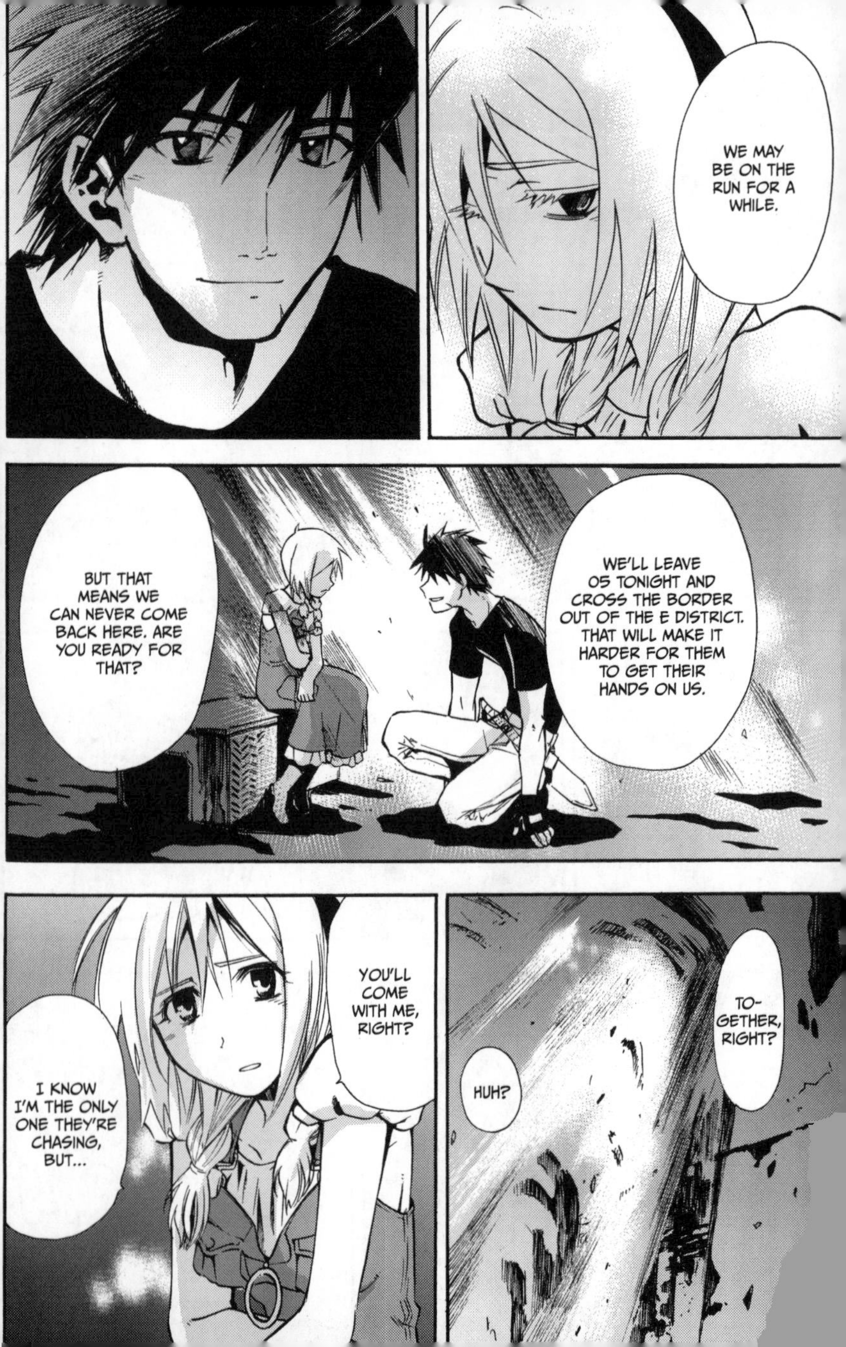
WE MAY BE ON THE RUN FOR A WHILE.
WE'LL LEAVE 05 TONIGHT AND CROSS THE BORDER OUT OF THE E DISTRICT. THAT WILL MAKE IT HARDER FOR THEM TO GET THEIR HANDS ON US.
BUT THAT MEANS WE CAN NEVER COME BACK HERE. ARE YOU READY FOR THAT?
TO-GETHER, RIGHT?
HUH?
YOU'LL COME WITH ME, RIGHT?
I KNOW I'M THE ONLY ONE THEY'RE CHASING, BUT...

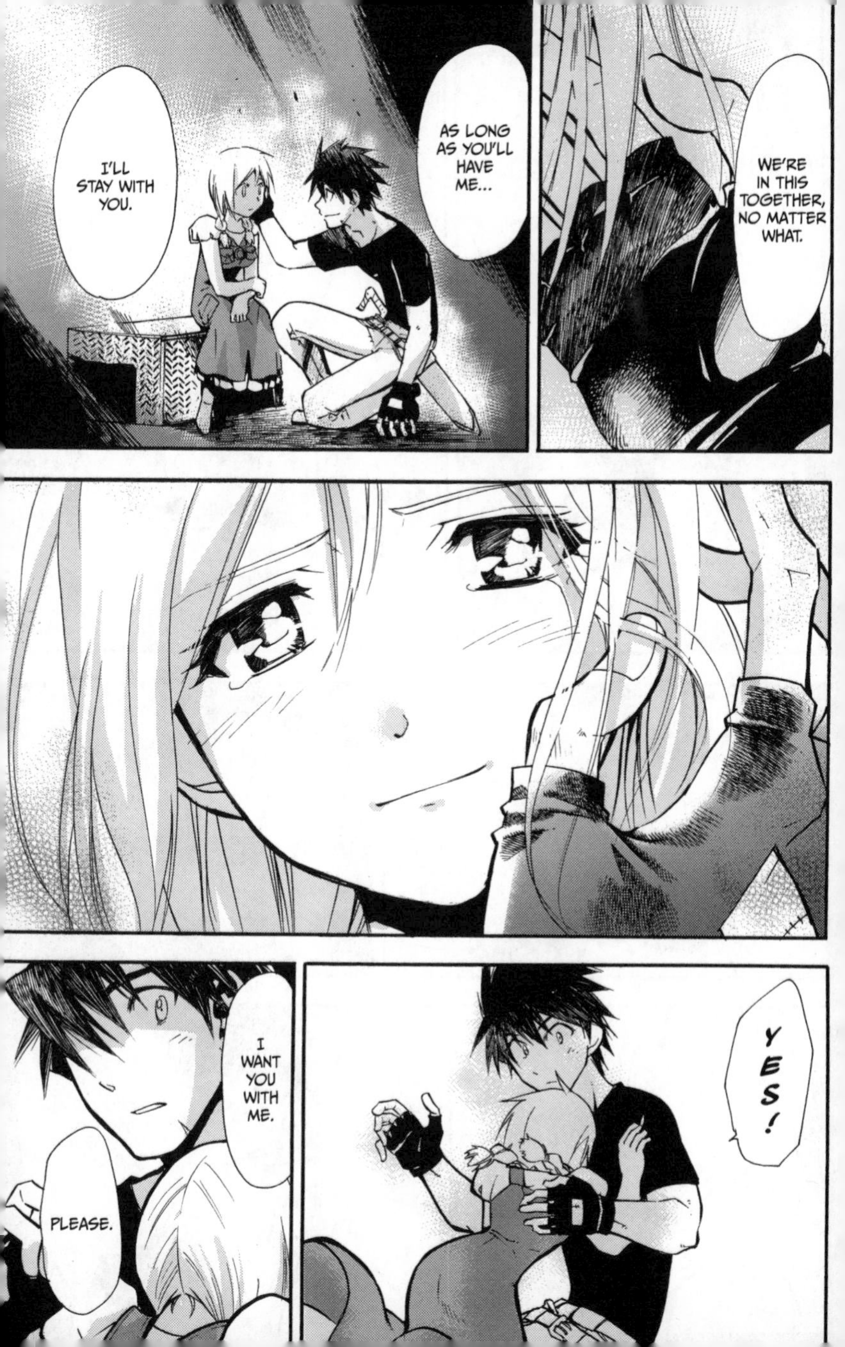
WE'RE IN THIS TOGETHER, NO MATTER WHAT.
AS LONG AS YOU'LL HAVE ME...
I'LL STAY WITH YOU.
YES!
I WANT YOU WITH ME.
PLEASE.

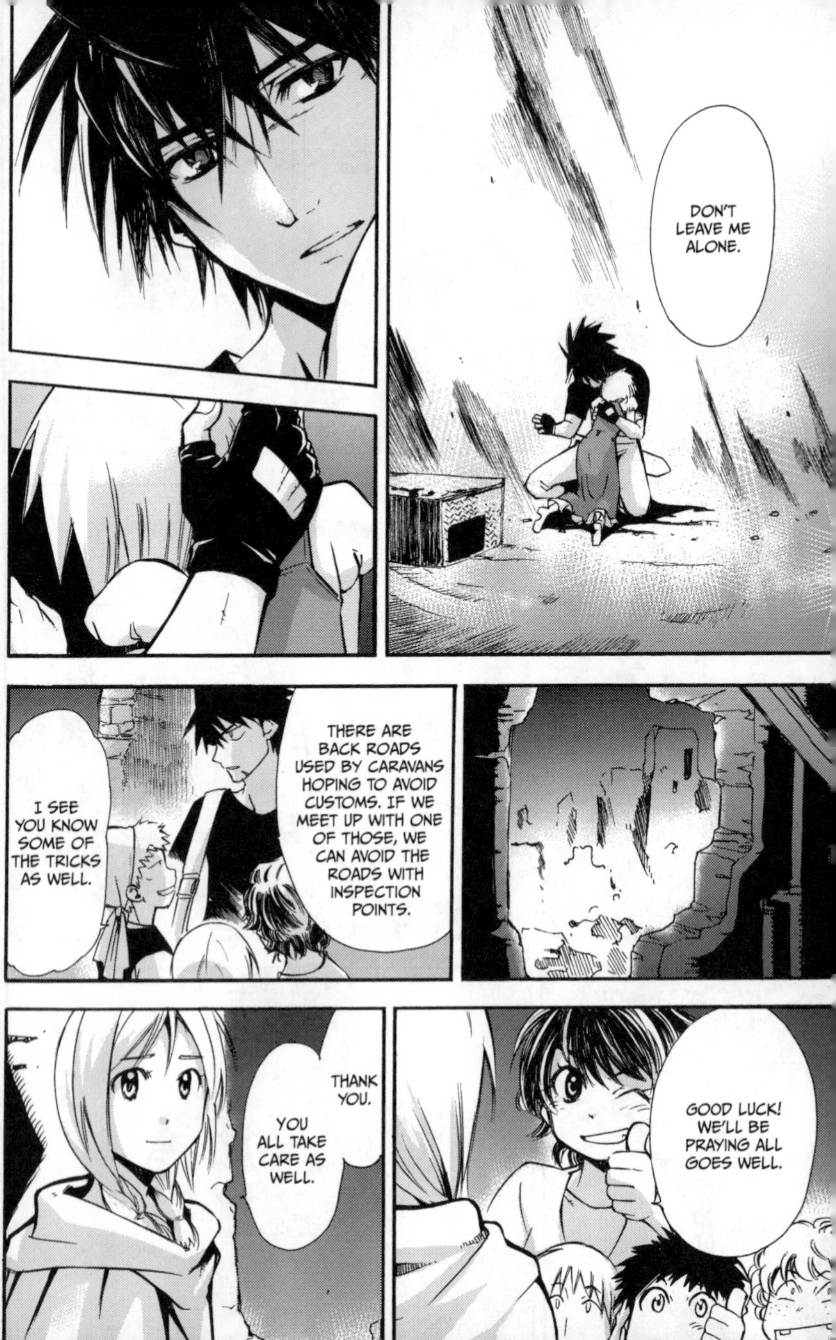
DON'T LEAVE ME ALONE.
THERE ARE BACK ROADS USED BY CARAVANS HOPING TO AVOID CUSTOMS. IF WE MEET UP WITH ONE OF THOSE, WE CAN AVOID THE ROADS WITH INSPECTION POINTS.
I SEE YOU KNOW SOME OF THE TRICKS AS WELL.
GOOD LUCK! WE'LL BE PRAYING ALL GOES WELL.
THANK YOU.
YOU ALL TAKE CARE AS WELL.

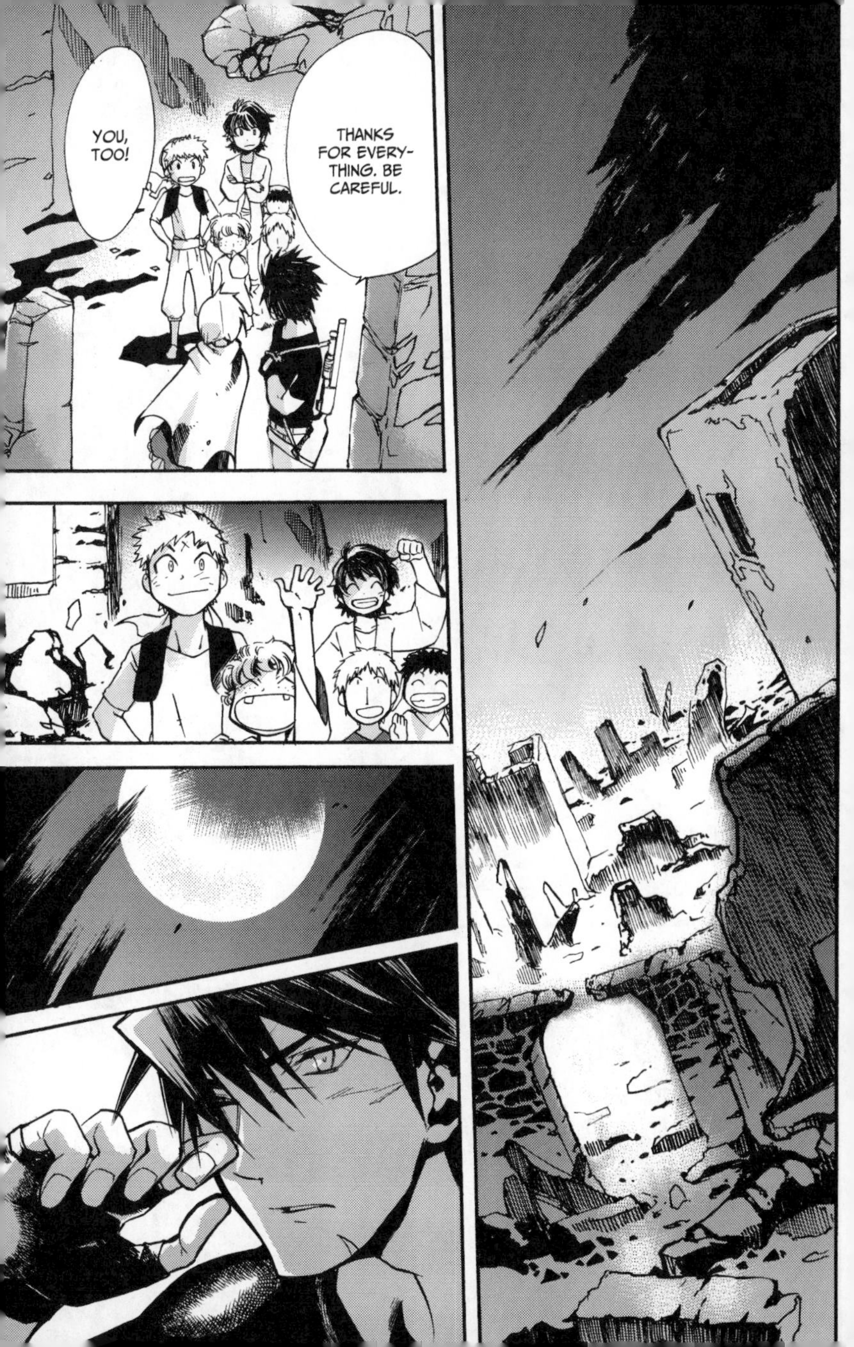
THANKS FOR EVERY-THING. BE CAREFUL.
YOU, TOO!

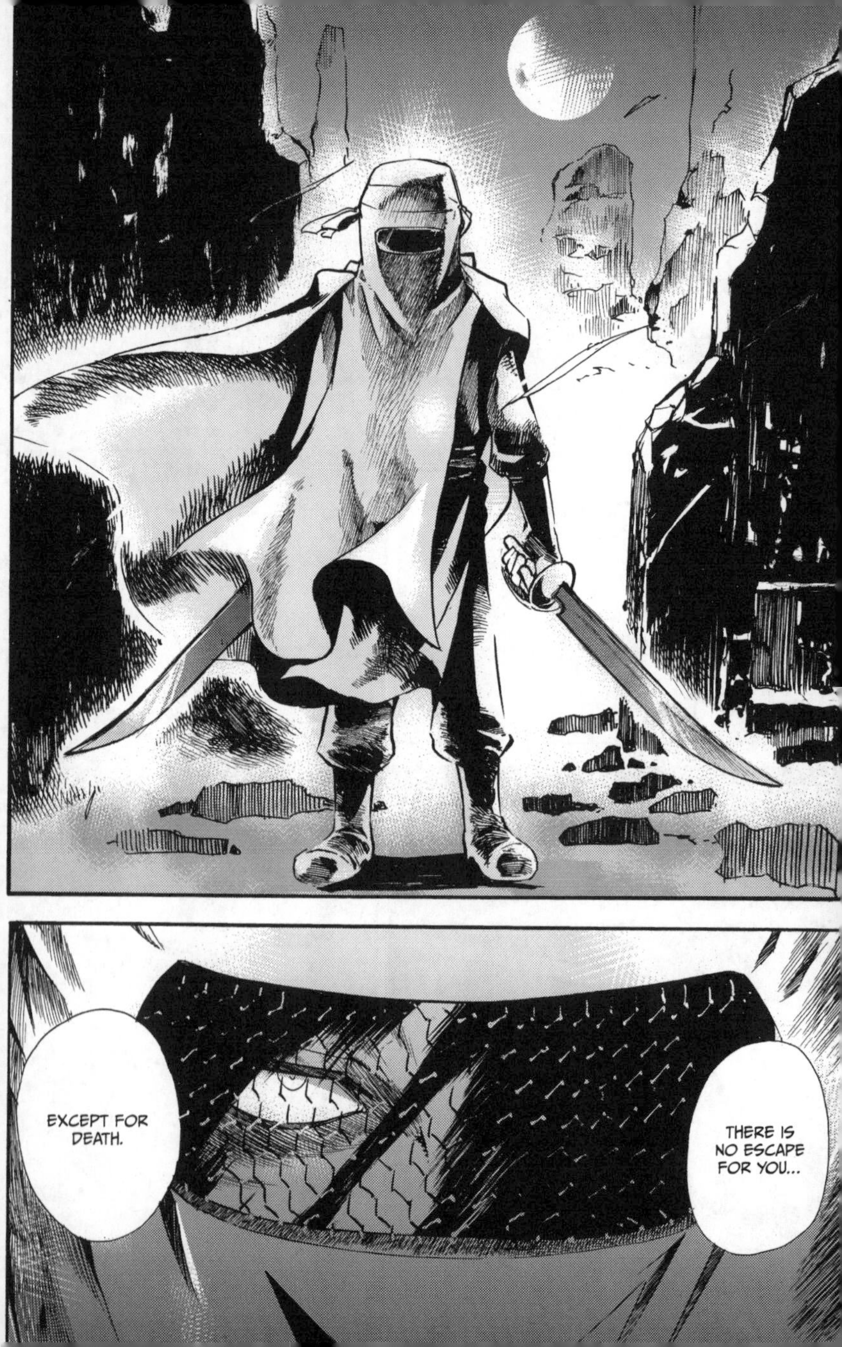
THERE IS NO ESCAPE FOR YOU...
EXCEPT FOR DEATH.

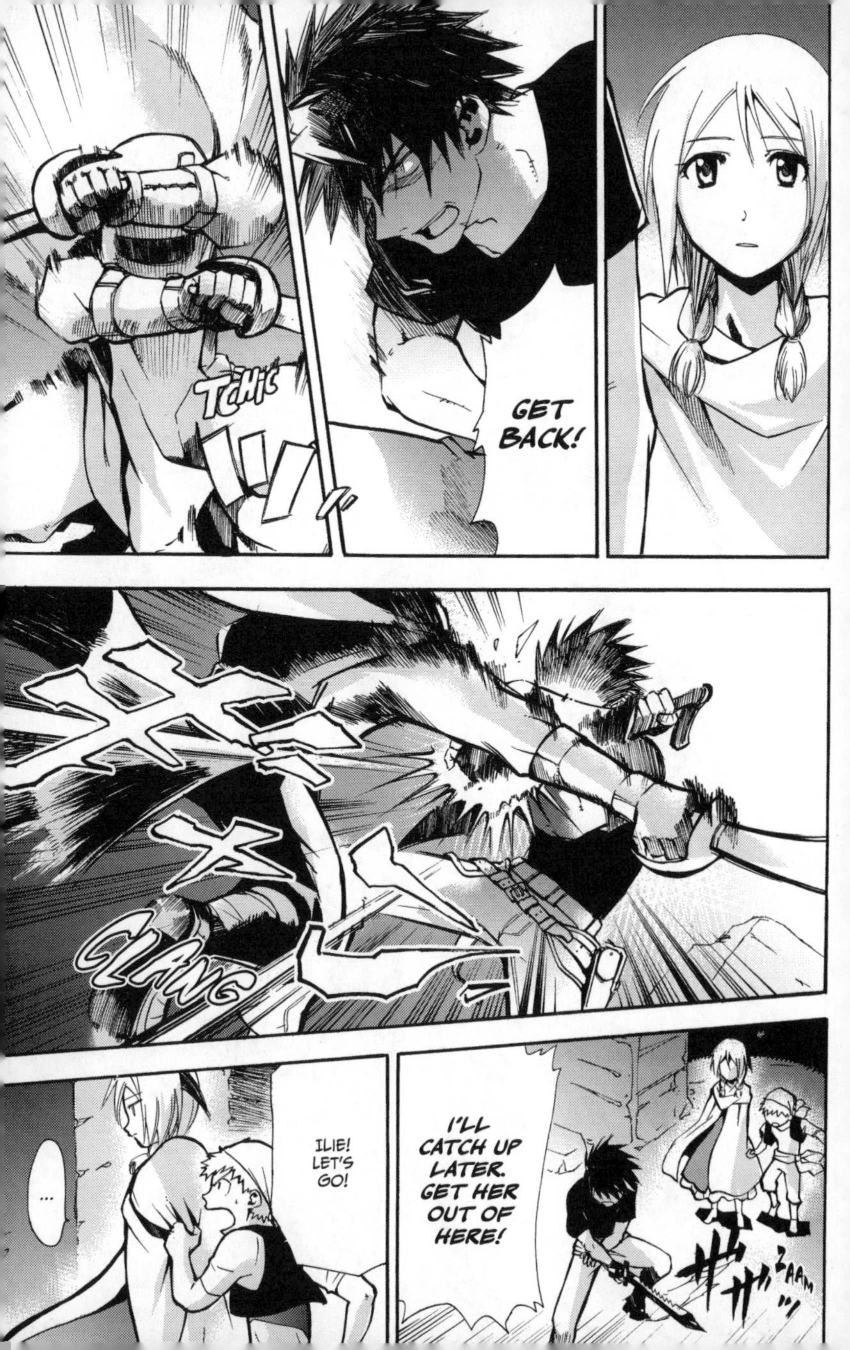
GET BACK!
TCHIC
CLANG
I'LL CATCH UP LATER. GET HER OUT OF HERE!
ZAAM
ILIE! LET'S GO!
...

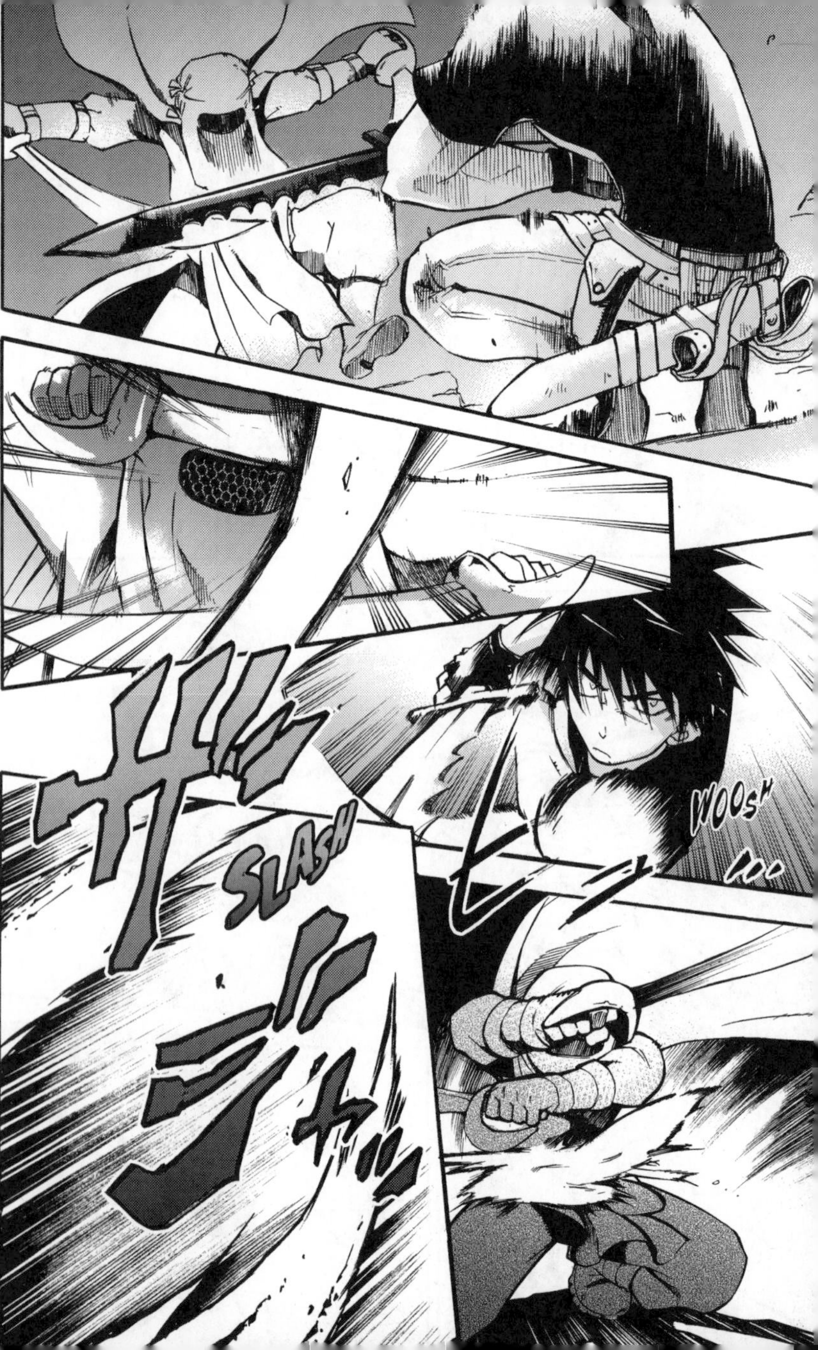
WOOSH
SLASH

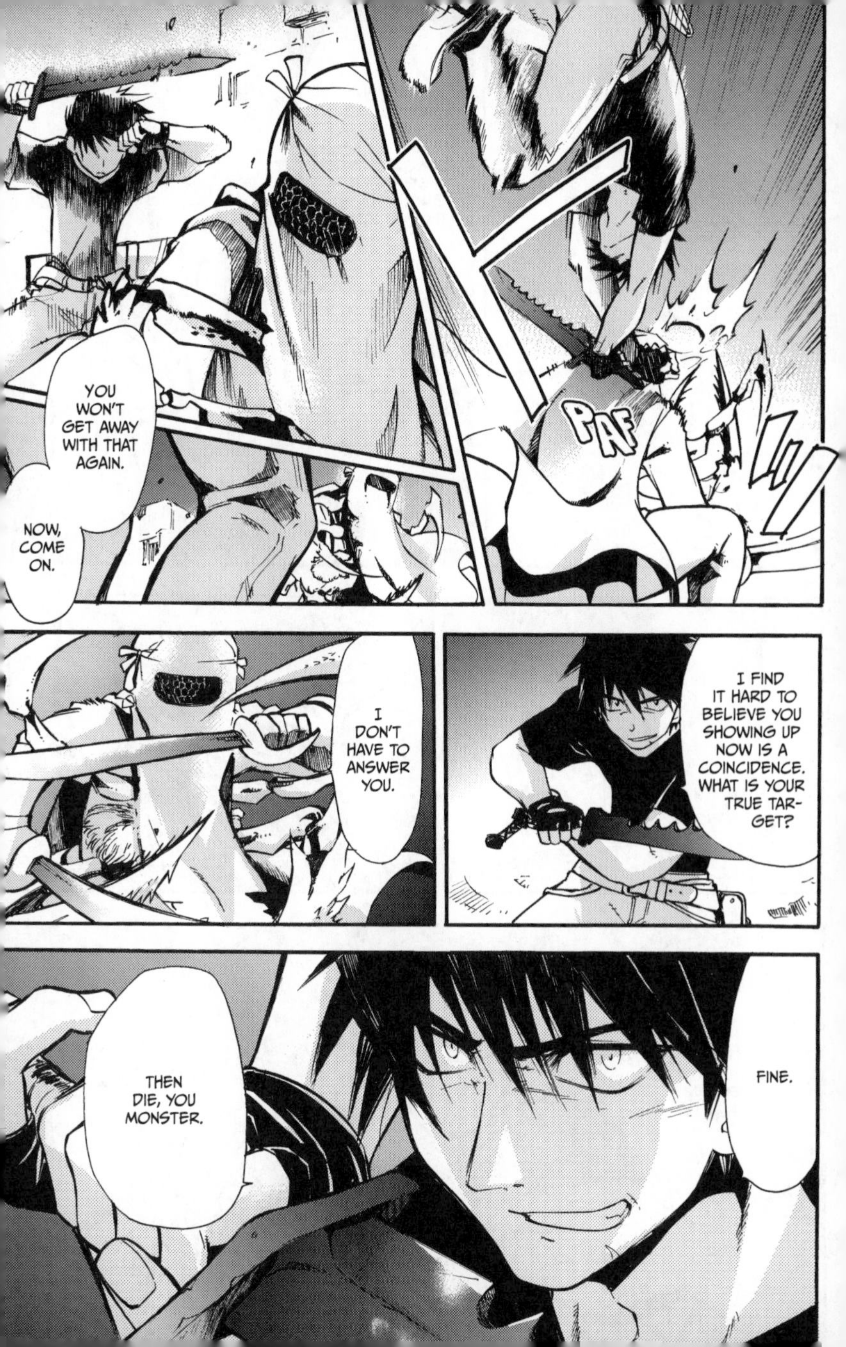
PAF
YOU WON'T GET AWAY WITH THAT AGAIN.
NOW, COME ON.
I FIND IT HARD TO BELIEVE YOU SHOWING UP NOW IS A COINCIDENCE. WHAT IS YOUR TRUE TAR-GET?
I DON'T HAVE TO ANSWER YOU.
FINE.
THEN DIE, YOU MONSTER.

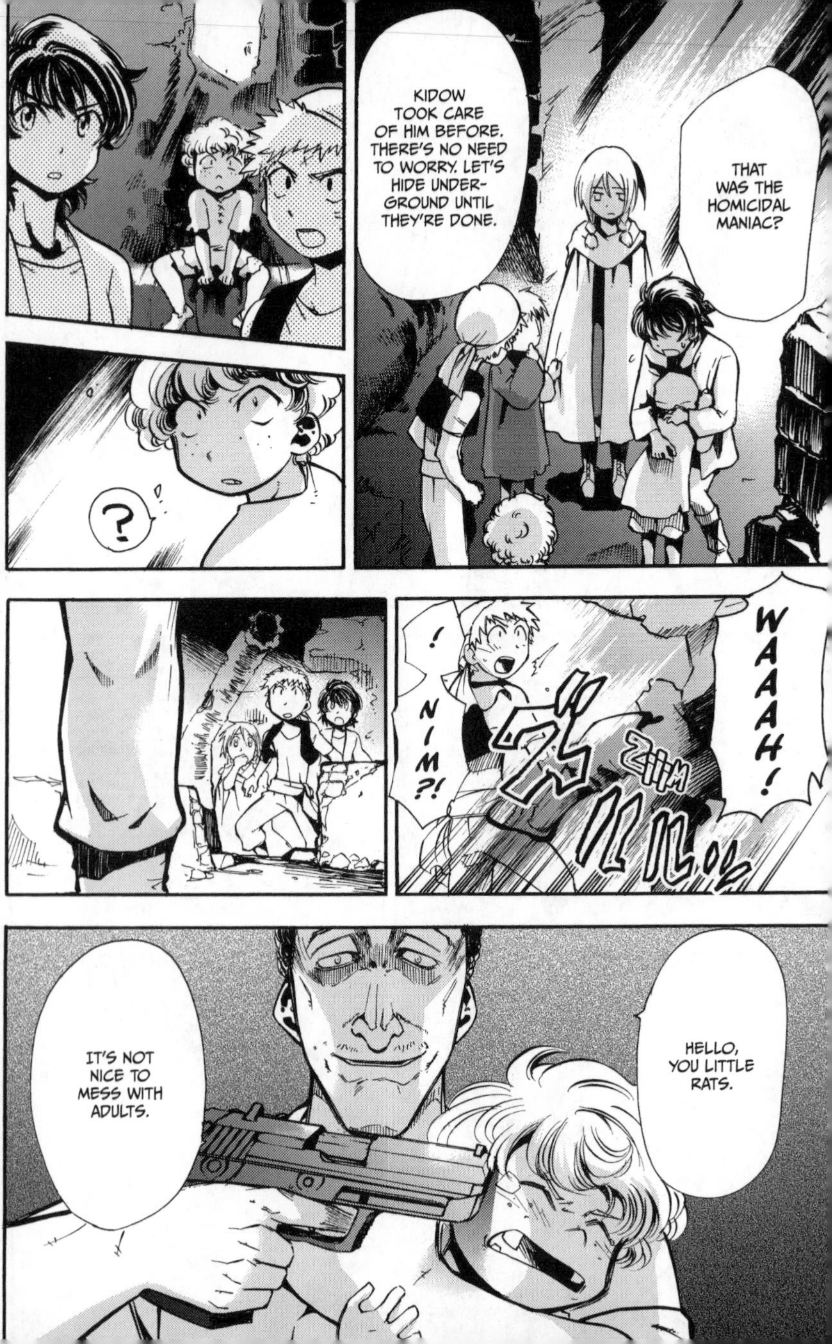
THAT WAS THE HOMICIDAL MANIAC?
KIDOW TOOK CARE OF HIM BEFORE. THERE'S NO NEED TO WORRY. LET'S HIDE UNDER-GROUND UNTIL THEY'RE DONE.
?
WAAAAH!
NIM?!
!
HELLO, YOU LITTLE RATS.
IT'S NOT NICE TO MESS WITH ADULTS.

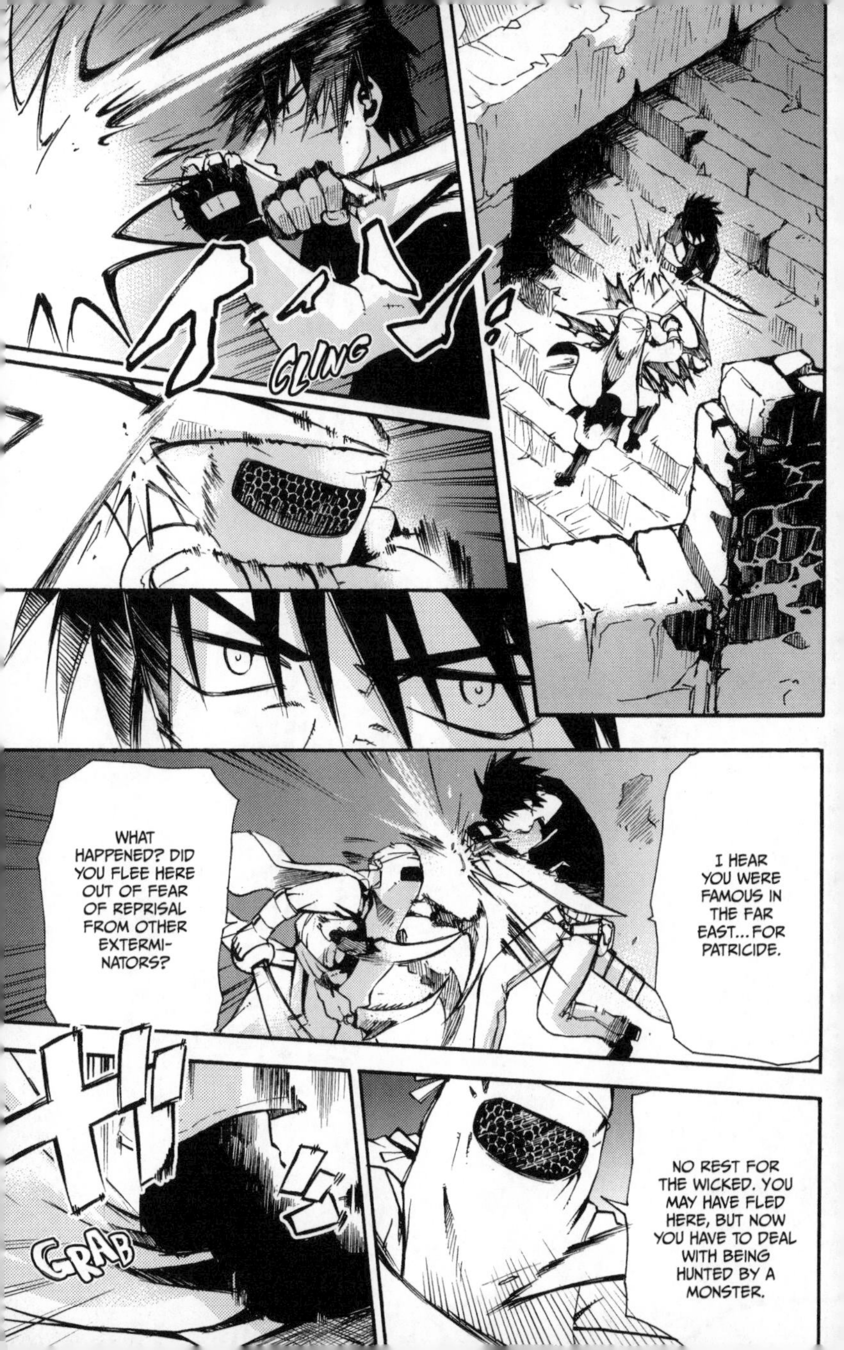
CLING
I HEAR YOU WERE FAMOUS IN THE FAR EAST...FOR PATRICIDE.
WHAT HAPPENED? DID YOU FLEE HERE OUT OF FEAR OF REPRISAL FROM OTHER EXTERMI-NATORS?
NO REST FOR THE WICKED. YOU MAY HAVE FLED HERE, BUT NOW YOU HAVE TO DEAL WITH BEING HUNTED BY A MONSTER.
GRAB

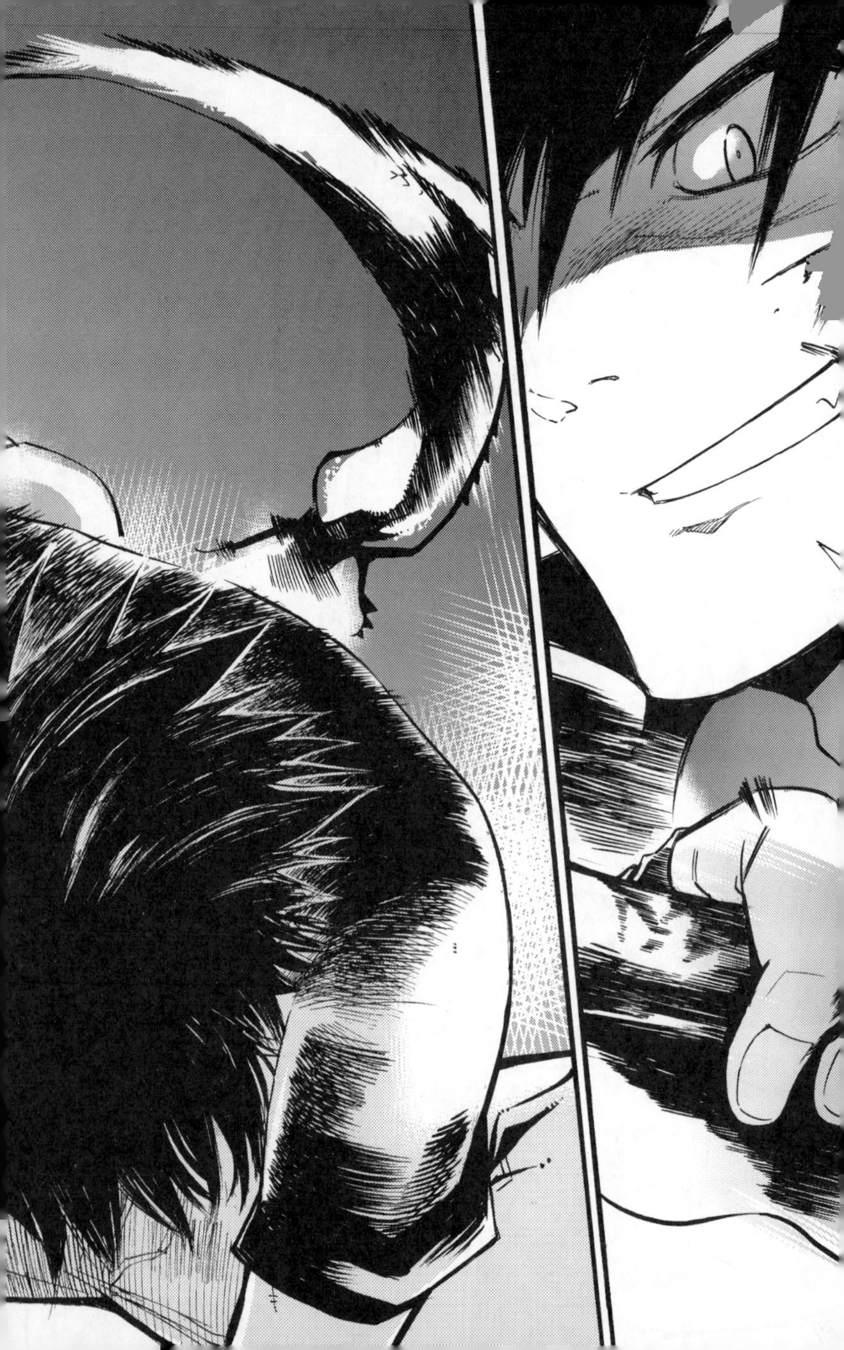

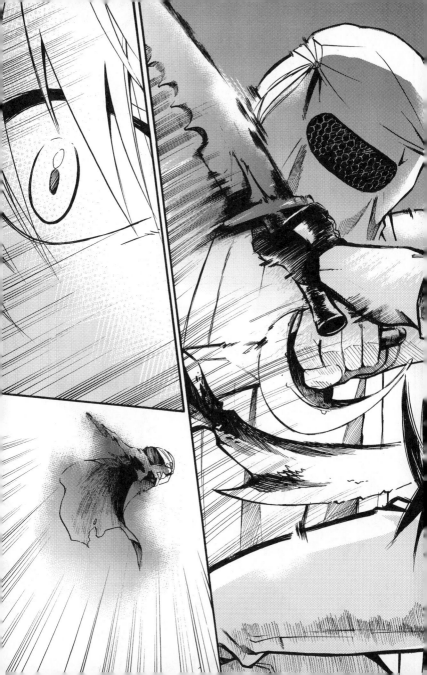

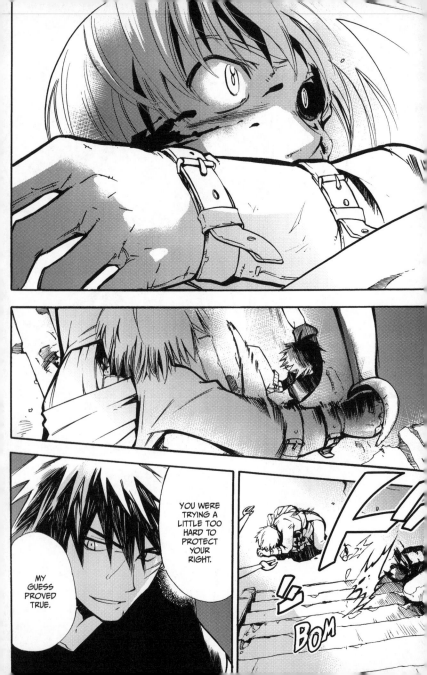

YOU WERE TRYING A LITTLE TOO HARD TO PROTECT YOUR RIGHT.

MY GUESS PROVED TRUE.

BOM

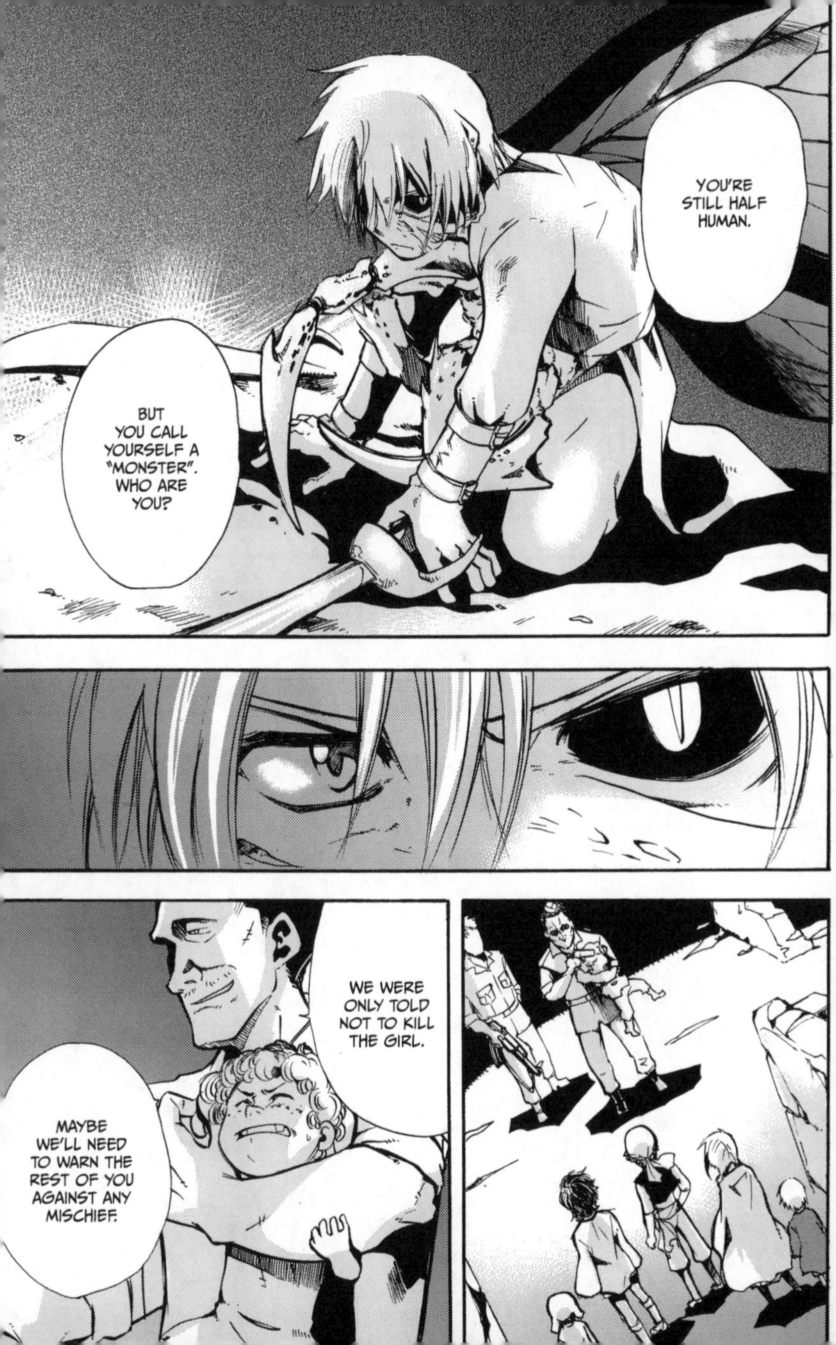
YOU'RE STILL HALF HUMAN.
BUT YOU CALL YOURSELF A "MONSTER". WHO ARE YOU?
WE WERE ONLY TOLD NOT TO KILL THE GIRL.
MAYBE WE'LL NEED TO WARN THE REST OF YOU AGAINST ANY MISCHIEF.

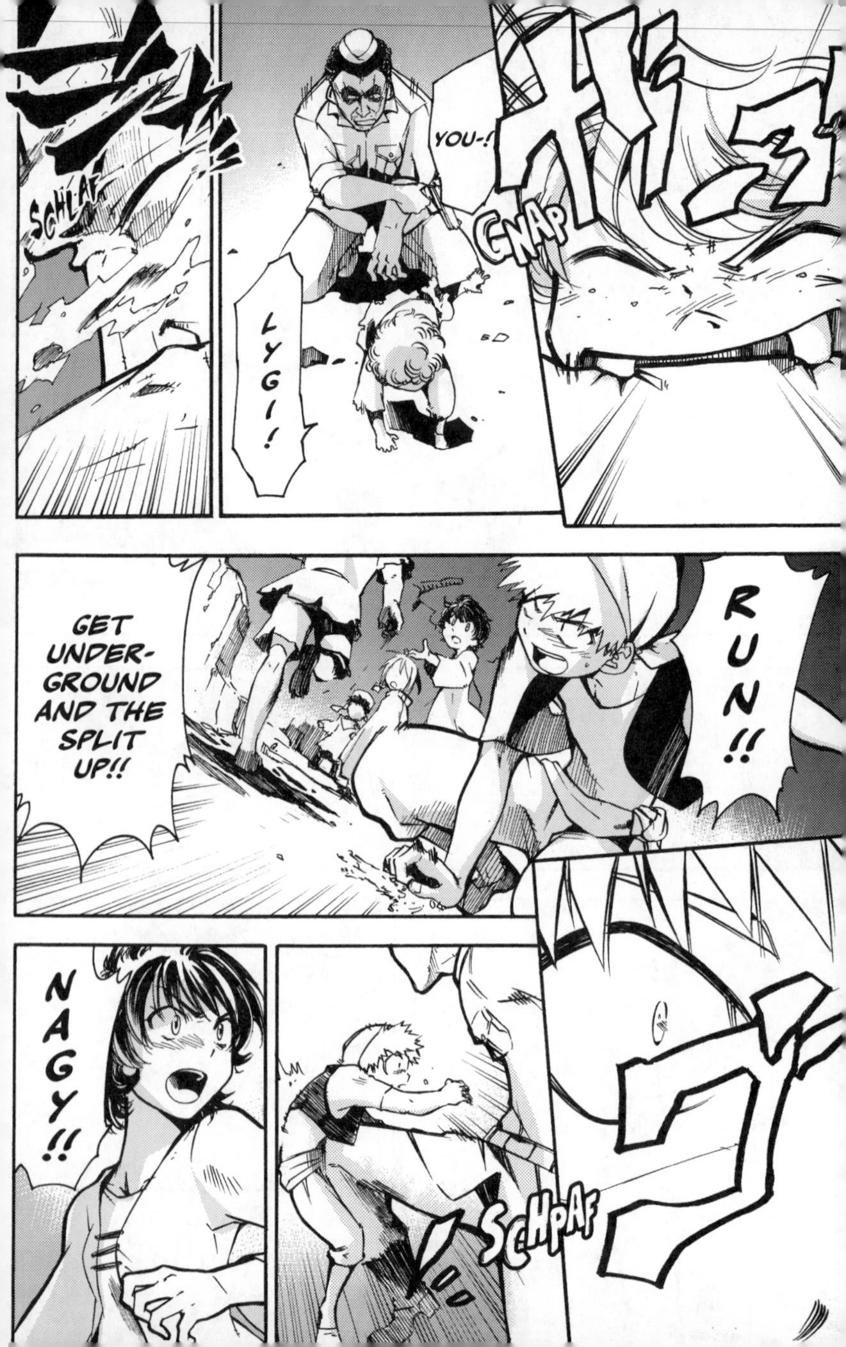
CNAP
YOU-!
LYGI!
SCHLAF
RUN!!
GET UNDER-GROUND AND THE SPLIT UP!!
SCHPAF
NAGY!!

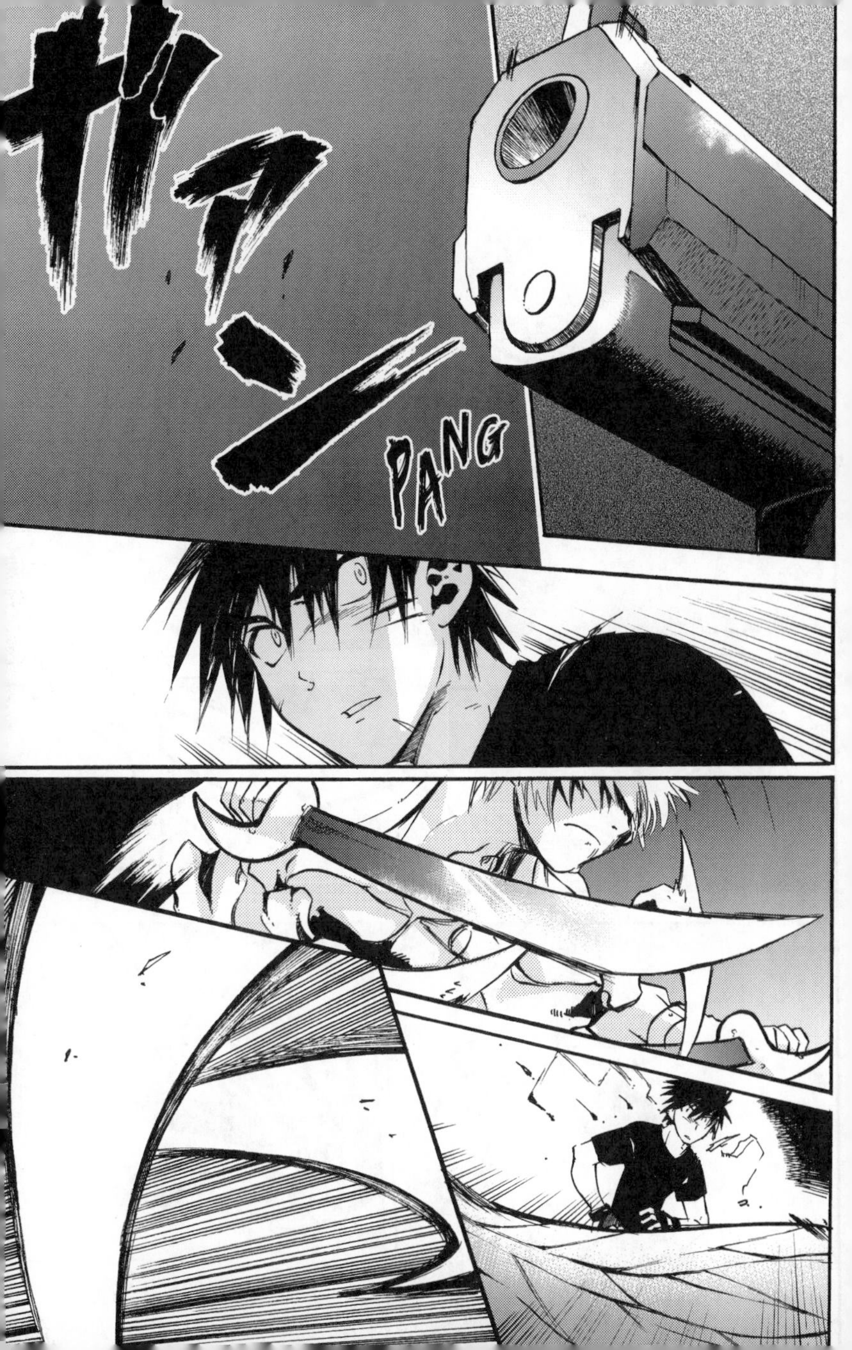
ザァン
PANG

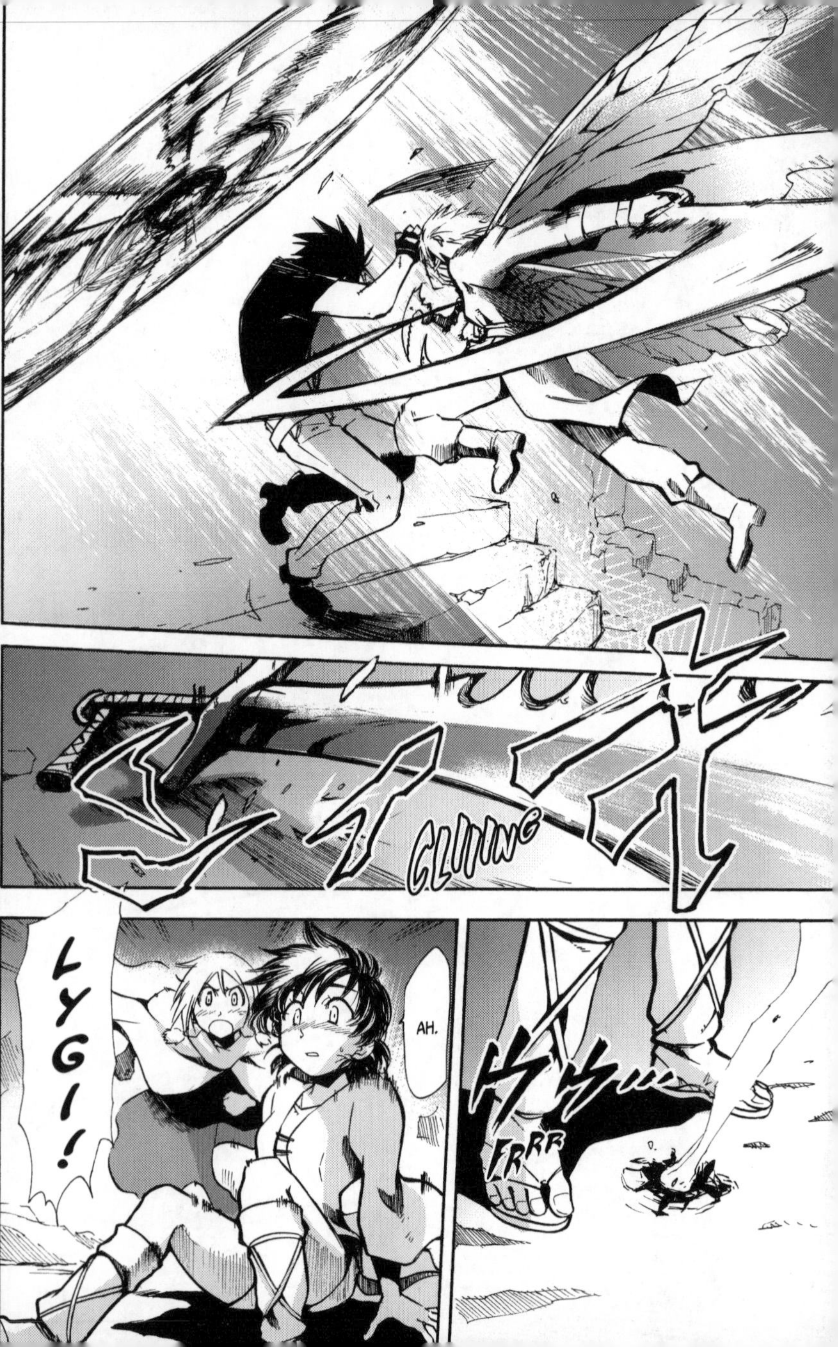
CLIIING
FRRR
AH.
LYGI!!

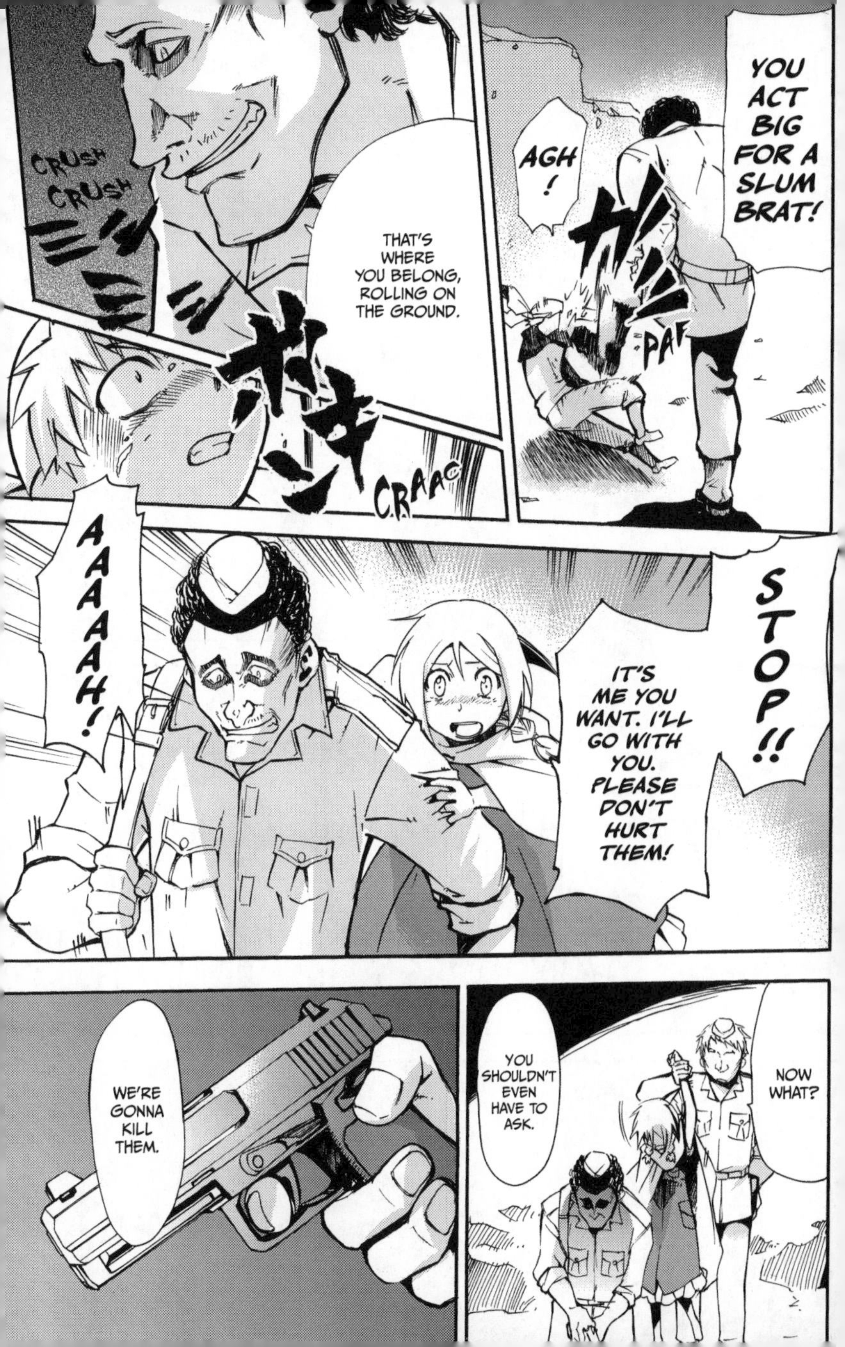
YOU ACT BIG FOR A SLUM BRAT!
AGH!
PAF
CRUSH
CRUSH
THAT'S WHERE YOU BELONG, ROLLING ON THE GROUND.
CRAAC
STOP!!
IT'S ME YOU WANT. I'LL GO WITH YOU. PLEASE DON'T HURT THEM!
AAAAAH!
NOW WHAT?
YOU SHOULDN'T EVEN HAVE TO ASK.
WE'RE GONNA KILL THEM.

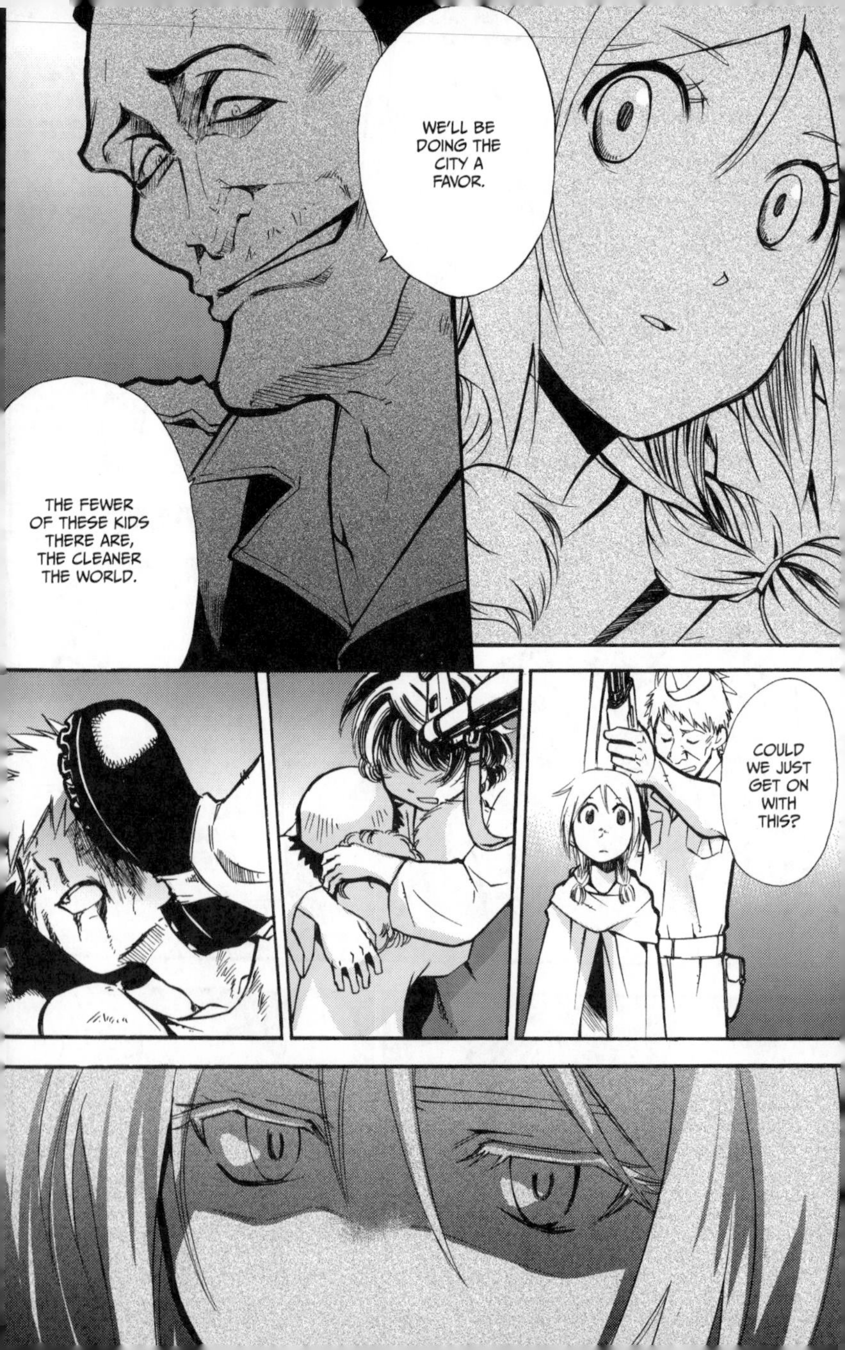
WE'LL BE DOING THE CITY A FAVOR.
THE FEWER OF THESE KIDS THERE ARE, THE CLEANER THE WORLD.
COULD WE JUST GET ON WITH THIS?

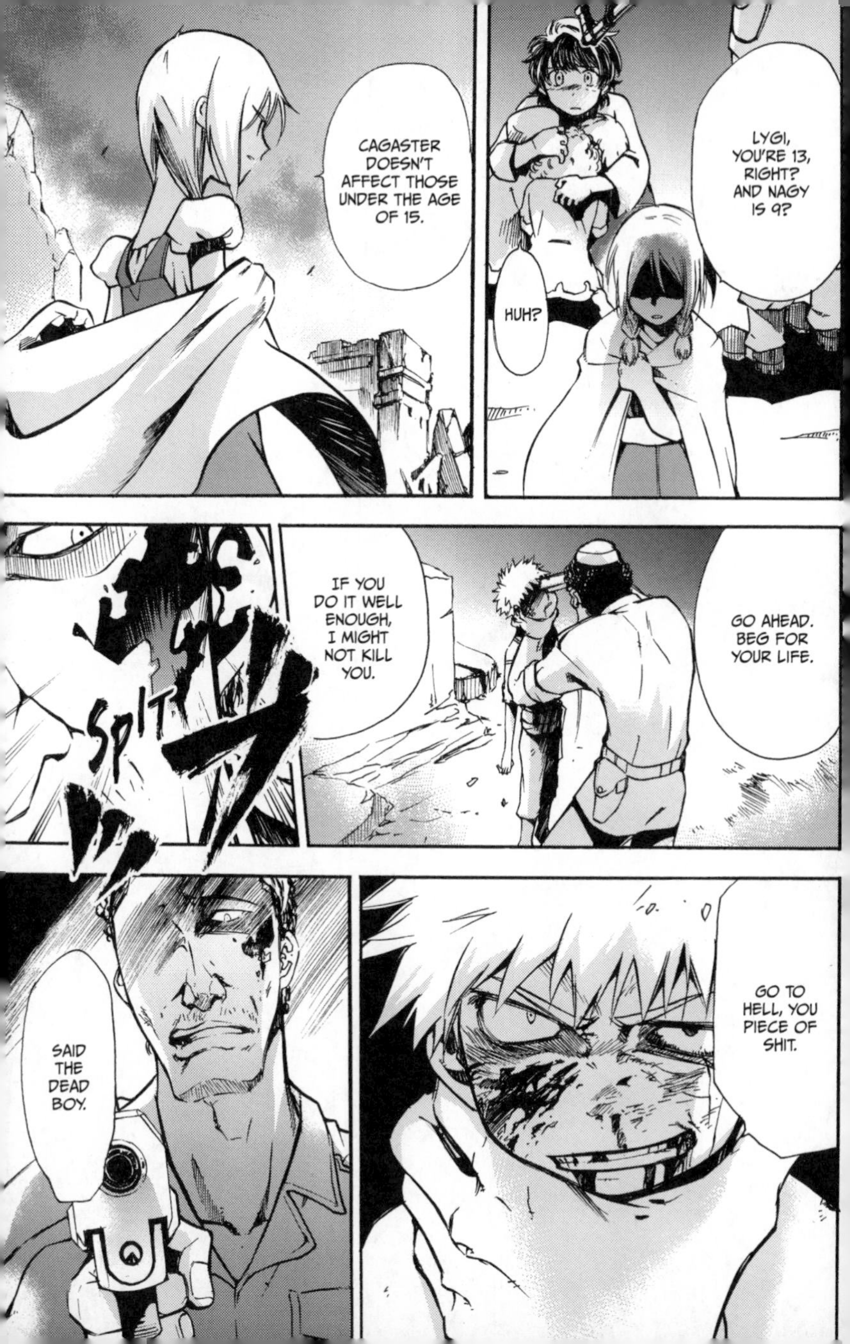
LYGI, YOU'RE 13, RIGHT? AND NAGY IS 9?
HUH?
CAGASTER DOESN'T AFFECT THOSE UNDER THE AGE OF 15.
GO AHEAD. BEG FOR YOUR LIFE.
IF YOU DO IT WELL ENOUGH, I MIGHT NOT KILL YOU.
SPIT
GO TO HELL, YOU PIECE OF SHIT.
SAID THE DEAD BOY.

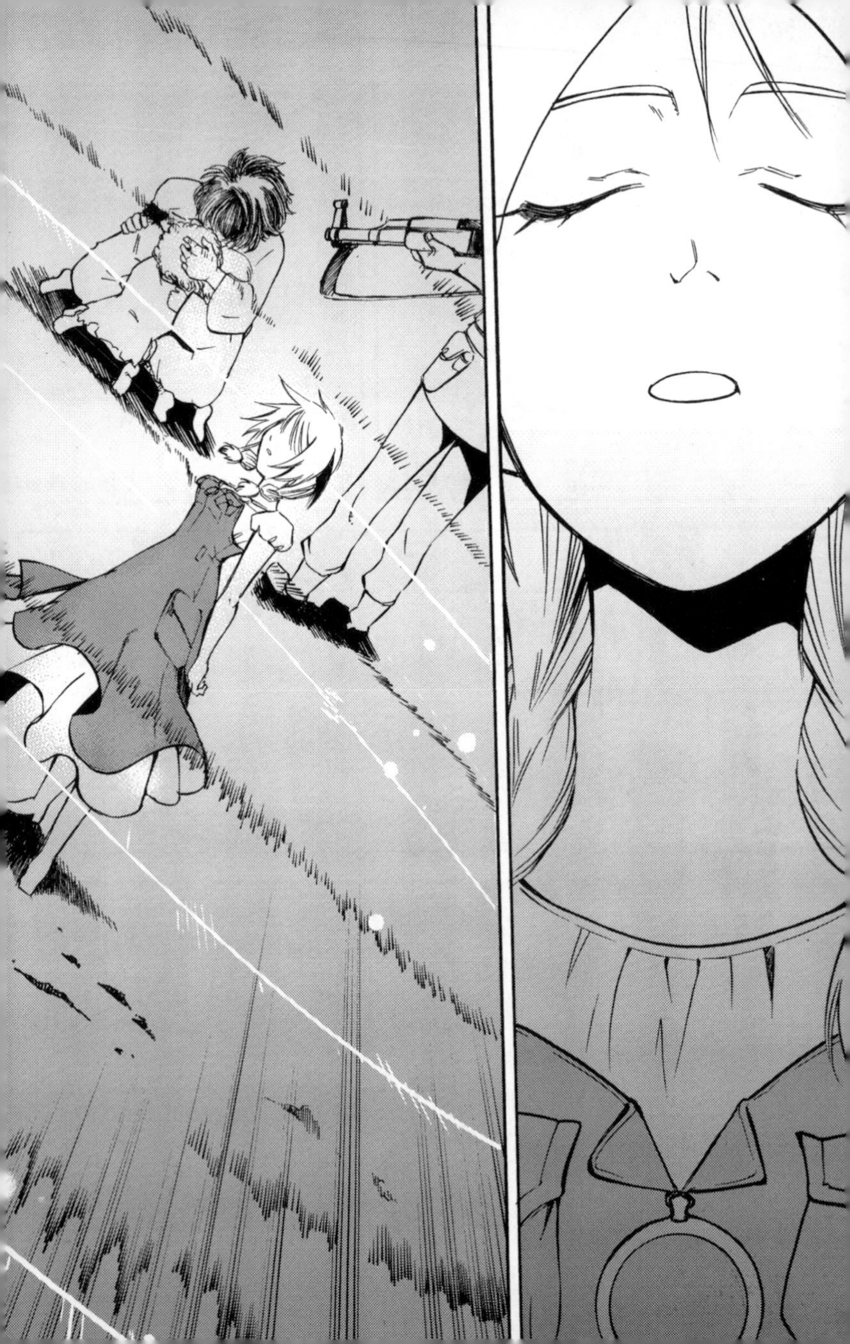

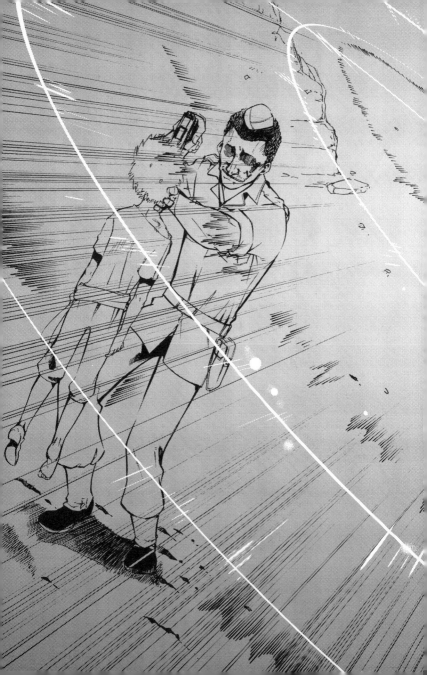

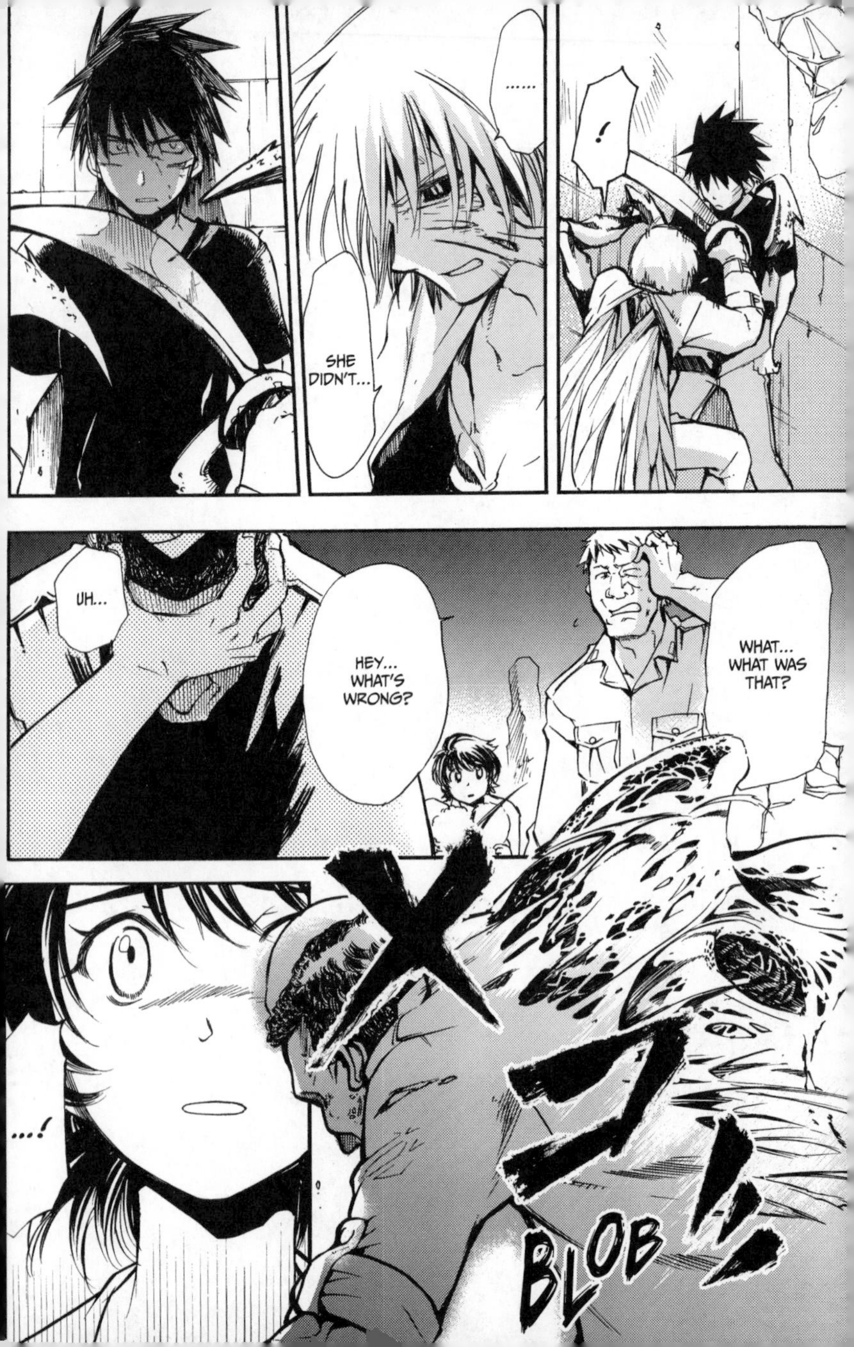
!
......
SHE DIDN'T...
WHAT... WHAT WAS THAT?
HEY... WHAT'S WRONG?
UH...
BLOB
...!

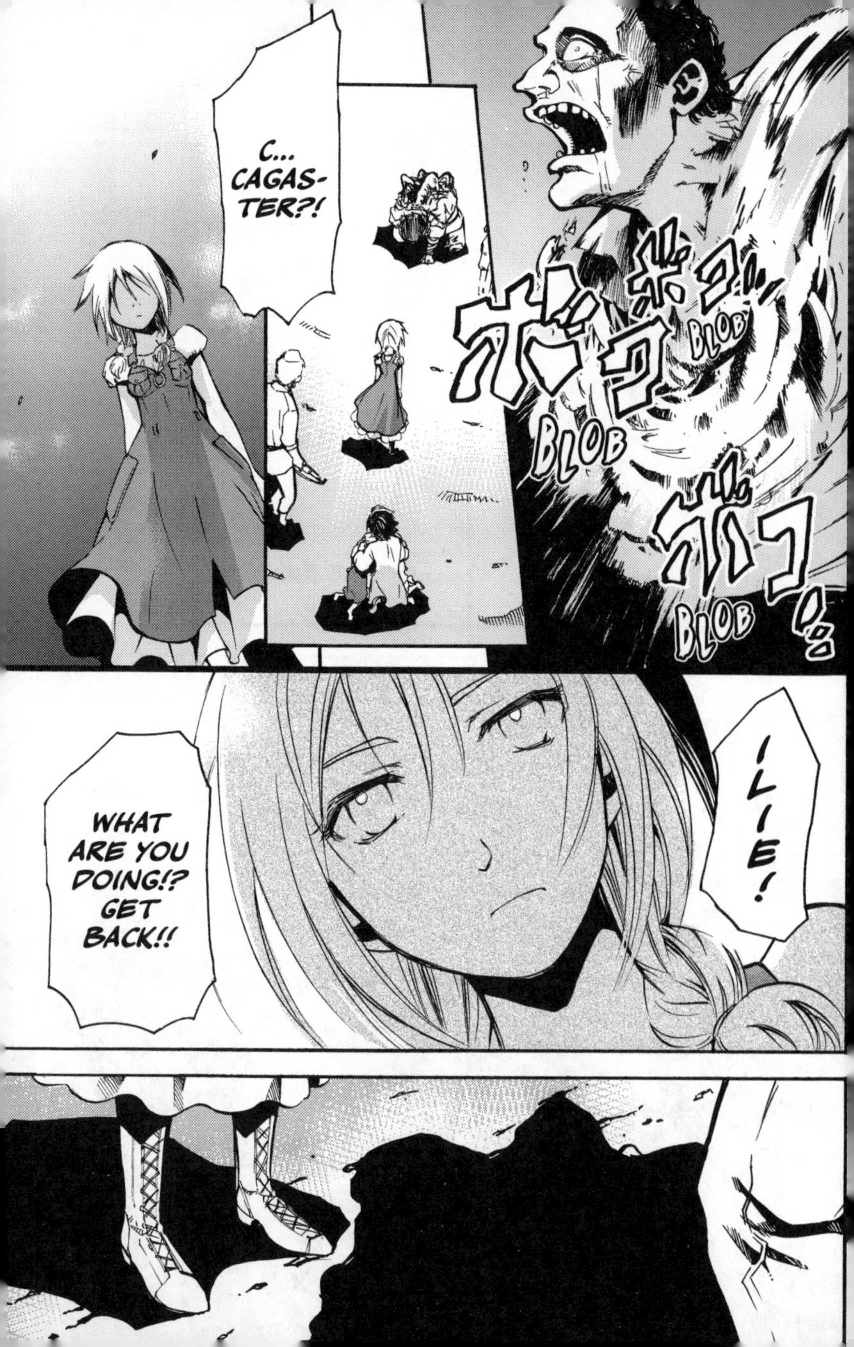
BLOB
BLOB
BLOB
C... CAGASTER?!
ILLIE!
WHAT ARE YOU DOING!? GET BACK!!

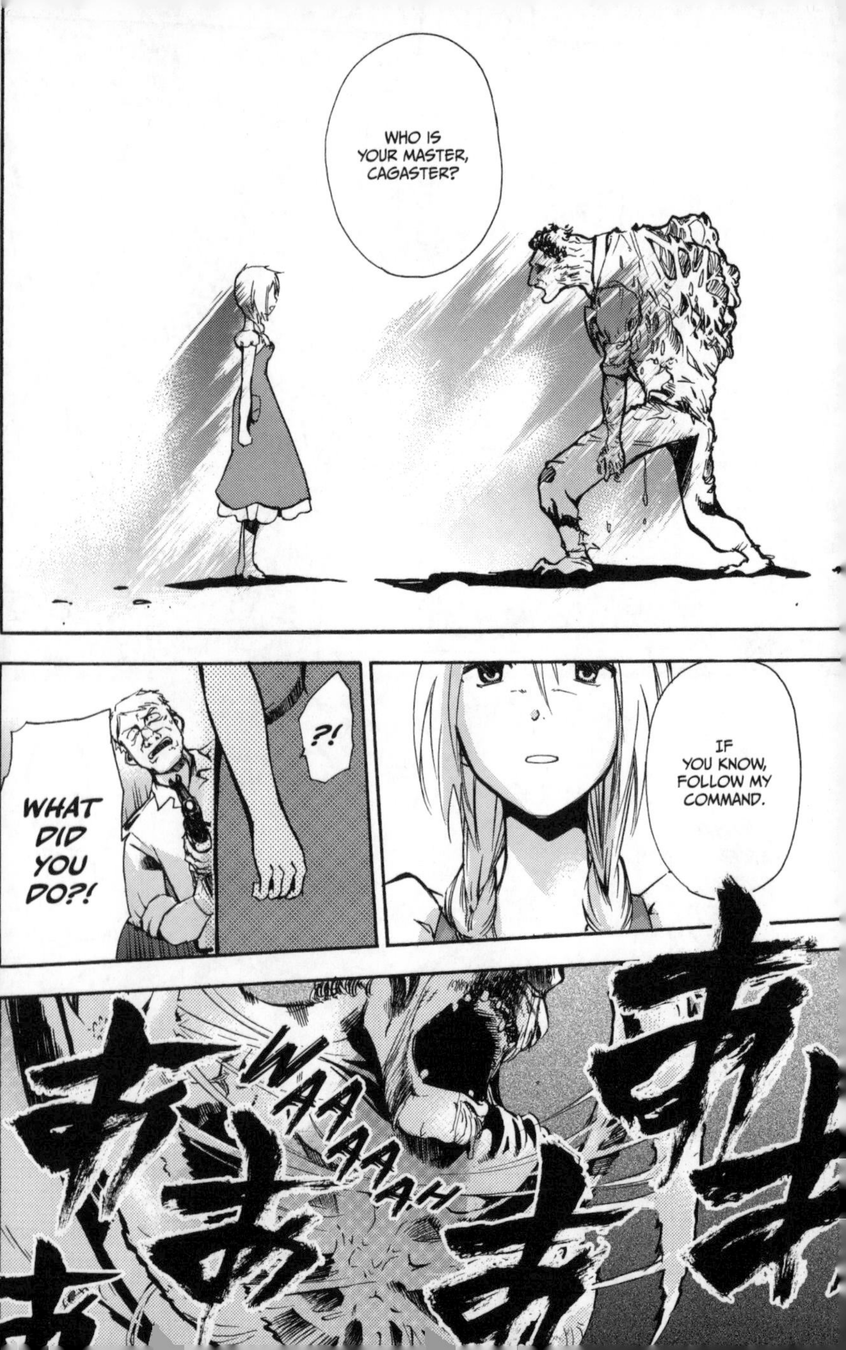
WHO IS YOUR MASTER, CAGASTER?
IF YOU KNOW, FOLLOW MY COMMAND.
?!
WHAT DID YOU DO?!
WAAAAAAH

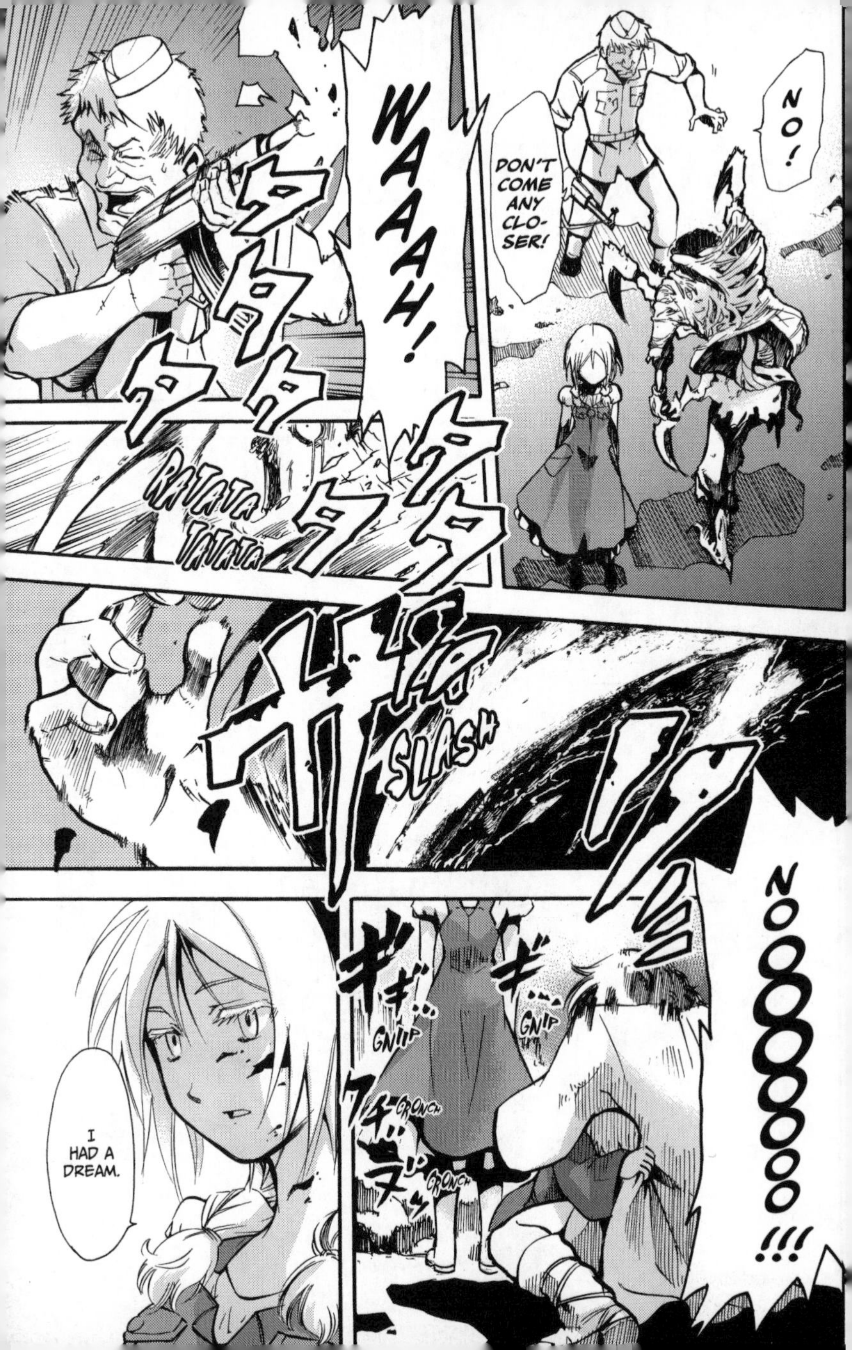
NO!
DON'T COME ANY CLO-SER!
WAAAAH!
RATATA TATATA
SLASH
NOOOOOOOOOOO!!!
GNIP
GNIP
CRONCH
CRONCH
I HAD A DREAM.

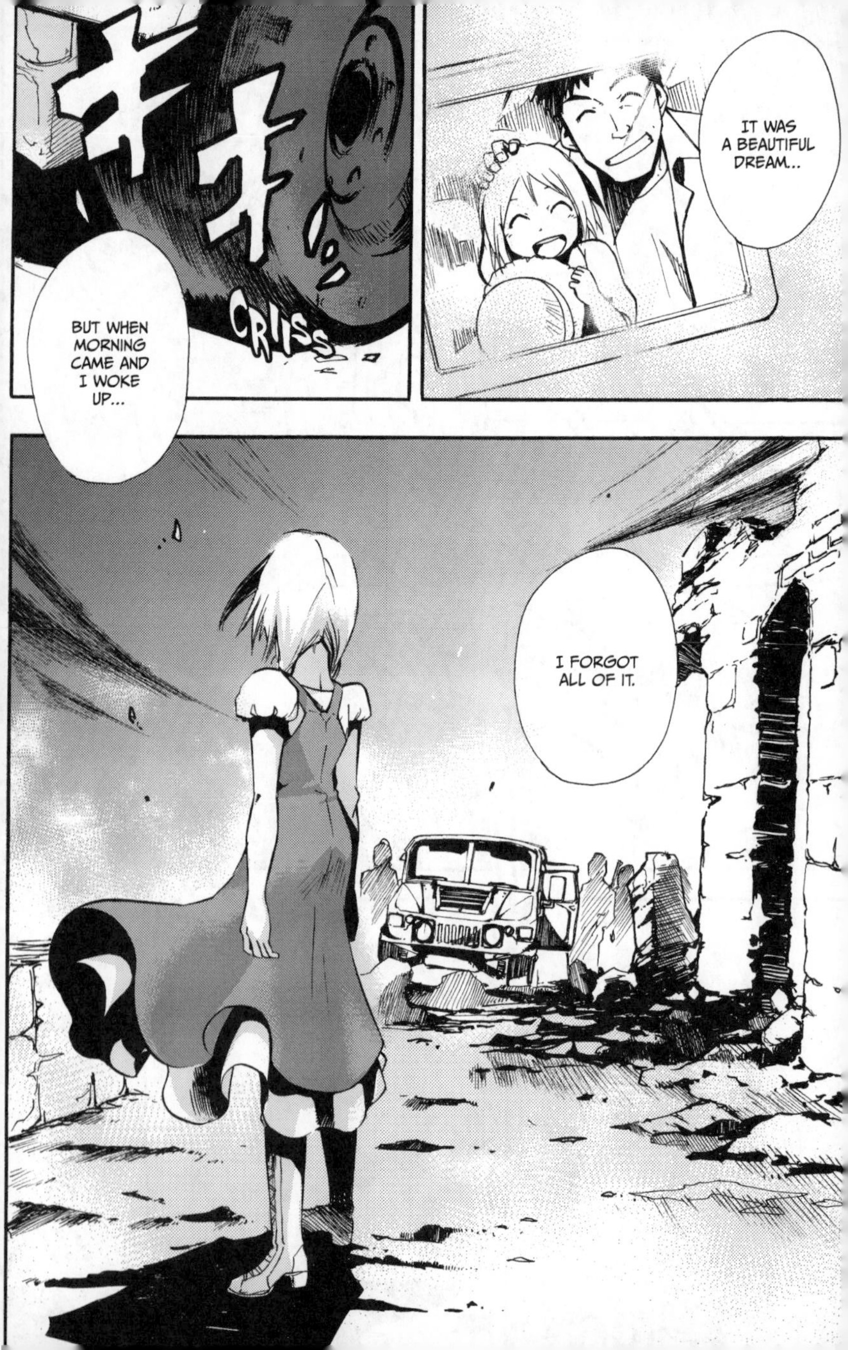
IT WAS A BEAUTIFUL DREAM...
CRISS
BUT WHEN MORNING CAME AND I WOKE UP...
I FORGOT ALL OF IT.

[CHAPTER 14]

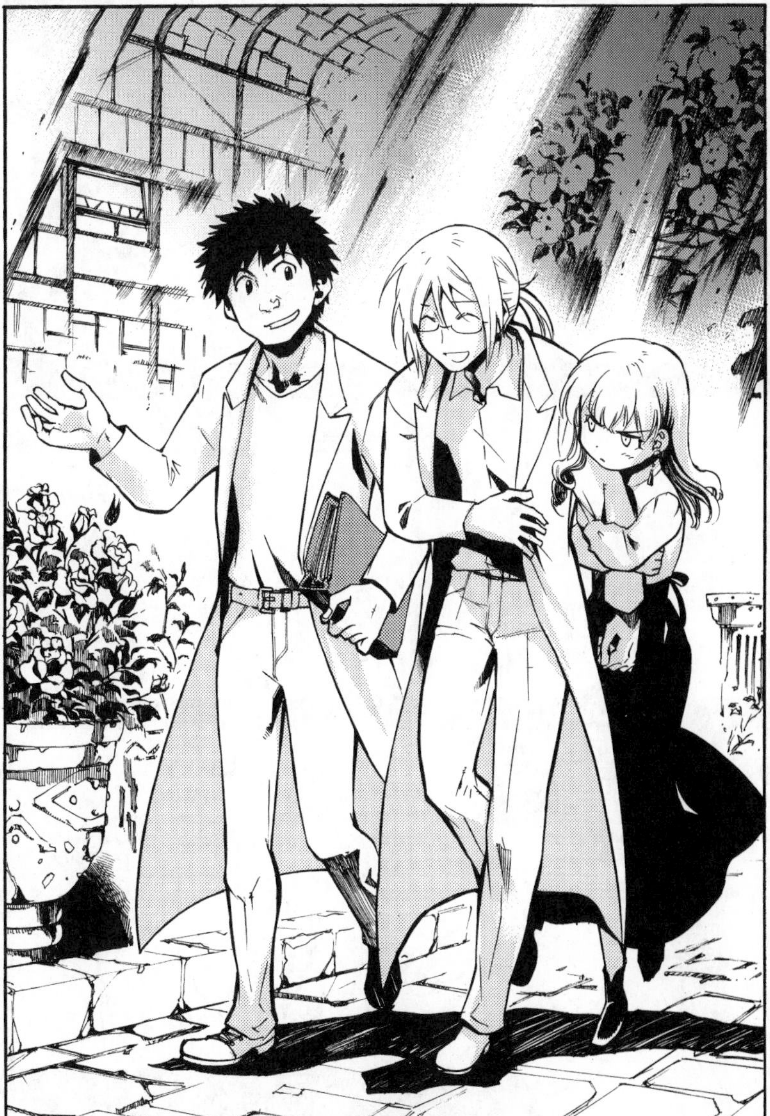

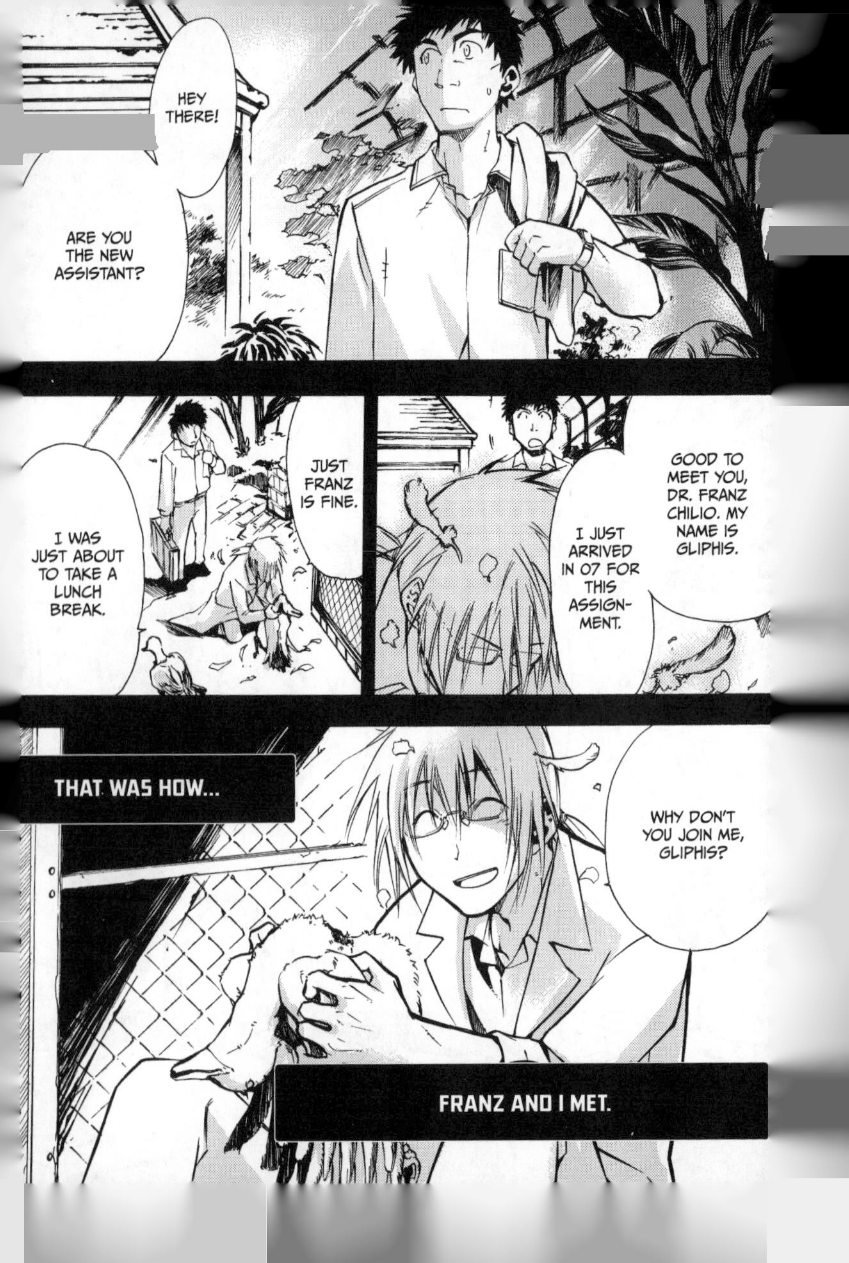
HEY THERE!
ARE YOU THE NEW ASSISTANT?
GOOD TO MEET YOU, DR. FRANZ CHILIO. MY NAME IS GLIPHIS.
I JUST ARRIVED IN 07 FOR THIS ASSIGNMENT.
JUST FRANZ IS FINE.
I WAS JUST ABOUT TO TAKE A LUNCH BREAK.
WHY DON'T YOU JOIN ME, GLIPHIS?
THAT WAS HOW...
FRANZ AND I MET.

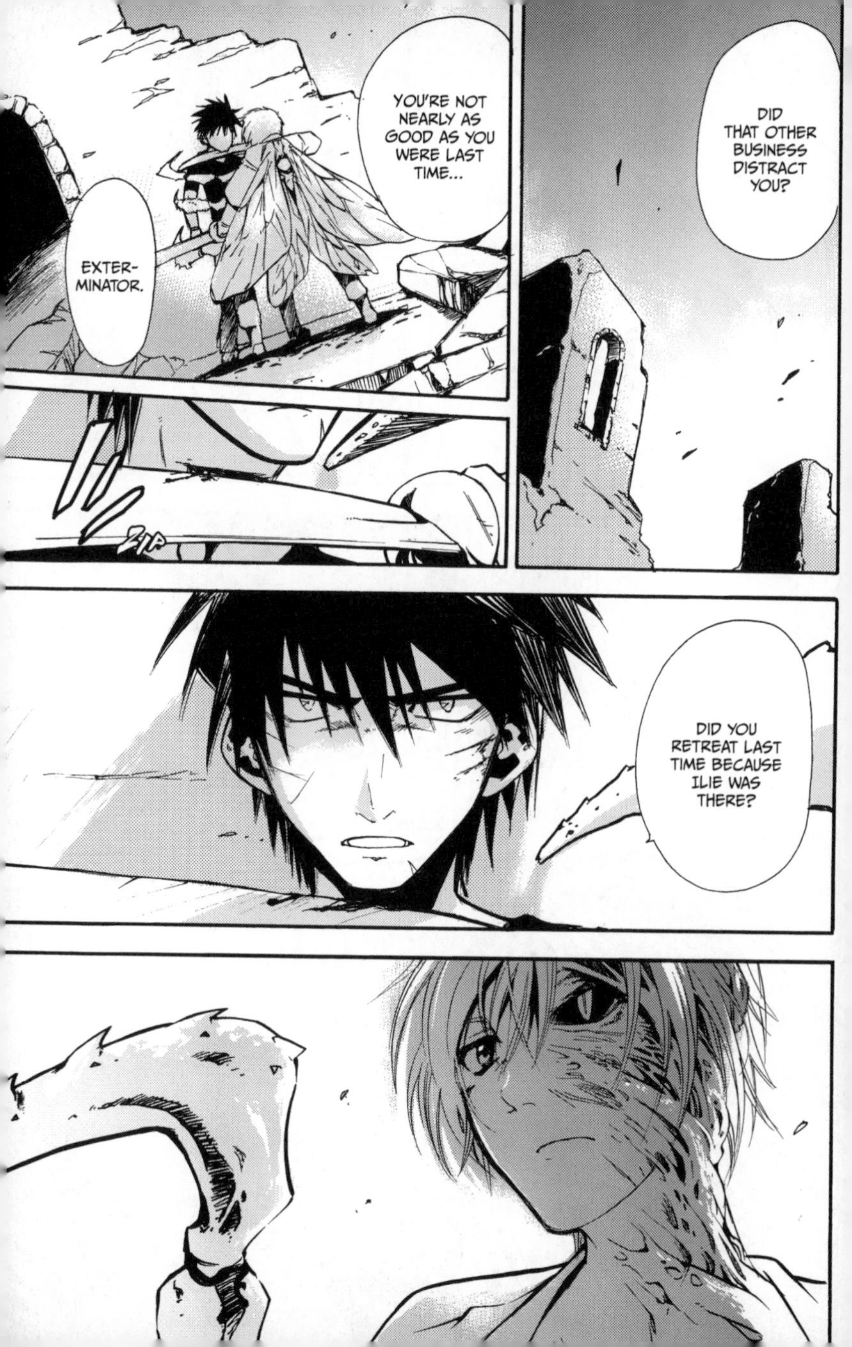
DID THAT OTHER BUSINESS DISTRACT YOU?
YOU'RE NOT NEARLY AS GOOD AS YOU WERE LAST TIME...
EXTER-MINATOR.
ZIP
DID YOU RETREAT LAST TIME BECAUSE ILIE WAS THERE?

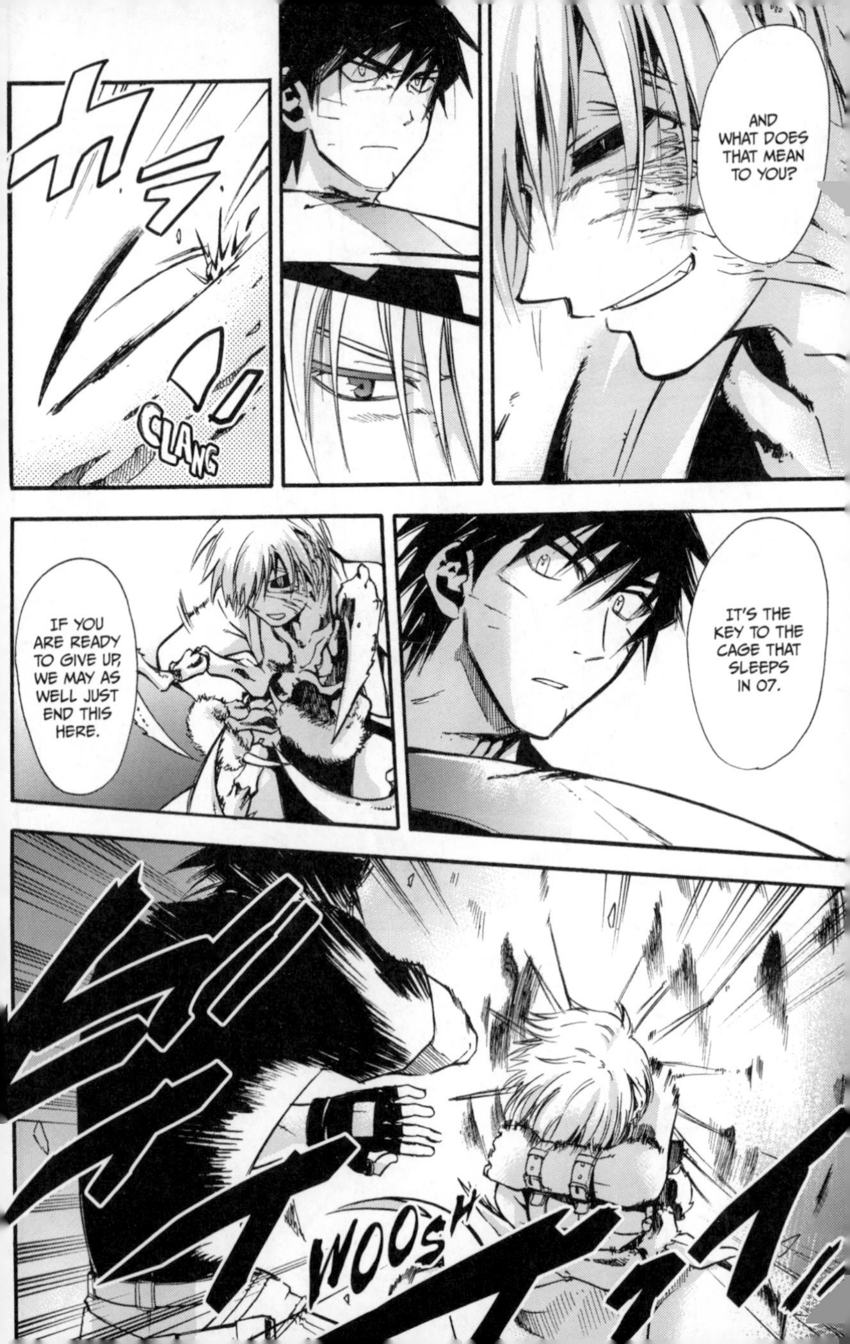
AND WHAT DOES THAT MEAN TO YOU?
CLANG
IT'S THE KEY TO THE CAGE THAT SLEEPS IN 07.
IF YOU ARE READY TO GIVE UP, WE MAY AS WELL JUST END THIS HERE.
WOOSH

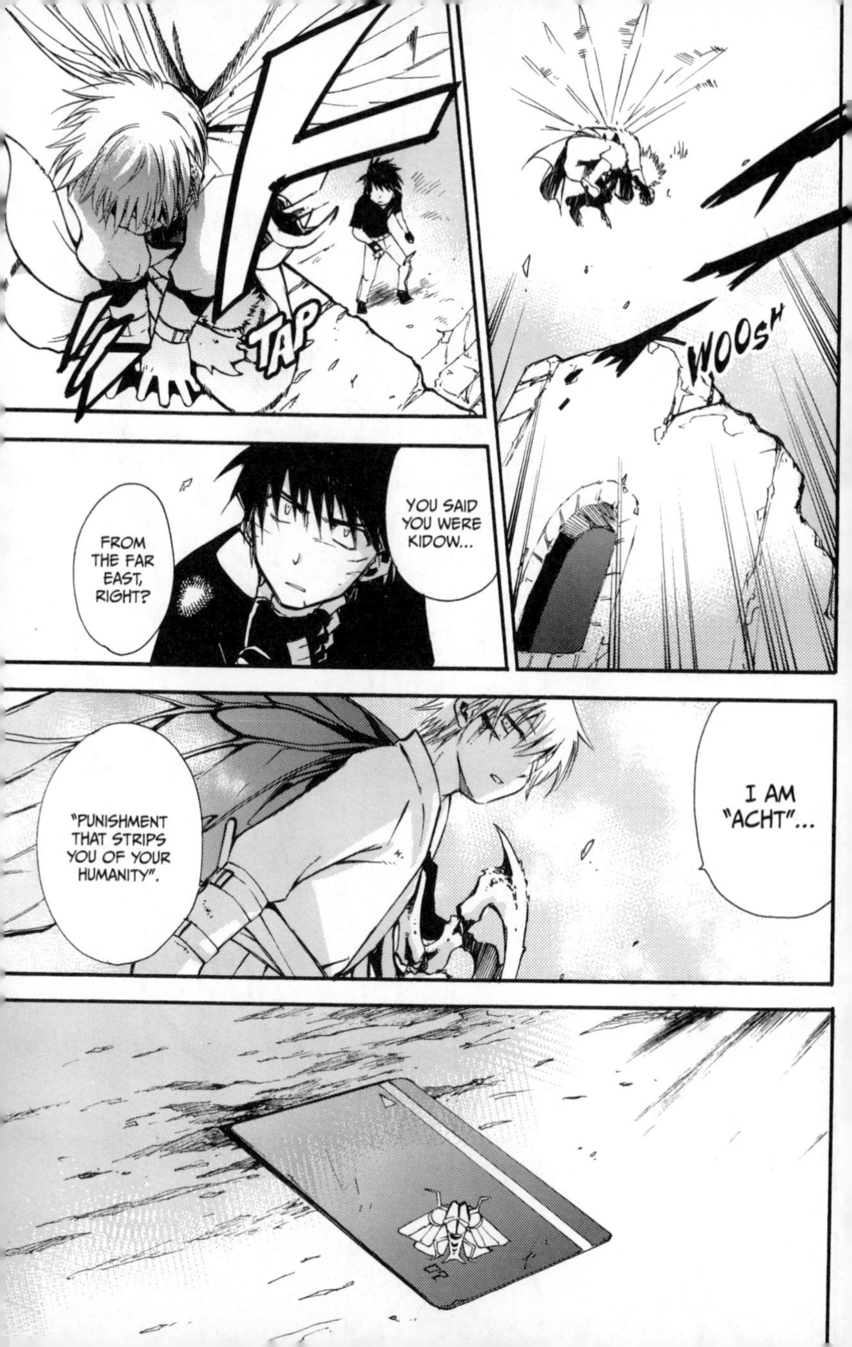
WOOSH
TAP
YOU SAID YOU WERE KIDOW...
FROM THE FAR EAST, RIGHT?
I AM "ACHT"...
"PUNISHMENT THAT STRIPS YOU OF YOUR HUMANITY".

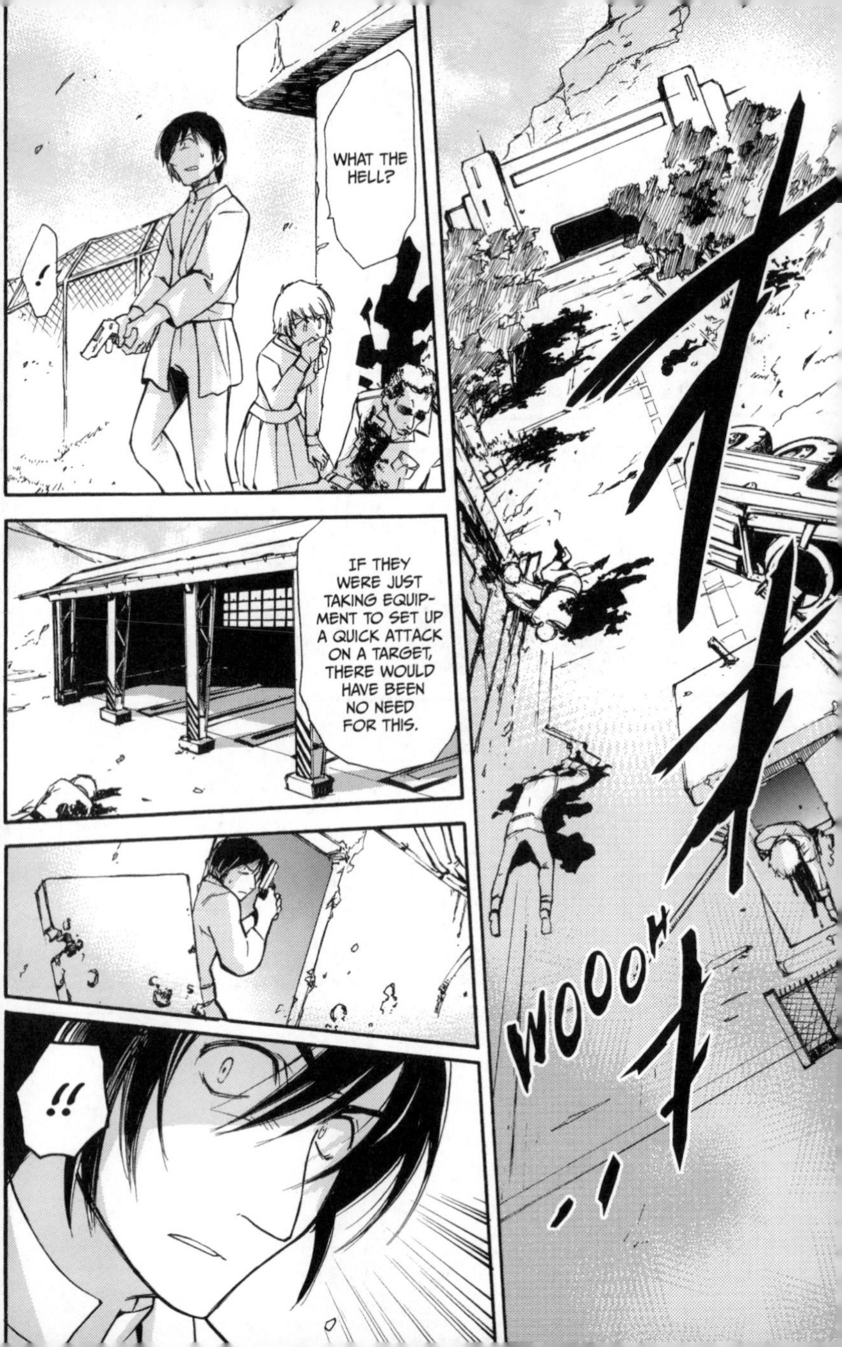
WOOOH
WHAT THE HELL?
!
IF THEY WERE JUST TAKING EQUIPMENT TO SET UP A QUICK ATTACK ON A TARGET, THERE WOULD HAVE BEEN NO NEED FOR THIS.
!!

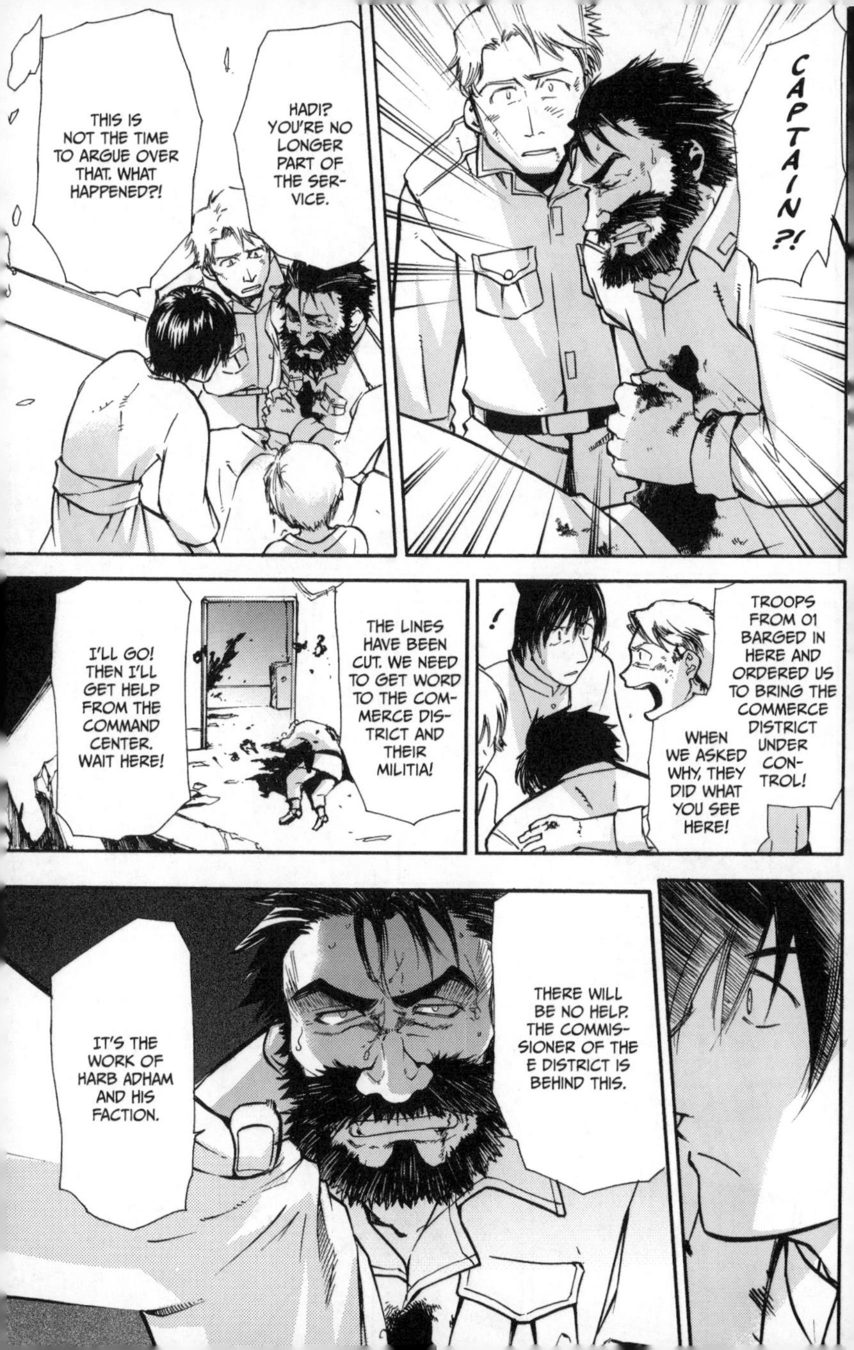
CAPTAIN?!
HADI? YOU'RE NO LONGER PART OF THE SERVICE.
THIS IS NOT THE TIME TO ARGUE OVER THAT. WHAT HAPPENED?!
TROOPS FROM 01 BARGED IN HERE AND ORDERED US TO BRING THE COMMERCE DISTRICT UNDER CONTROL!
WHEN WE ASKED WHY, THEY DID WHAT YOU SEE HERE!
THE LINES HAVE BEEN CUT. WE NEED TO GET WORD TO THE COMMERCE DISTRICT AND THEIR MILITIA!
I'LL GO! THEN I'LL GET HELP FROM THE COMMAND CENTER. WAIT HERE!
THERE WILL BE NO HELP. THE COMMISSIONER OF THE E DISTRICT IS BEHIND THIS.
IT'S THE WORK OF HARB ADHAM AND HIS FACTION.

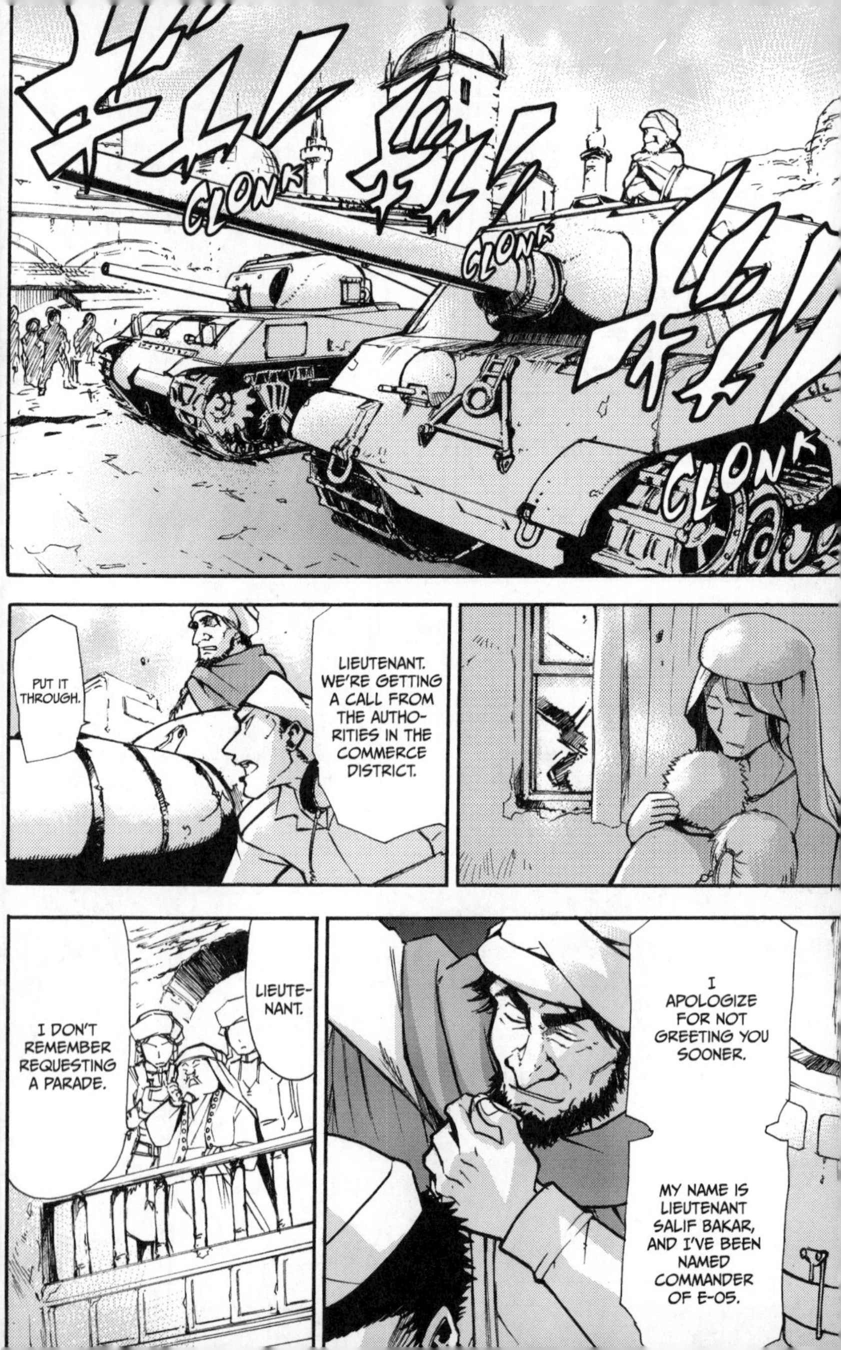
CLONK
CLONK
CLONK
LIEUTENANT. WE'RE GETTING A CALL FROM THE AUTHORITIES IN THE COMMERCE DISTRICT.
PUT IT THROUGH.
I APOLOGIZE FOR NOT GREETING YOU SOONER.
MY NAME IS LIEUTENANT SALIF BAKAR, AND I'VE BEEN NAMED COMMANDER OF E-05.
LIEUTENANT.
I DON'T REMEMBER REQUESTING A PARADE.

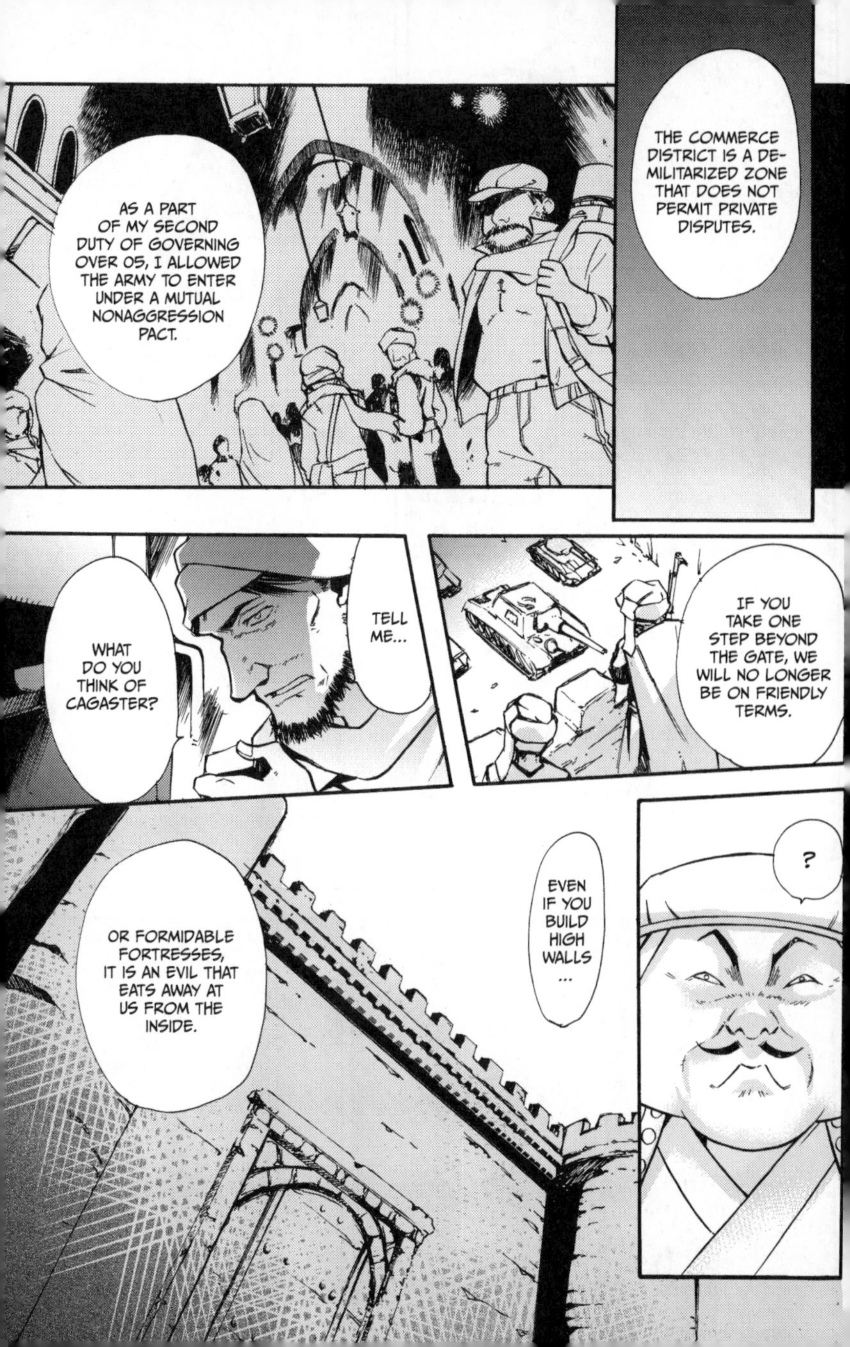
THE COMMERCE DISTRICT IS A DE-MILITARIZED ZONE THAT DOES NOT PERMIT PRIVATE DISPUTES.
AS A PART OF MY SECOND DUTY OF GOVERNING OVER 05, I ALLOWED THE ARMY TO ENTER UNDER A MUTUAL NONAGGRESSION PACT.
IF YOU TAKE ONE STEP BEYOND THE GATE, WE WILL NO LONGER BE ON FRIENDLY TERMS.
TELL ME...
WHAT DO YOU THINK OF CAGASTER?
?
EVEN IF YOU BUILD HIGH WALLS ...
OR FORMIDABLE FORTRESSES, IT IS AN EVIL THAT EATS AWAY AT US FROM THE INSIDE.

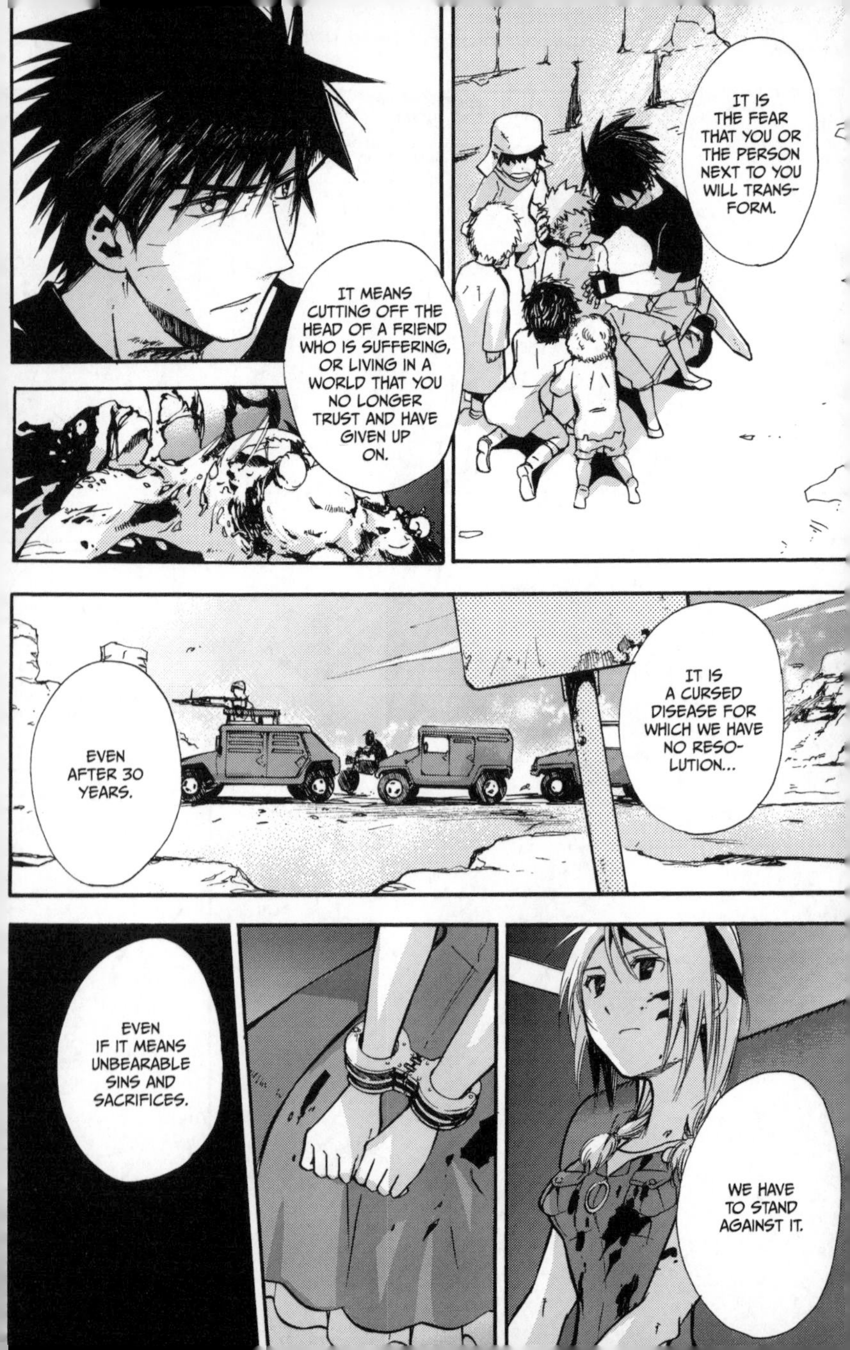
IT IS THE FEAR THAT YOU OR THE PERSON NEXT TO YOU WILL TRANS-FORM.
IT MEANS CUTTING OFF THE HEAD OF A FRIEND WHO IS SUFFERING, OR LIVING IN A WORLD THAT YOU NO LONGER TRUST AND HAVE GIVEN UP ON.
IT IS A CURSED DISEASE FOR WHICH WE HAVE NO RESO-LUTION...
EVEN AFTER 30 YEARS.
WE HAVE TO STAND AGAINST IT.
EVEN IF IT MEANS UNBEARABLE SINS AND SACRIFICES.

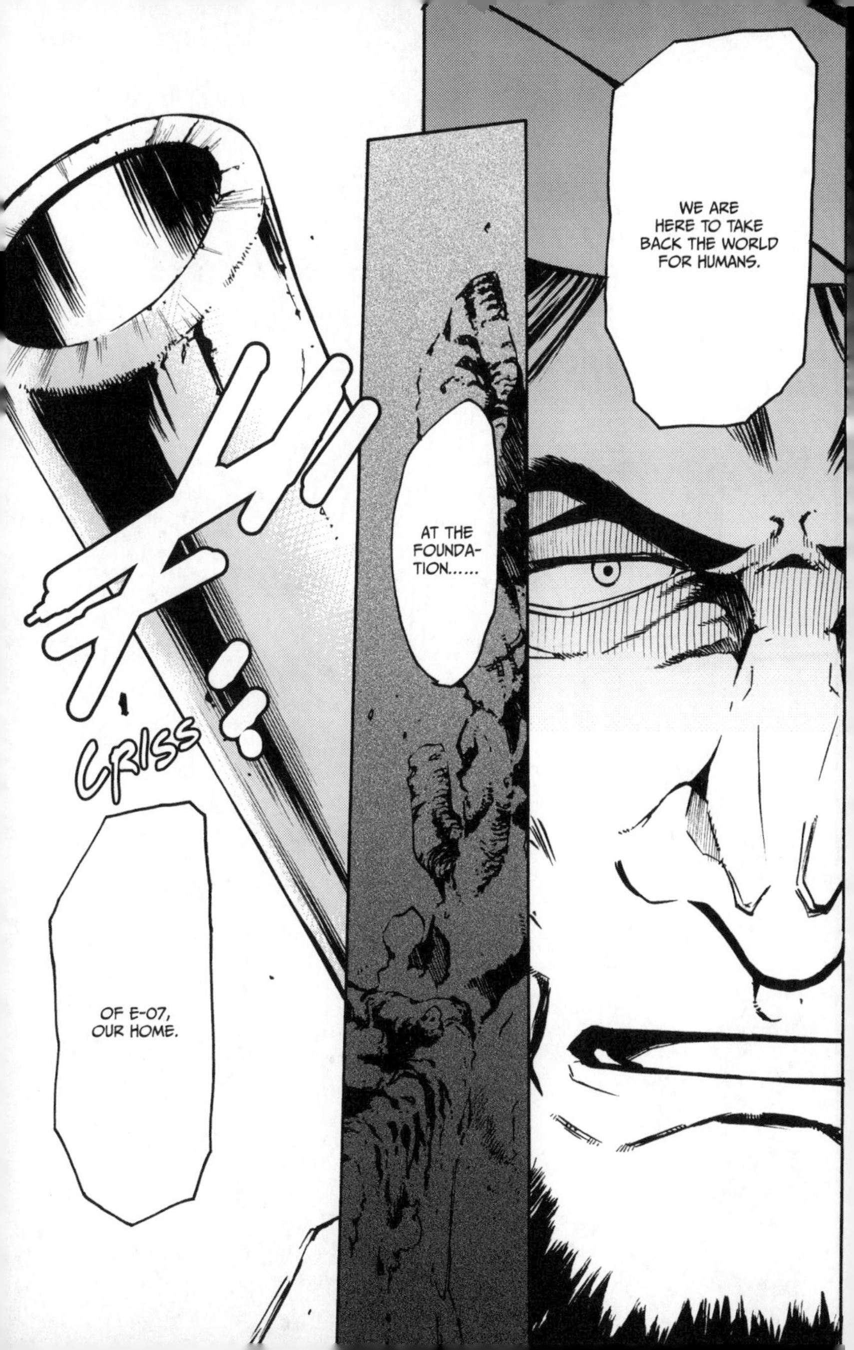
WE ARE HERE TO TAKE BACK THE WORLD FOR HUMANS.
AT THE FOUNDA-TION......
CRISS
OF E-07, OUR HOME.

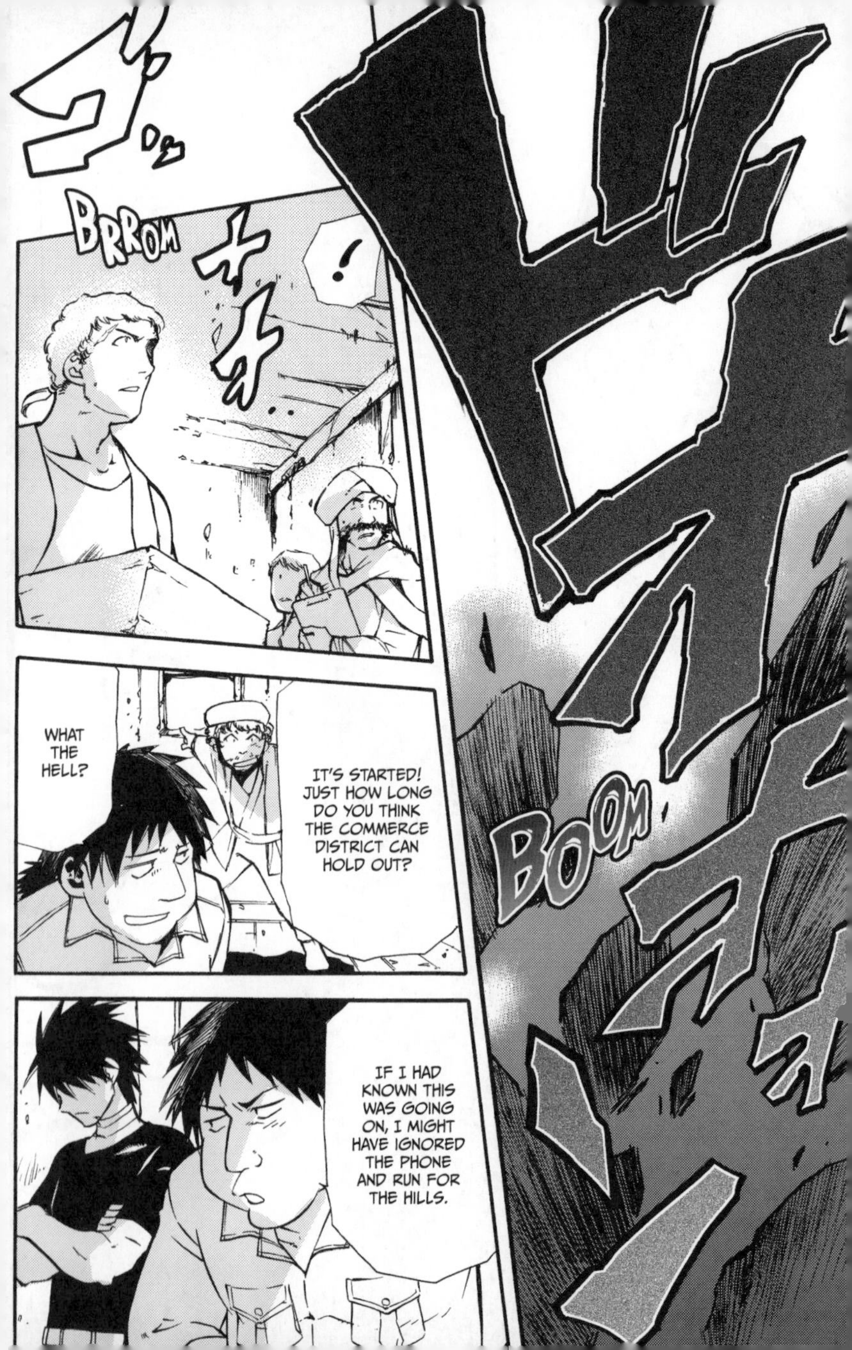
BOOM
BRROM
!
IT'S STARTED! JUST HOW LONG DO YOU THINK THE COMMERCE DISTRICT CAN HOLD OUT?
WHAT THE HELL?
IF I HAD KNOWN THIS WAS GOING ON, I MIGHT HAVE IGNORED THE PHONE AND RUN FOR THE HILLS.

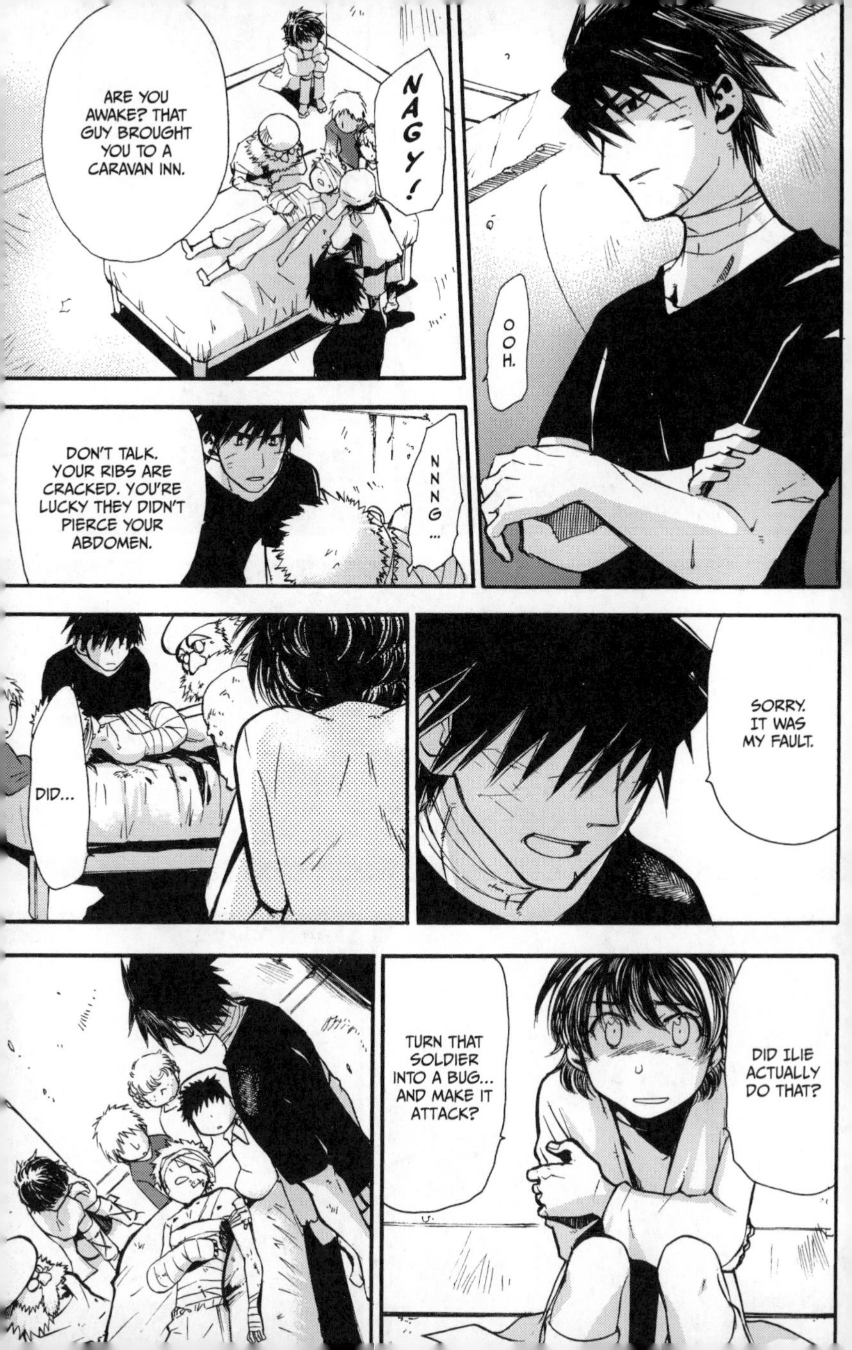
OOH.
NAGY!
ARE YOU AWAKE? THAT GUY BROUGHT YOU TO A CARAVAN INN.
NNNG...
DON'T TALK. YOUR RIBS ARE CRACKED. YOU'RE LUCKY THEY DIDN'T PIERCE YOUR ABDOMEN.
SORRY. IT WAS MY FAULT.
DID...
DID ILIE ACTUALLY DO THAT?
TURN THAT SOLDIER INTO A BUG... AND MAKE IT ATTACK?

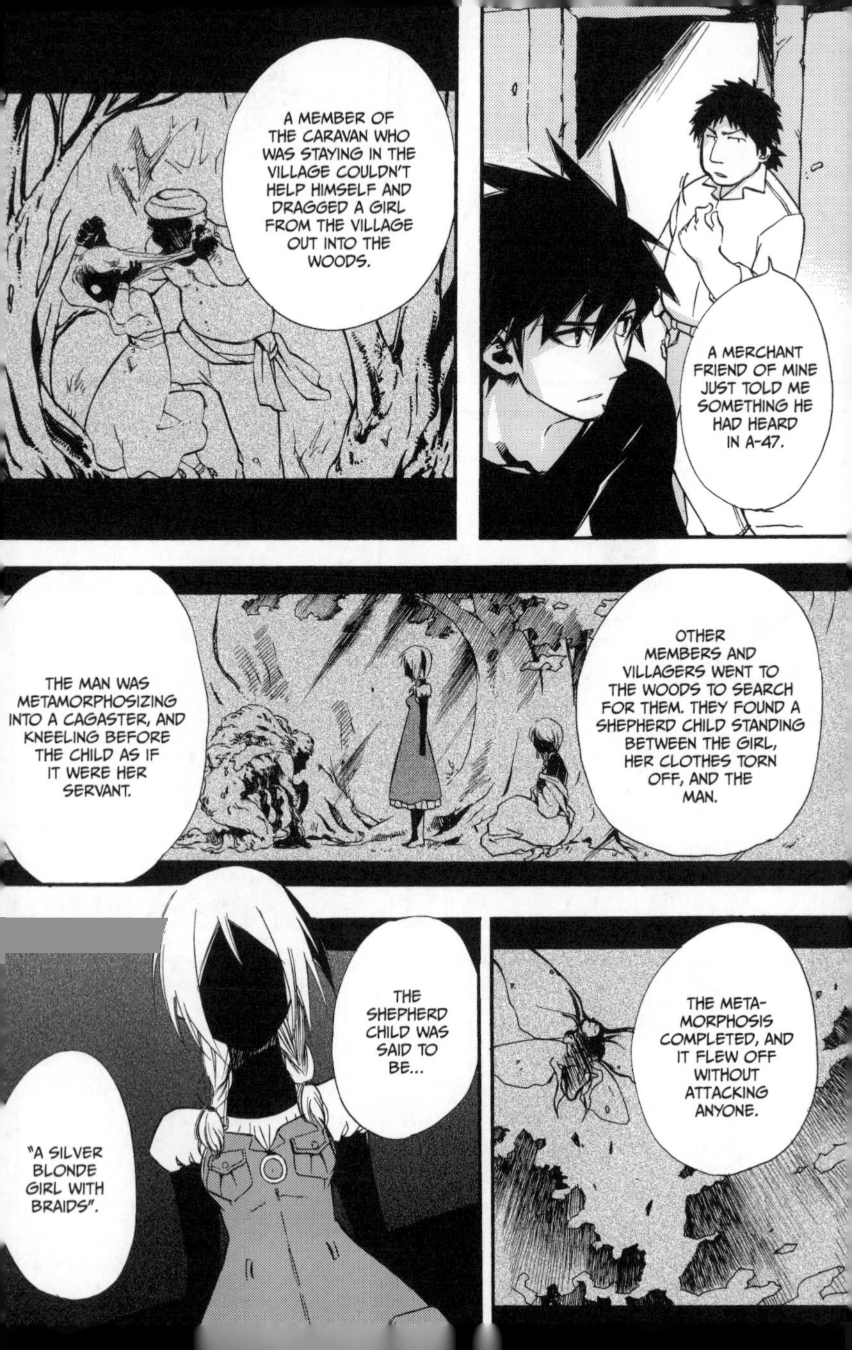
A MERCHANT FRIEND OF MINE JUST TOLD ME SOMETHING HE HAD HEARD IN A-47.
A MEMBER OF THE CARAVAN WHO WAS STAYING IN THE VILLAGE COULDN'T HELP HIMSELF AND DRAGGED A GIRL FROM THE VILLAGE OUT INTO THE WOODS.
OTHER MEMBERS AND VILLAGERS WENT TO THE WOODS TO SEARCH FOR THEM. THEY FOUND A SHEPHERD CHILD STANDING BETWEEN THE GIRL, HER CLOTHES TORN OFF, AND THE MAN.
THE MAN WAS METAMORPHOSIZING INTO A CAGASTER, AND KNEELING BEFORE THE CHILD AS IF IT WERE HER SERVANT.
THE META-MORPHOSIS COMPLETED, AND IT FLEW OFF WITHOUT ATTACKING ANYONE.
THE SHEPHERD CHILD WAS SAID TO BE...
"A SILVER BLONDE GIRL WITH BRAIDS".

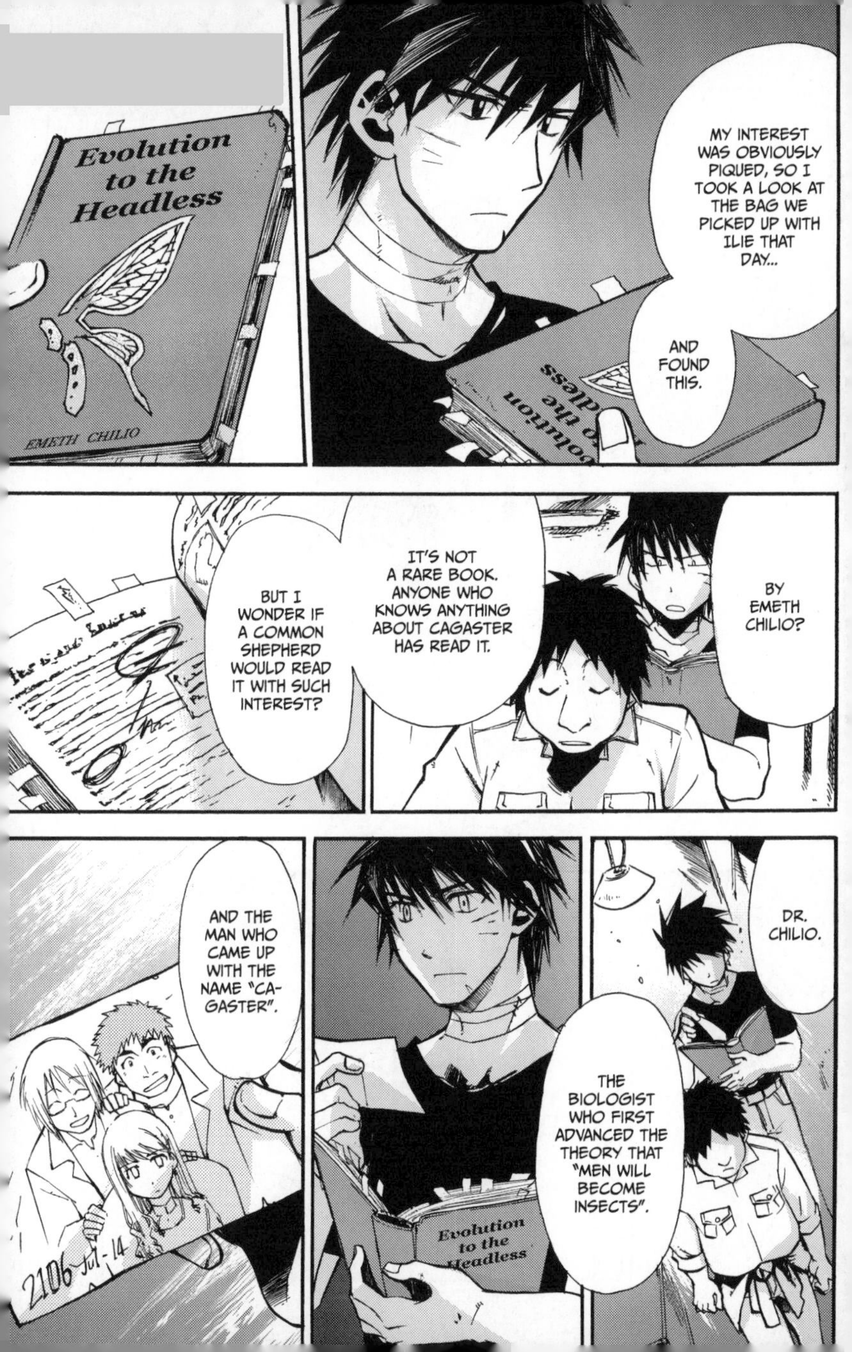
MY INTEREST WAS OBVIOUSLY PIQUED, SO I TOOK A LOOK AT THE BAG WE PICKED UP WITH ILIE THAT DAY...
AND FOUND THIS.
Evolution to the Headless
EMETH CHILIO
BY EMETH CHILIO?
IT'S NOT A RARE BOOK. ANYONE WHO KNOWS ANYTHING ABOUT CAGASTER HAS READ IT.
BUT I WONDER IF A COMMON SHEPHERD WOULD READ IT WITH SUCH INTEREST?
DR. CHILIO.
THE BIOLOGIST WHO FIRST ADVANCED THE THEORY THAT "MEN WILL BECOME INSECTS".
Evolution to the Headless
AND THE MAN WHO CAME UP WITH THE NAME "CA-GASTER".
2106 Jul-14

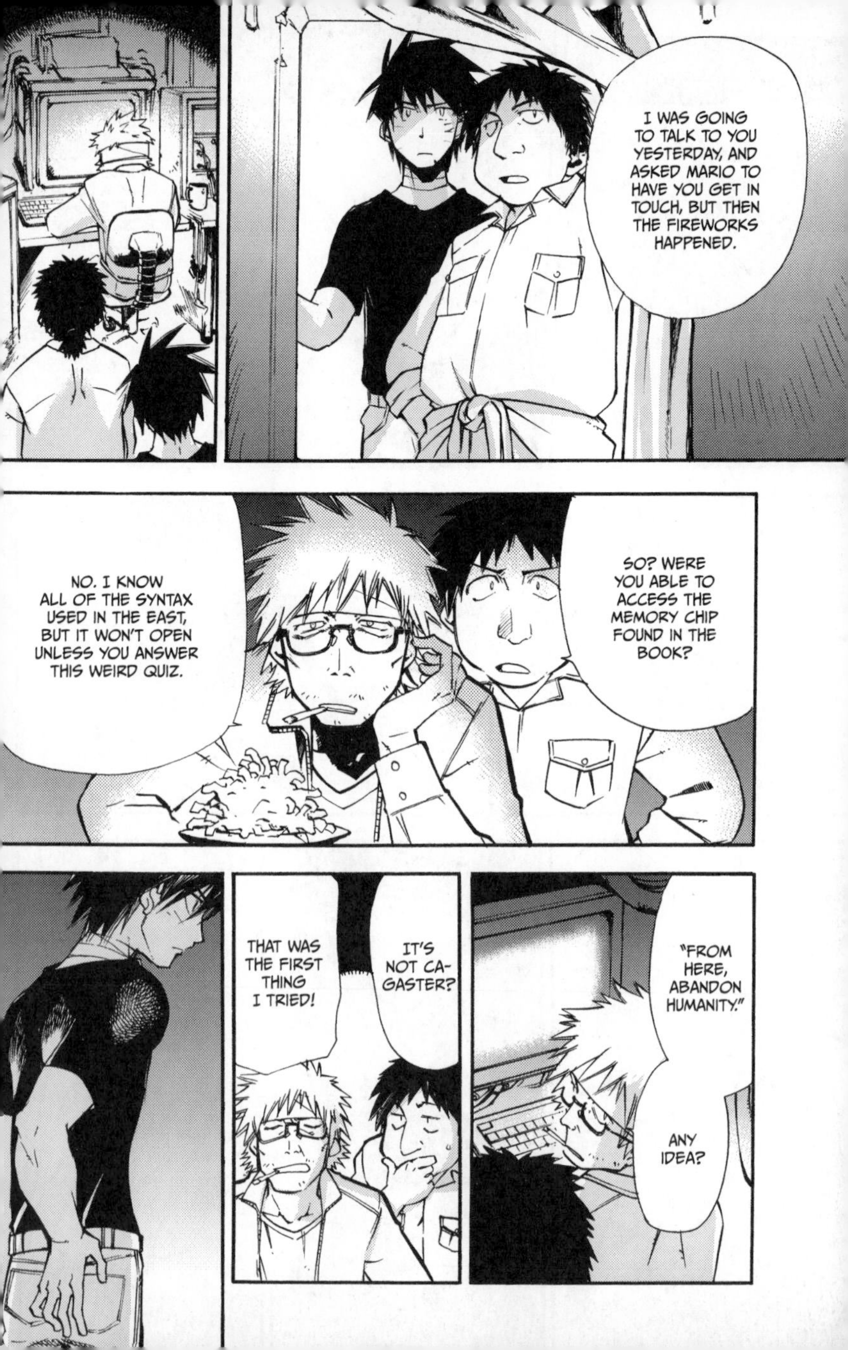
I WAS GOING TO TALK TO YOU YESTERDAY, AND ASKED MARIO TO HAVE YOU GET IN TOUCH, BUT THEN THE FIREWORKS HAPPENED.
SO? WERE YOU ABLE TO ACCESS THE MEMORY CHIP FOUND IN THE BOOK?
NO. I KNOW ALL OF THE SYNTAX USED IN THE EAST, BUT IT WON'T OPEN UNLESS YOU ANSWER THIS WEIRD QUIZ.
"FROM HERE, ABANDON HUMANITY."
ANY IDEA?
IT'S NOT CA-GASTER?
THAT WAS THE FIRST THING I TRIED!

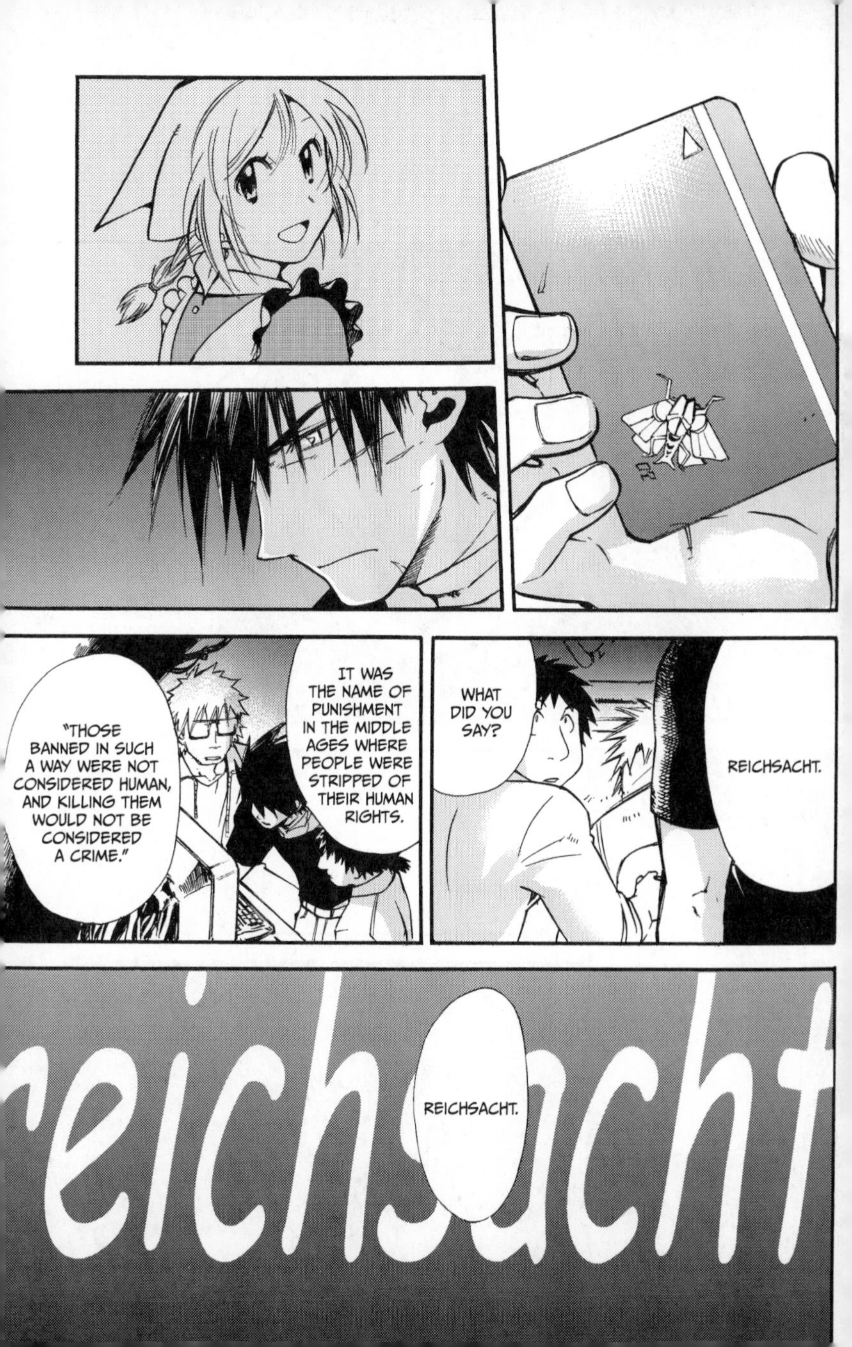
REICHSACHT.
WHAT DID YOU SAY?
IT WAS THE NAME OF PUNISHMENT IN THE MIDDLE AGES WHERE PEOPLE WERE STRIPPED OF THEIR HUMAN RIGHTS.
"THOSE BANNED IN SUCH A WAY WERE NOT CONSIDERED HUMAN, AND KILLING THEM WOULD NOT BE CONSIDERED A CRIME."
REICHSACHT.

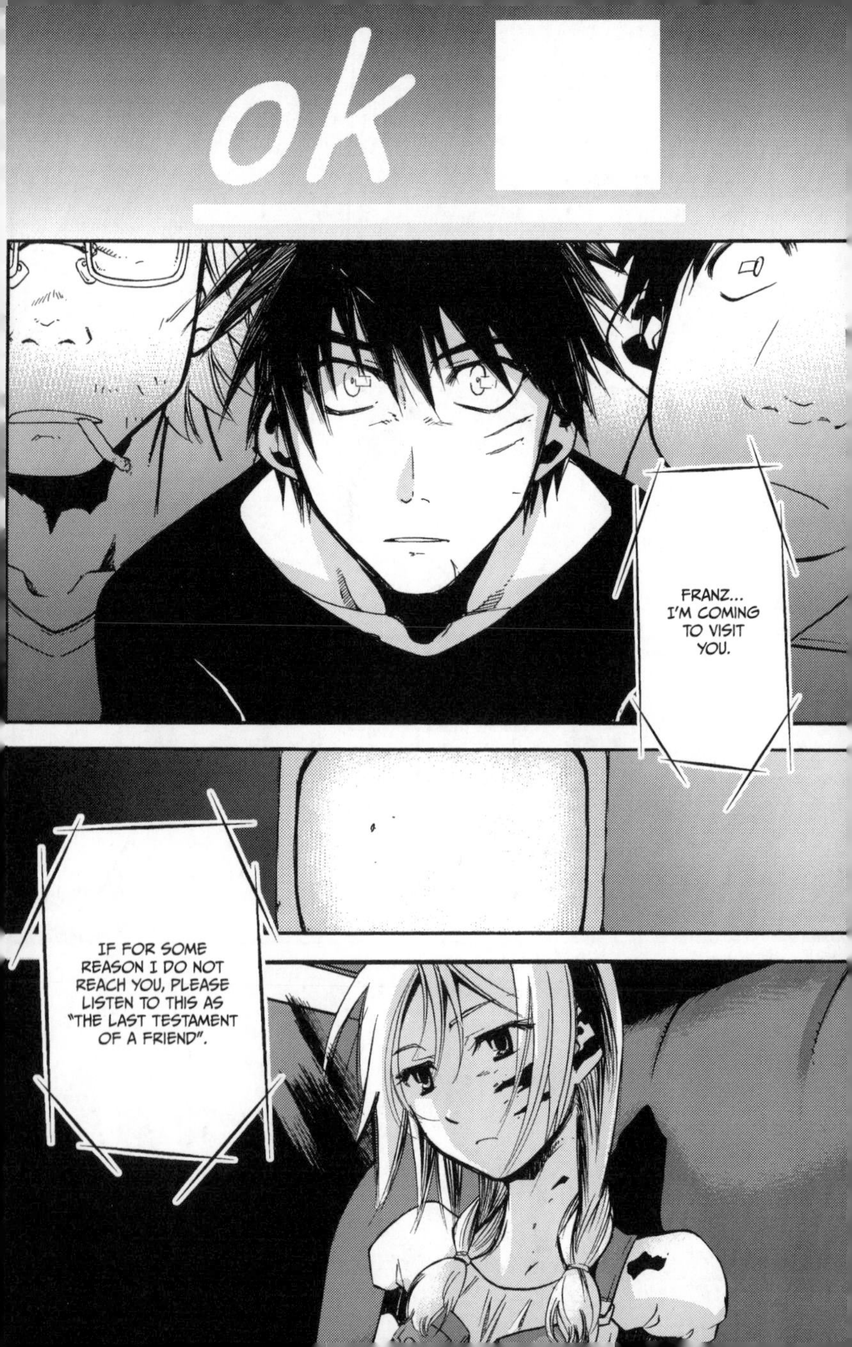
ok
FRANZ... I'M COMING TO VISIT YOU.
IF FOR SOME REASON I DO NOT REACH YOU, PLEASE LISTEN TO THIS AS "THE LAST TESTAMENT OF A FRIEND".

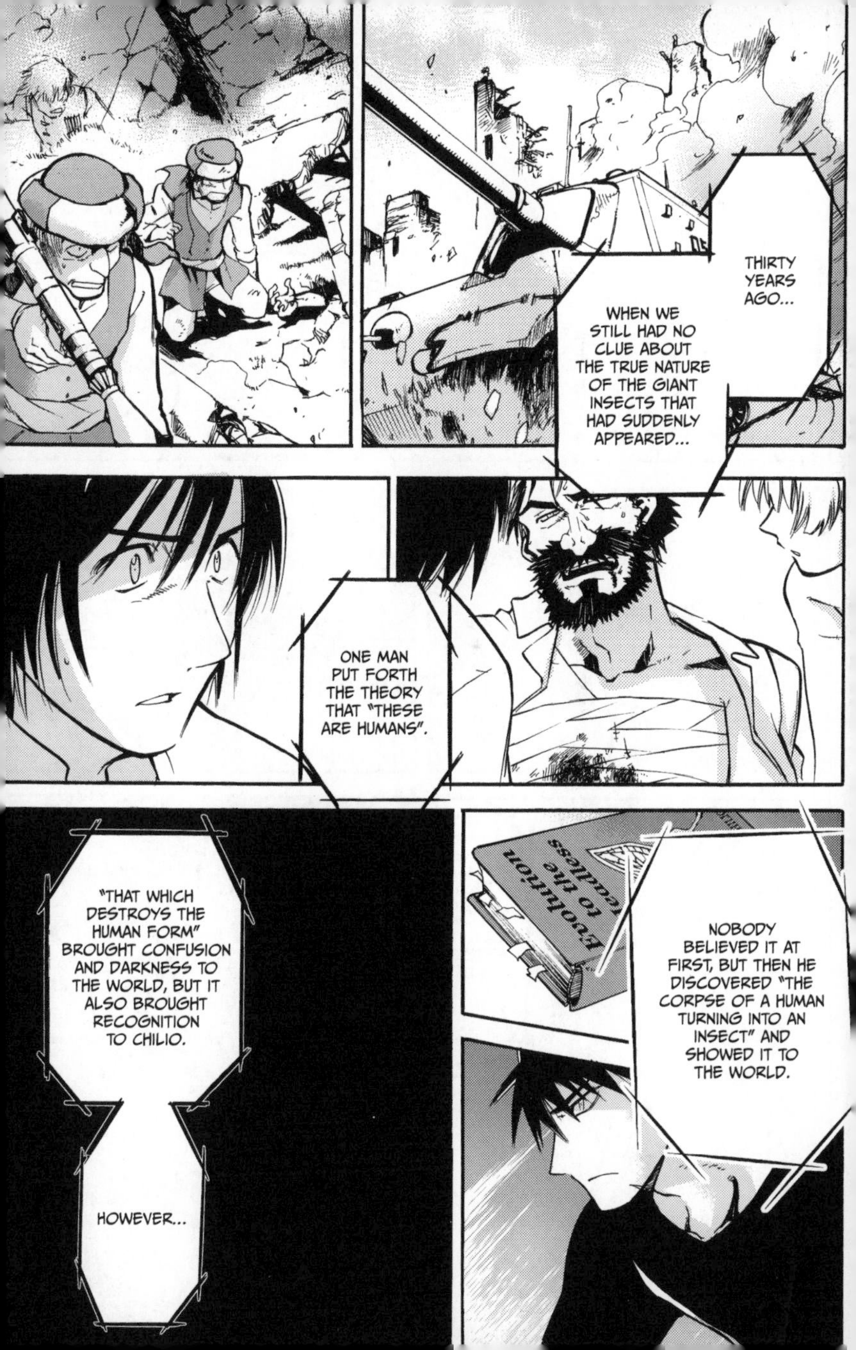
THIRTY YEARS AGO...
WHEN WE STILL HAD NO CLUE ABOUT THE TRUE NATURE OF THE GIANT INSECTS THAT HAD SUDDENLY APPEARED...
ONE MAN PUT FORTH THE THEORY THAT "THESE ARE HUMANS".
NOBODY BELIEVED IT AT FIRST, BUT THEN HE DISCOVERED "THE CORPSE OF A HUMAN TURNING INTO AN INSECT" AND SHOWED IT TO THE WORLD.
"THAT WHICH DESTROYS THE HUMAN FORM" BROUGHT CONFUSION AND DARKNESS TO THE WORLD, BUT IT ALSO BROUGHT RECOGNITION TO CHILIO.
HOWEVER...

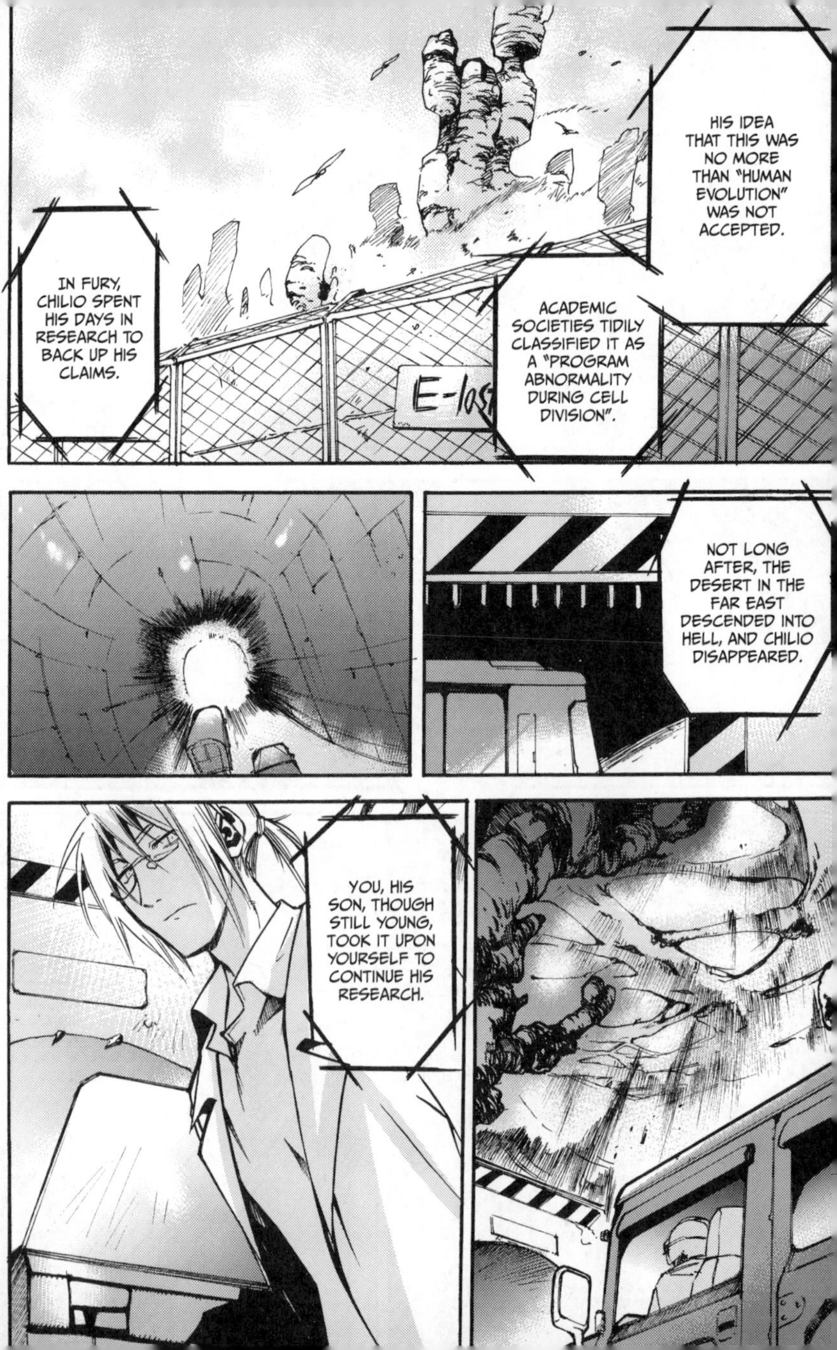
HIS IDEA THAT THIS WAS NO MORE THAN "HUMAN EVOLUTION" WAS NOT ACCEPTED.
ACADEMIC SOCIETIES TIDILY CLASSIFIED IT AS A "PROGRAM ABNORMALITY DURING CELL DIVISION".
IN FURY, CHILIO SPENT HIS DAYS IN RESEARCH TO BACK UP HIS CLAIMS.
NOT LONG AFTER, THE DESERT IN THE FAR EAST DESCENDED INTO HELL, AND CHILIO DISAPPEARED.
YOU, HIS SON, THOUGH STILL YOUNG, TOOK IT UPON YOURSELF TO CONTINUE HIS RESEARCH.

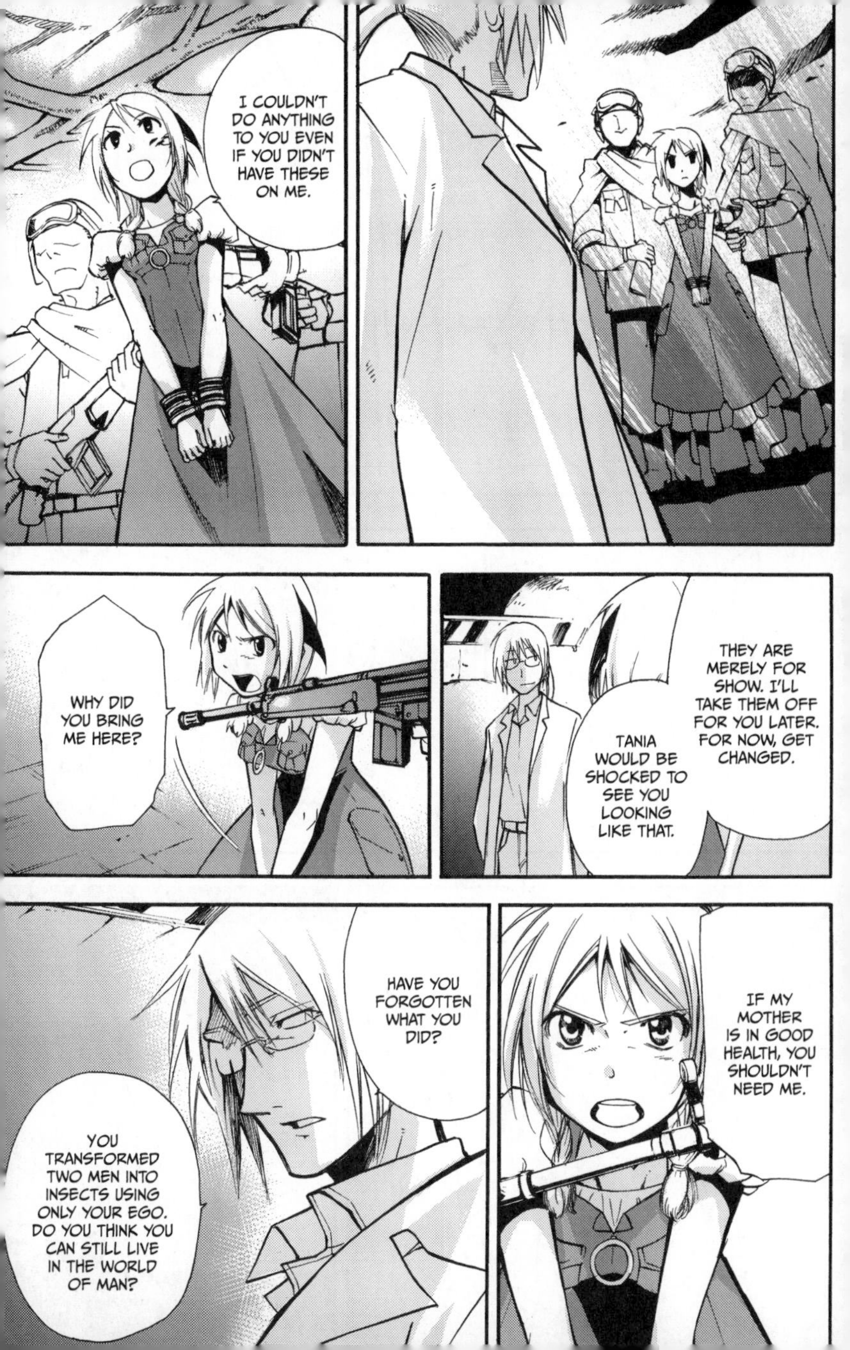
I COULDN'T DO ANYTHING TO YOU EVEN IF YOU DIDN'T HAVE THESE ON ME.
THEY ARE MERELY FOR SHOW. I'LL TAKE THEM OFF FOR YOU LATER. FOR NOW, GET CHANGED.
TANIA WOULD BE SHOCKED TO SEE YOU LOOKING LIKE THAT.
WHY DID YOU BRING ME HERE?
IF MY MOTHER IS IN GOOD HEALTH, YOU SHOULDN'T NEED ME.
HAVE YOU FORGOTTEN WHAT YOU DID?
YOU TRANSFORMED TWO MEN INTO INSECTS USING ONLY YOUR EGO. DO YOU THINK YOU CAN STILL LIVE IN THE WORLD OF MAN?

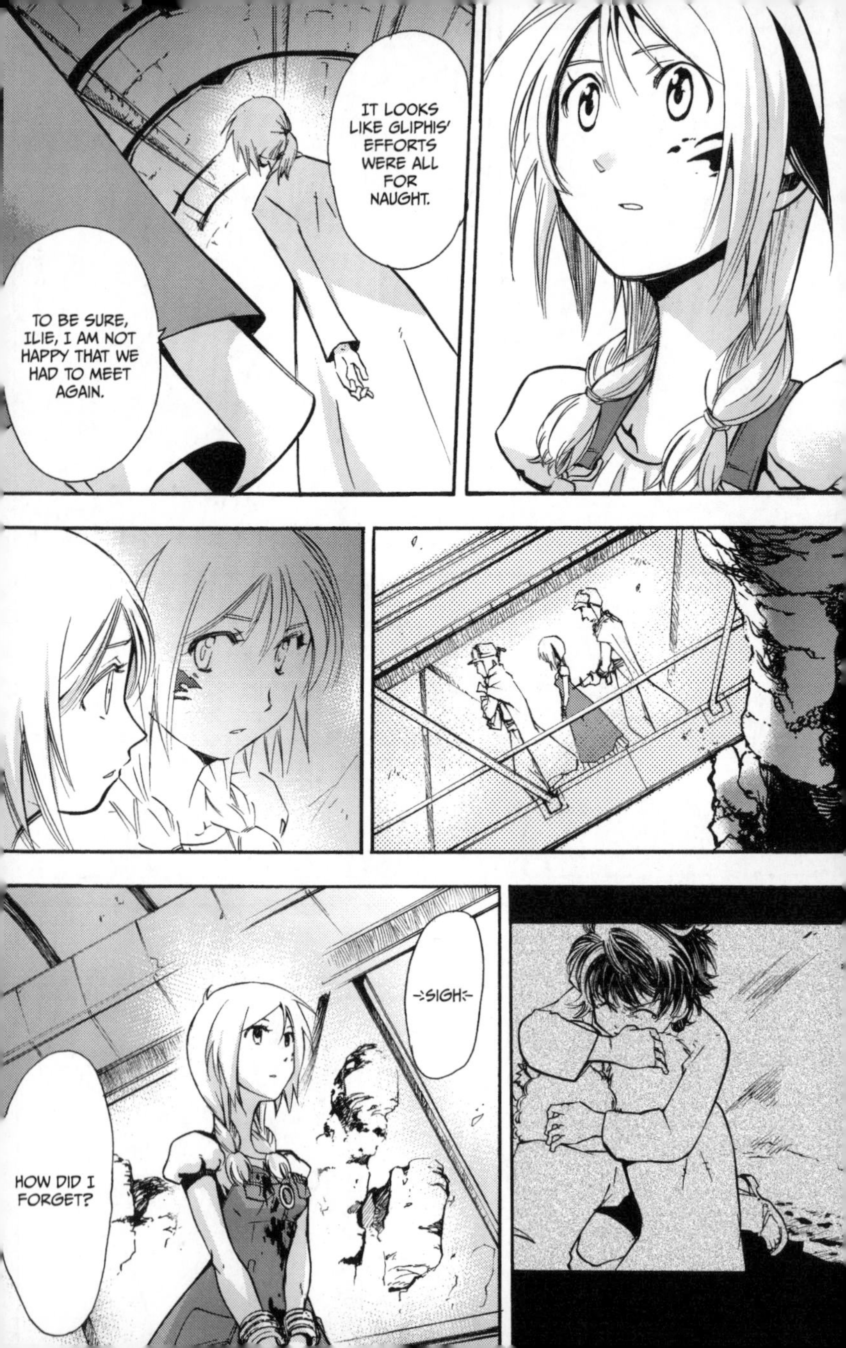
IT LOOKS LIKE GLIPHIS' EFFORTS WERE ALL FOR NAUGHT.
TO BE SURE, ILIE, I AM NOT HAPPY THAT WE HAD TO MEET AGAIN.
-SIGH-
HOW DID I FORGET?

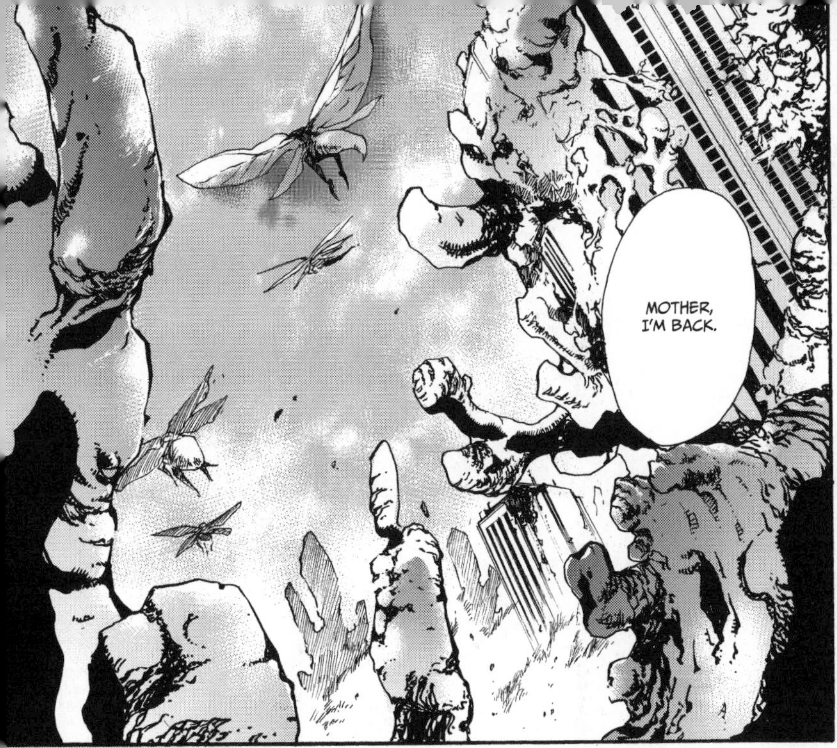
MOTHER, I'M BACK.

2104 A.D. E-07

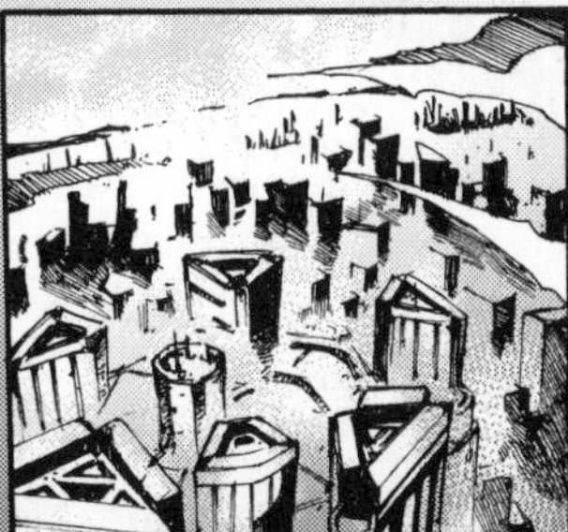

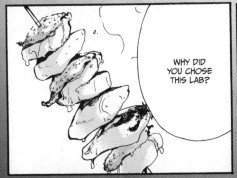

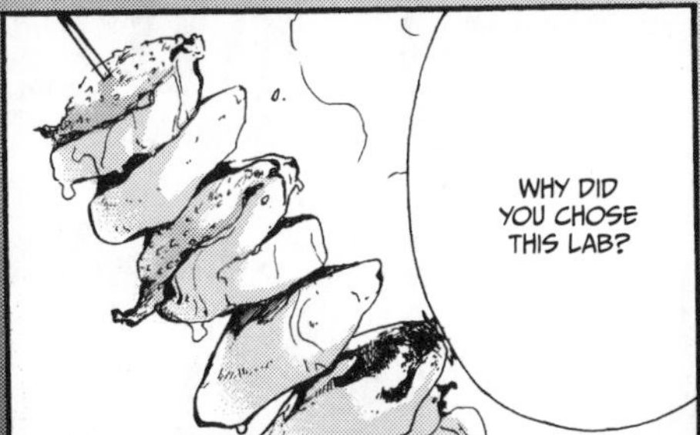
WHY DID YOU CHOSE THIS LAB?

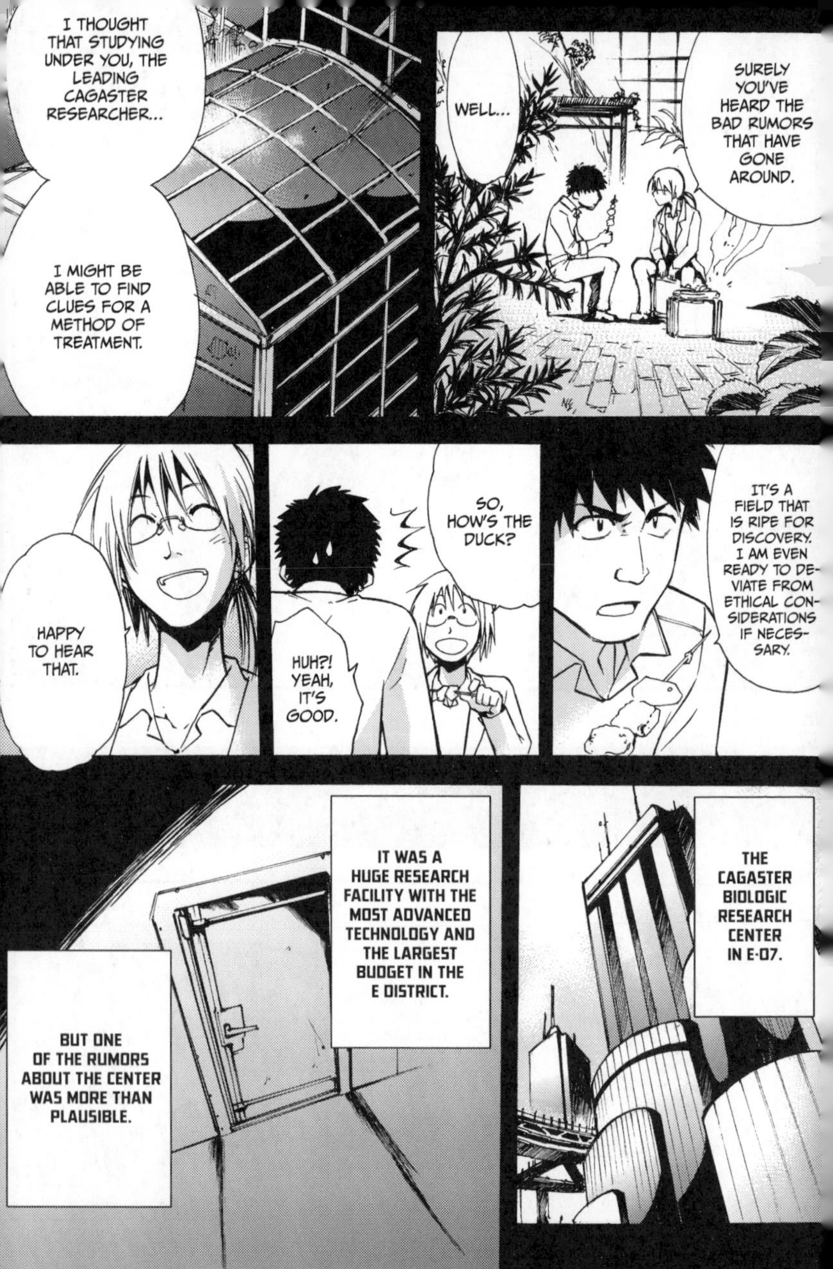
SURELY YOU'VE HEARD THE BAD RUMORS THAT HAVE GONE AROUND.
WELL...
I THOUGHT THAT STUDYING UNDER YOU, THE LEADING CAGASTER RESEARCHER...
I MIGHT BE ABLE TO FIND CLUES FOR A METHOD OF TREATMENT.
IT'S A FIELD THAT IS RIPE FOR DISCOVERY. I AM EVEN READY TO DE-VIATE FROM ETHICAL CON-SIDERATIONS IF NECES-SARY.
SO, HOW'S THE DUCK?
HUH?! YEAH, IT'S GOOD.
HAPPY TO HEAR THAT.
THE CAGASTER BIOLOGIC RESEARCH CENTER IN E-07.
IT WAS A HUGE RESEARCH FACILITY WITH THE MOST ADVANCED TECHNOLOGY AND THE LARGEST BUDGET IN THE E DISTRICT.
BUT ONE OF THE RUMORS ABOUT THE CENTER WAS MORE THAN PLAUSIBLE.

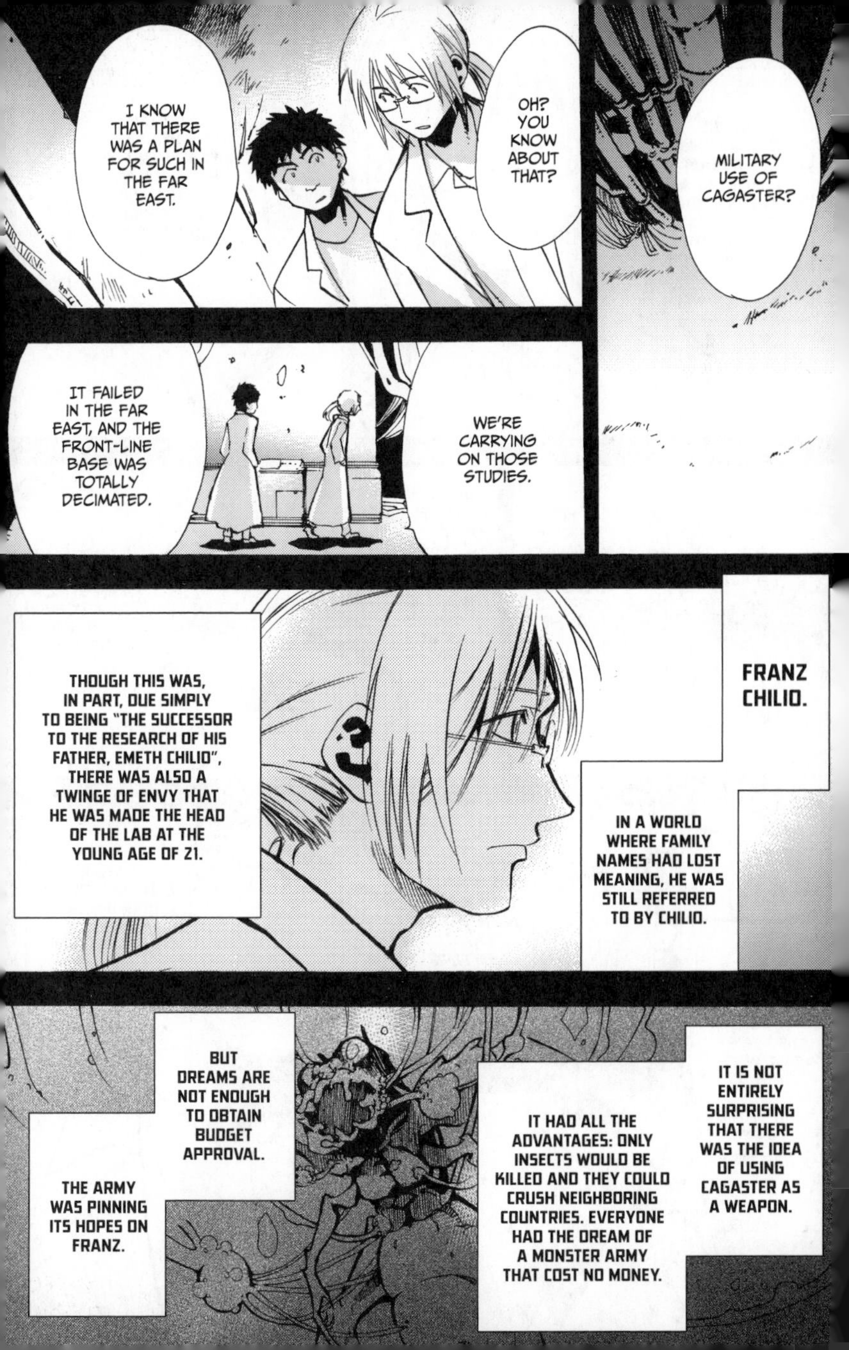
MILITARY USE OF CAGASTER?
OH? YOU KNOW ABOUT THAT?
I KNOW THAT THERE WAS A PLAN FOR SUCH IN THE FAR EAST.
WE'RE CARRYING ON THOSE STUDIES.
IT FAILED IN THE FAR EAST, AND THE FRONT-LINE BASE WAS TOTALLY DECIMATED.
FRANZ CHILIO.
IN A WORLD WHERE FAMILY NAMES HAD LOST MEANING, HE WAS STILL REFERRED TO BY CHILIO.
THOUGH THIS WAS, IN PART, DUE SIMPLY TO BEING "THE SUCCESSOR TO THE RESEARCH OF HIS FATHER, EMETH CHILIO", THERE WAS ALSO A TWINGE OF ENVY THAT HE WAS MADE THE HEAD OF THE LAB AT THE YOUNG AGE OF 21.
IT IS NOT ENTIRELY SURPRISING THAT THERE WAS THE IDEA OF USING CAGASTER AS A WEAPON.
IT HAD ALL THE ADVANTAGES: ONLY INSECTS WOULD BE KILLED AND THEY COULD CRUSH NEIGHBORING COUNTRIES. EVERYONE HAD THE DREAM OF A MONSTER ARMY THAT COST NO MONEY.
BUT DREAMS ARE NOT ENOUGH TO OBTAIN BUDGET APPROVAL.
THE ARMY WAS PINNING ITS HOPES ON FRANZ.

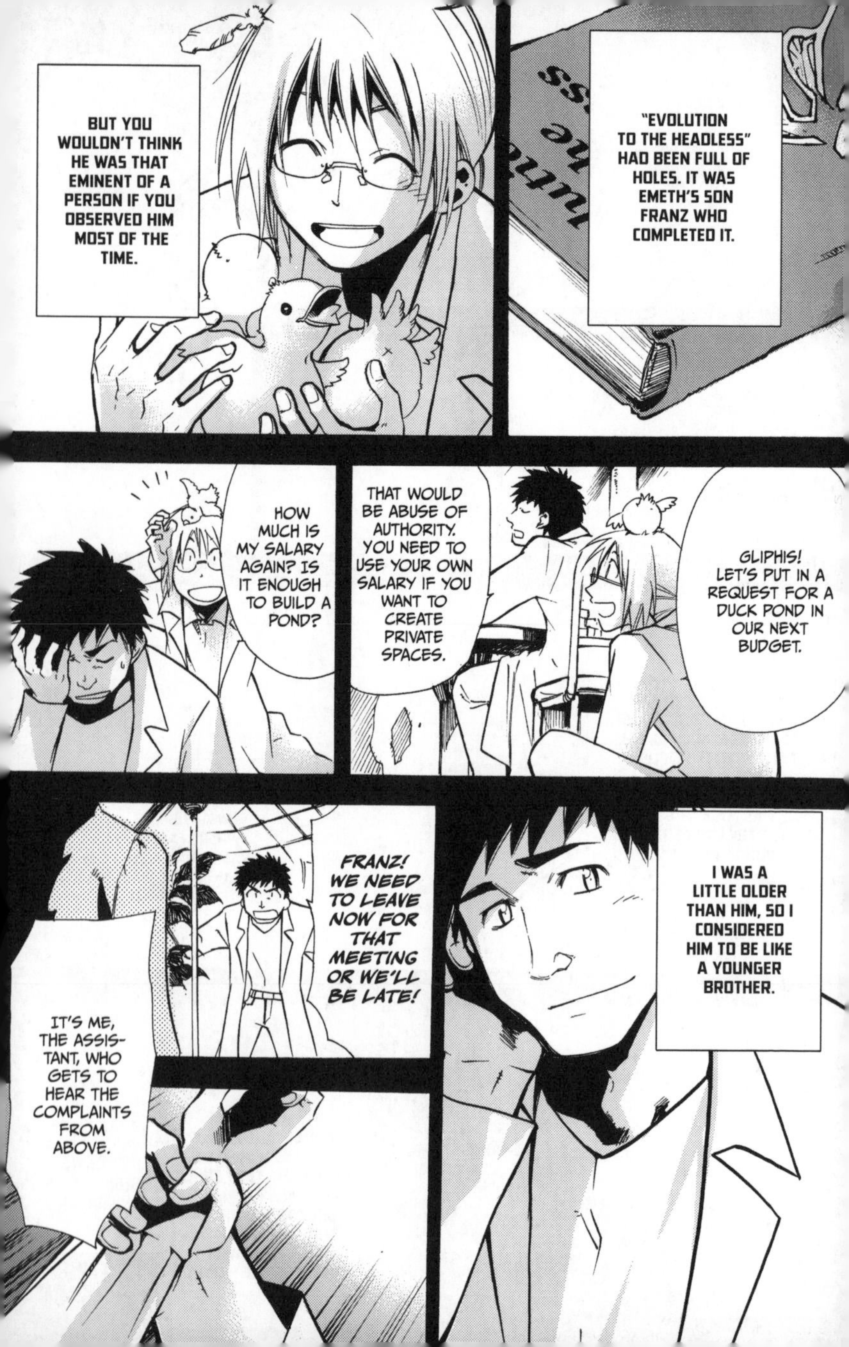
"EVOLUTION TO THE HEADLESS" HAD BEEN FULL OF HOLES. IT WAS EMETH'S SON FRANZ WHO COMPLETED IT.
BUT YOU WOULDN'T THINK HE WAS THAT EMINENT OF A PERSON IF YOU OBSERVED HIM MOST OF THE TIME.
GLIPHIS! LET'S PUT IN A REQUEST FOR A DUCK POND IN OUR NEXT BUDGET.
THAT WOULD BE ABUSE OF AUTHORITY. YOU NEED TO USE YOUR OWN SALARY IF YOU WANT TO CREATE PRIVATE SPACES.
HOW MUCH IS MY SALARY AGAIN? IS IT ENOUGH TO BUILD A POND?
I WAS A LITTLE OLDER THAN HIM, SO I CONSIDERED HIM TO BE LIKE A YOUNGER BROTHER.
FRANZ! WE NEED TO LEAVE NOW FOR THAT MEETING OR WE'LL BE LATE!
IT'S ME, THE ASSISTANT, WHO GETS TO HEAR THE COMPLAINTS FROM ABOVE.

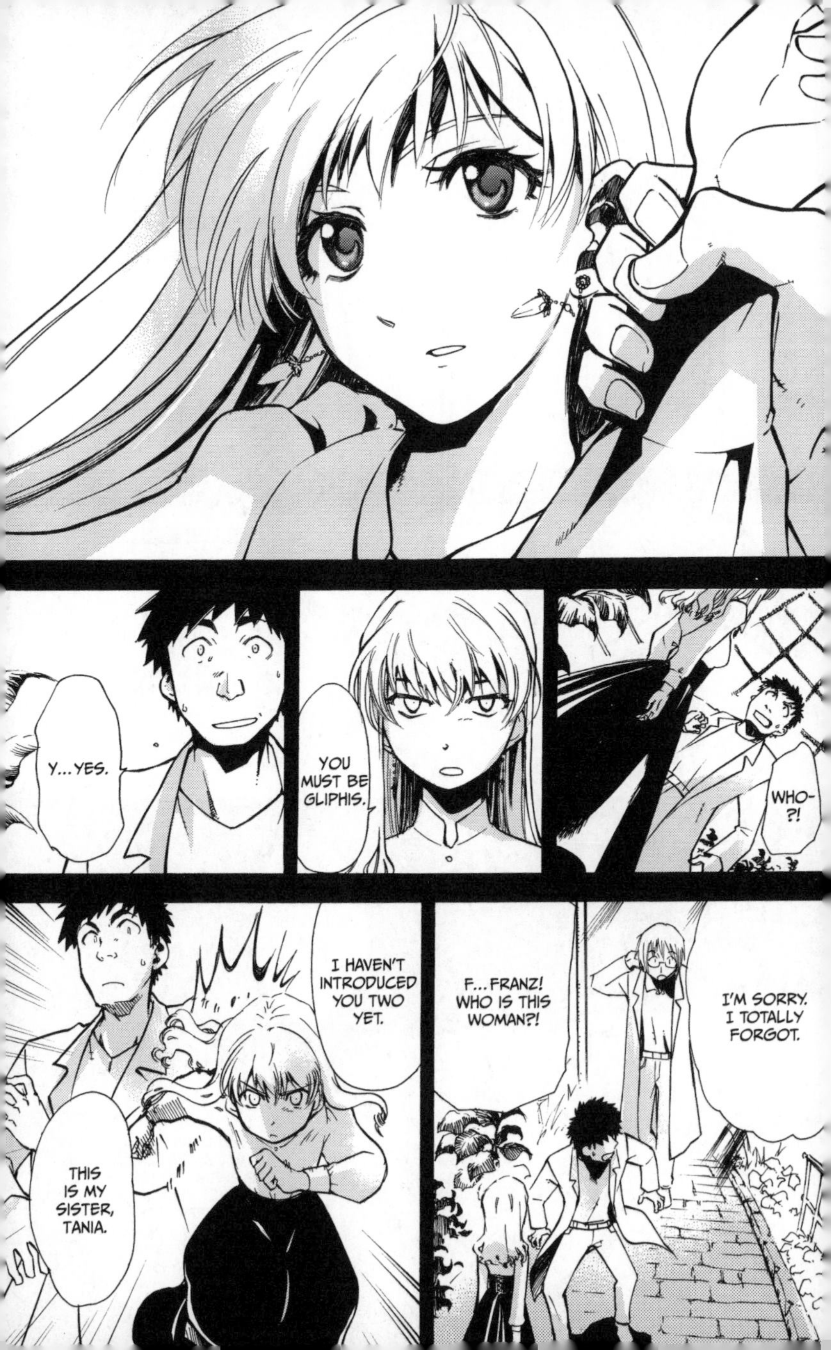
WHO-?!
YOU MUST BE GLIPHIS.
Y...YES.
F...FRANZ! WHO IS THIS WOMAN?!
I'M SORRY. I TOTALLY FORGOT.
I HAVEN'T INTRODUCED YOU TWO YET.
THIS IS MY SISTER, TANIA.

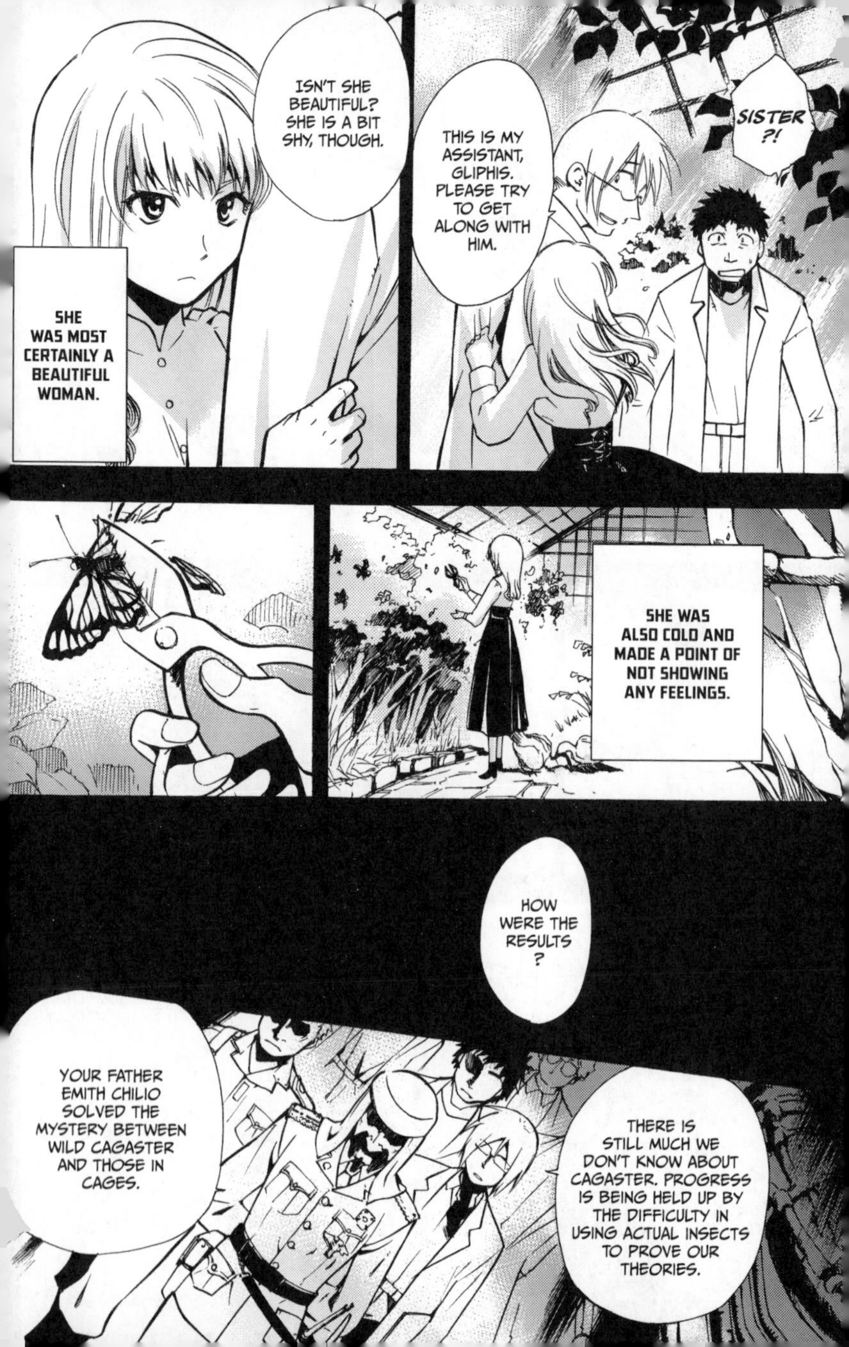
SISTER ?!
THIS IS MY ASSISTANT, GLIPHIS. PLEASE TRY TO GET ALONG WITH HIM.
ISN'T SHE BEAUTIFUL? SHE IS A BIT SHY, THOUGH.
SHE WAS MOST CERTAINLY A BEAUTIFUL WOMAN.
SHE WAS ALSO COLD AND MADE A POINT OF NOT SHOWING ANY FEELINGS.
HOW WERE THE RESULTS ?
THERE IS STILL MUCH WE DON'T KNOW ABOUT CAGASTER. PROGRESS IS BEING HELD UP BY THE DIFFICULTY IN USING ACTUAL INSECTS TO PROVE OUR THEORIES.
YOUR FATHER EMITH CHILIO SOLVED THE MYSTERY BETWEEN WILD CAGASTER AND THOSE IN CAGES.

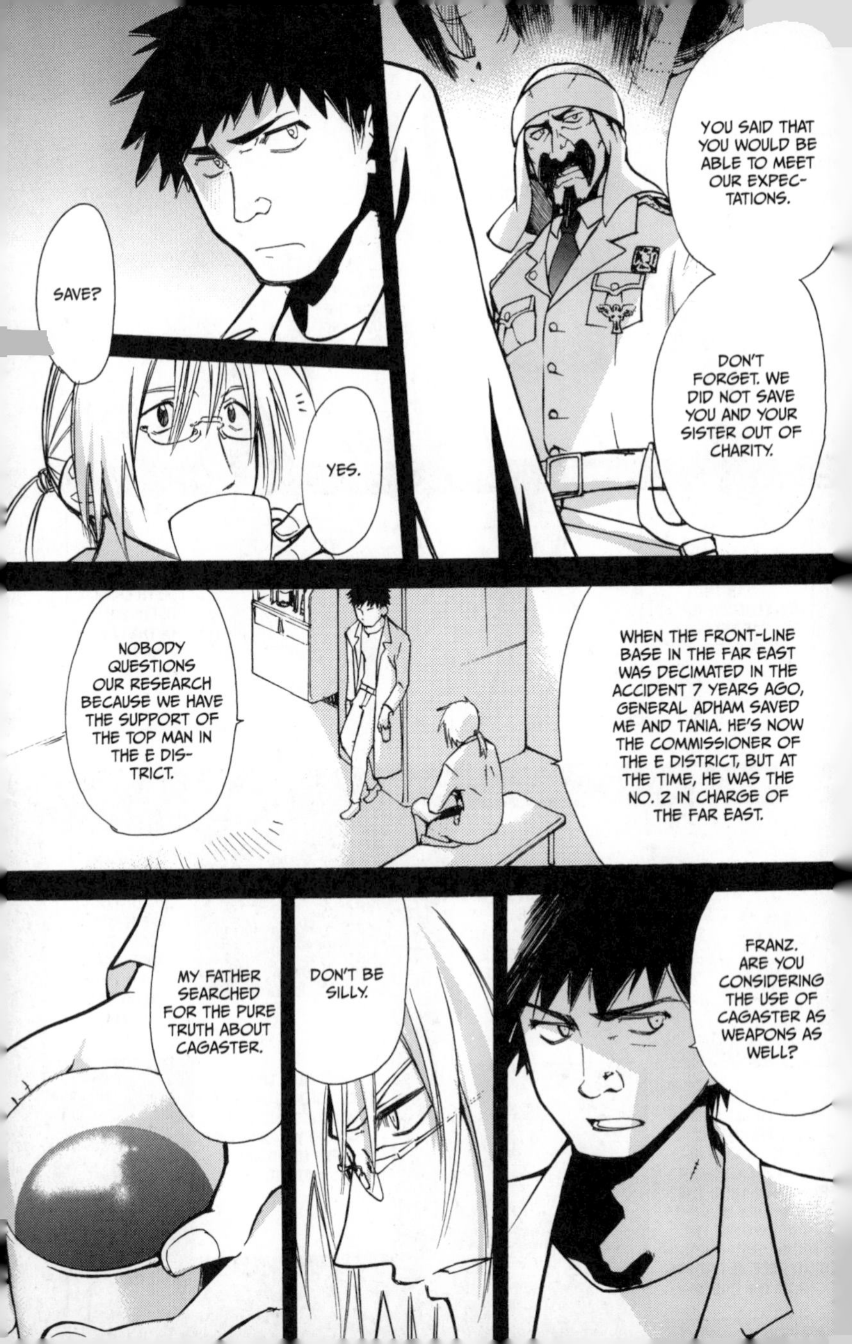
YOU SAID THAT YOU WOULD BE ABLE TO MEET OUR EXPEC-TATIONS.
DON'T FORGET. WE DID NOT SAVE YOU AND YOUR SISTER OUT OF CHARITY.
SAVE?
YES.
WHEN THE FRONT-LINE BASE IN THE FAR EAST WAS DECIMATED IN THE ACCIDENT 7 YEARS AGO, GENERAL ADHAM SAVED ME AND TANIA. HE'S NOW THE COMMISSIONER OF THE E DISTRICT, BUT AT THE TIME, HE WAS THE NO. 2 IN CHARGE OF THE FAR EAST.
NOBODY QUESTIONS OUR RESEARCH BECAUSE WE HAVE THE SUPPORT OF THE TOP MAN IN THE E DIS-TRICT.
FRANZ. ARE YOU CONSIDERING THE USE OF CAGASTER AS WEAPONS AS WELL?
DON'T BE SILLY.
MY FATHER SEARCHED FOR THE PURE TRUTH ABOUT CAGASTER.

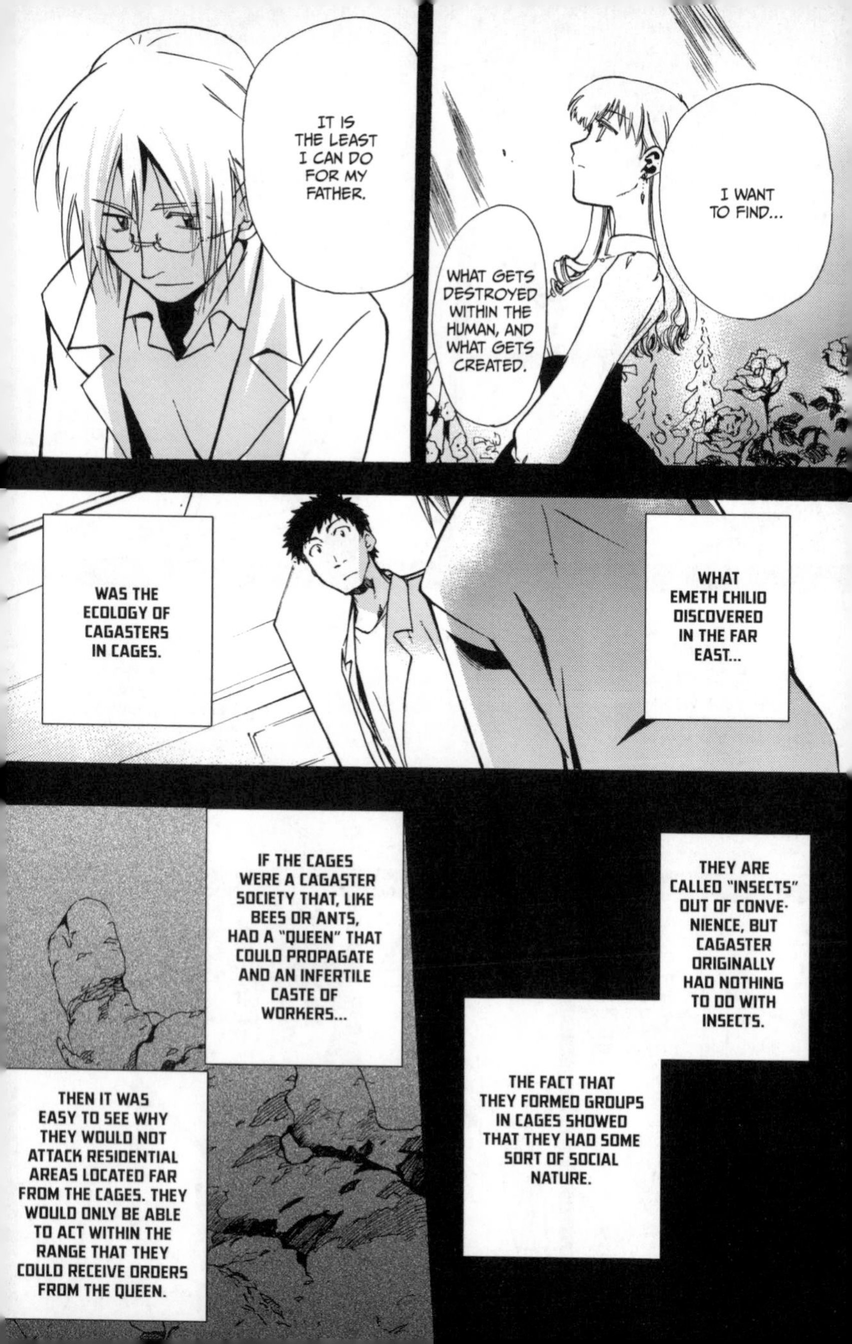
I WANT TO FIND...
WHAT GETS DESTROYED WITHIN THE HUMAN, AND WHAT GETS CREATED.
IT IS THE LEAST I CAN DO FOR MY FATHER.
WHAT EMETH CHILIO DISCOVERED IN THE FAR EAST...
WAS THE ECOLOGY OF CAGASTERS IN CAGES.
THEY ARE CALLED "INSECTS" OUT OF CONVENIENCE, BUT CAGASTER ORIGINALLY HAD NOTHING TO DO WITH INSECTS.
THE FACT THAT THEY FORMED GROUPS IN CAGES SHOWED THAT THEY HAD SOME SORT OF SOCIAL NATURE.
IF THE CAGES WERE A CAGASTER SOCIETY THAT, LIKE BEES OR ANTS, HAD A "QUEEN" THAT COULD PROPAGATE AND AN INFERTILE CASTE OF WORKERS...
THEN IT WAS EASY TO SEE WHY THEY WOULD NOT ATTACK RESIDENTIAL AREAS LOCATED FAR FROM THE CAGES. THEY WOULD ONLY BE ABLE TO ACT WITHIN THE RANGE THAT THEY COULD RECEIVE ORDERS FROM THE QUEEN.

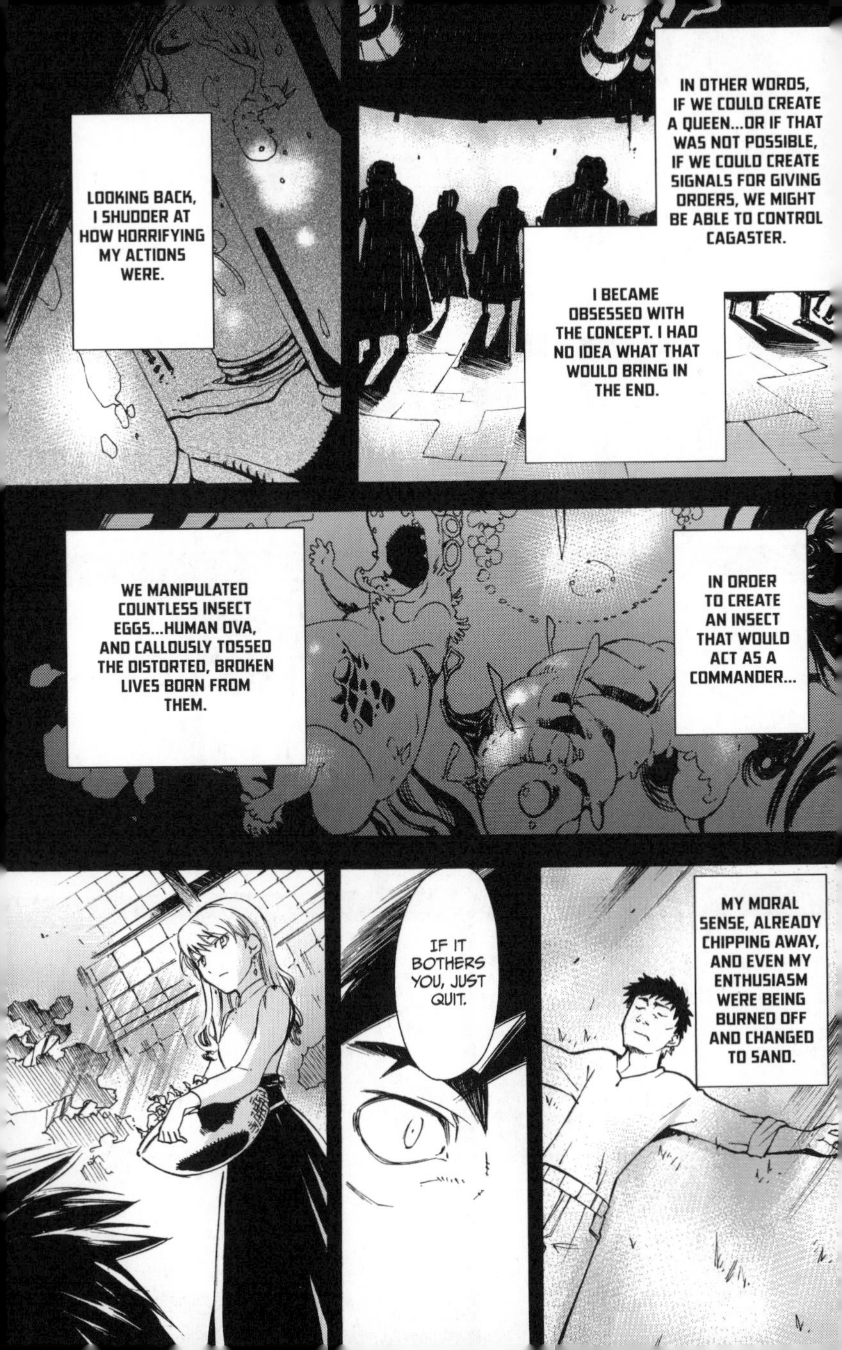
IN OTHER WORDS, IF WE COULD CREATE A QUEEN...OR IF THAT WAS NOT POSSIBLE, IF WE COULD CREATE SIGNALS FOR GIVING ORDERS, WE MIGHT BE ABLE TO CONTROL CAGASTER.
I BECAME OBSESSED WITH THE CONCEPT. I HAD NO IDEA WHAT THAT WOULD BRING IN THE END.
LOOKING BACK, I SHUDDER AT HOW HORRIFYING MY ACTIONS WERE.
IN ORDER TO CREATE AN INSECT THAT WOULD ACT AS A COMMANDER...
WE MANIPULATED COUNTLESS INSECT EGGS...HUMAN OVA, AND CALLOUSLY TOSSED THE DISTORTED, BROKEN LIVES BORN FROM THEM.
MY MORAL SENSE, ALREADY CHIPPING AWAY, AND EVEN MY ENTHUSIASM WERE BEING BURNED OFF AND CHANGED TO SAND.
IF IT BOTHERS YOU, JUST QUIT.

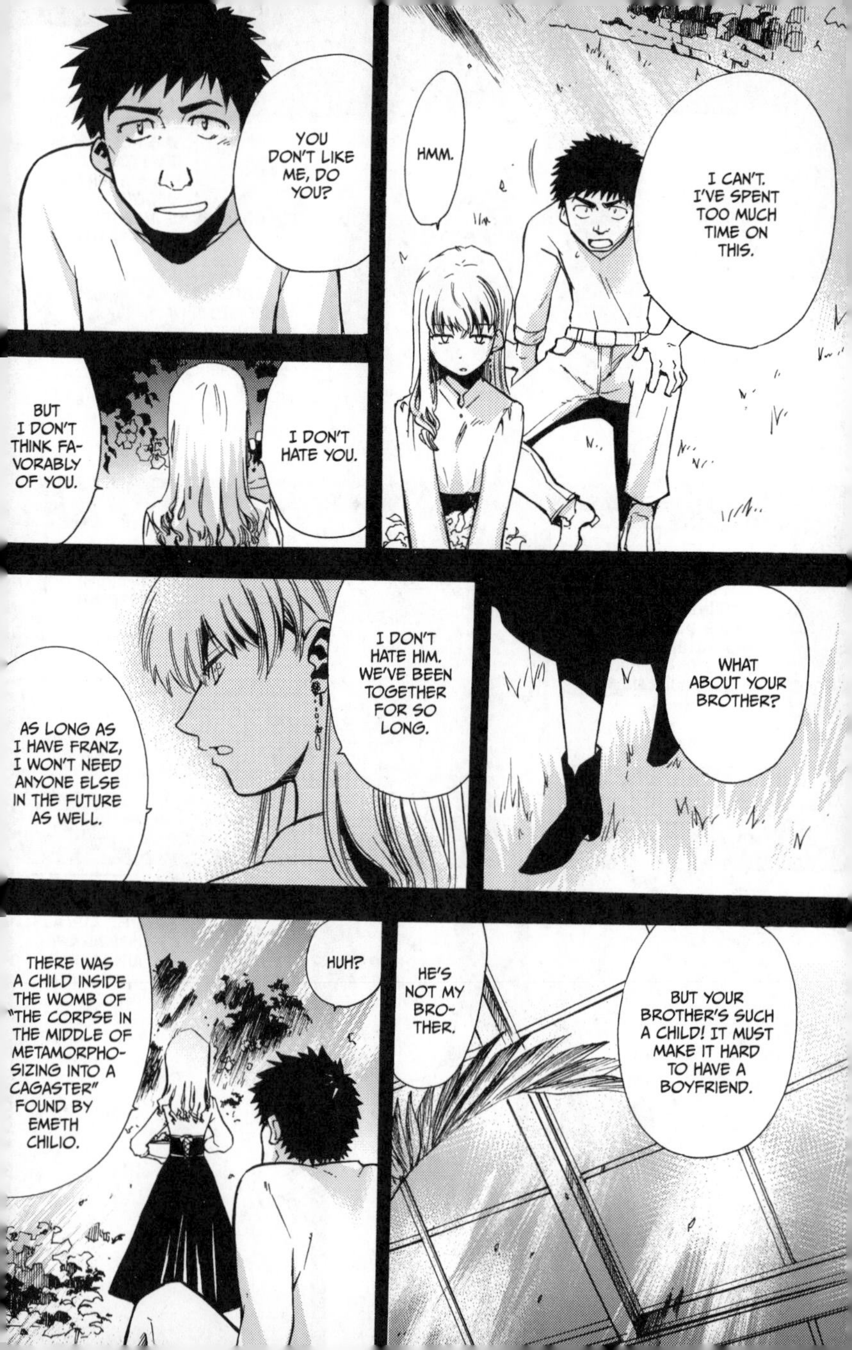

I CAN'T. I'VE SPENT TOO MUCH TIME ON THIS.
HMM.
YOU DON'T LIKE ME, DO YOU?
I DON'T HATE YOU.
BUT I DON'T THINK FA-VORABLY OF YOU.
WHAT ABOUT YOUR BROTHER?
I DON'T HATE HIM. WE'VE BEEN TOGETHER FOR SO LONG.
AS LONG AS I HAVE FRANZ, I WON'T NEED ANYONE ELSE IN THE FUTURE AS WELL.
BUT YOUR BROTHER'S SUCH A CHILD! IT MUST MAKE IT HARD TO HAVE A BOYFRIEND.
HE'S NOT MY BRO-THER.
HUH?
THERE WAS A CHILD INSIDE THE WOMB OF "THE CORPSE IN THE MIDDLE OF METAMORPHO-SIZING INTO A CAGASTER" FOUND BY EMETH CHILIO.

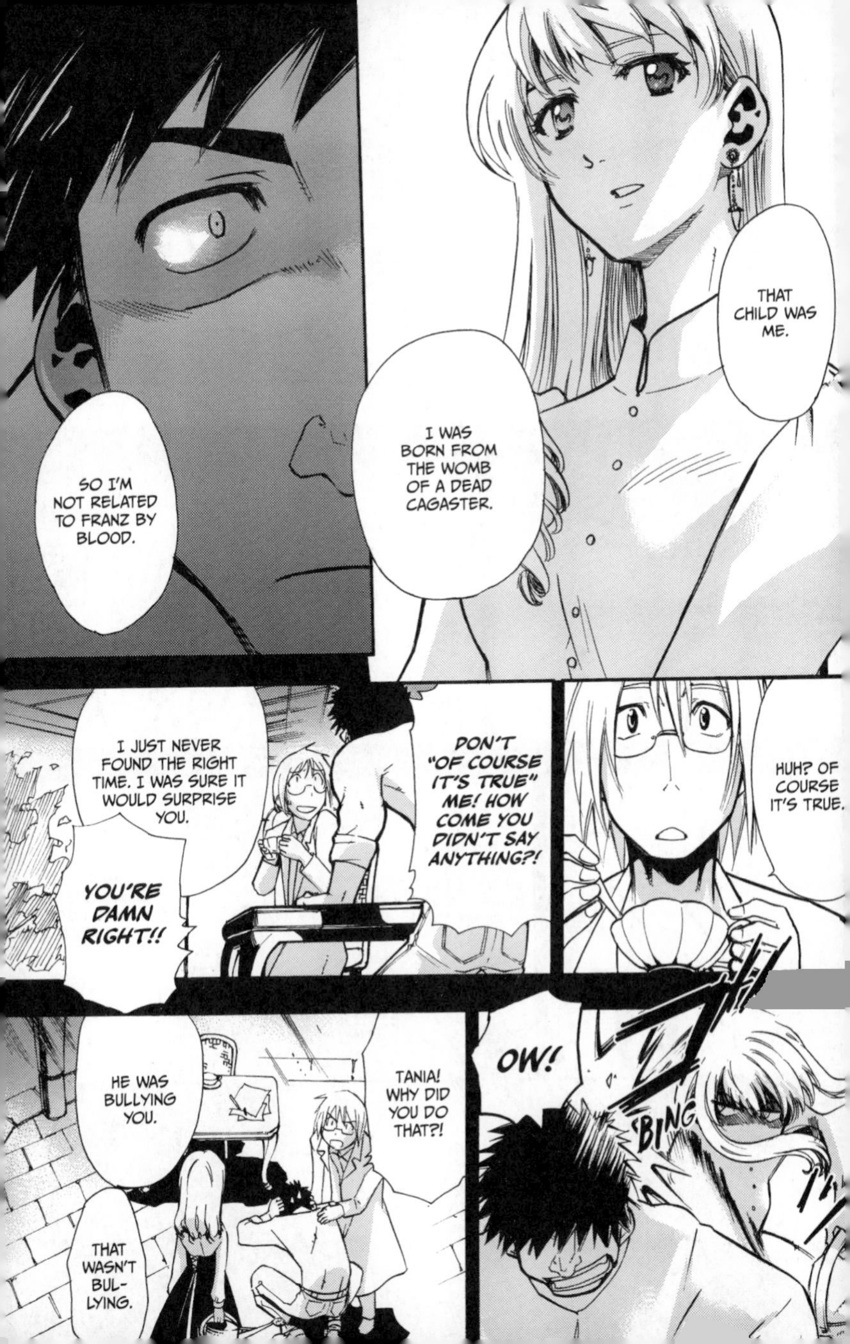
THAT CHILD WAS ME.
I WAS BORN FROM THE WOMB OF A DEAD CAGASTER.
SO I'M NOT RELATED TO FRANZ BY BLOOD.
HUH? OF COURSE IT'S TRUE.
DON'T "OF COURSE IT'S TRUE" ME! HOW COME YOU DIDN'T SAY ANYTHING?!
I JUST NEVER FOUND THE RIGHT TIME. I WAS SURE IT WOULD SURPRISE YOU.
YOU'RE DAMN RIGHT!!
OW!
BING
TANIA! WHY DID YOU DO THAT?!
HE WAS BULLYING YOU.
THAT WASN'T BUL-LYING.

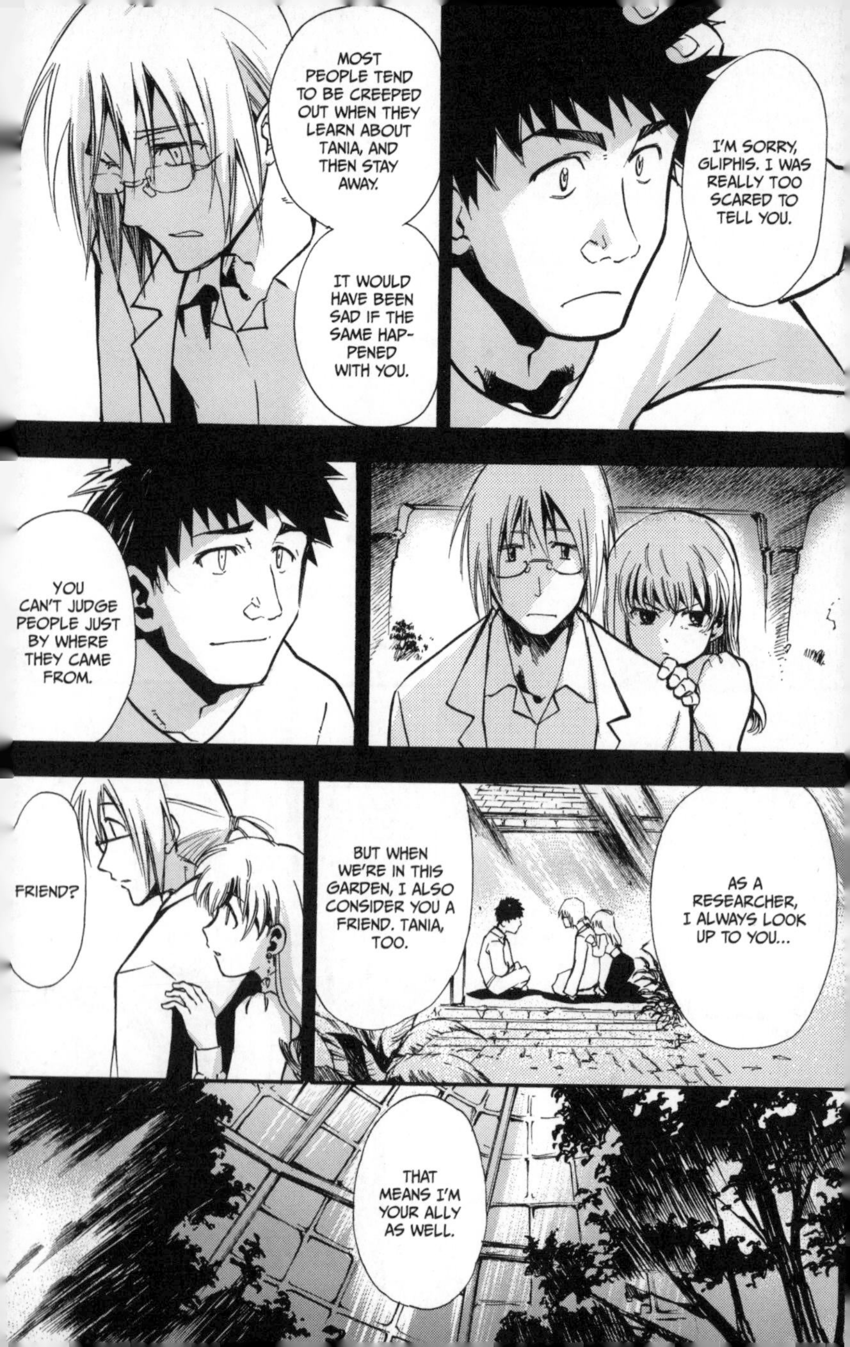
I'M SORRY, GLIPHIS. I WAS REALLY TOO SCARED TO TELL YOU.
MOST PEOPLE TEND TO BE CREEPED OUT WHEN THEY LEARN ABOUT TANIA, AND THEN STAY AWAY.
IT WOULD HAVE BEEN SAD IF THE SAME HAP-PENED WITH YOU.
YOU CAN'T JUDGE PEOPLE JUST BY WHERE THEY CAME FROM.
AS A RESEARCHER, I ALWAYS LOOK UP TO YOU...
BUT WHEN WE'RE IN THIS GARDEN, I ALSO CONSIDER YOU A FRIEND. TANIA, TOO.
FRIEND?
THAT MEANS I'M YOUR ALLY AS WELL.

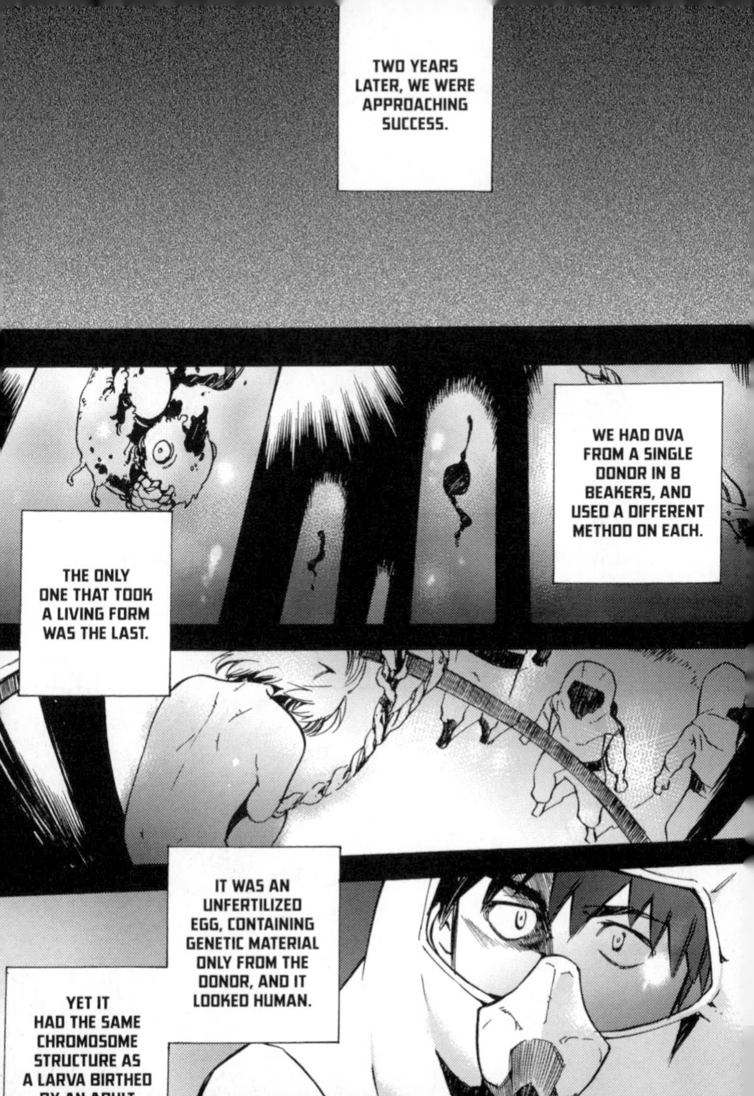
TWO YEARS LATER, WE WERE APPROACHING SUCCESS.
WE HAD OVA FROM A SINGLE DONOR IN 8 BEAKERS, AND USED A DIFFERENT METHOD ON EACH.
THE ONLY ONE THAT TOOK A LIVING FORM WAS THE LAST.
IT WAS AN UNFERTILIZED EGG, CONTAINING GENETIC MATERIAL ONLY FROM THE DONOR, AND IT LOOKED HUMAN.
YET IT HAD THE SAME CHROMOSOME STRUCTURE AS A LARVA BIRTHED BY AN ADULT

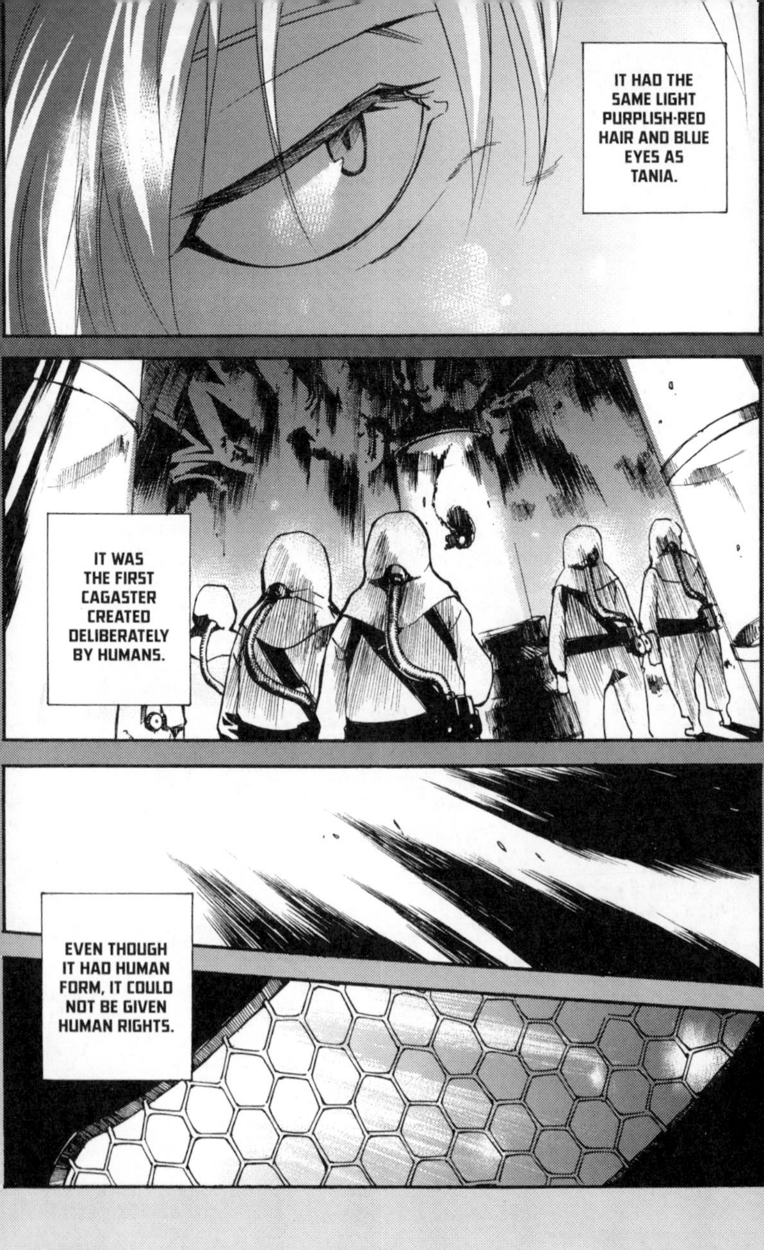
IT HAD THE SAME LIGHT PURPLISH-RED HAIR AND BLUE EYES AS TANIA.
IT WAS THE FIRST CAGASTER CREATED DELIBERATELY BY HUMANS.
EVEN THOUGH IT HAD HUMAN FORM, IT COULD NOT BE GIVEN HUMAN RIGHTS.

GNIP

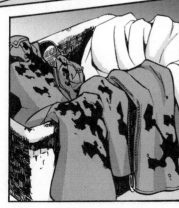

WE NAMED THE CHILD "ACHT".

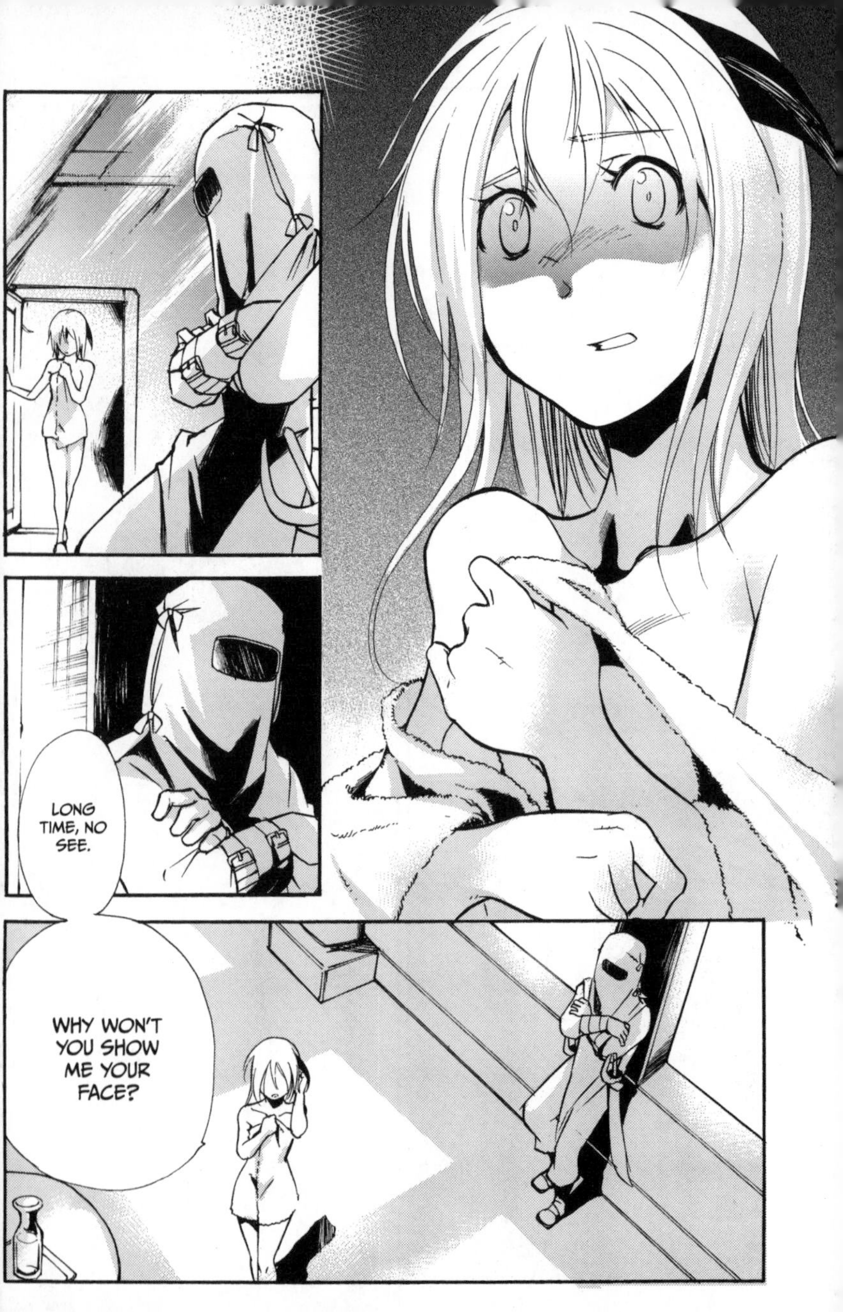
LONG TIME, NO SEE.
WHY WON'T YOU SHOW ME YOUR FACE?

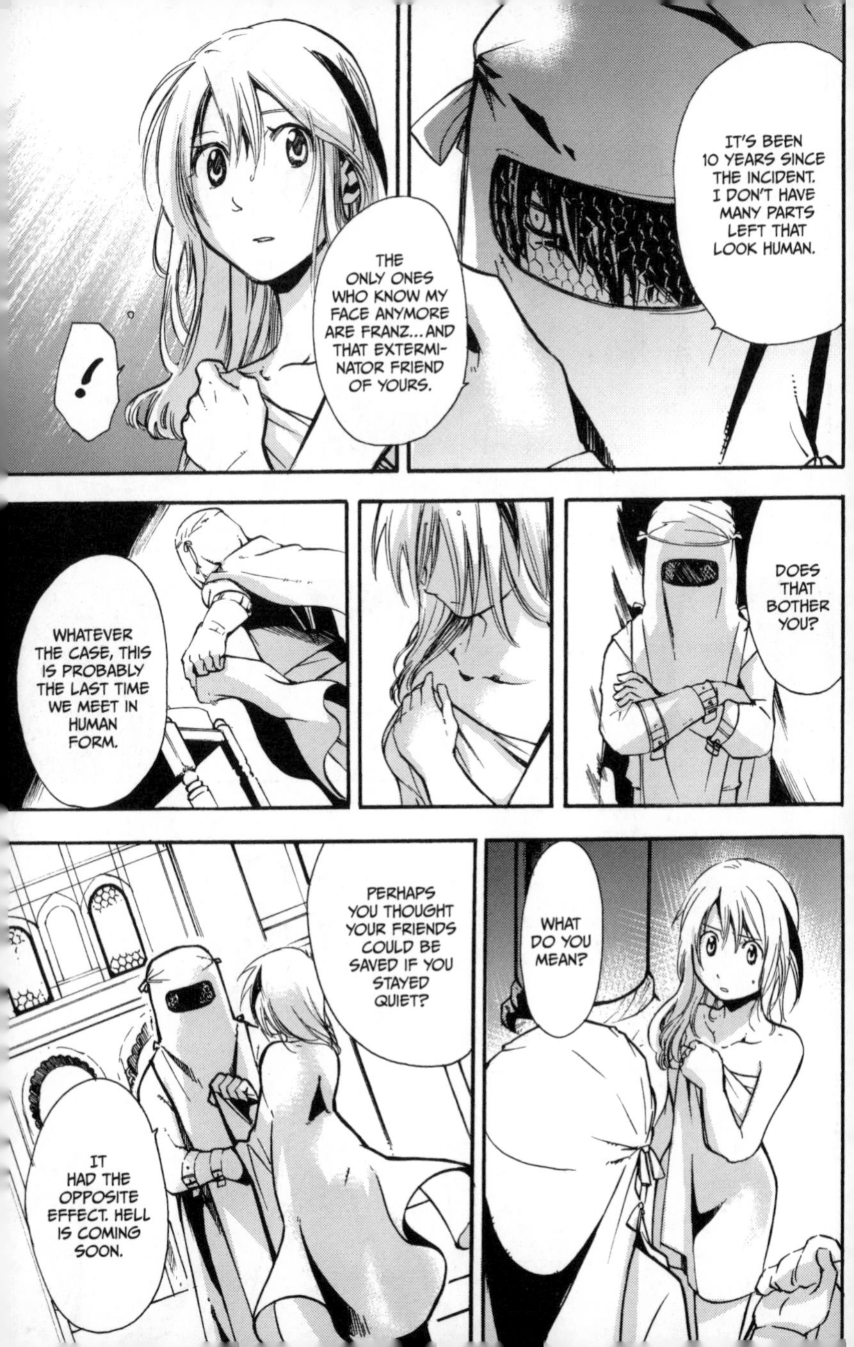
IT'S BEEN 10 YEARS SINCE THE INCIDENT. I DON'T HAVE MANY PARTS LEFT THAT LOOK HUMAN.
THE ONLY ONES WHO KNOW MY FACE ANYMORE ARE FRANZ...AND THAT EXTERMINATOR FRIEND OF YOURS.
!
DOES THAT BOTHER YOU?
WHATEVER THE CASE, THIS IS PROBABLY THE LAST TIME WE MEET IN HUMAN FORM.
WHAT DO YOU MEAN?
PERHAPS YOU THOUGHT YOUR FRIENDS COULD BE SAVED IF YOU STAYED QUIET?
IT HAD THE OPPOSITE EFFECT. HELL IS COMING SOON.

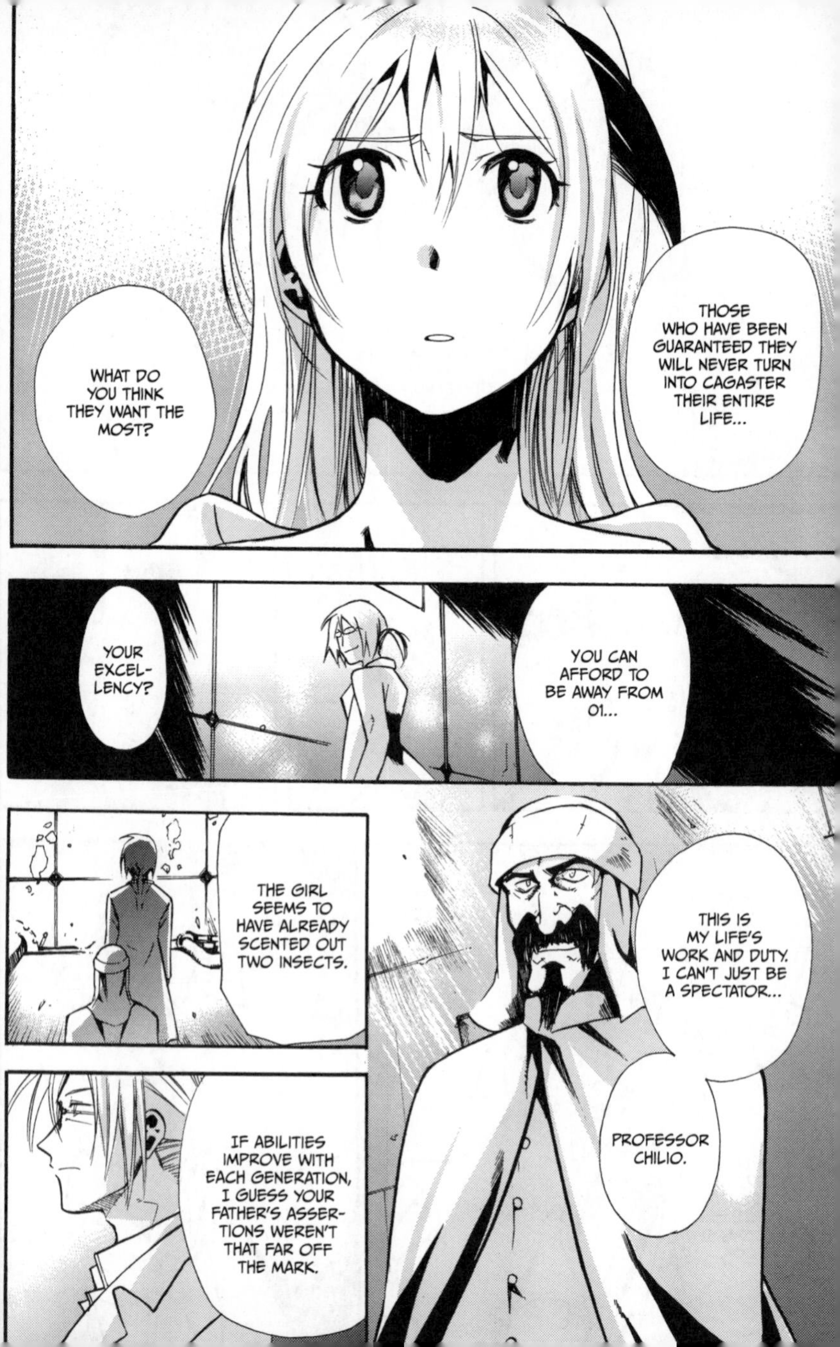
THOSE WHO HAVE BEEN GUARANTEED THEY WILL NEVER TURN INTO CAGASTER THEIR ENTIRE LIFE...
WHAT DO YOU THINK THEY WANT THE MOST?
YOU CAN AFFORD TO BE AWAY FROM 01...
YOUR EXCEL-LENCY?
THIS IS MY LIFE'S WORK AND DUTY. I CAN'T JUST BE A SPECTATOR...
PROFESSOR CHILIO.
THE GIRL SEEMS TO HAVE ALREADY SCENTED OUT TWO INSECTS.
IF ABILITIES IMPROVE WITH EACH GENERATION, I GUESS YOUR FATHER'S ASSER-TIONS WEREN'T THAT FAR OFF THE MARK.

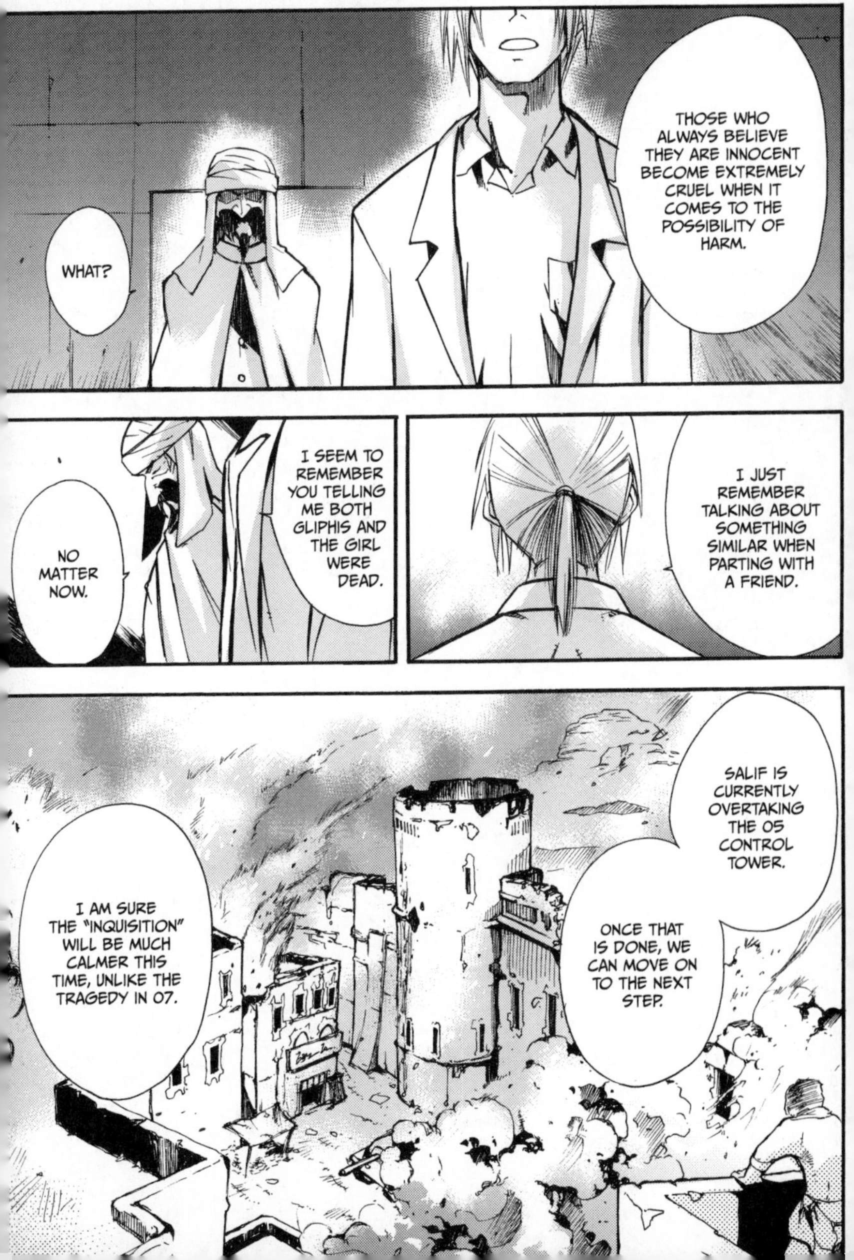
THOSE WHO ALWAYS BELIEVE THEY ARE INNOCENT BECOME EXTREMELY CRUEL WHEN IT COMES TO THE POSSIBILITY OF HARM.
WHAT?
I JUST REMEMBER TALKING ABOUT SOMETHING SIMILAR WHEN PARTING WITH A FRIEND.
I SEEM TO REMEMBER YOU TELLING ME BOTH GLIPHIS AND THE GIRL WERE DEAD.
NO MATTER NOW.
SALIF IS CURRENTLY OVERTAKING THE 05 CONTROL TOWER.
ONCE THAT IS DONE, WE CAN MOVE ON TO THE NEXT STEP.
I AM SURE THE "INQUISITION" WILL BE MUCH CALMER THIS TIME, UNLIKE THE TRAGEDY IN 07.

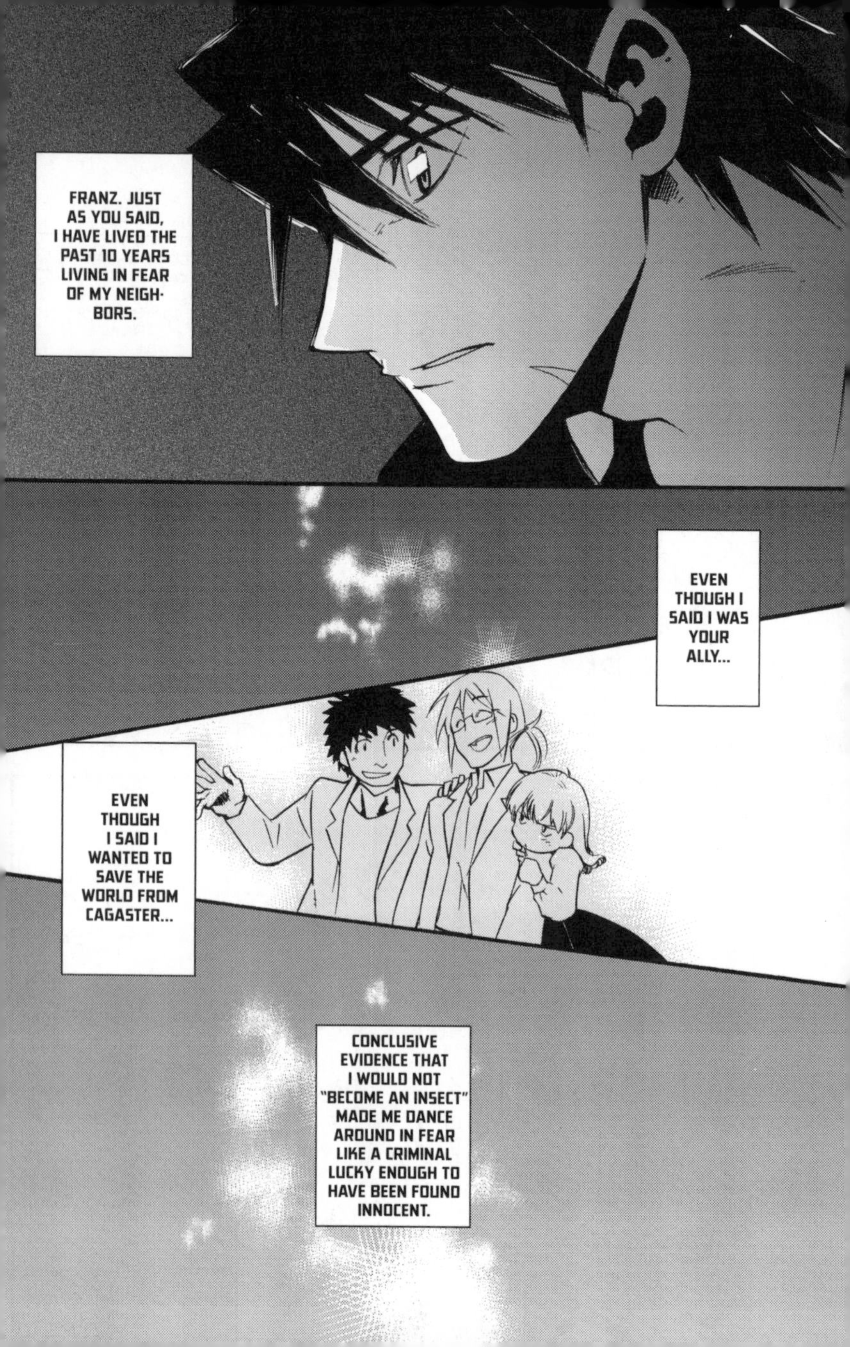
FRANZ. JUST AS YOU SAID, I HAVE LIVED THE PAST 10 YEARS LIVING IN FEAR OF MY NEIGH-BORS.
EVEN THOUGH I SAID I WAS YOUR ALLY...
EVEN THOUGH I SAID I WANTED TO SAVE THE WORLD FROM CAGASTER...
CONCLUSIVE EVIDENCE THAT I WOULD NOT "BECOME AN INSECT" MADE ME DANCE AROUND IN FEAR LIKE A CRIMINAL LUCKY ENOUGH TO HAVE BEEN FOUND INNOCENT.

[CHAPTER 15]

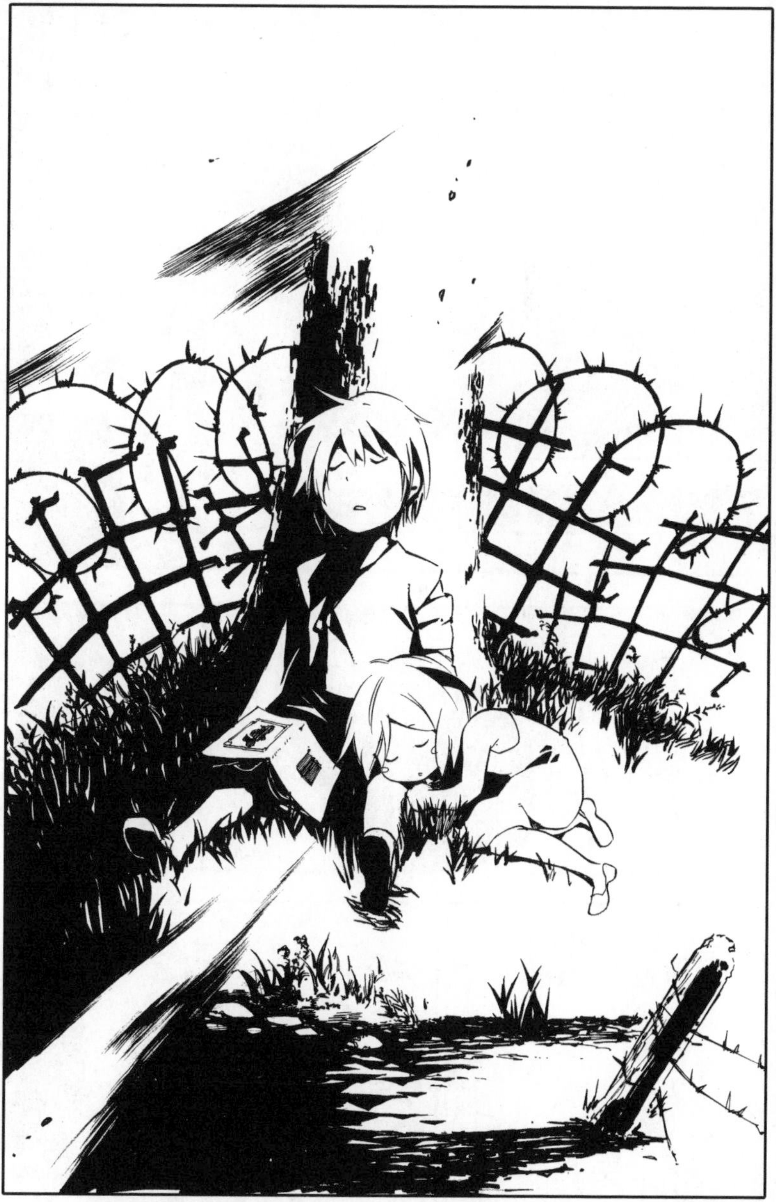

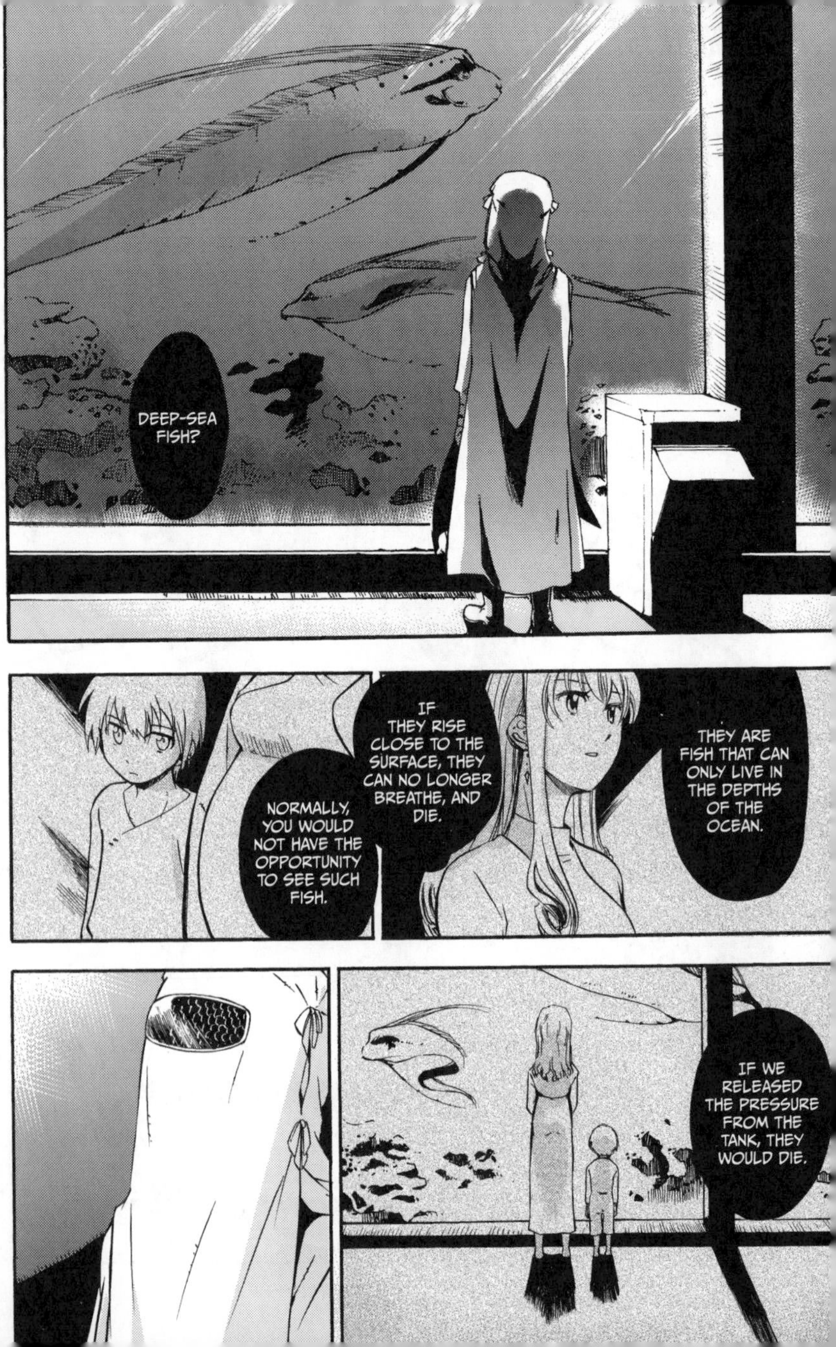
DEEP-SEA FISH?
THEY ARE FISH THAT CAN ONLY LIVE IN THE DEPTHS OF THE OCEAN.
IF THEY RISE CLOSE TO THE SURFACE, THEY CAN NO LONGER BREATHE, AND DIE.
NORMALLY, YOU WOULD NOT HAVE THE OPPORTUNITY TO SEE SUCH FISH.
IF WE RELEASED THE PRESSURE FROM THE TANK, THEY WOULD DIE.

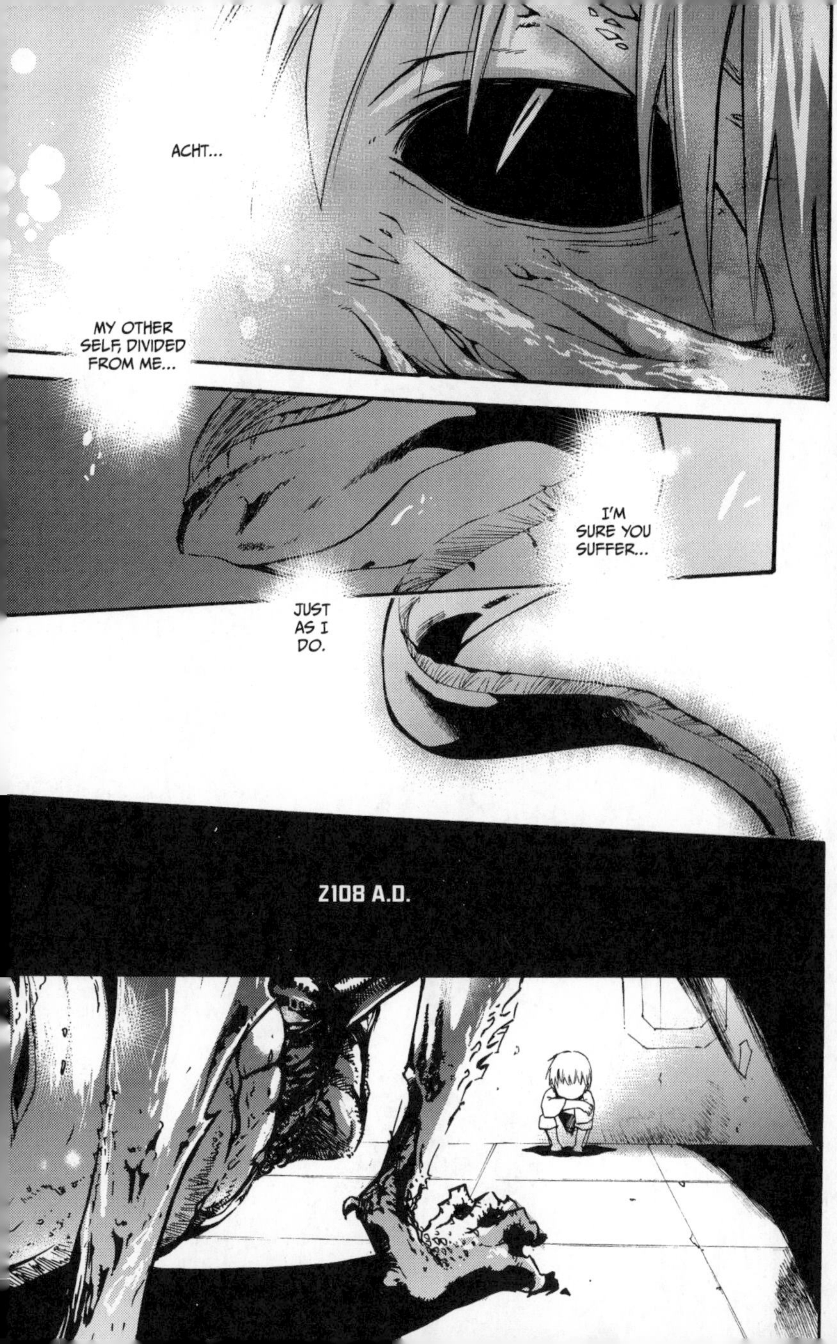
ACHT...
MY OTHER SELF, DIVIDED FROM ME...
I'M SURE YOU SUFFER...
JUST AS I DO.
2108 A.D.

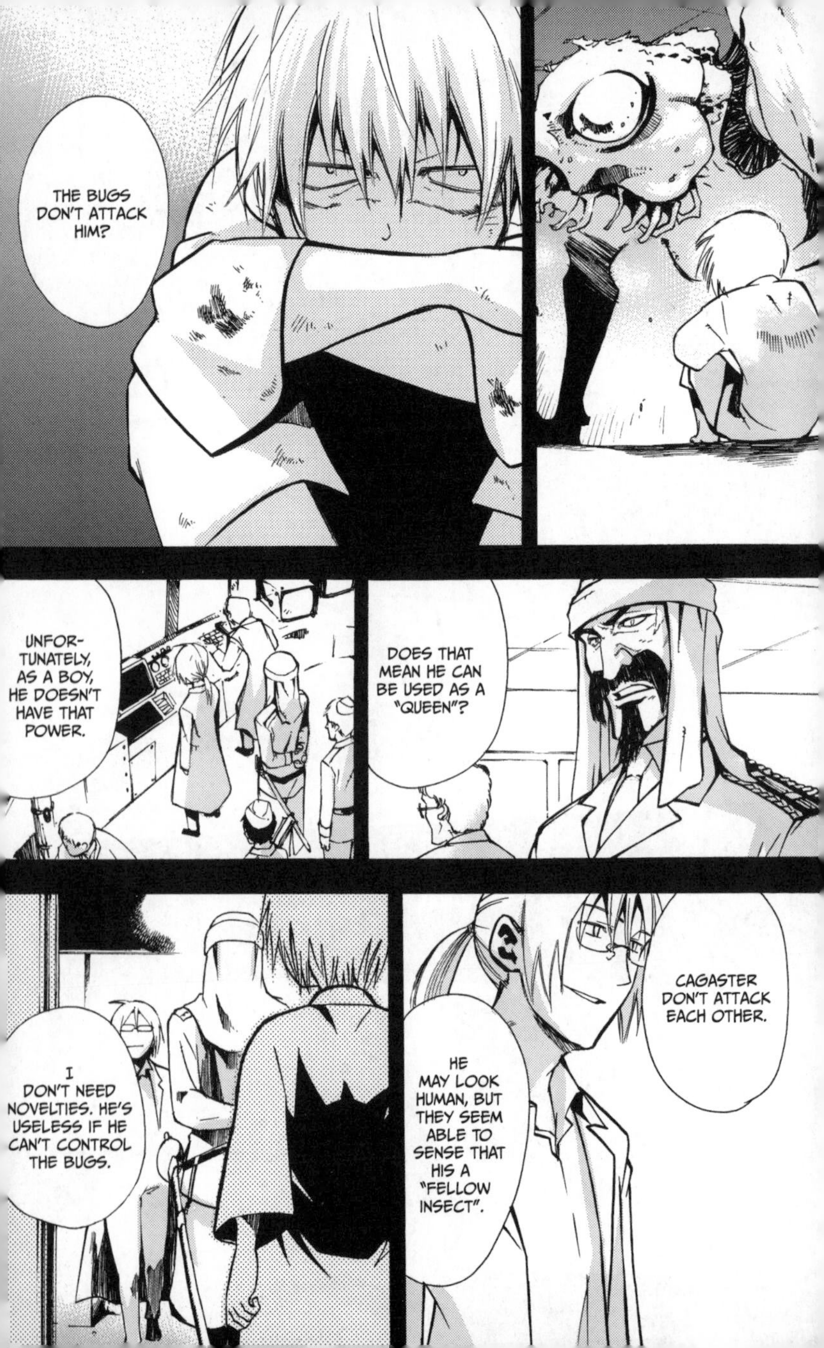
THE BUGS DON'T ATTACK HIM?
DOES THAT MEAN HE CAN BE USED AS A "QUEEN"?
UNFOR-TUNATELY, AS A BOY, HE DOESN'T HAVE THAT POWER.
CAGASTER DON'T ATTACK EACH OTHER.
HE MAY LOOK HUMAN, BUT THEY SEEM ABLE TO SENSE THAT HIS A "FELLOW INSECT".
I DON'T NEED NOVELTIES. HE'S USELESS IF HE CAN'T CONTROL THE BUGS.

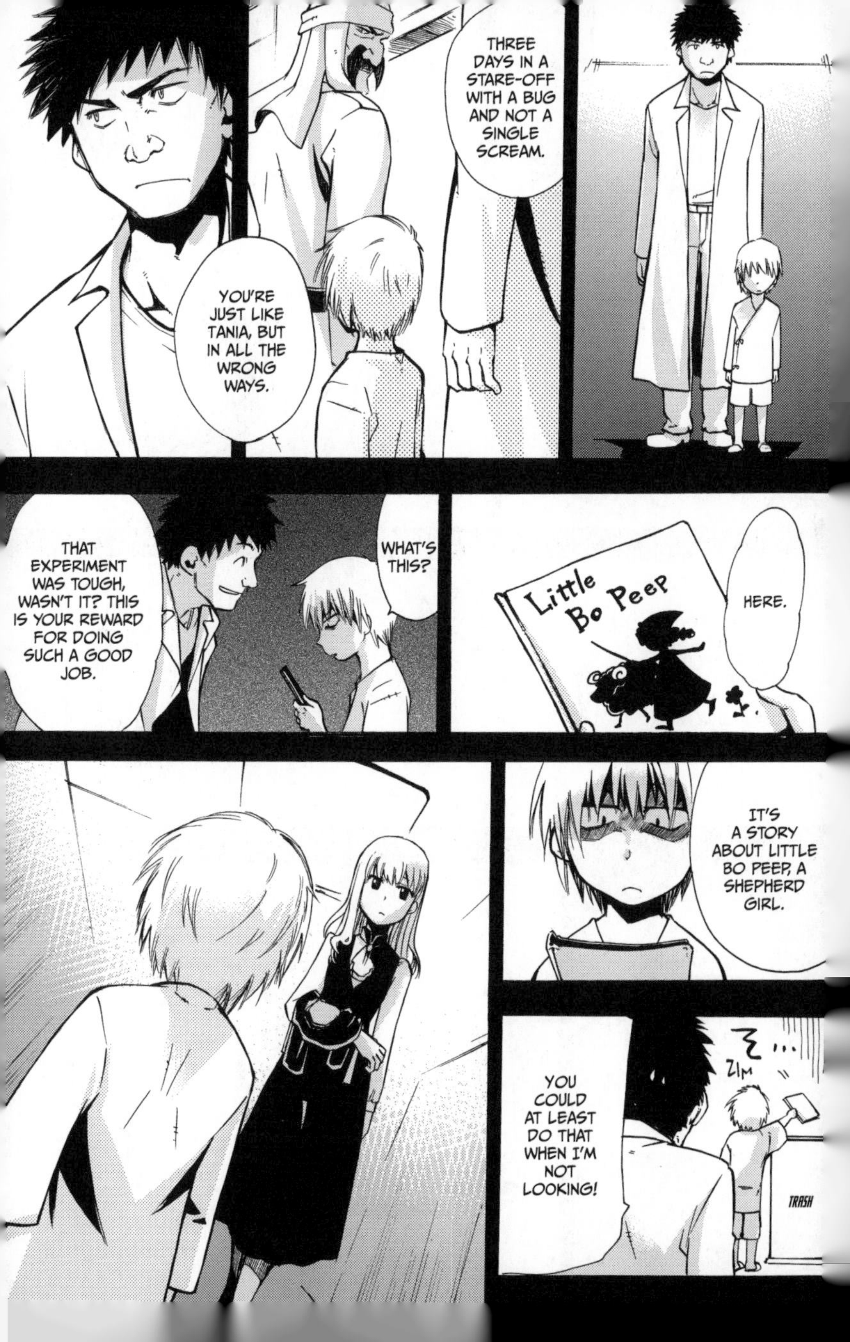
THREE DAYS IN A STARE-OFF WITH A BUG AND NOT A SINGLE SCREAM.
YOU'RE JUST LIKE TANIA, BUT IN ALL THE WRONG WAYS.
HERE.
Little Bo Peep
WHAT'S THIS?
THAT EXPERIMENT WAS TOUGH, WASN'T IT? THIS IS YOUR REWARD FOR DOING SUCH A GOOD JOB.
IT'S A STORY ABOUT LITTLE BO PEEP, A SHEPHERD GIRL.
ZIM
YOU COULD AT LEAST DO THAT WHEN I'M NOT LOOKING!
TRASH

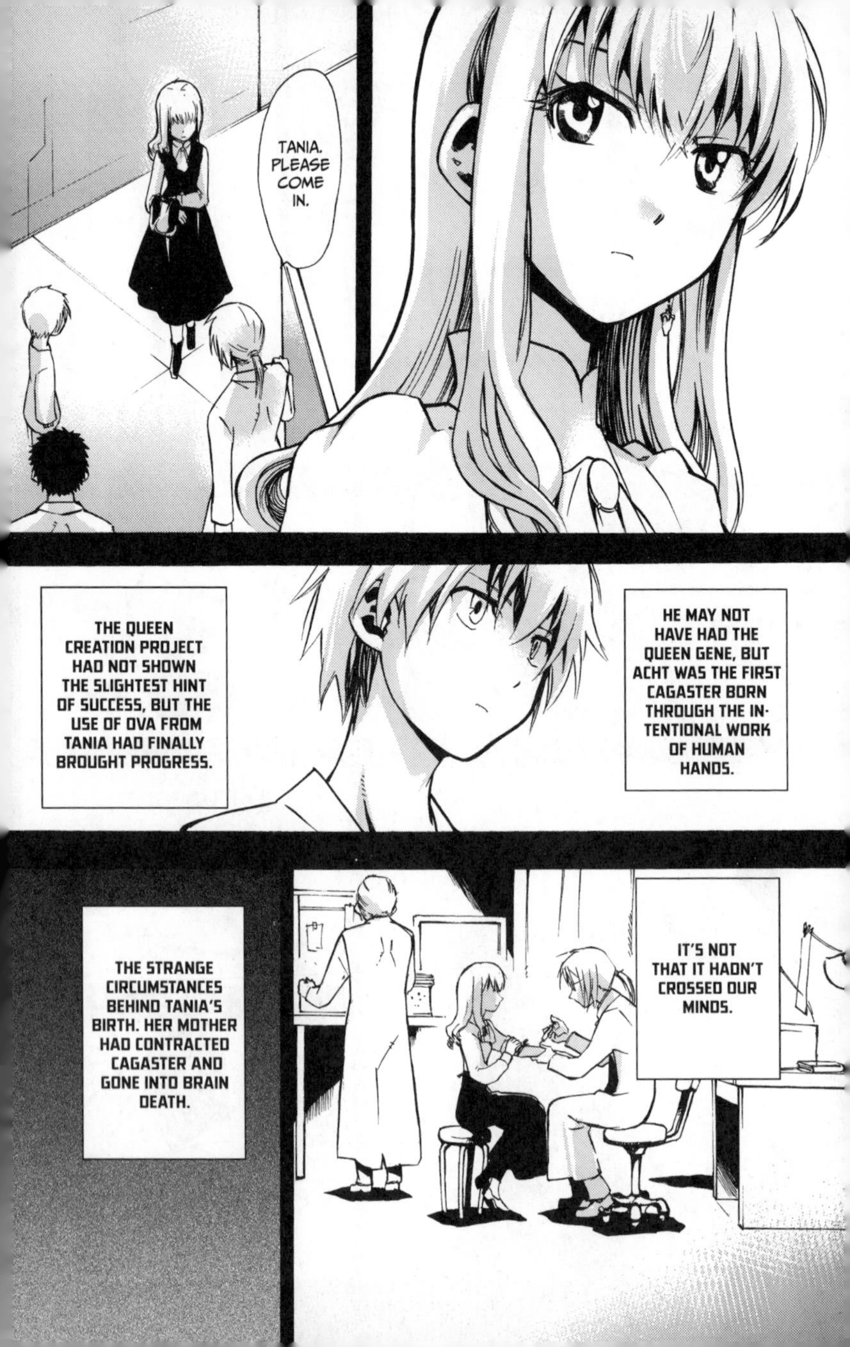
TANIA. PLEASE COME IN.
HE MAY NOT HAVE HAD THE QUEEN GENE, BUT ACHT WAS THE FIRST CAGASTER BORN THROUGH THE IN-TENTIONAL WORK OF HUMAN HANDS.
THE QUEEN CREATION PROJECT HAD NOT SHOWN THE SLIGHTEST HINT OF SUCCESS, BUT THE USE OF OVA FROM TANIA HAD FINALLY BROUGHT PROGRESS.
IT'S NOT THAT IT HADN'T CROSSED OUR MINDS.
THE STRANGE CIRCUMSTANCES BEHIND TANIA'S BIRTH. HER MOTHER HAD CONTRACTED CAGASTER AND GONE INTO BRAIN DEATH.

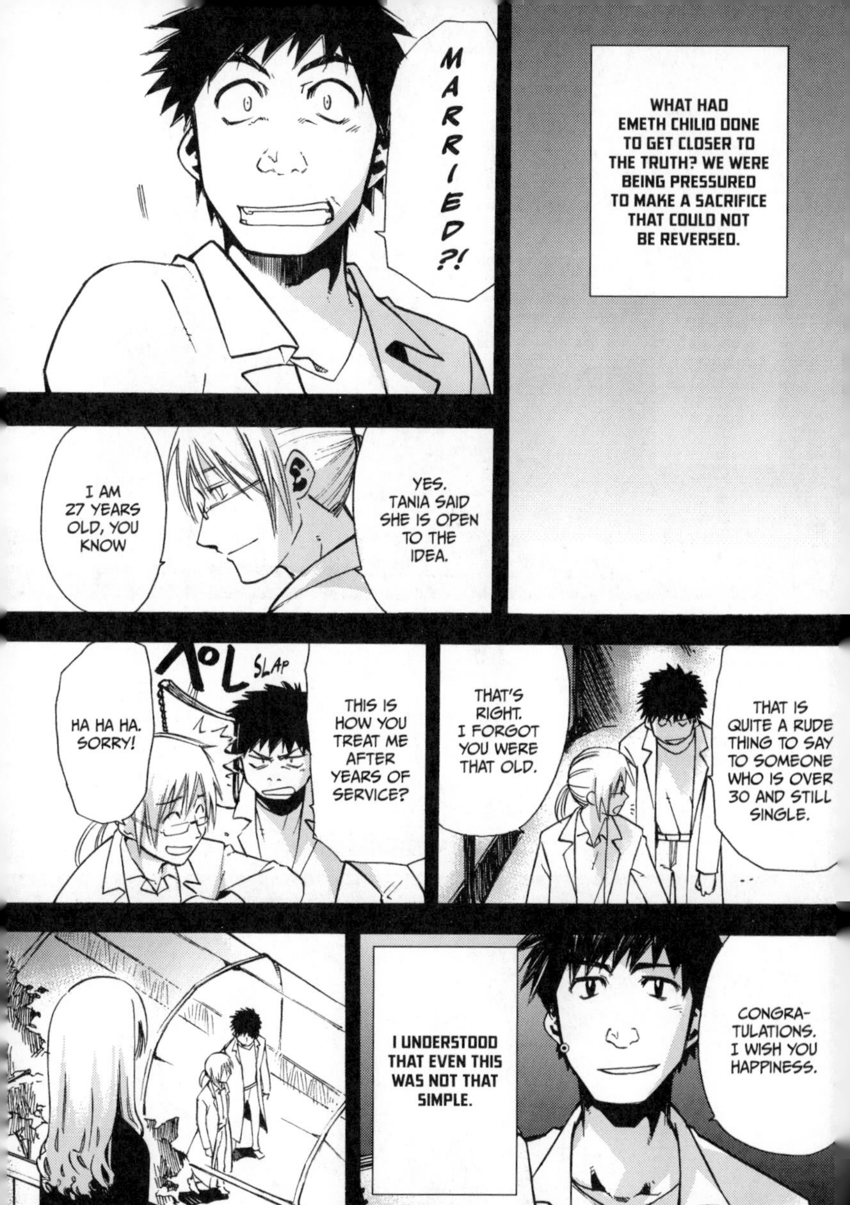
WHAT HAD EMETH CHILIO DONE TO GET CLOSER TO THE TRUTH? WE WERE BEING PRESSURED TO MAKE A SACRIFICE THAT COULD NOT BE REVERSED.
MARRIED?!
YES. TANIA SAID SHE IS OPEN TO THE IDEA.
I AM 27 YEARS OLD, YOU KNOW
THAT IS QUITE A RUDE THING TO SAY TO SOMEONE WHO IS OVER 30 AND STILL SINGLE.
THAT'S RIGHT. I FORGOT YOU WERE THAT OLD.
THIS IS HOW YOU TREAT ME AFTER YEARS OF SERVICE?
SLAP
HA HA HA. SORRY!
CONGRA-TULATIONS. I WISH YOU HAPPINESS.
I UNDERSTOOD THAT EVEN THIS WAS NOT THAT SIMPLE.

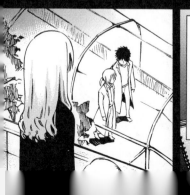

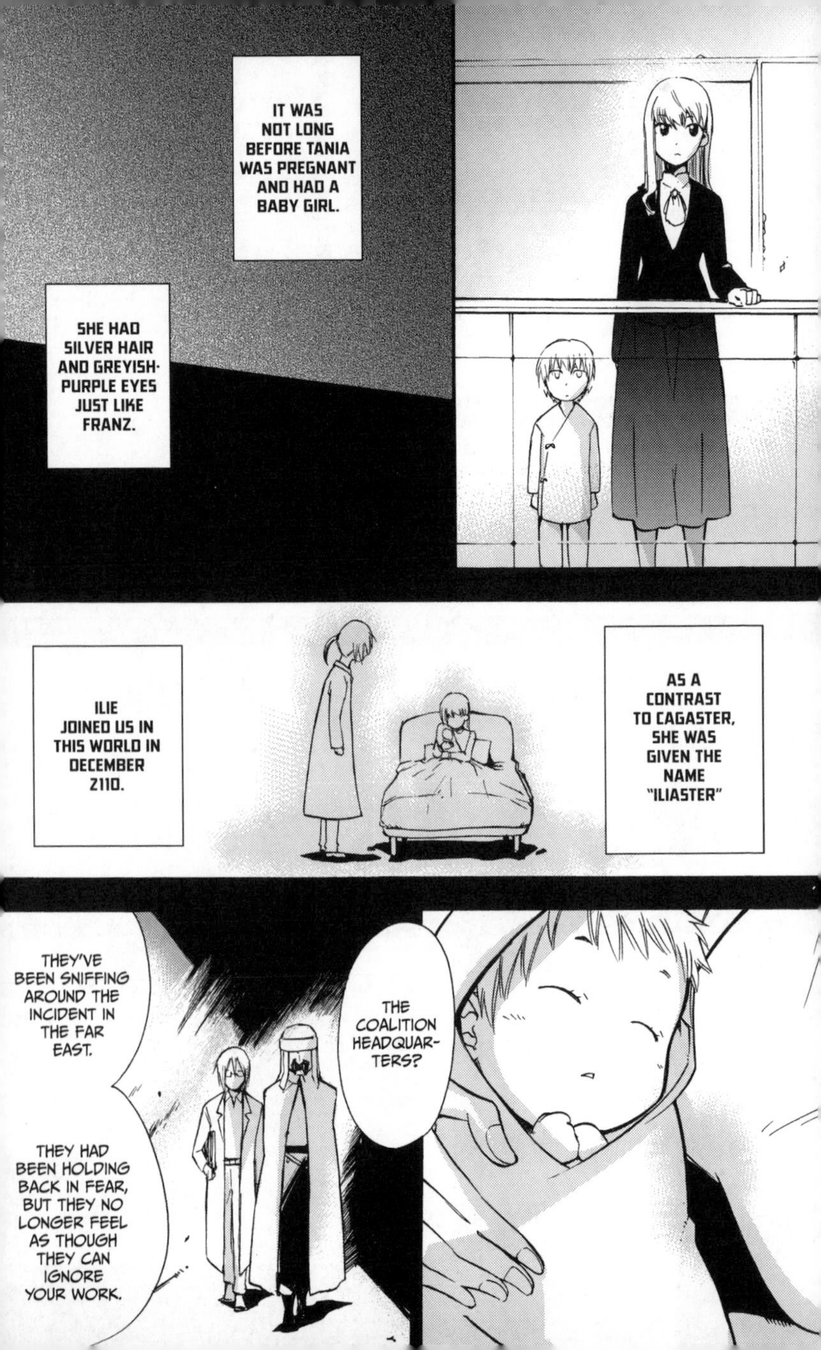
IT WAS NOT LONG BEFORE TANIA WAS PREGNANT AND HAD A BABY GIRL.
SHE HAD SILVER HAIR AND GREYISH-PURPLE EYES JUST LIKE FRANZ.
AS A CONTRAST TO CAGASTER, SHE WAS GIVEN THE NAME "ILIASTER"
ILIE JOINED US IN THIS WORLD IN DECEMBER 2110.
THE COALITION HEADQUARTERS?
THEY'VE BEEN SNIFFING AROUND THE INCIDENT IN THE FAR EAST.
THEY HAD BEEN HOLDING BACK IN FEAR, BUT THEY NO LONGER FEEL AS THOUGH THEY CAN IGNORE YOUR WORK.

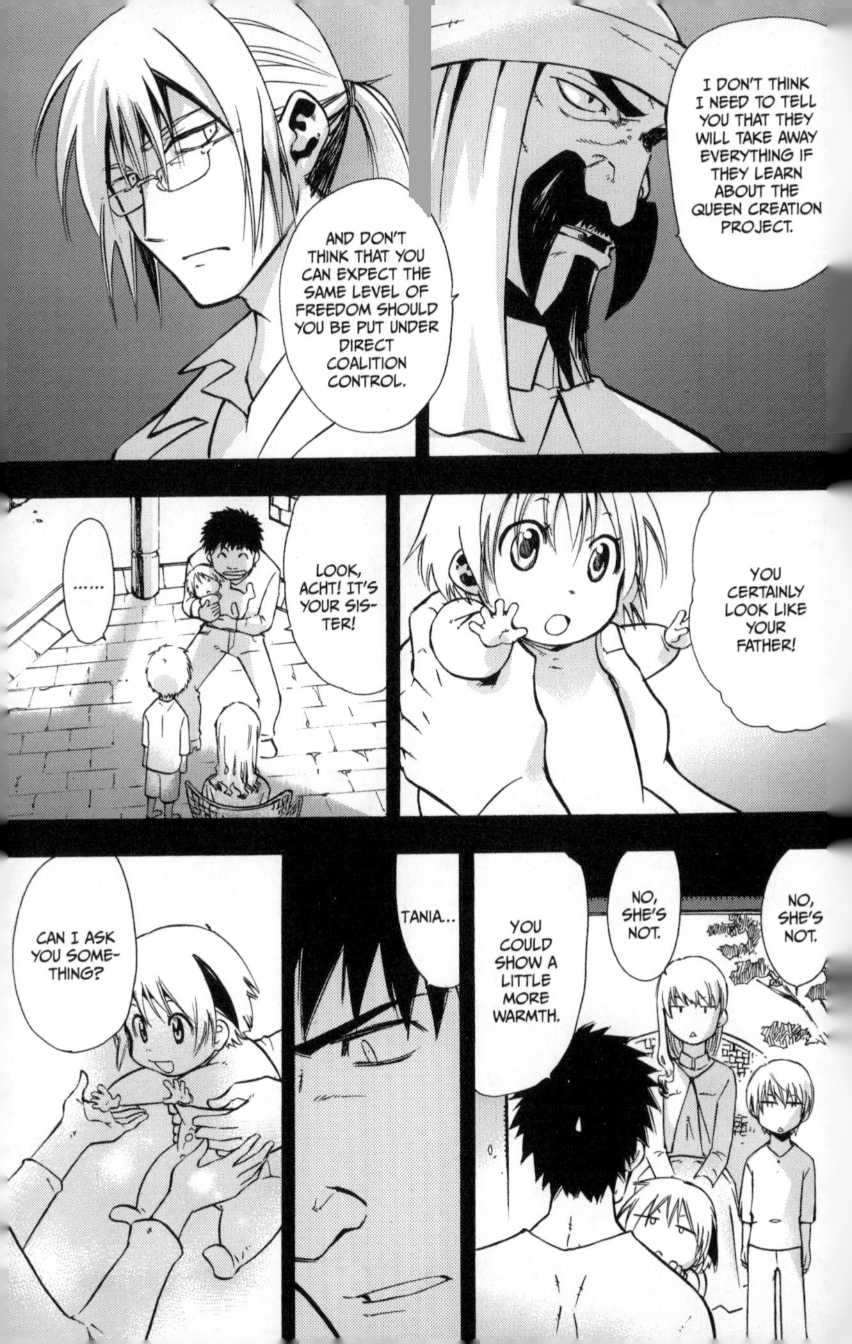
I DON'T THINK I NEED TO TELL YOU THAT THEY WILL TAKE AWAY EVERYTHING IF THEY LEARN ABOUT THE QUEEN CREATION PROJECT.
AND DON'T THINK THAT YOU CAN EXPECT THE SAME LEVEL OF FREEDOM SHOULD YOU BE PUT UNDER DIRECT COALITION CONTROL.
YOU CERTAINLY LOOK LIKE YOUR FATHER!
LOOK, ACHT! IT'S YOUR SIS-TER!
......
NO, SHE'S NOT.
NO, SHE'S NOT.
YOU COULD SHOW A LITTLE MORE WARMTH.
TANIA...
CAN I ASK YOU SOME-THING?

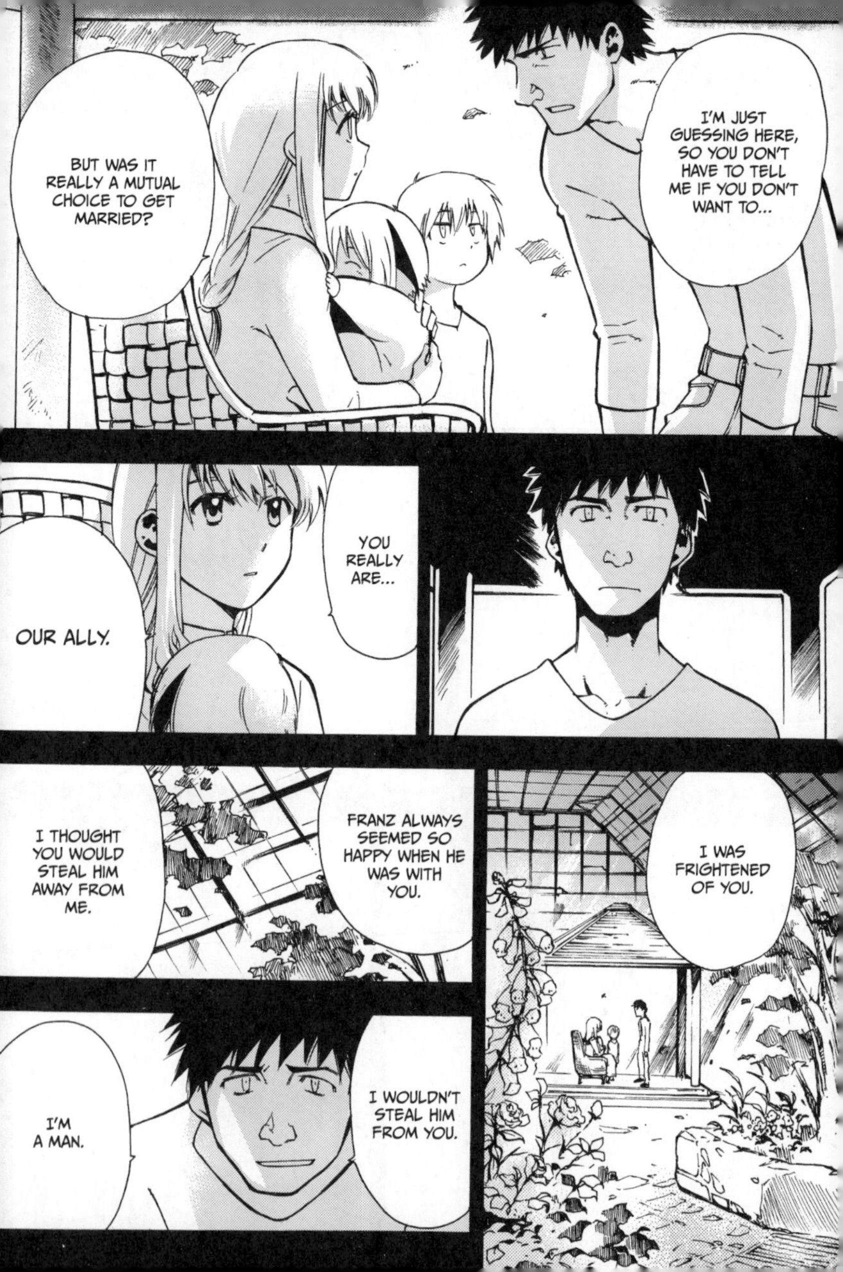
I'M JUST GUESSING HERE, SO YOU DON'T HAVE TO TELL ME IF YOU DON'T WANT TO...
BUT WAS IT REALLY A MUTUAL CHOICE TO GET MARRIED?
YOU REALLY ARE...
OUR ALLY.
I WAS FRIGHTENED OF YOU.
FRANZ ALWAYS SEEMED SO HAPPY WHEN HE WAS WITH YOU.
I THOUGHT YOU WOULD STEAL HIM AWAY FROM ME.
I WOULDN'T STEAL HIM FROM YOU.
I'M A MAN.

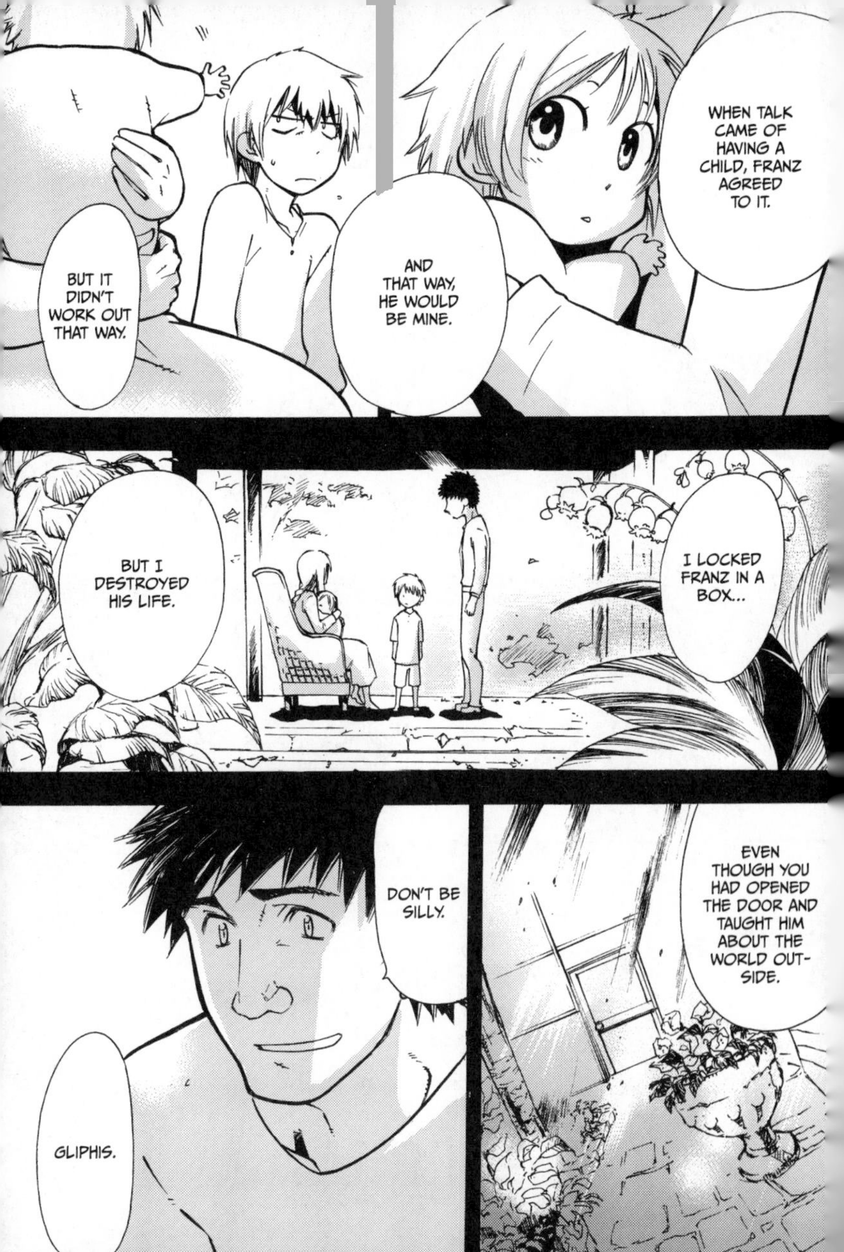
WHEN TALK CAME OF HAVING A CHILD, FRANZ AGREED TO IT.
AND THAT WAY, HE WOULD BE MINE.
BUT IT DIDN'T WORK OUT THAT WAY.
I LOCKED FRANZ IN A BOX...
BUT I DESTROYED HIS LIFE.
EVEN THOUGH YOU HAD OPENED THE DOOR AND TAUGHT HIM ABOUT THE WORLD OUT-SIDE.
DON'T BE SILLY.
GLIPHIS.

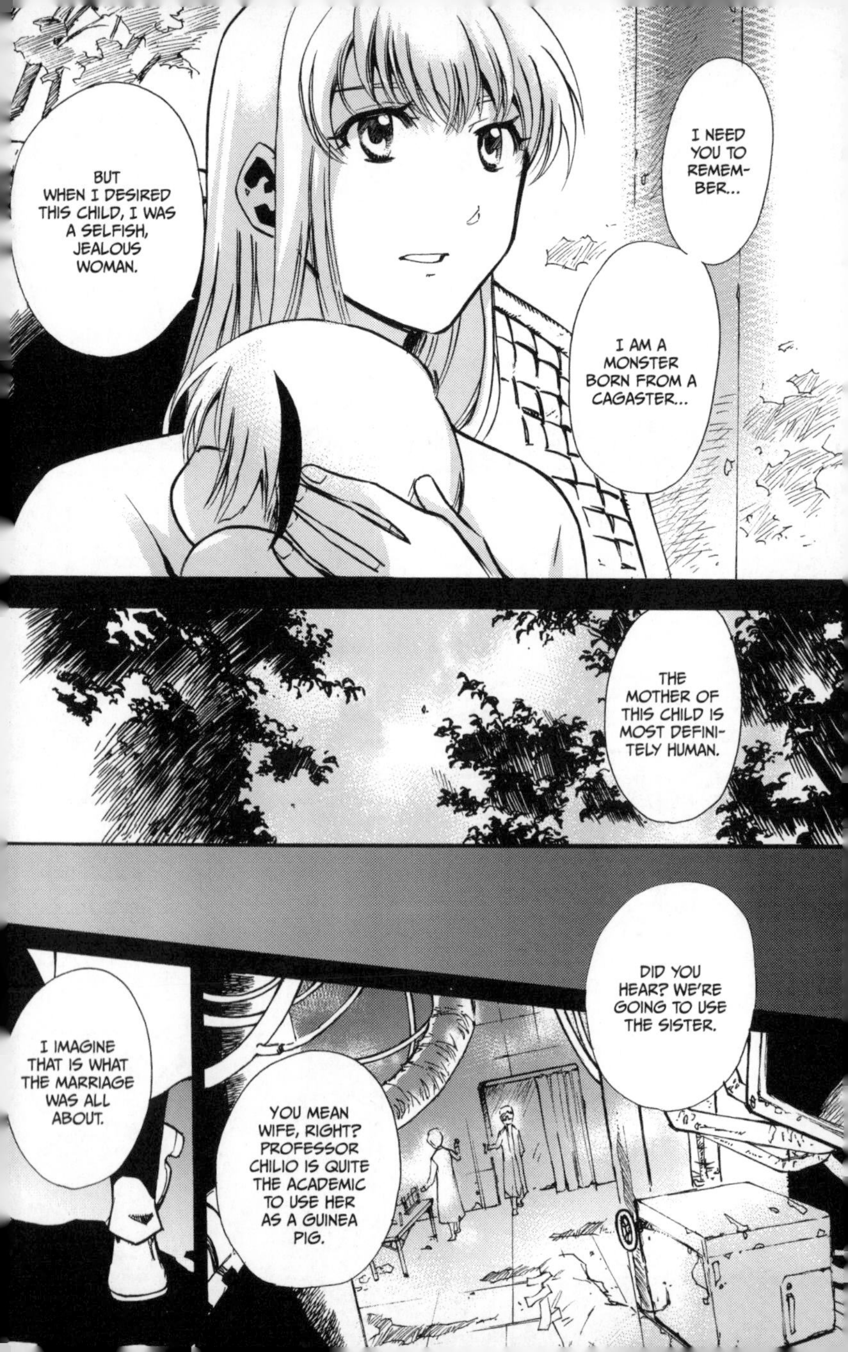
I NEED YOU TO REMEMBER...
I AM A MONSTER BORN FROM A CAGASTER...
BUT WHEN I DESIRED THIS CHILD, I WAS A SELFISH, JEALOUS WOMAN.
THE MOTHER OF THIS CHILD IS MOST DEFINITELY HUMAN.
DID YOU HEAR? WE'RE GOING TO USE THE SISTER.
YOU MEAN WIFE, RIGHT? PROFESSOR CHILIO IS QUITE THE ACADEMIC TO USE HER AS A GUINEA PIG.
I IMAGINE THAT IS WHAT THE MARRIAGE WAS ALL ABOUT.

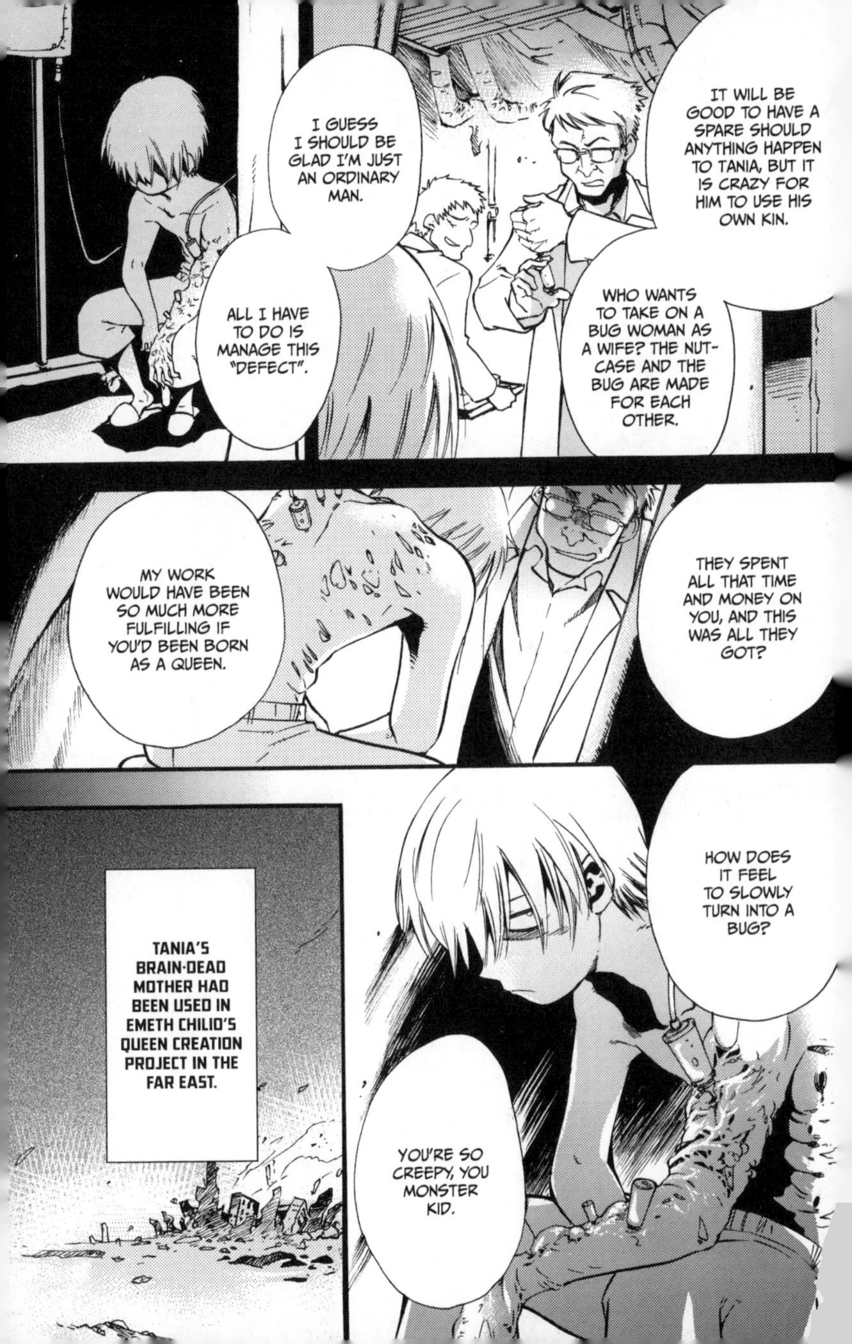
IT WILL BE GOOD TO HAVE A SPARE SHOULD ANYTHING HAPPEN TO TANIA, BUT IT IS CRAZY FOR HIM TO USE HIS OWN KIN.
WHO WANTS TO TAKE ON A BUG WOMAN AS A WIFE? THE NUT-CASE AND THE BUG ARE MADE FOR EACH OTHER.
I GUESS I SHOULD BE GLAD I'M JUST AN ORDINARY MAN.
ALL I HAVE TO DO IS MANAGE THIS "DEFECT".
THEY SPENT ALL THAT TIME AND MONEY ON YOU, AND THIS WAS ALL THEY GOT?
MY WORK WOULD HAVE BEEN SO MUCH MORE FULFILLING IF YOU'D BEEN BORN AS A QUEEN.
HOW DOES IT FEEL TO SLOWLY TURN INTO A BUG?
YOU'RE SO CREEPY, YOU MONSTER KID.
TANIA'S BRAIN-DEAD MOTHER HAD BEEN USED IN EMETH CHILIO'S QUEEN CREATION PROJECT IN THE FAR EAST.

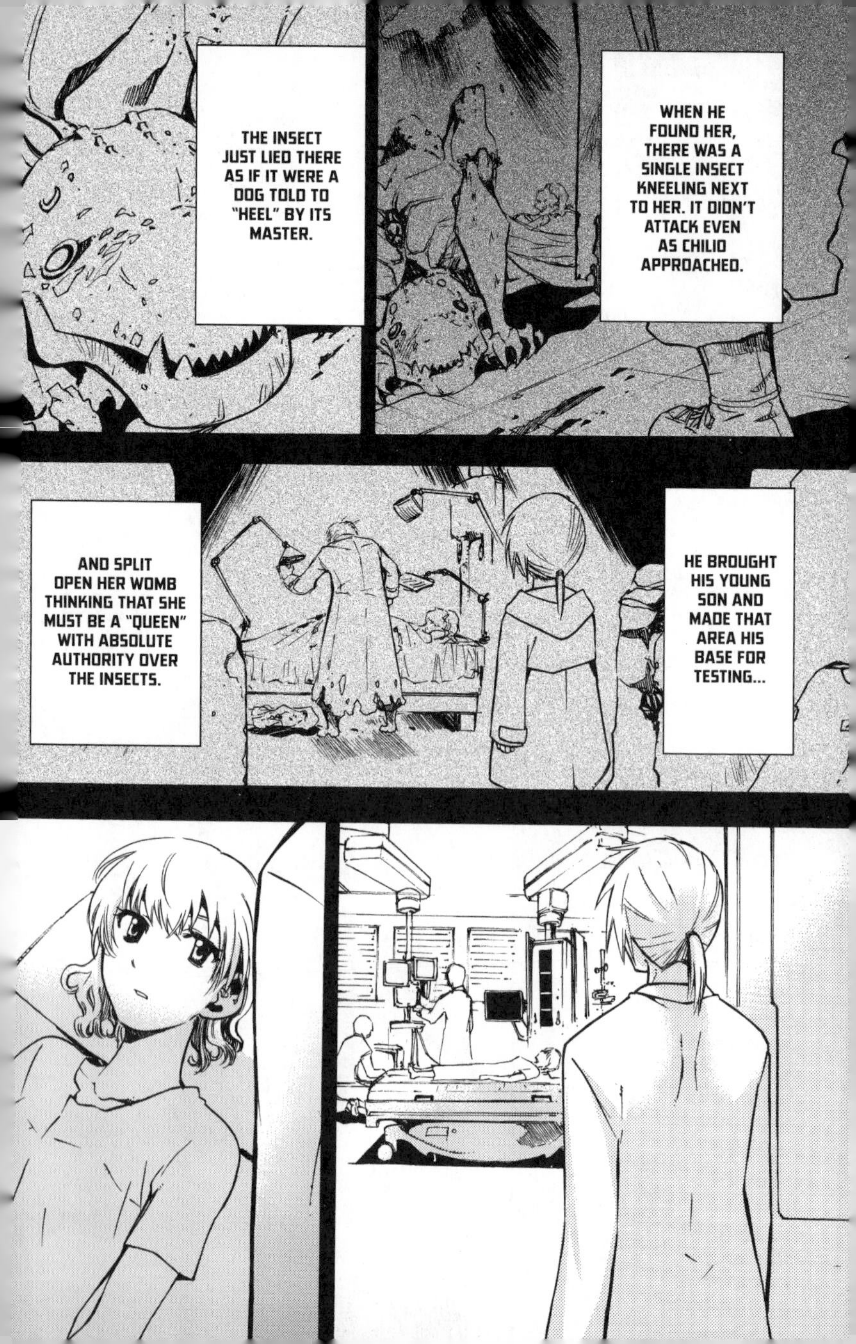
WHEN HE FOUND HER, THERE WAS A SINGLE INSECT KNEELING NEXT TO HER. IT DIDN'T ATTACK EVEN AS CHILIO APPROACHED.
THE INSECT JUST LIED THERE AS IF IT WERE A DOG TOLD TO "HEEL" BY ITS MASTER.
HE BROUGHT HIS YOUNG SON AND MADE THAT AREA HIS BASE FOR TESTING...
AND SPLIT OPEN HER WOMB THINKING THAT SHE MUST BE A "QUEEN" WITH ABSOLUTE AUTHORITY OVER THE INSECTS.

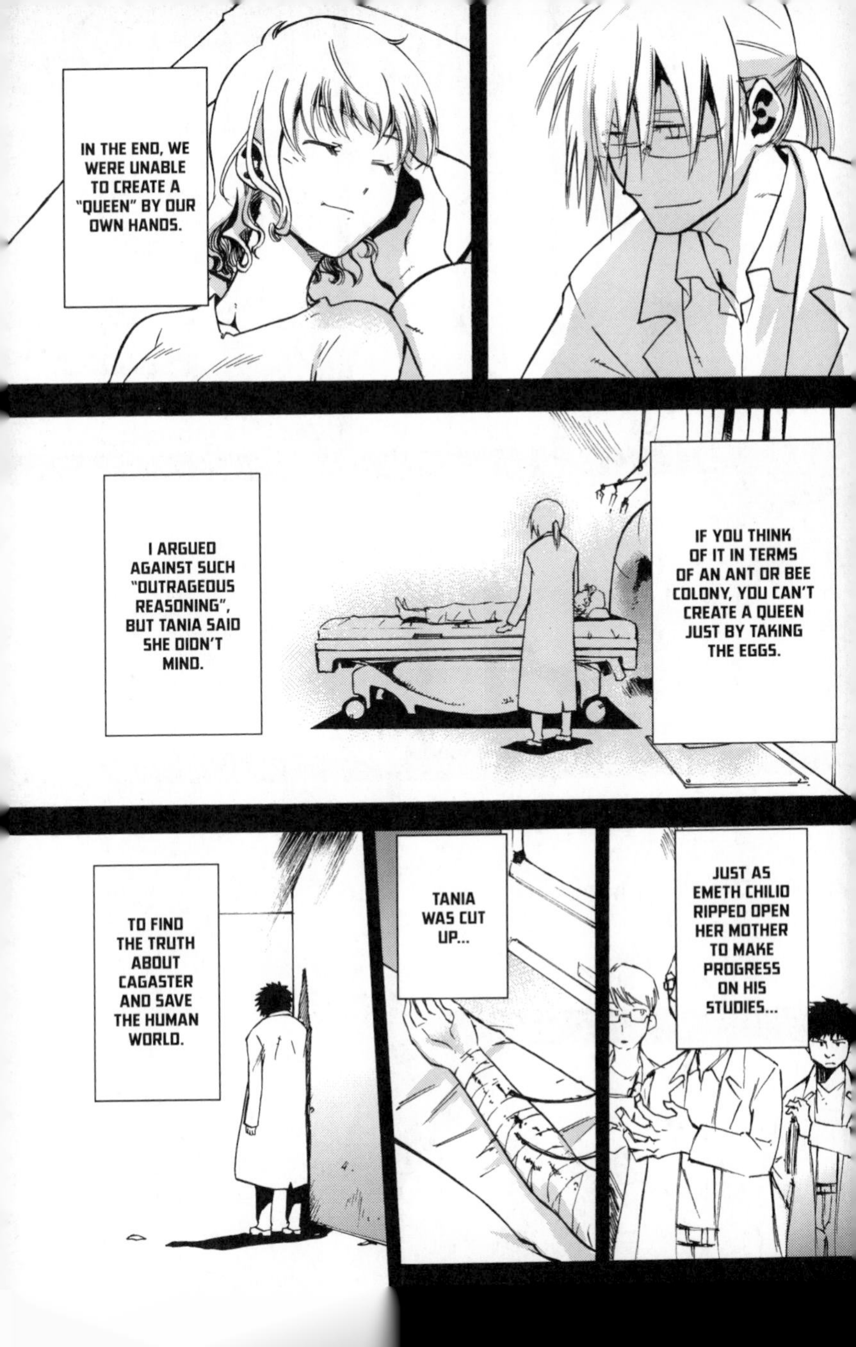
IN THE END, WE WERE UNABLE TO CREATE A "QUEEN" BY OUR OWN HANDS.
IF YOU THINK OF IT IN TERMS OF AN ANT OR BEE COLONY, YOU CAN'T CREATE A QUEEN JUST BY TAKING THE EGGS.
I ARGUED AGAINST SUCH "OUTRAGEOUS REASONING", BUT TANIA SAID SHE DIDN'T MIND.
JUST AS EMETH CHILIO RIPPED OPEN HER MOTHER TO MAKE PROGRESS ON HIS STUDIES...
TANIA WAS CUT UP...
TO FIND THE TRUTH ABOUT CAGASTER AND SAVE THE HUMAN WORLD.

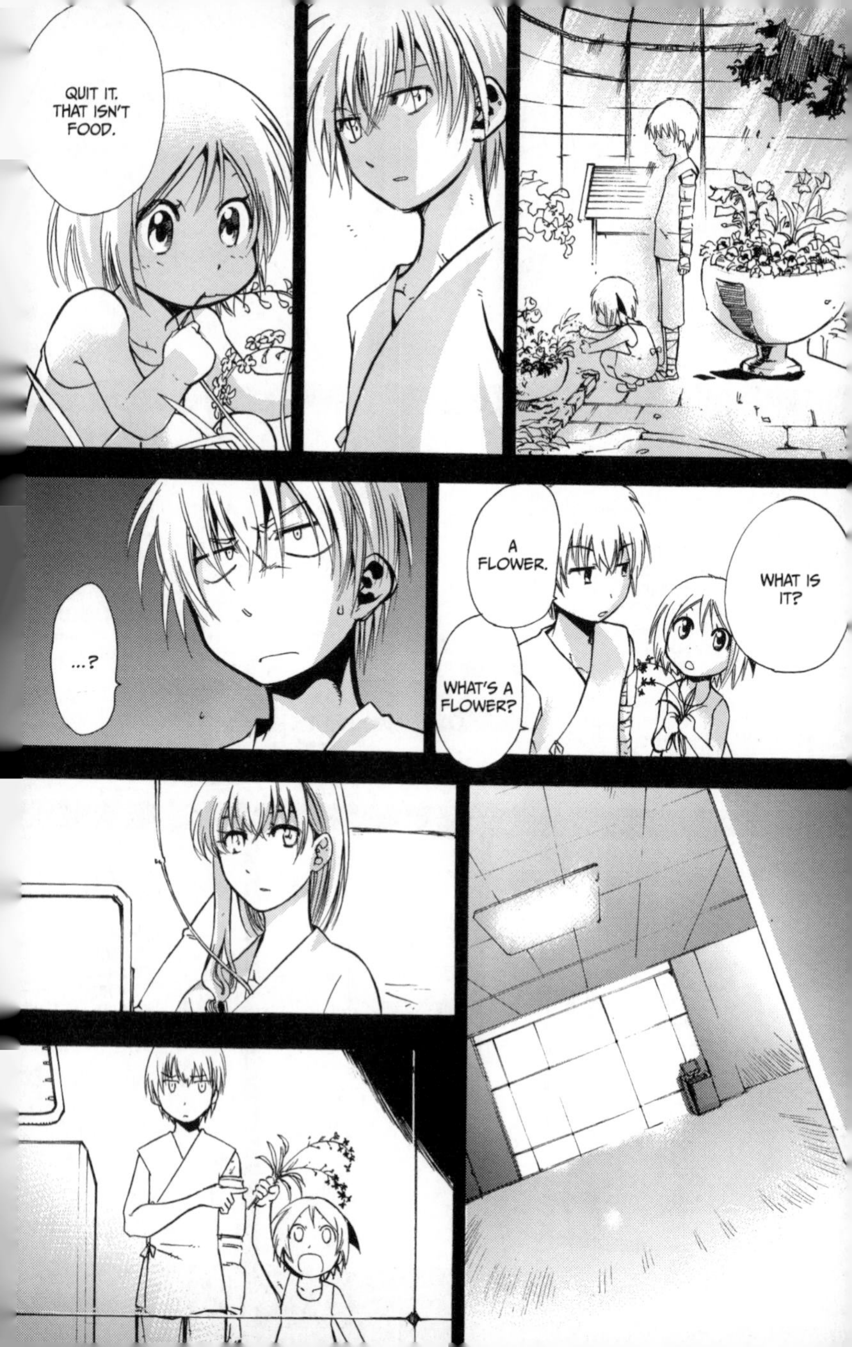
QUIT IT. THAT ISN'T FOOD.
WHAT IS IT?
A FLOWER.
WHAT'S A FLOWER?
...?

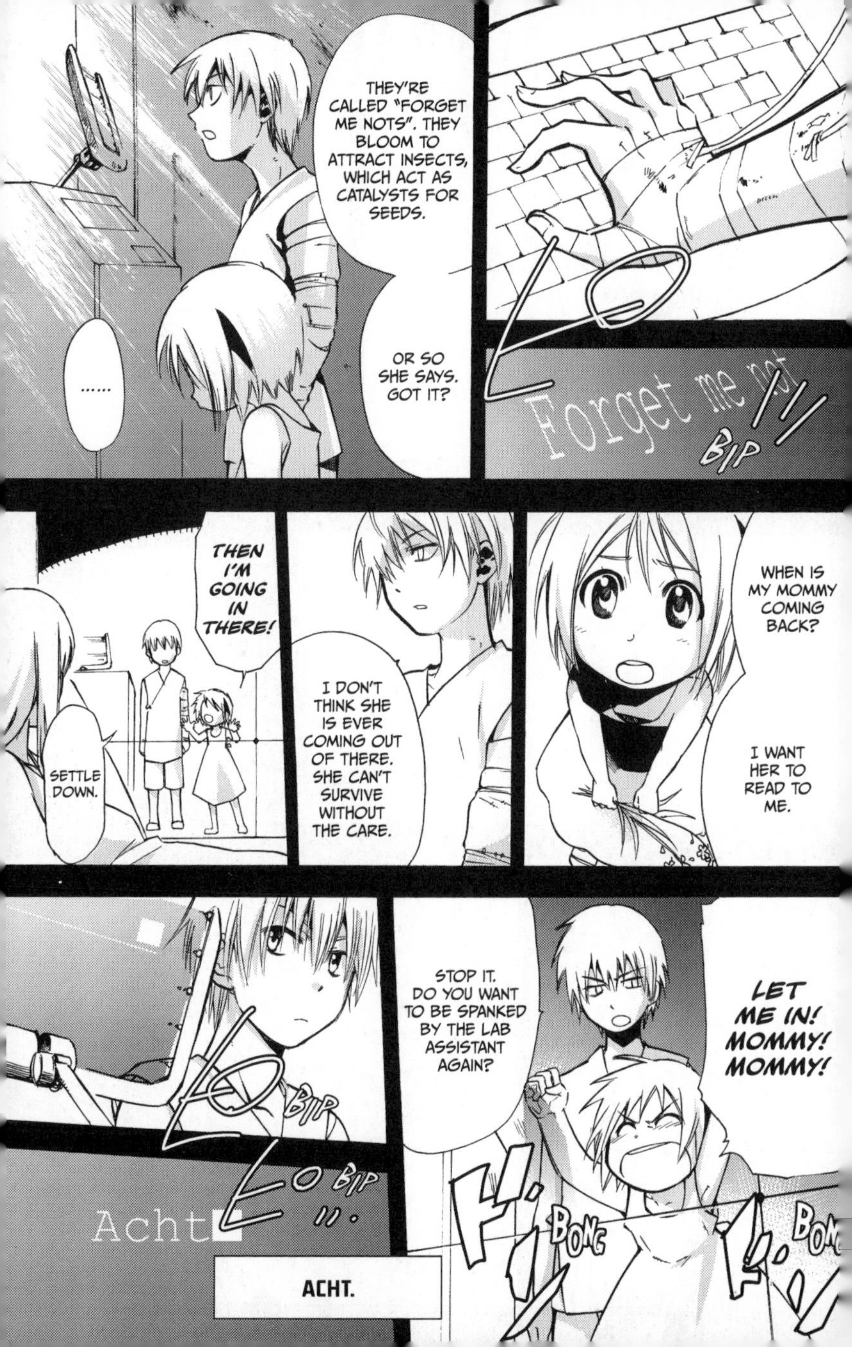
Forget me not
BIP
THEY'RE CALLED "FORGET ME NOTS". THEY BLOOM TO ATTRACT INSECTS, WHICH ACT AS CATALYSTS FOR SEEDS.
OR SO SHE SAYS. GOT IT?
......
WHEN IS MY MOMMY COMING BACK?
I WANT HER TO READ TO ME.
I DON'T THINK SHE IS EVER COMING OUT OF THERE. SHE CAN'T SURVIVE WITHOUT THE CARE.
THEN I'M GOING IN THERE!
SETTLE DOWN.
LET ME IN! MOMMY! MOMMY!
STOP IT. DO YOU WANT TO BE SPANKED BY THE LAB ASSISTANT AGAIN?
BONG
BONG
BIP
BIP
Acht
ACHT.

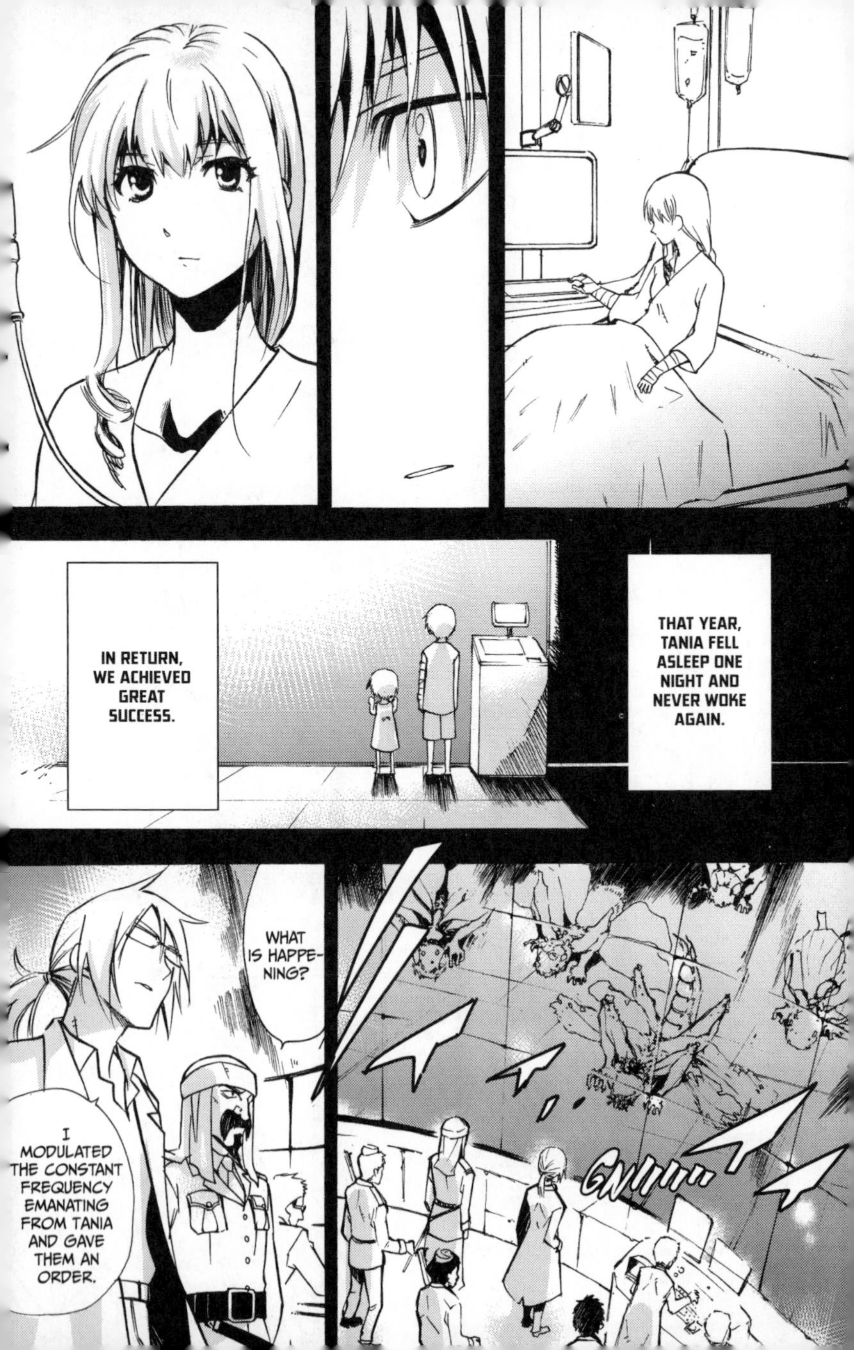
THAT YEAR, TANIA FELL ASLEEP ONE NIGHT AND NEVER WOKE AGAIN.
IN RETURN, WE ACHIEVED GREAT SUCCESS.
WHAT IS HAPPENING?
I MODULATED THE CONSTANT FREQUENCY EMANATING FROM TANIA AND GAVE THEM AN ORDER.

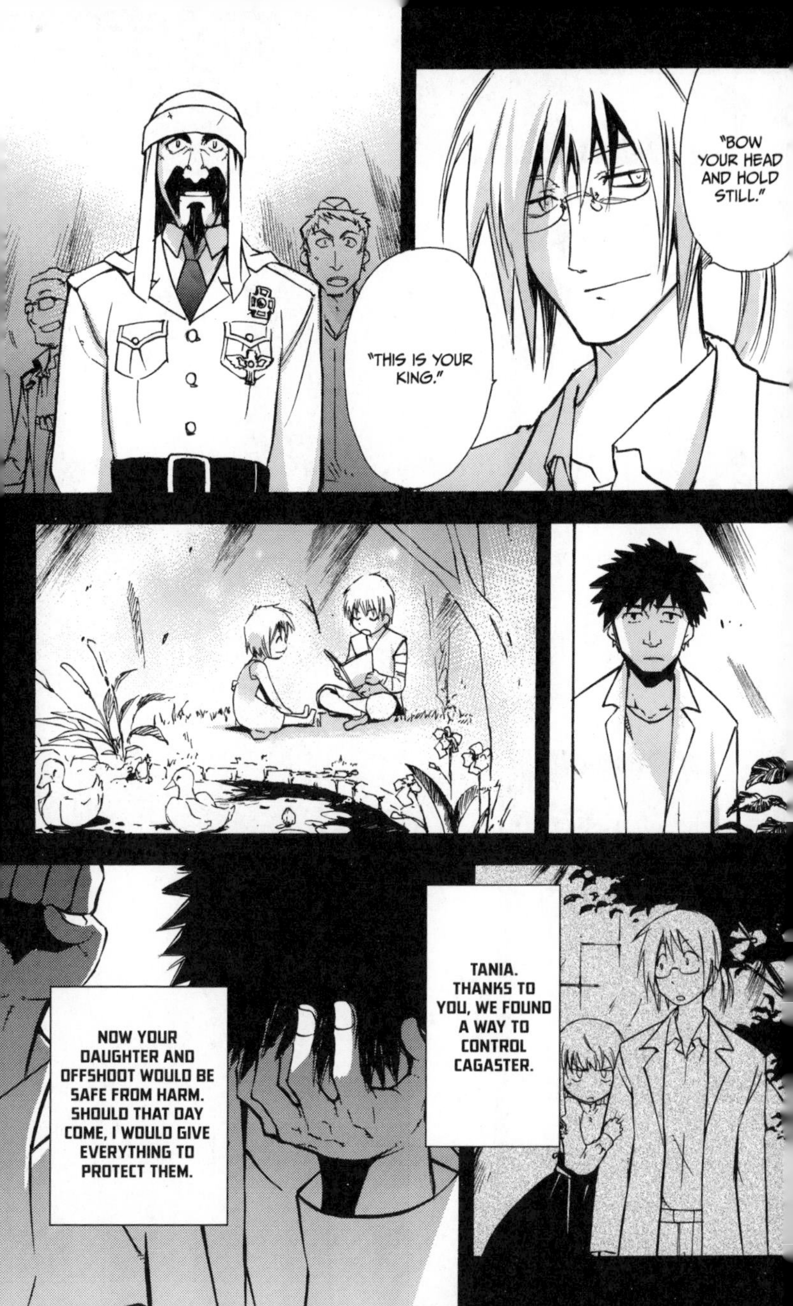
"BOW YOUR HEAD AND HOLD STILL."
"THIS IS YOUR KING."
TANIA. THANKS TO YOU, WE FOUND A WAY TO CONTROL CAGASTER.
NOW YOUR DAUGHTER AND OFFSHOOT WOULD BE SAFE FROM HARM. SHOULD THAT DAY COME, I WOULD GIVE EVERYTHING TO PROTECT THEM.

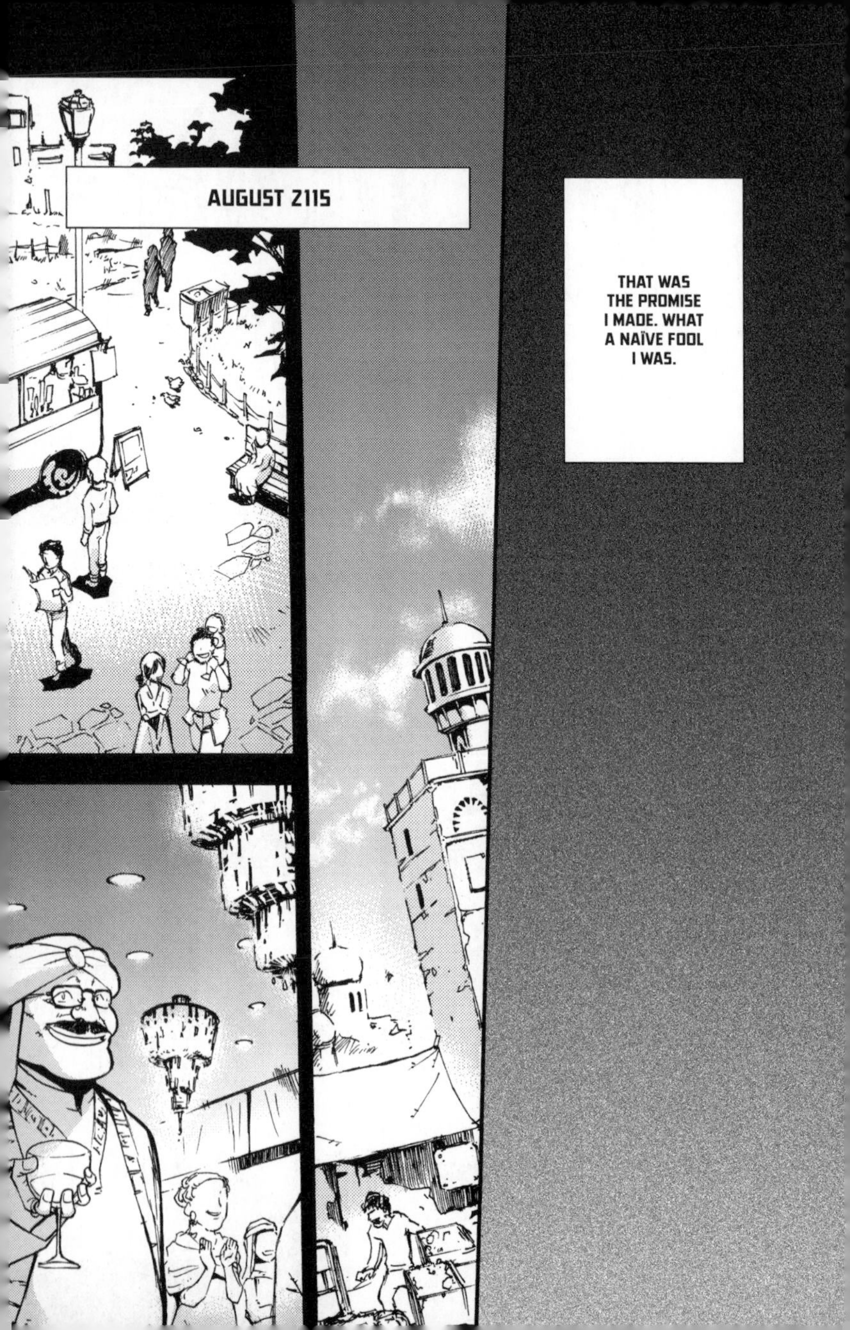
THAT WAS THE PROMISE I MADE. WHAT A NAÏVE FOOL I WAS.
AUGUST 2115

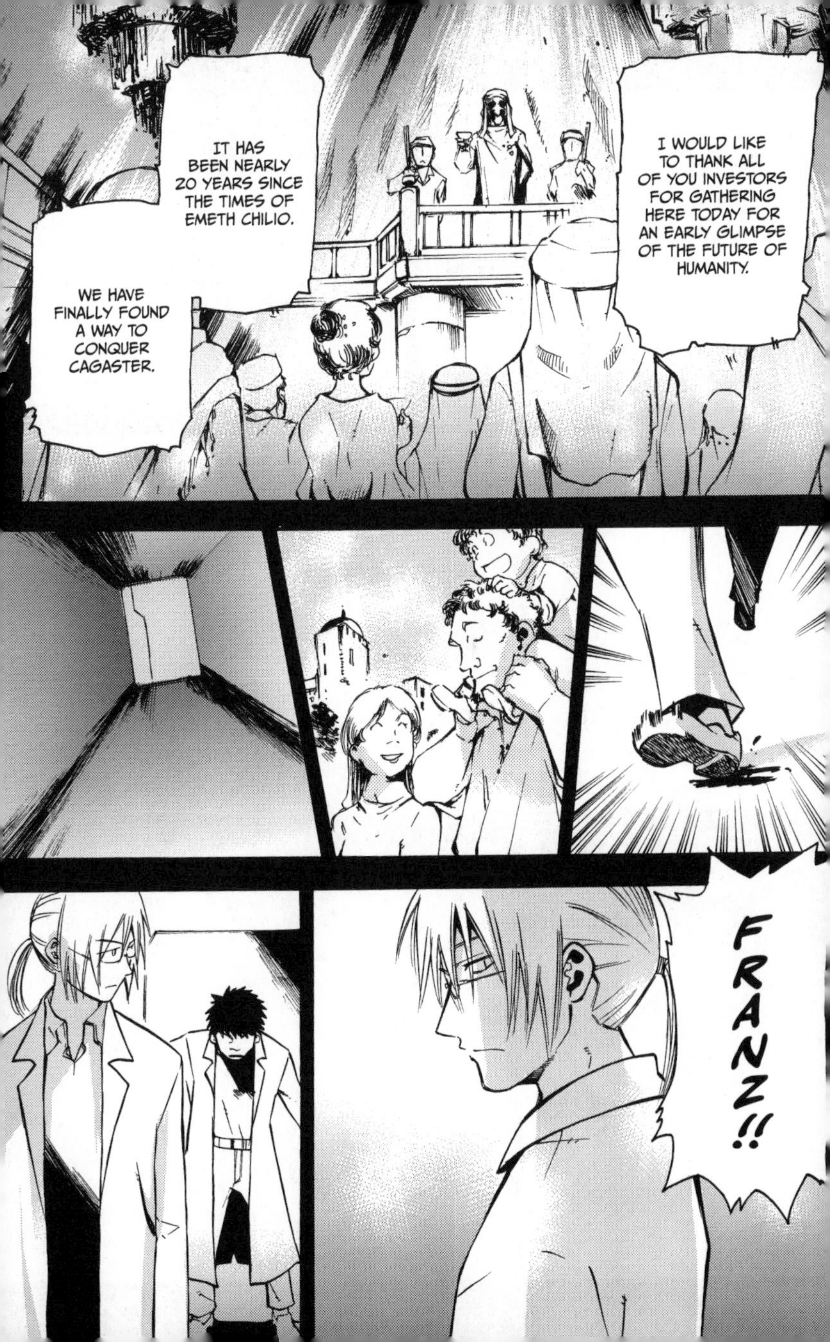
I WOULD LIKE TO THANK ALL OF YOU INVESTORS FOR GATHERING HERE TODAY FOR AN EARLY GLIMPSE OF THE FUTURE OF HUMANITY.
IT HAS BEEN NEARLY 20 YEARS SINCE THE TIMES OF EMETH CHILIO.
WE HAVE FINALLY FOUND A WAY TO CONQUER CAGASTER.
FRANZ!!

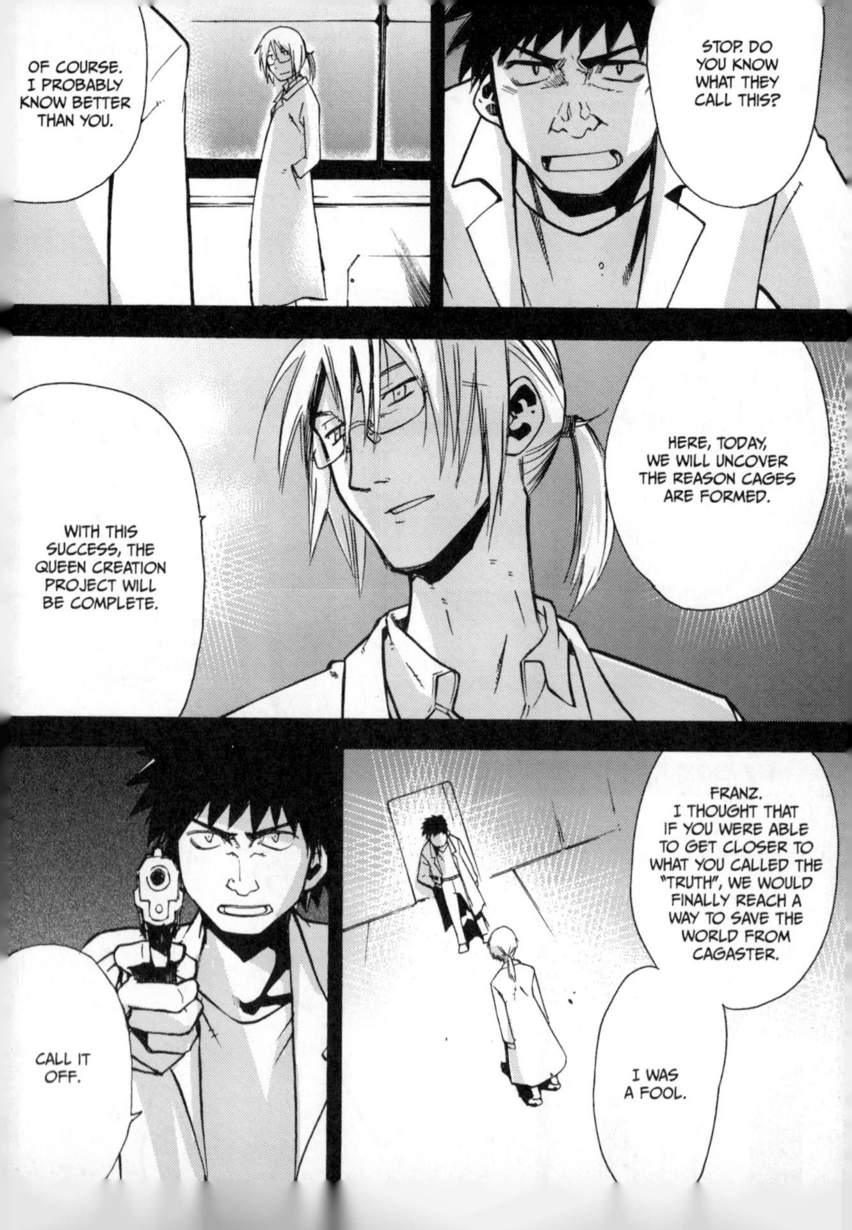
STOP. DO YOU KNOW WHAT THEY CALL THIS?
OF COURSE. I PROBABLY KNOW BETTER THAN YOU.
HERE, TODAY, WE WILL UNCOVER THE REASON CAGES ARE FORMED.
WITH THIS SUCCESS, THE QUEEN CREATION PROJECT WILL BE COMPLETE.
FRANZ. I THOUGHT THAT IF YOU WERE ABLE TO GET CLOSER TO WHAT YOU CALLED THE "TRUTH", WE WOULD FINALLY REACH A WAY TO SAVE THE WORLD FROM CAGASTER.
I WAS A FOOL.
CALL IT OFF.

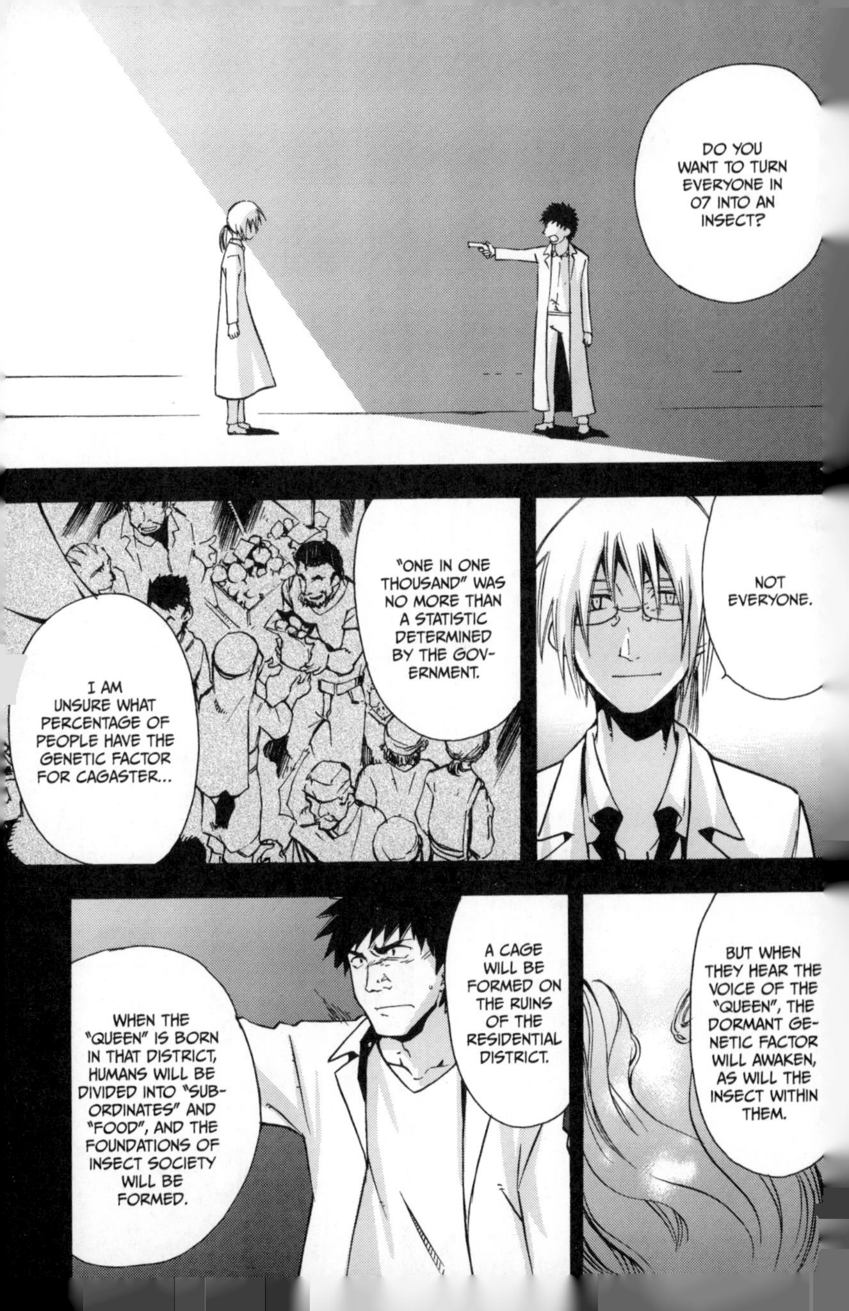
DO YOU WANT TO TURN EVERYONE IN 07 INTO AN INSECT?
NOT EVERYONE.
"ONE IN ONE THOUSAND" WAS NO MORE THAN A STATISTIC DETERMINED BY THE GOV-ERNMENT.
I AM UNSURE WHAT PERCENTAGE OF PEOPLE HAVE THE GENETIC FACTOR FOR CAGASTER...
BUT WHEN THEY HEAR THE VOICE OF THE "QUEEN", THE DORMANT GE-NETIC FACTOR WILL AWAKEN, AS WILL THE INSECT WITHIN THEM.
A CAGE WILL BE FORMED ON THE RUINS OF THE RESIDENTIAL DISTRICT.
WHEN THE "QUEEN" IS BORN IN THAT DISTRICT, HUMANS WILL BE DIVIDED INTO "SUB-ORDINATES" AND "FOOD", AND THE FOUNDATIONS OF INSECT SOCIETY WILL BE FORMED.

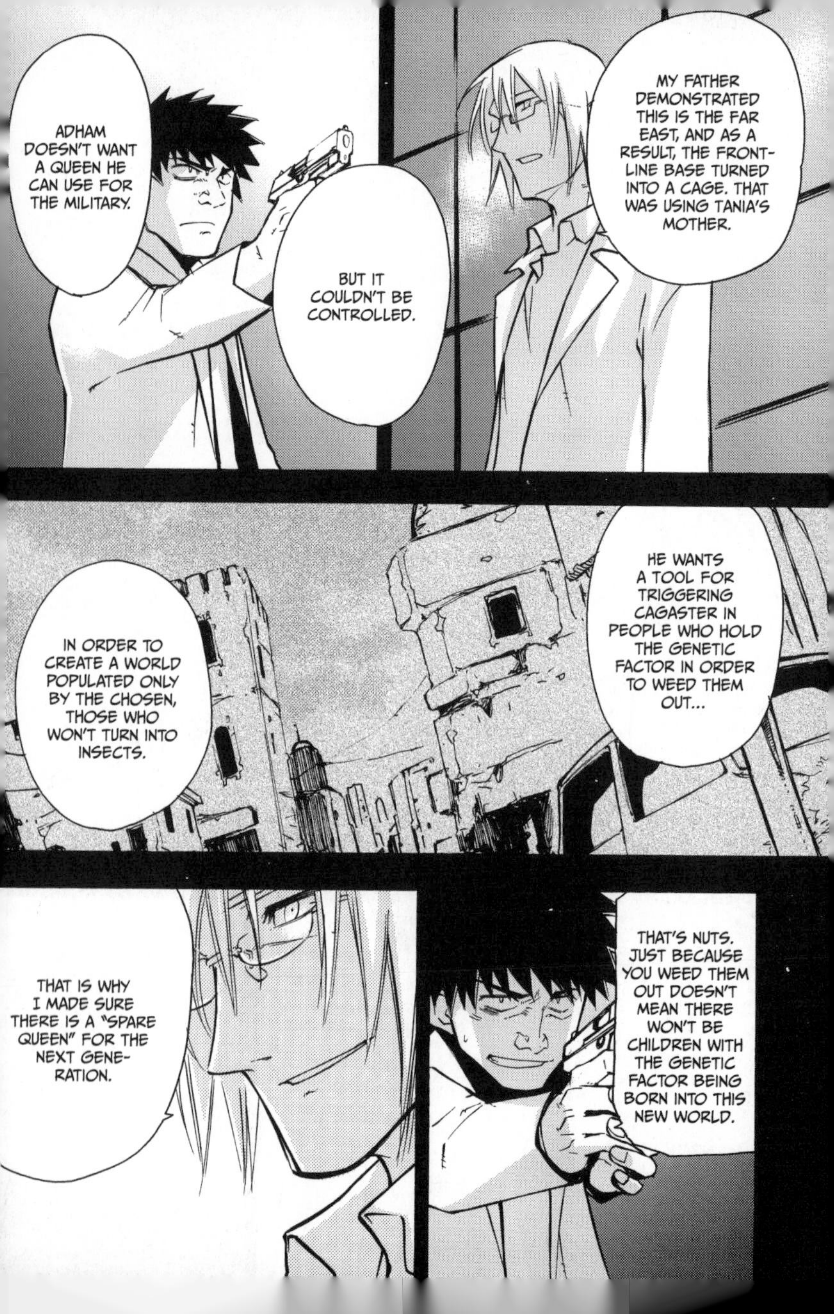
MY FATHER DEMONSTRATED THIS IS THE FAR EAST, AND AS A RESULT, THE FRONT-LINE BASE TURNED INTO A CAGE. THAT WAS USING TANIA'S MOTHER.
BUT IT COULDN'T BE CONTROLLED.
ADHAM DOESN'T WANT A QUEEN HE CAN USE FOR THE MILITARY.
HE WANTS A TOOL FOR TRIGGERING CAGASTER IN PEOPLE WHO HOLD THE GENETIC FACTOR IN ORDER TO WEED THEM OUT...
IN ORDER TO CREATE A WORLD POPULATED ONLY BY THE CHOSEN, THOSE WHO WON'T TURN INTO INSECTS.
THAT'S NUTS. JUST BECAUSE YOU WEED THEM OUT DOESN'T MEAN THERE WON'T BE CHILDREN WITH THE GENETIC FACTOR BEING BORN INTO THIS NEW WORLD.
THAT IS WHY I MADE SURE THERE IS A "SPARE QUEEN" FOR THE NEXT GENE-RATION.

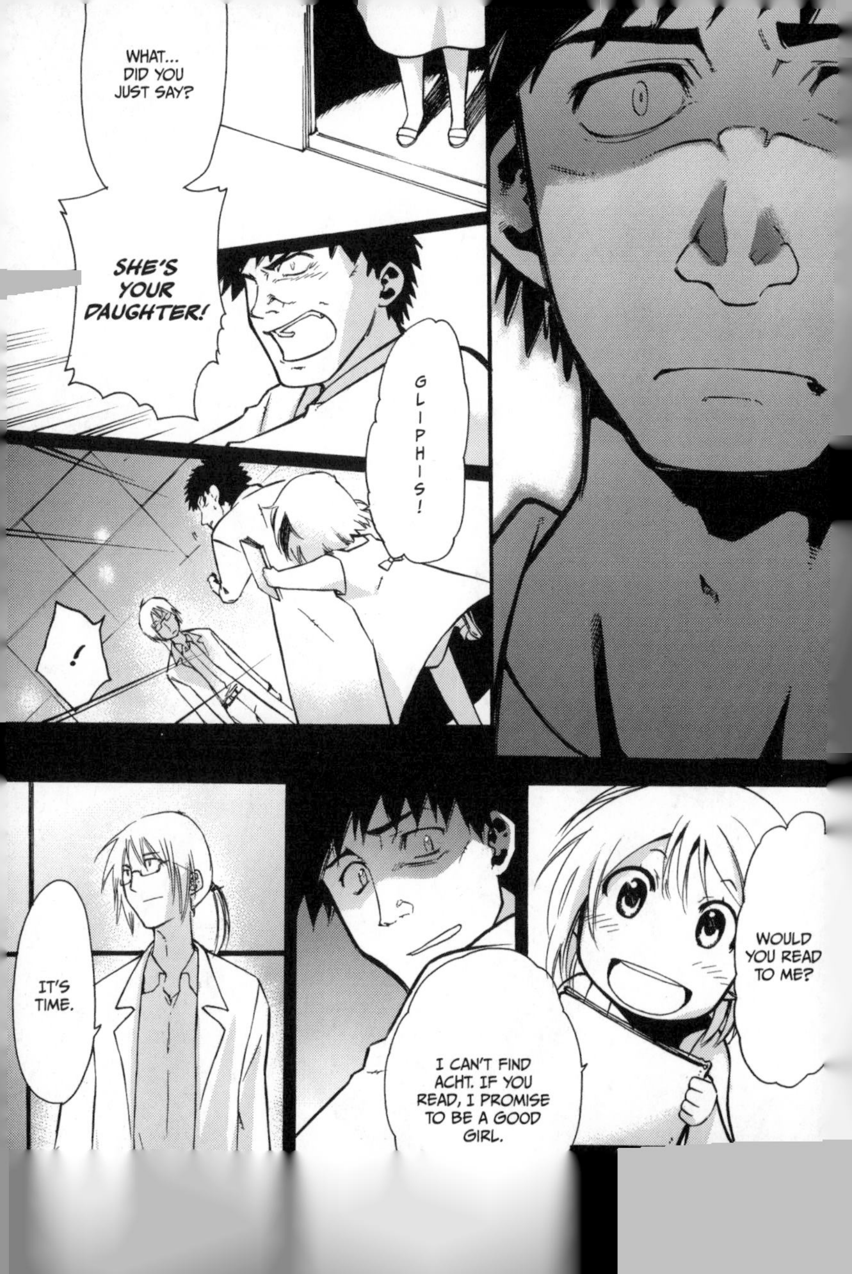
WHAT... DID YOU JUST SAY?
SHE'S YOUR DAUGHTER!
GLIPHIS!
!
WOULD YOU READ TO ME?
I CAN'T FIND ACHT. IF YOU READ, I PROMISE TO BE A GOOD GIRL.
IT'S TIME.

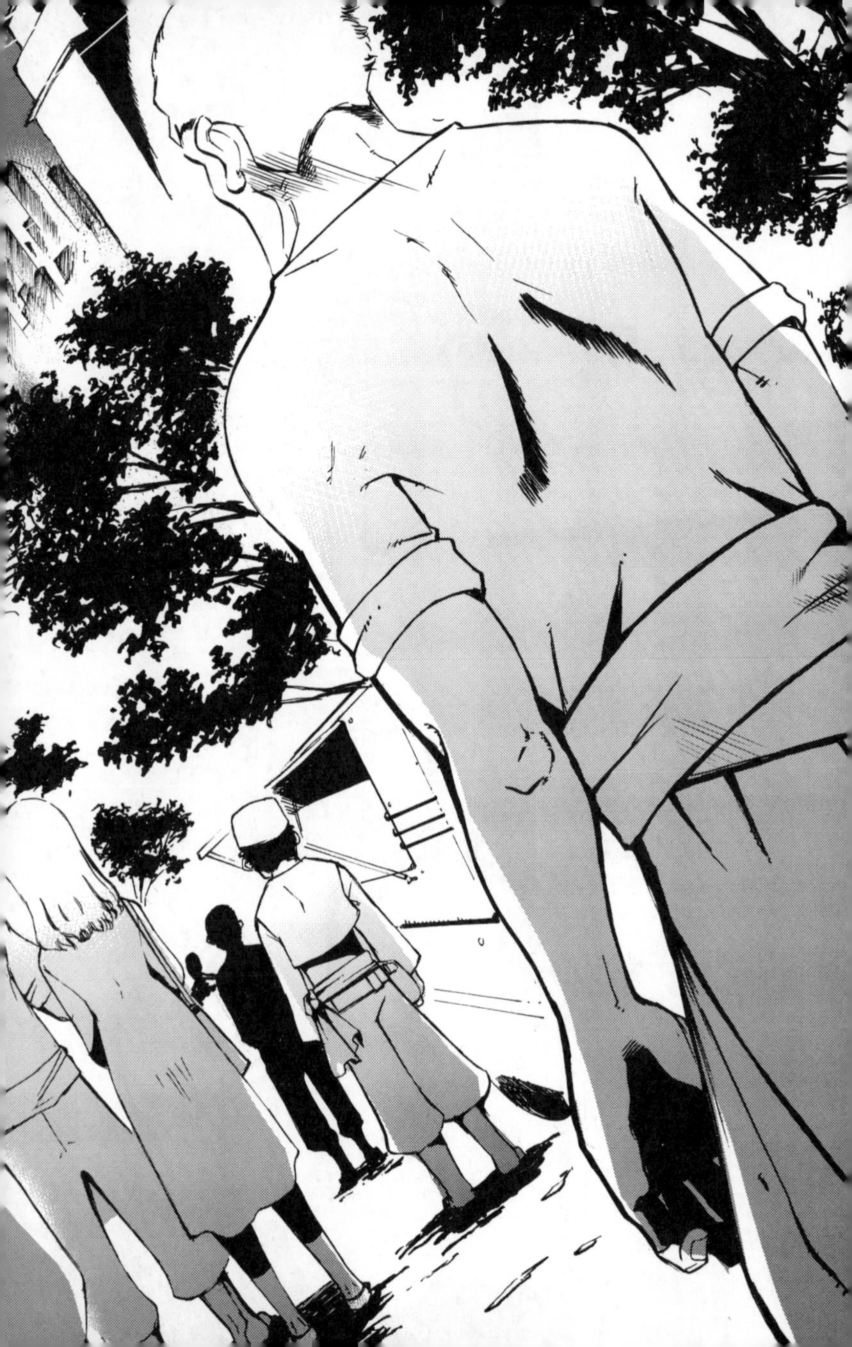

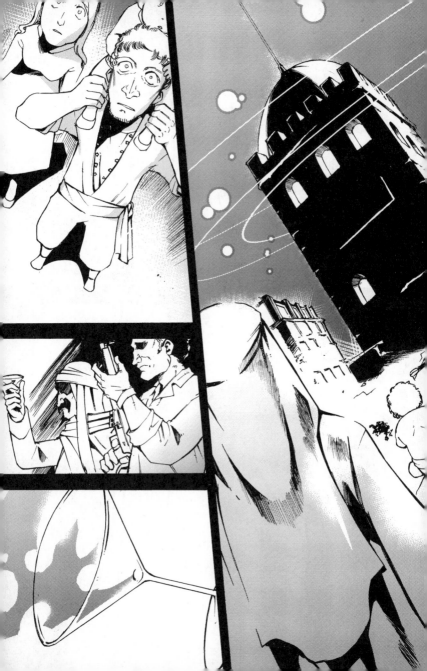

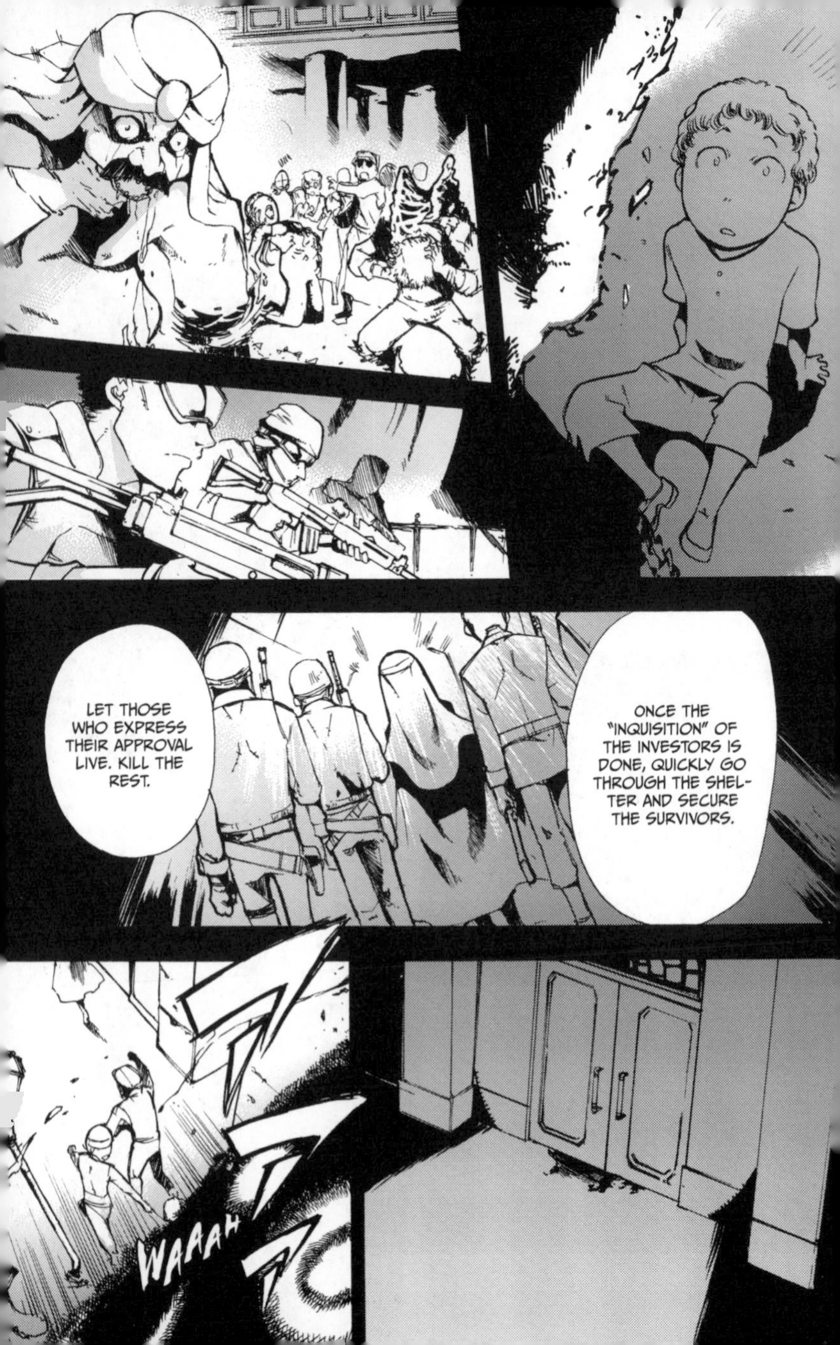
ONCE THE "INQUISITION" OF THE INVESTORS IS DONE, QUICKLY GO THROUGH THE SHEL-TER AND SECURE THE SURVIVORS.
LET THOSE WHO EXPRESS THEIR APPROVAL LIVE. KILL THE REST.
WAAAH

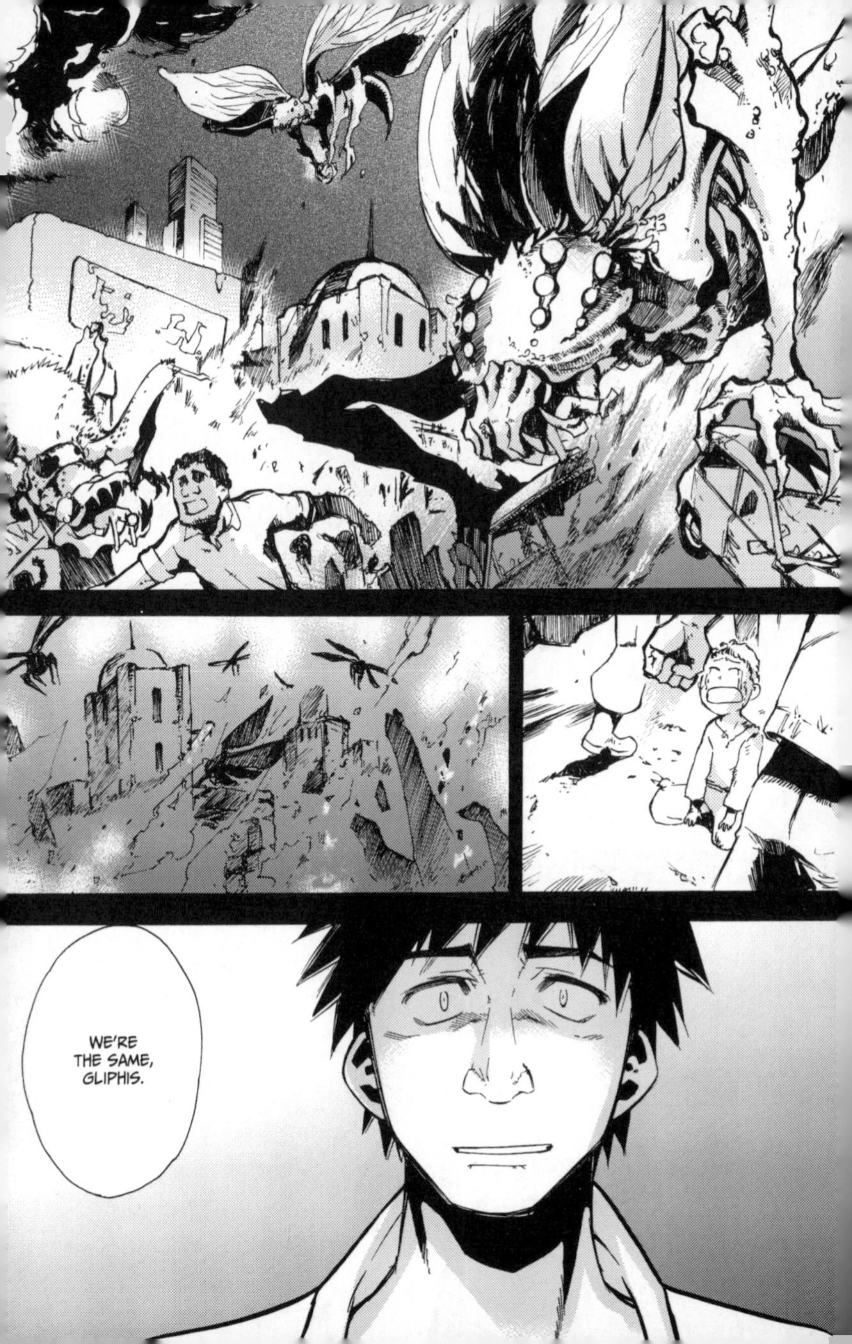
WE'RE THE SAME, GLIPHIS.

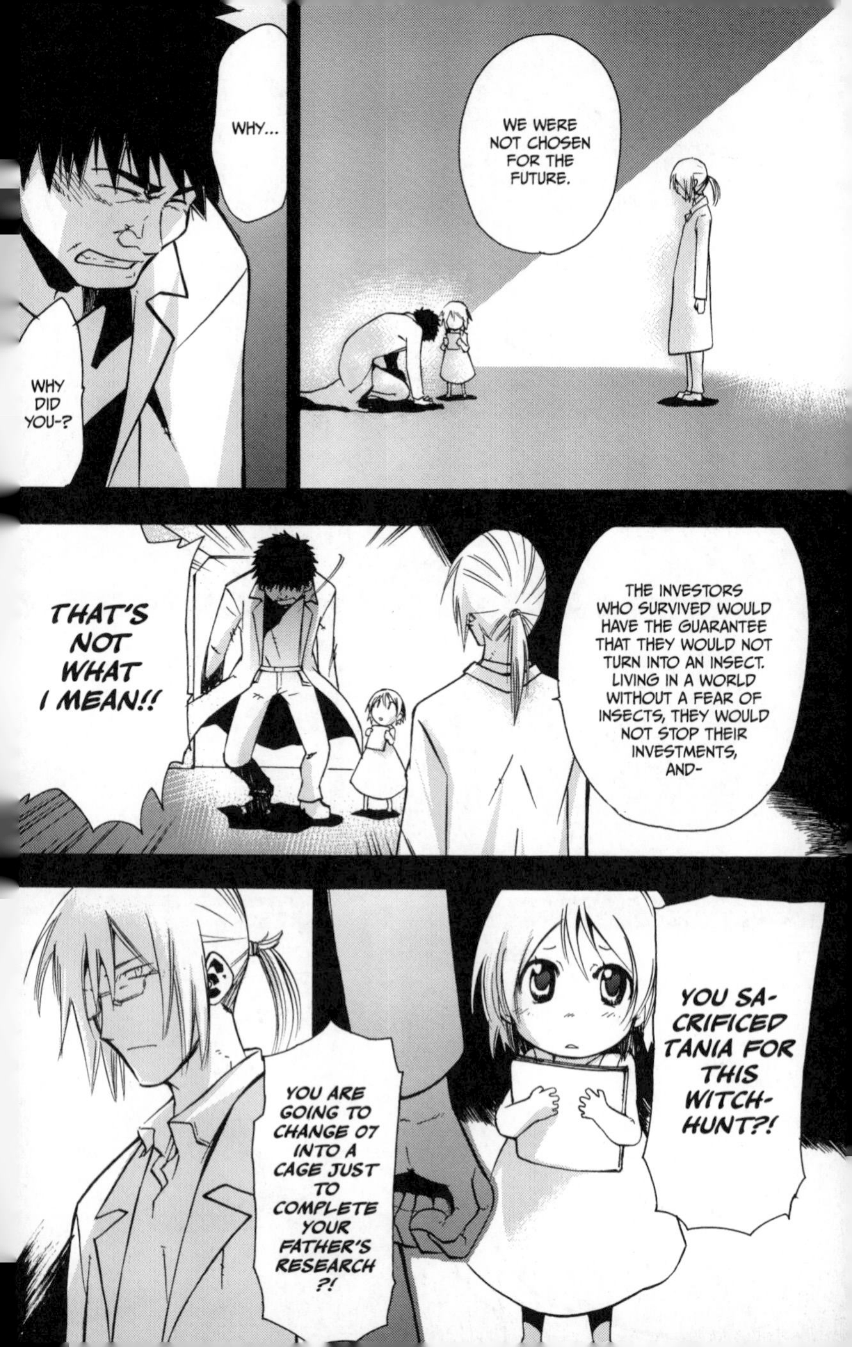
WE WERE NOT CHOSEN FOR THE FUTURE.
WHY...
WHY DID YOU-?
THE INVESTORS WHO SURVIVED WOULD HAVE THE GUARANTEE THAT THEY WOULD NOT TURN INTO AN INSECT. LIVING IN A WORLD WITHOUT A FEAR OF INSECTS, THEY WOULD NOT STOP THEIR INVESTMENTS, AND-
THAT'S NOT WHAT I MEAN!!
YOU SA-CRIFICED TANIA FOR THIS WITCH-HUNT?!
YOU ARE GOING TO CHANGE 07 INTO A CAGE JUST TO COMPLETE YOUR FATHER'S RESEARCH ?!

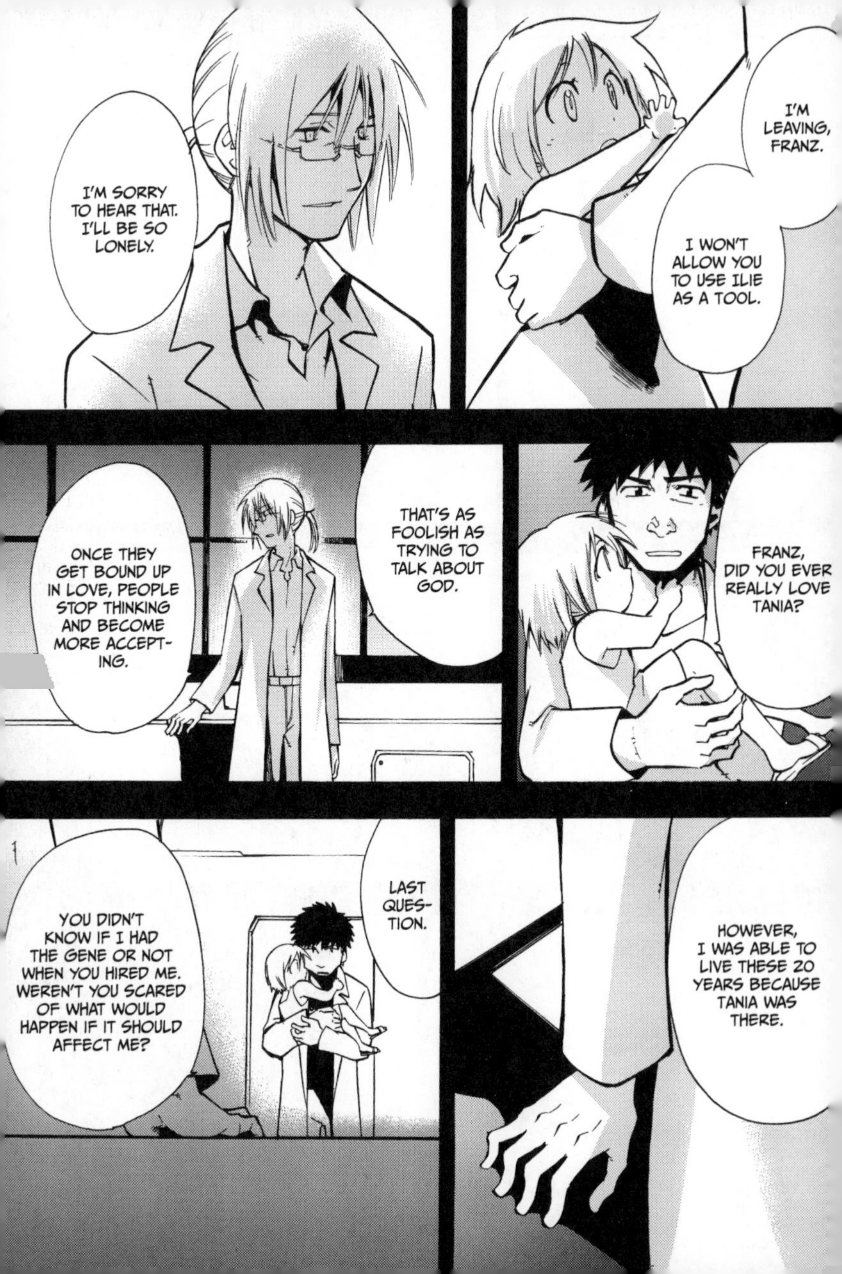
I'M LEAVING, FRANZ.
I WON'T ALLOW YOU TO USE ILIE AS A TOOL.
I'M SORRY TO HEAR THAT. I'LL BE SO LONELY.
FRANZ, DID YOU EVER REALLY LOVE TANIA?
THAT'S AS FOOLISH AS TRYING TO TALK ABOUT GOD.
ONCE THEY GET BOUND UP IN LOVE, PEOPLE STOP THINKING AND BECOME MORE ACCEPT-ING.
HOWEVER, I WAS ABLE TO LIVE THESE 20 YEARS BECAUSE TANIA WAS THERE.
LAST QUES-TION.
YOU DIDN'T KNOW IF I HAD THE GENE OR NOT WHEN YOU HIRED ME. WEREN'T YOU SCARED OF WHAT WOULD HAPPEN IF IT SHOULD AFFECT ME?

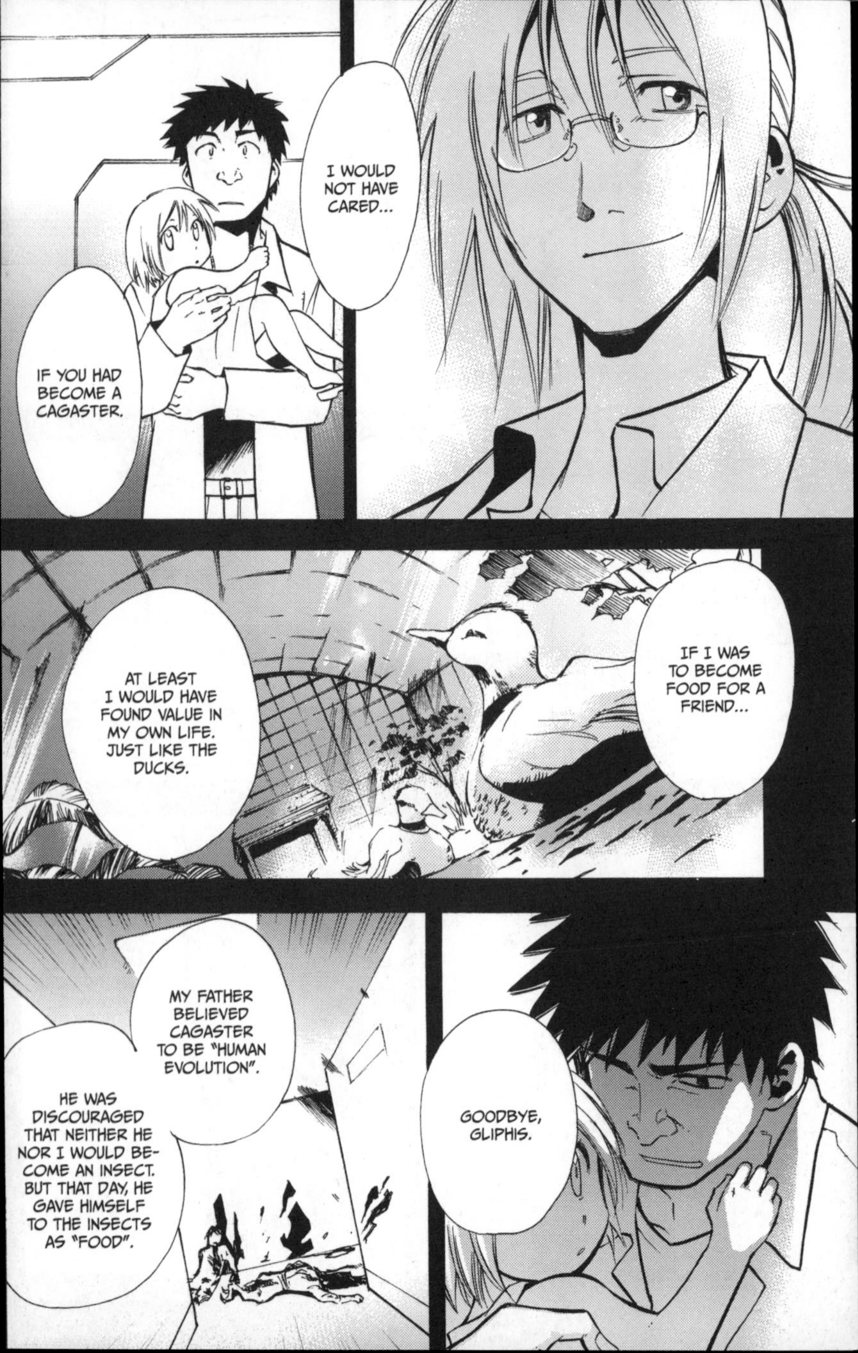
I WOULD NOT HAVE CARED...
IF YOU HAD BECOME A CAGASTER.
IF I WAS TO BECOME FOOD FOR A FRIEND...
AT LEAST I WOULD HAVE FOUND VALUE IN MY OWN LIFE. JUST LIKE THE DUCKS.
GOODBYE, GLIPHIS.
MY FATHER BELIEVED CAGASTER TO BE "HUMAN EVOLUTION".
HE WAS DISCOURAGED THAT NEITHER HE NOR I WOULD BE-COME AN INSECT. BUT THAT DAY, HE GAVE HIMSELF TO THE INSECTS AS "FOOD".

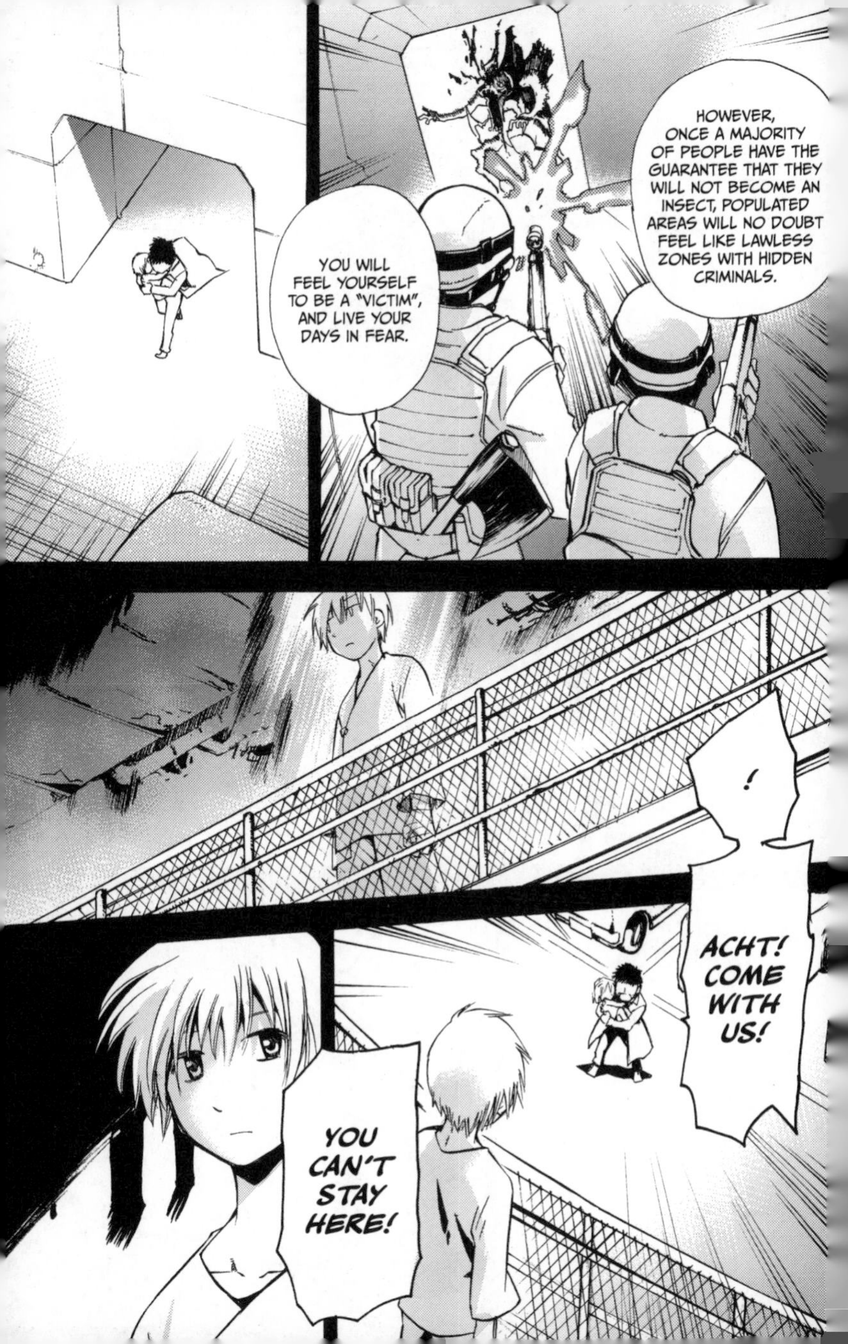
HOWEVER, ONCE A MAJORITY OF PEOPLE HAVE THE GUARANTEE THAT THEY WILL NOT BECOME AN INSECT, POPULATED AREAS WILL NO DOUBT FEEL LIKE LAWLESS ZONES WITH HIDDEN CRIMINALS.
YOU WILL FEEL YOURSELF TO BE A "VICTIM", AND LIVE YOUR DAYS IN FEAR.
!
ACHT! COME WITH US!
YOU CAN'T STAY HERE!

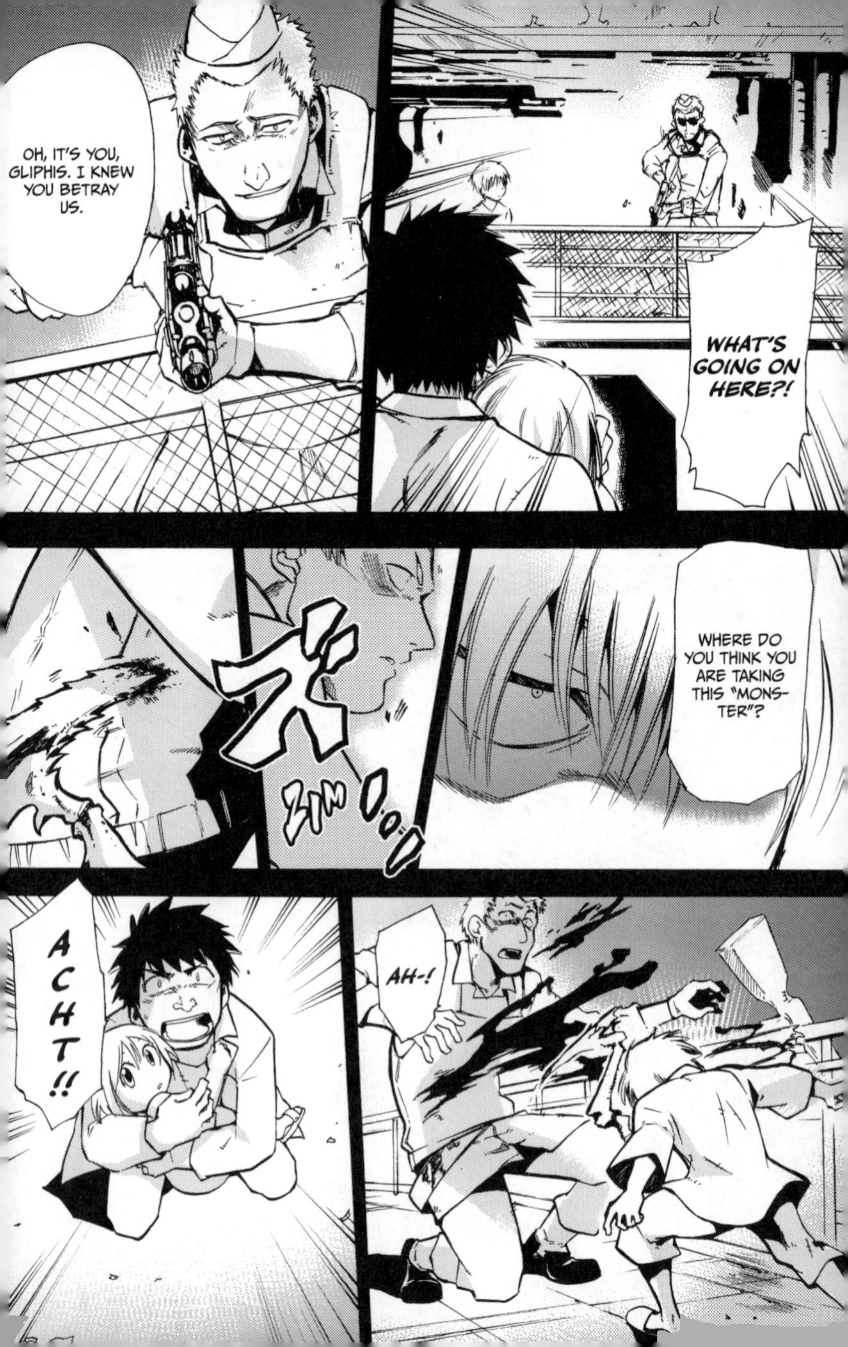
WHAT'S GOING ON HERE?!
OH, IT'S YOU, GLIPHIS. I KNEW YOU BETRAY US.
WHERE DO YOU THINK YOU ARE TAKING THIS "MONSTER"?
ZIM
AH-!
ACHT!!

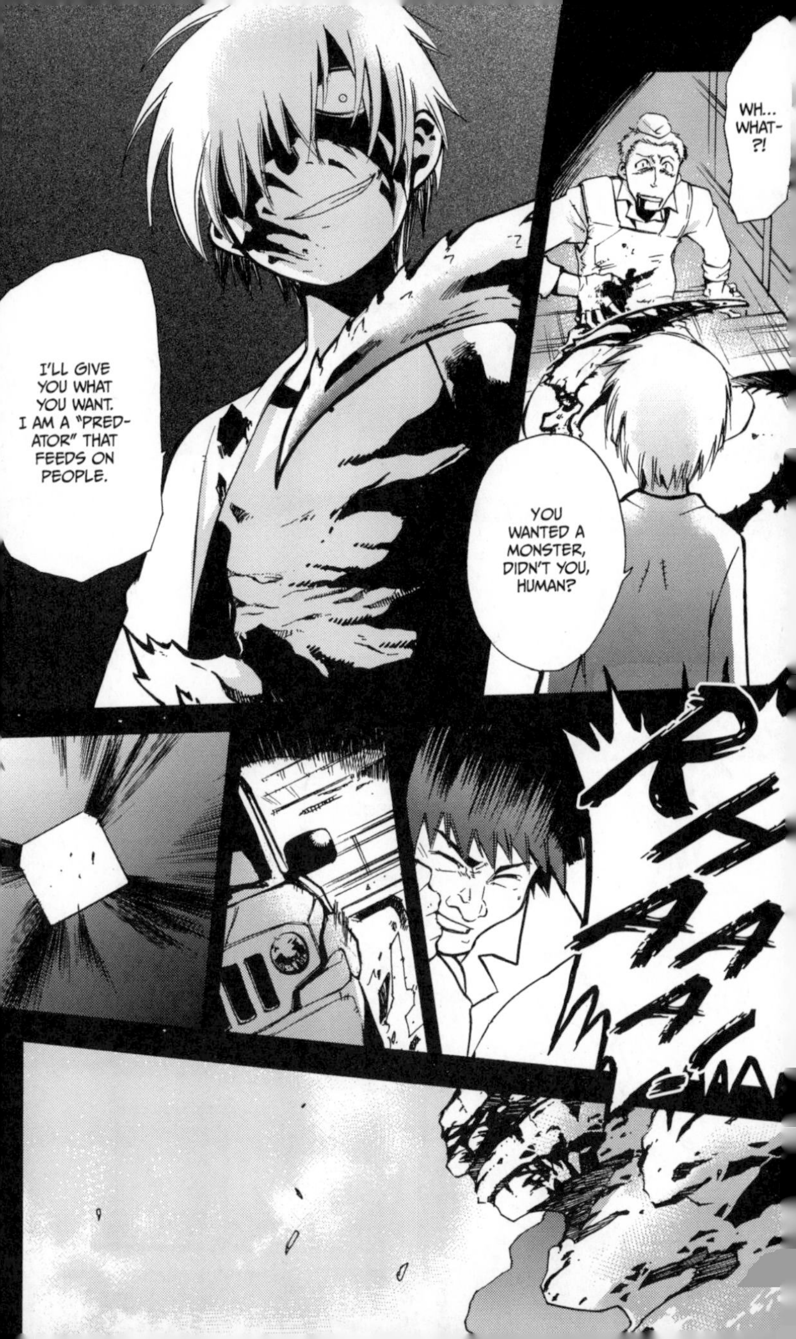
WH... WHAT-?!
YOU WANTED A MONSTER, DIDN'T YOU, HUMAN?
I'LL GIVE YOU WHAT YOU WANT. I AM A "PREDATOR" THAT FEEDS ON PEOPLE.

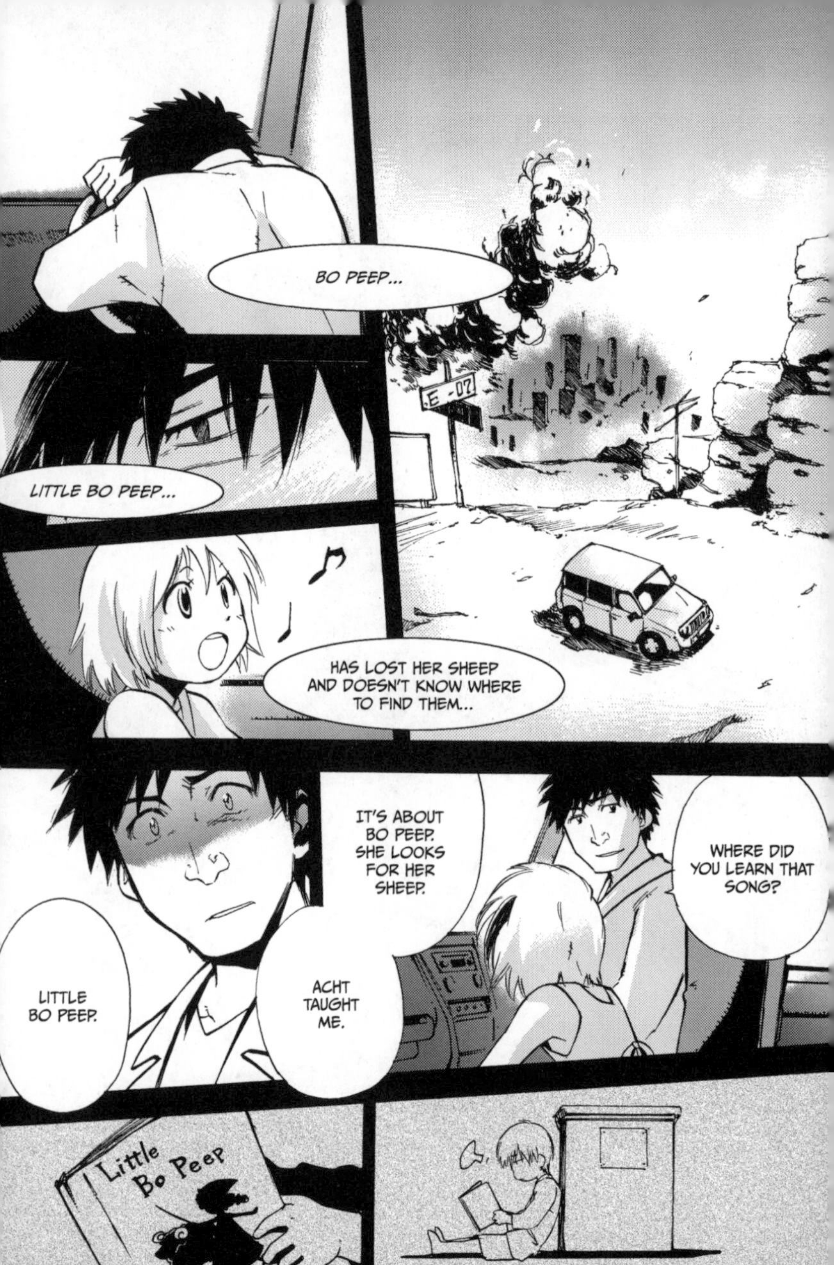
E-07
BO PEEP...
LITTLE BO PEEP...
HAS LOST HER SHEEP AND DOESN'T KNOW WHERE TO FIND THEM...
WHERE DID YOU LEARN THAT SONG?
IT'S ABOUT BO PEEP. SHE LOOKS FOR HER SHEEP.
ACHT TAUGHT ME.
LITTLE BO PEEP.
Little Bo Peep

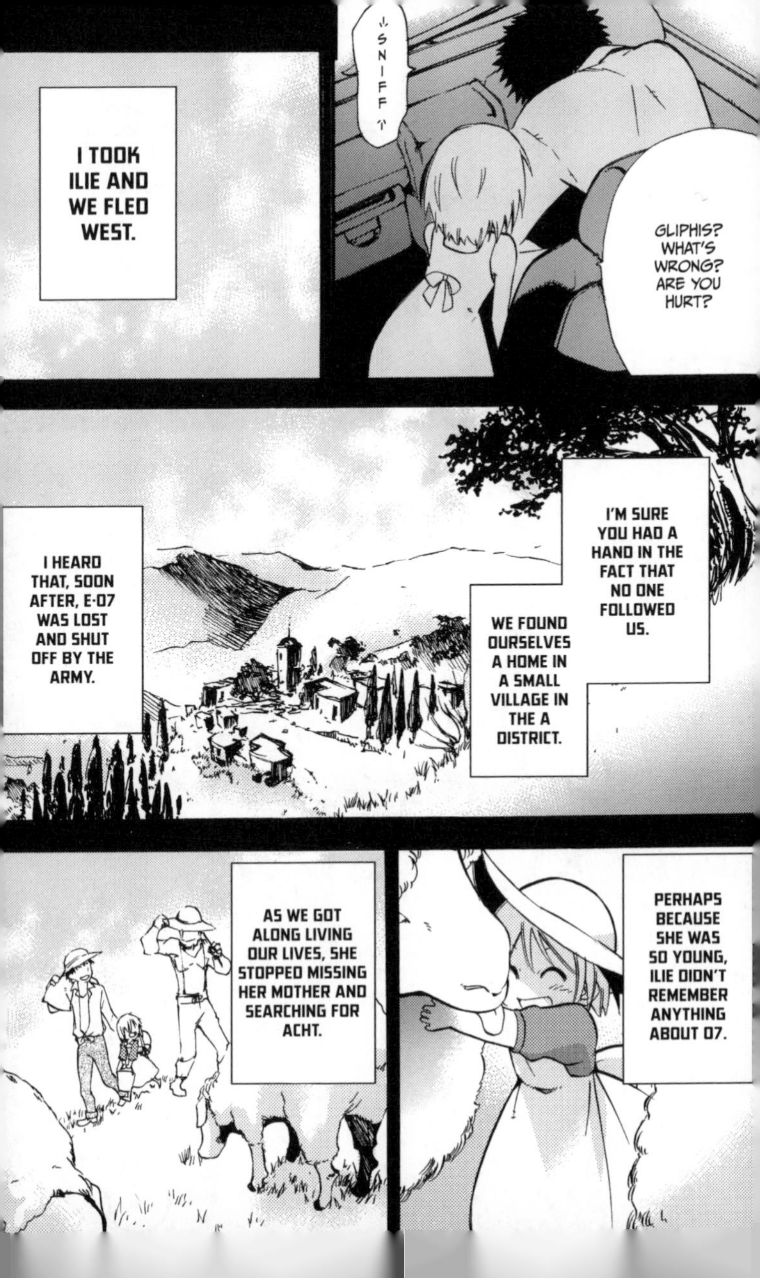
SNIFF
GLIPHIS? WHAT'S WRONG? ARE YOU HURT?
I TOOK ILIE AND WE FLED WEST.
I'M SURE YOU HAD A HAND IN THE FACT THAT NO ONE FOLLOWED US.
WE FOUND OURSELVES A HOME IN A SMALL VILLAGE IN THE A DISTRICT.
I HEARD THAT, SOON AFTER, E-07 WAS LOST AND SHUT OFF BY THE ARMY.
PERHAPS BECAUSE SHE WAS SO YOUNG, ILIE DIDN'T REMEMBER ANYTHING ABOUT 07.
AS WE GOT ALONG LIVING OUR LIVES, SHE STOPPED MISSING HER MOTHER AND SEARCHING FOR ACHT.

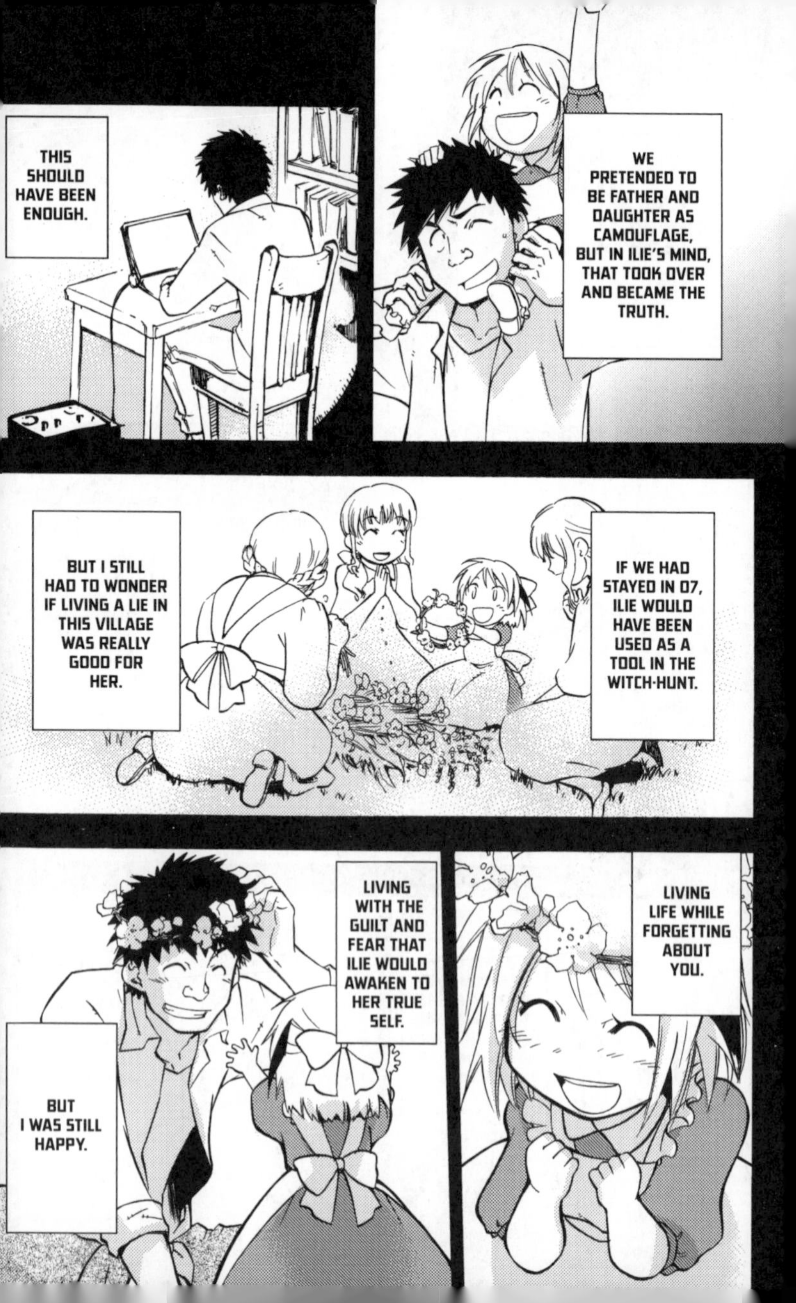
WE PRETENDED TO BE FATHER AND DAUGHTER AS CAMOUFLAGE, BUT IN ILIE'S MIND, THAT TOOK OVER AND BECAME THE TRUTH.
THIS SHOULD HAVE BEEN ENOUGH.
IF WE HAD STAYED IN 07, ILIE WOULD HAVE BEEN USED AS A TOOL IN THE WITCH-HUNT.
BUT I STILL HAD TO WONDER IF LIVING A LIE IN THIS VILLAGE WAS REALLY GOOD FOR HER.
LIVING LIFE WHILE FORGETTING ABOUT YOU.
LIVING WITH THE GUILT AND FEAR THAT ILIE WOULD AWAKEN TO HER TRUE SELF.
BUT I WAS STILL HAPPY.

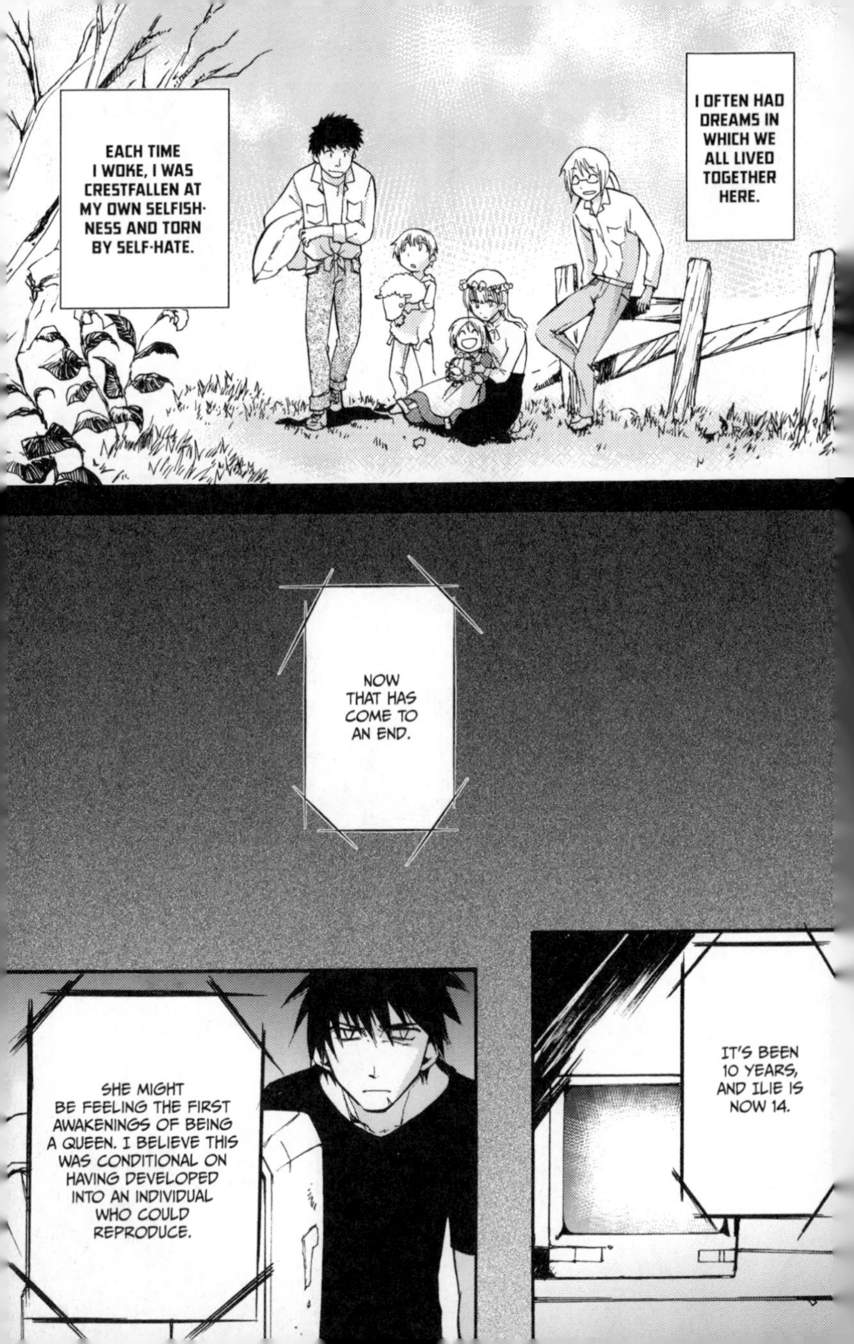
I OFTEN HAD DREAMS IN WHICH WE ALL LIVED TOGETHER HERE.
EACH TIME I WOKE, I WAS CRESTFALLEN AT MY OWN SELFISH-NESS AND TORN BY SELF-HATE.
NOW THAT HAS COME TO AN END.
IT'S BEEN 10 YEARS, AND ILIE IS NOW 14.
SHE MIGHT BE FEELING THE FIRST AWAKENINGS OF BEING A QUEEN. I BELIEVE THIS WAS CONDITIONAL ON HAVING DEVELOPED INTO AN INDIVIDUAL WHO COULD REPRODUCE.

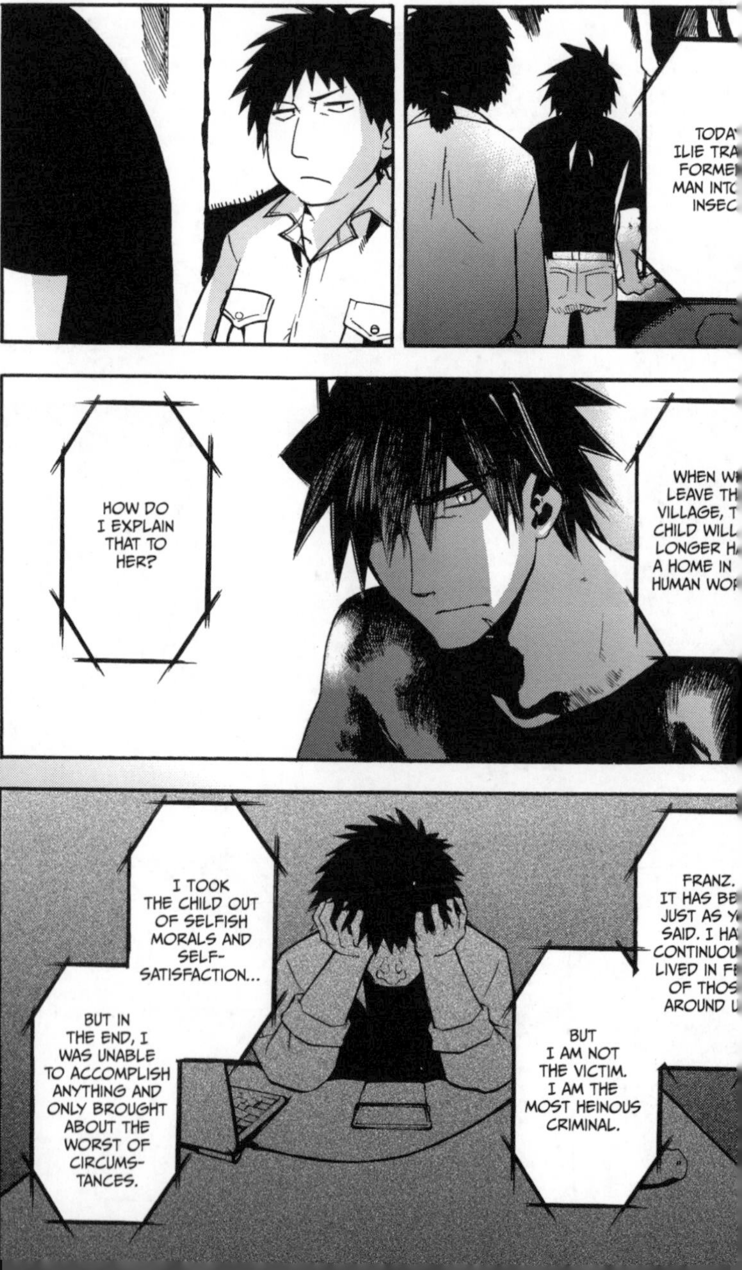
TODA' ILIE TRA FORME MAN INTO INSEC
WHEN W LEAVE TH VILLAGE, T CHILD WILL LONGER H A HOME IN HUMAN WOR
HOW DO I EXPLAIN THAT TO HER?
FRANZ. IT HAS BE JUST AS Y SAID. I HA CONTINUOU LIVED IN F OF THOS AROUND U
BUT I AM NOT THE VICTIM. I AM THE MOST HEINOUS CRIMINAL.
I TOOK THE CHILD OUT OF SELFISH MORALS AND SELF-SATISFACTION...
BUT IN THE END, I WAS UNABLE TO ACCOMPLISH ANYTHING AND ONLY BROUGHT ABOUT THE WORST OF CIRCUMS-TANCES.

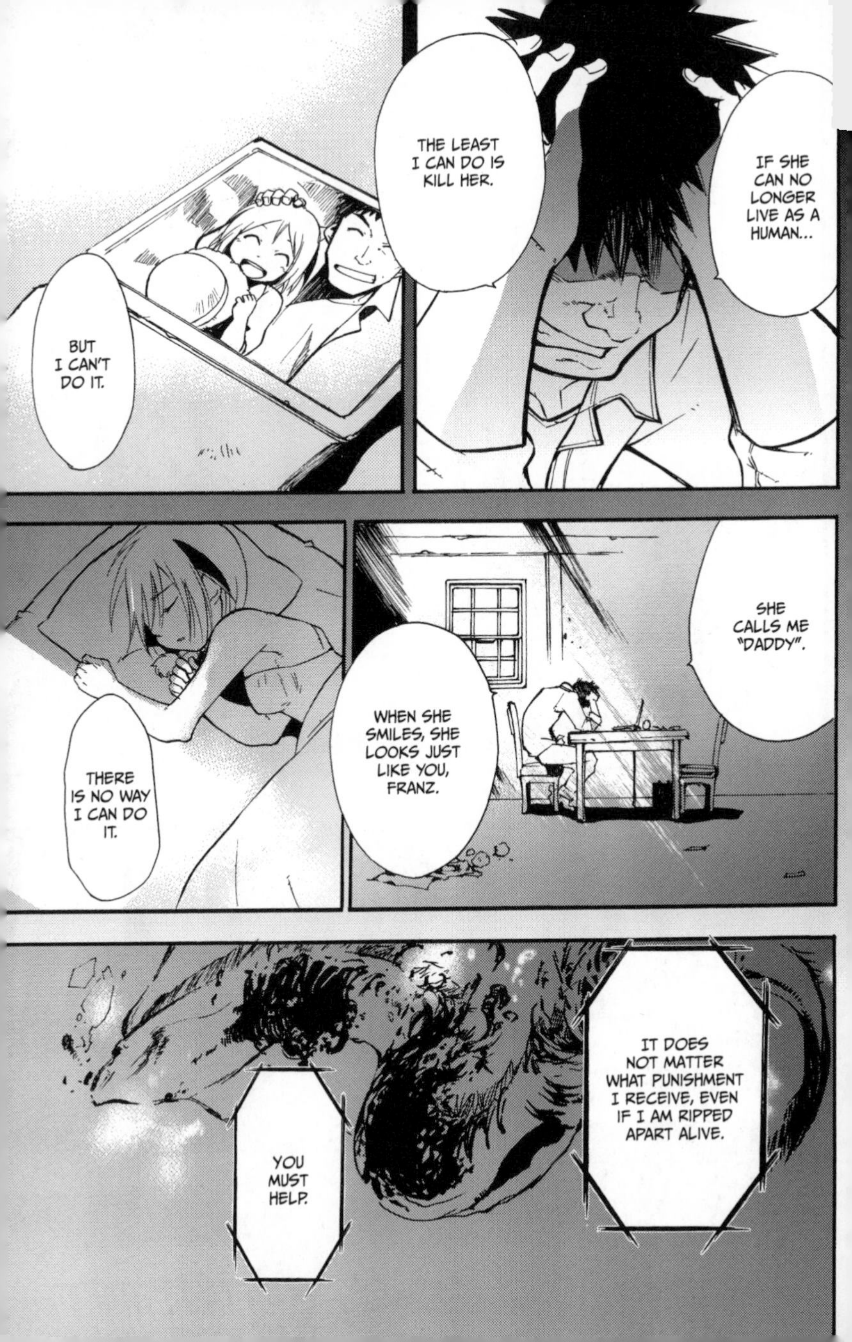
IF SHE CAN NO LONGER LIVE AS A HUMAN...
THE LEAST I CAN DO IS KILL HER.
BUT I CAN'T DO IT.
SHE CALLS ME "DADDY".
WHEN SHE SMILES, SHE LOOKS JUST LIKE YOU, FRANZ.
THERE IS NO WAY I CAN DO IT.
IT DOES NOT MATTER WHAT PUNISHMENT I RECEIVE, EVEN IF I AM RIPPED APART ALIVE.
YOU MUST HELP.

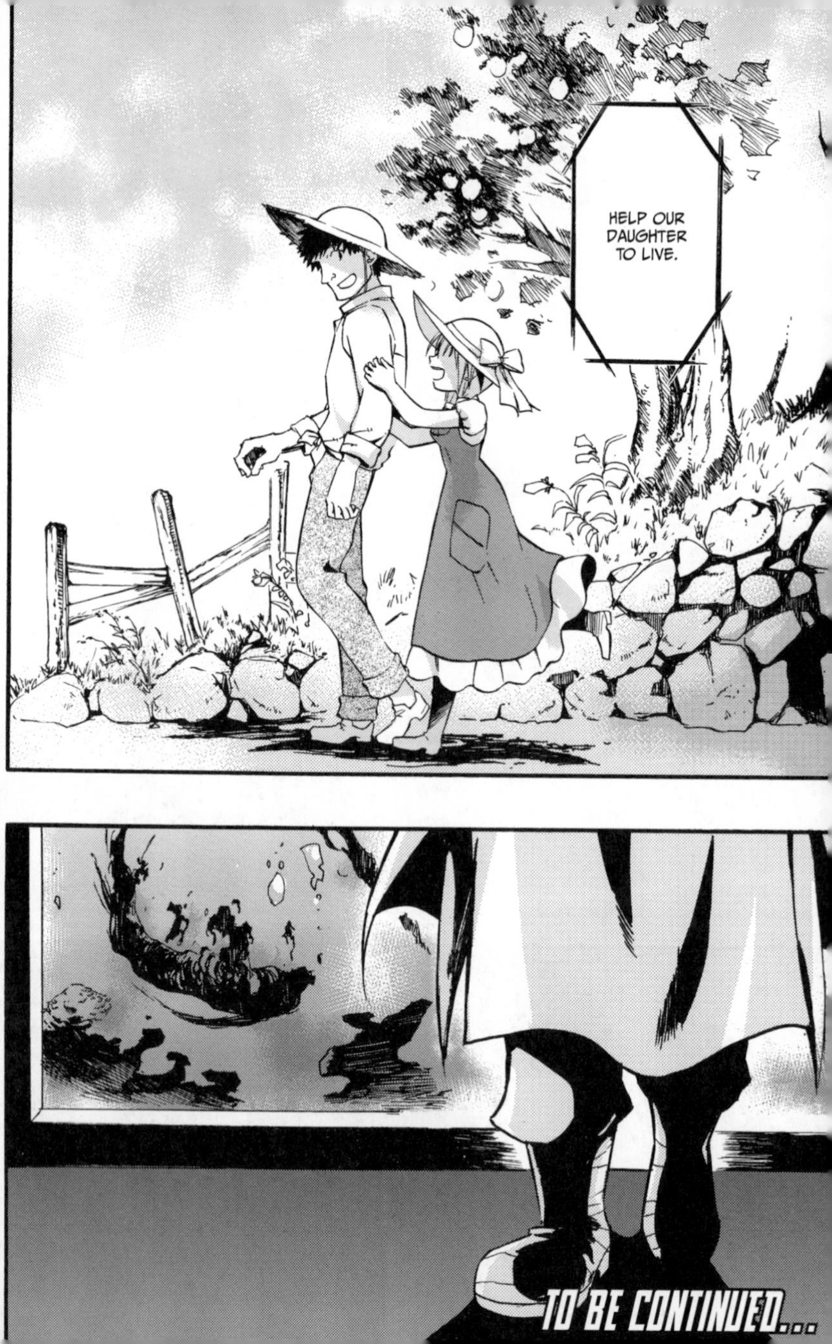
HELP OUR DAUGHTER TO LIVE.
TO BE CONTINUED...

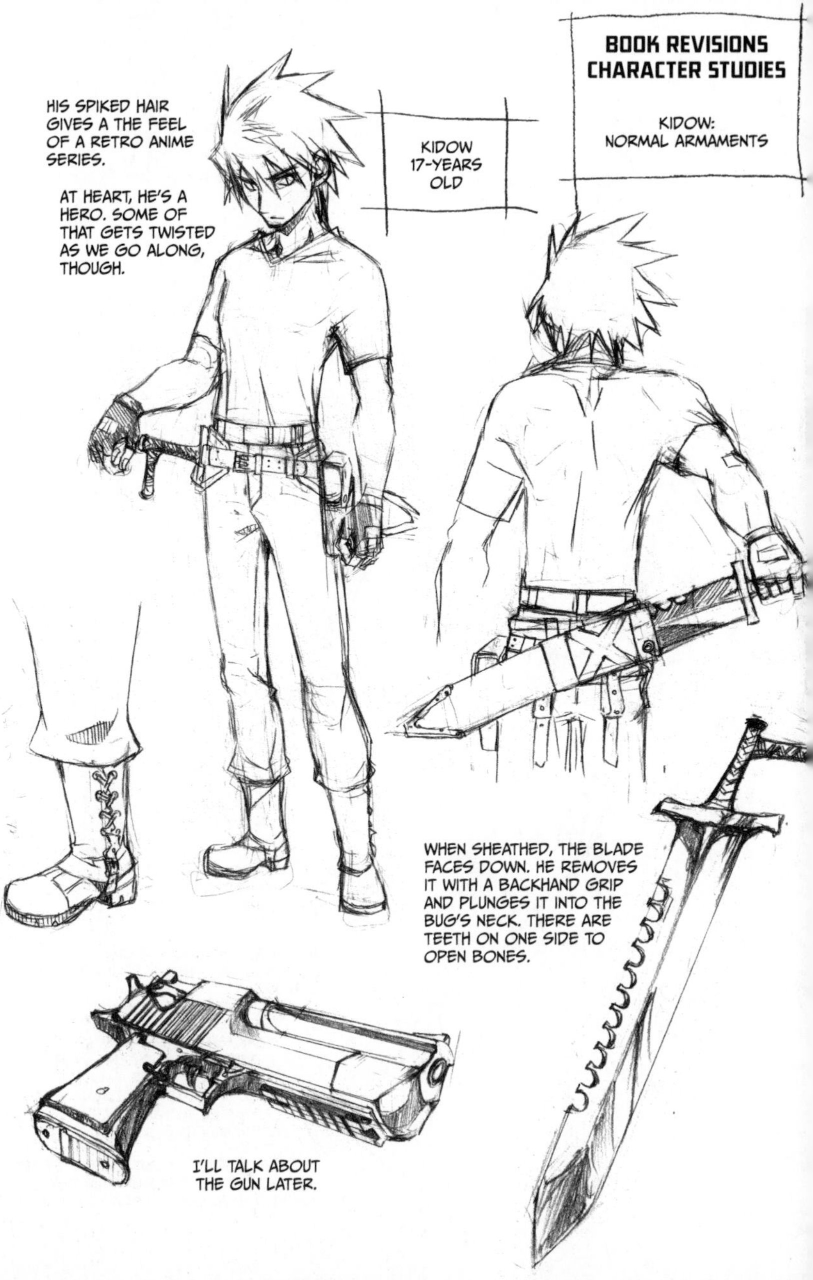
BOOK REVISIONS
CHARACTER STUDIES
KIDOW:
NORMAL ARMAMENTS
KIDOW
17-YEARS
OLD
HIS SPIKED HAIR GIVES A THE FEEL OF A RETRO ANIME SERIES.
AT HEART, HE'S A HERO. SOME OF THAT GETS TWISTED AS WE GO ALONG, THOUGH.
WHEN SHEATHED, THE BLADE FACES DOWN. HE REMOVES IT WITH A BACKHAND GRIP AND PLUNGES IT INTO THE BUG'S NECK. THERE ARE TEETH ON ONE SIDE TO OPEN BONES.
I'LL TALK ABOUT THE GUN LATER.

CLOTHES WORN OUTSIDE IN CHAPTER 7

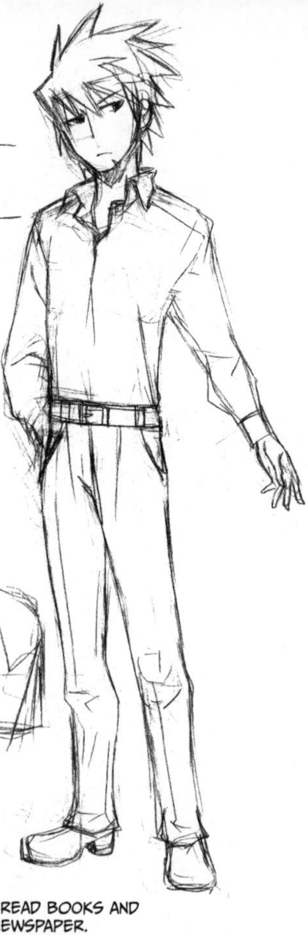

CLOTHES WHEN IN HIS ROOM.

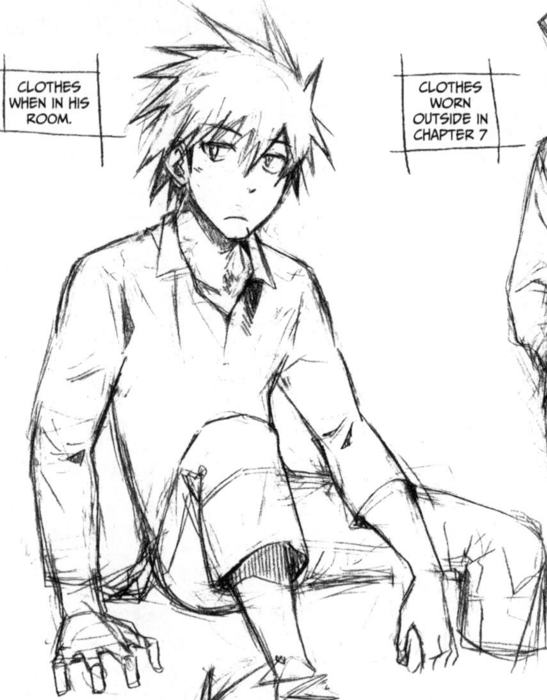

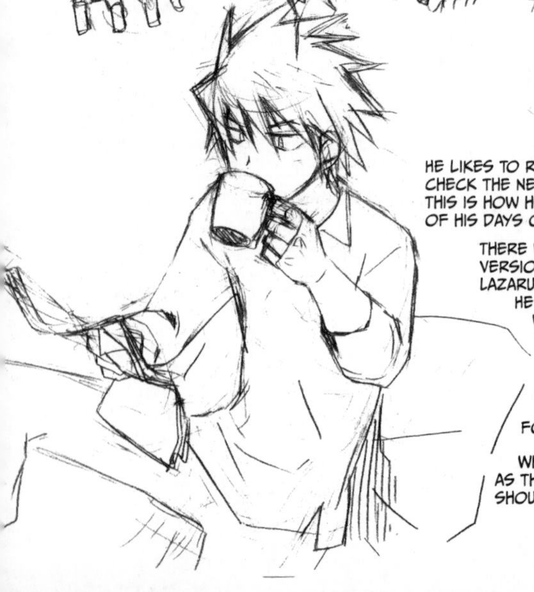

HE LIKES TO READ BOOKS AND CHECK THE NEWSPAPER.
THIS IS HOW HE SPENDS MOST OF HIS DAYS OFF.

THERE WAS EPISODE ADDED TO THE BOOK VERSION ABOUT "BEING EDUCATED BY LAZARUS".
HE WAS IMAGINED THIS WAY TO BEGIN WITH, BUT WHEN DECIDING WHAT TO KEEP AFTER DRAWING THE EPISODES ABOUT HIS PAST, I COULDN'T FIND A WAY TO INCORPORATE IT NATURALLY, SO AFTER GOING BACK AND FORTH FOR SOME TIME, I CUT IT.

WHEN I THINK ABOUT IT NOW, I FEEL AS THOUGH I CUT SOMETHING THAT SHOULD HAVE BEEN THERE.

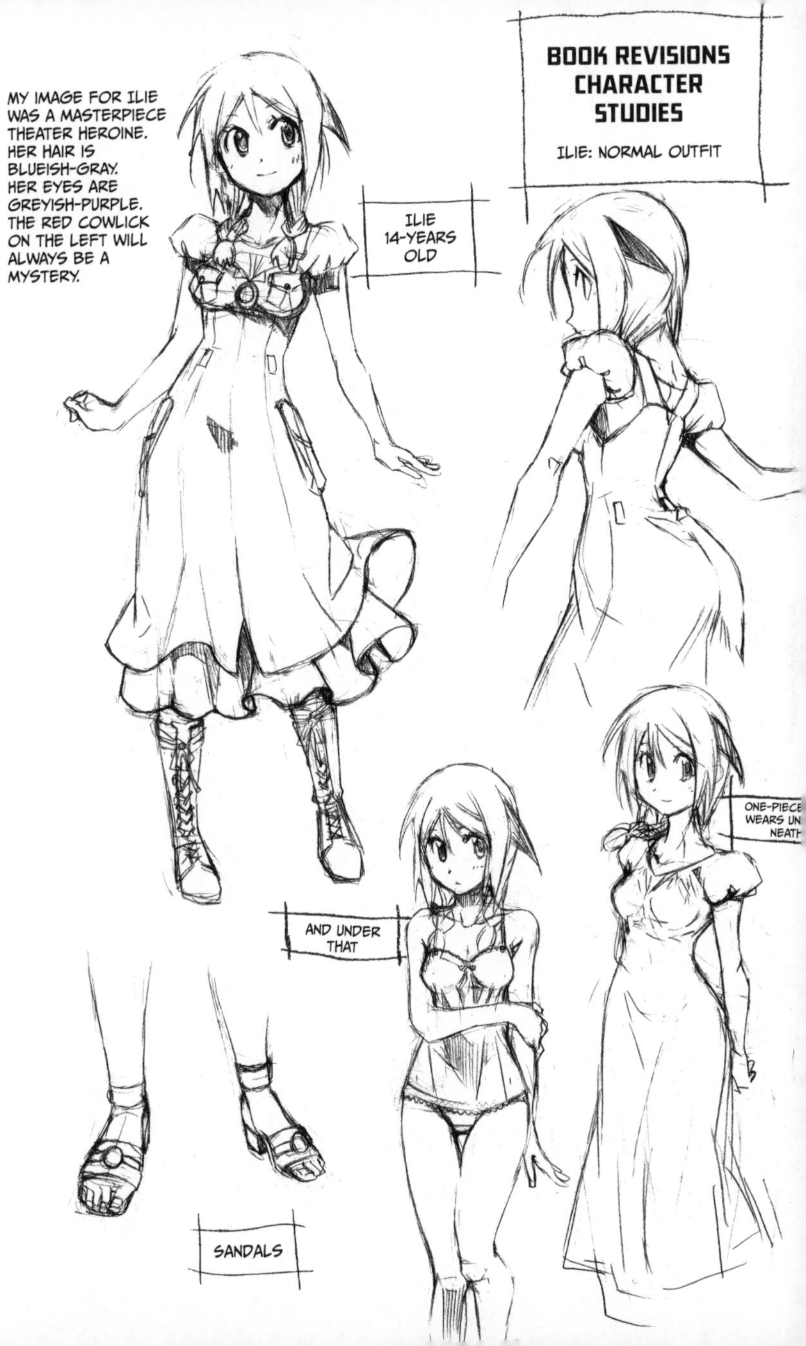
BOOK REVISIONS CHARACTER STUDIES
ILIE: NORMAL OUTFIT
MY IMAGE FOR ILIE WAS A MASTERPIECE THEATER HEROINE. HER HAIR IS BLUEISH-GRAY. HER EYES ARE GREYISH-PURPLE. THE RED COWLICK ON THE LEFT WILL ALWAYS BE A MYSTERY.
ILIE 14-YEARS OLD
ONE-PIECE
WEARS UN
NEATH
AND UNDER THAT
SANDALS

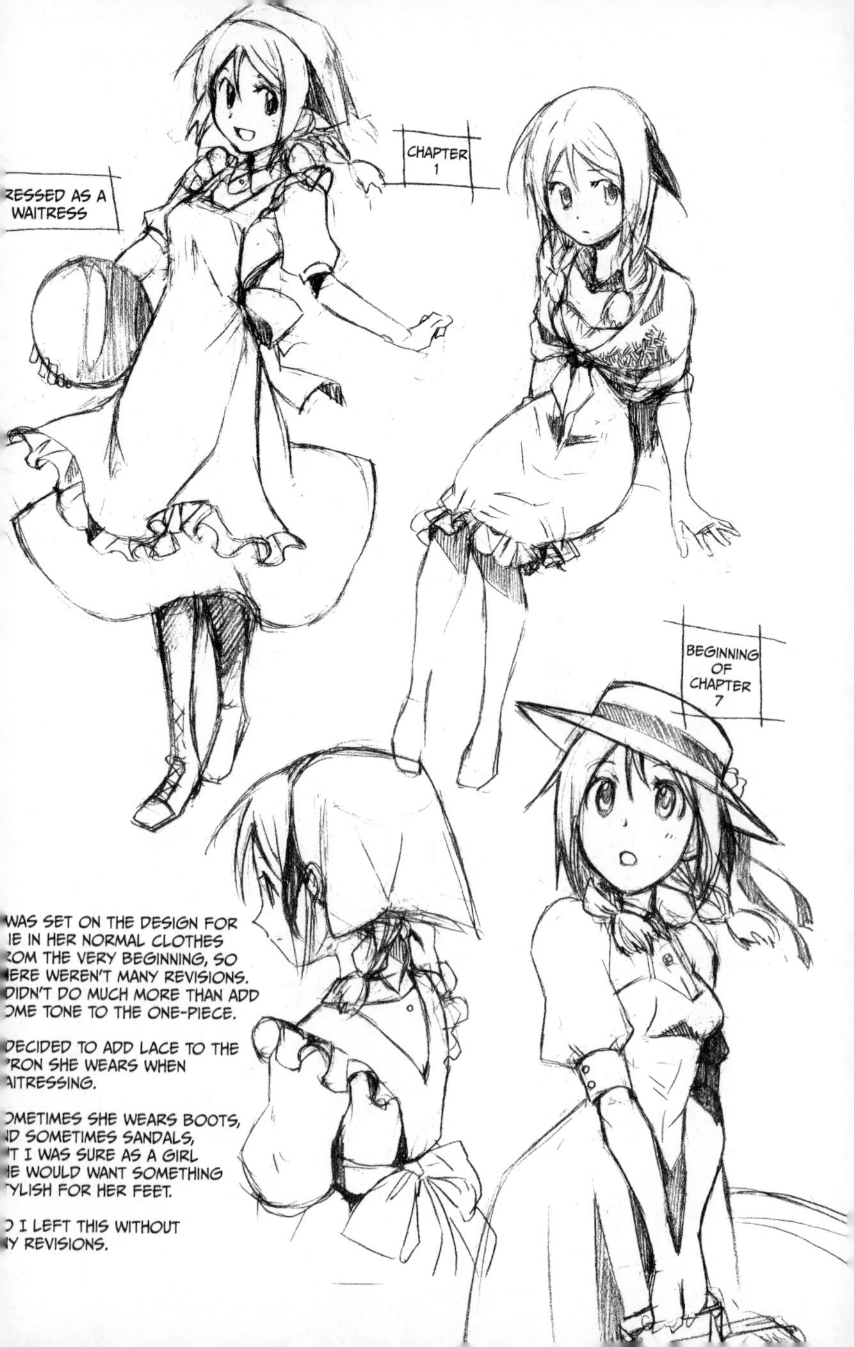
CHAPTER 1
RESSED AS A WAITRESS
BEGINNING OF CHAPTER 7

WAS SET ON THE DESIGN FOR
IE IN HER NORMAL CLOTHES
ROM THE VERY BEGINNING, SO
HERE WEREN'T MANY REVISIONS.
DIDN'T DO MUCH MORE THAN ADD
OME TONE TO THE ONE-PIECE.

DECIDED TO ADD LACE TO THE
PRON SHE WEARS WHEN
AITRESSING.

OMETIMES SHE WEARS BOOTS,
ND SOMETIMES SANDALS,
T I WAS SURE AS A GIRL
HE WOULD WANT SOMETHING
TYLISH FOR HER FEET.

O I LEFT THIS WITHOUT
NY REVISIONS.

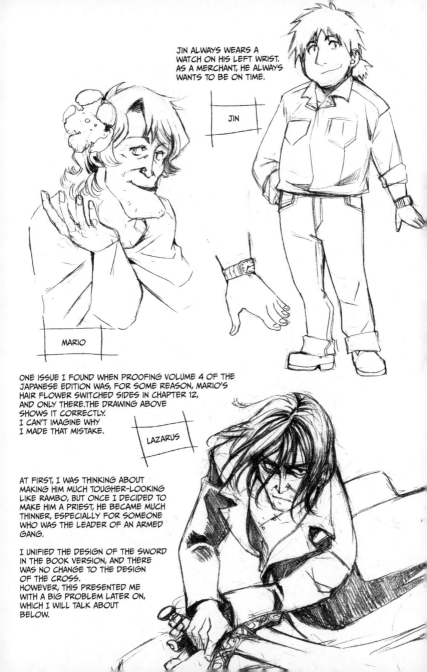

JIN ALWAYS WEARS A WATCH ON HIS LEFT WRIST. AS A MERCHANT, HE ALWAYS WANTS TO BE ON TIME.

JIN

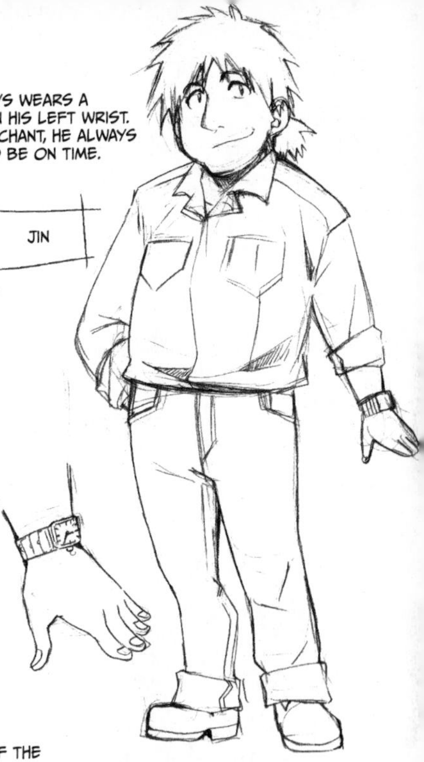

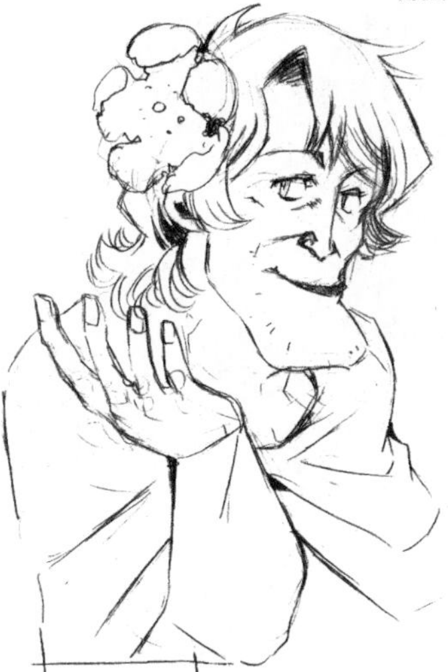

MARIO

ONE ISSUE I FOUND WHEN PROOFING VOLUME 4 OF THE JAPANESE EDITION WAS, FOR SOME REASON, MARIO'S HAIR FLOWER SWITCHED SIDES IN CHAPTER 12, AND ONLY THERE.THE DRAWING ABOVE SHOWS IT CORRECTLY.
I CAN'T IMAGINE WHY I MADE THAT MISTAKE.

LAZARUS

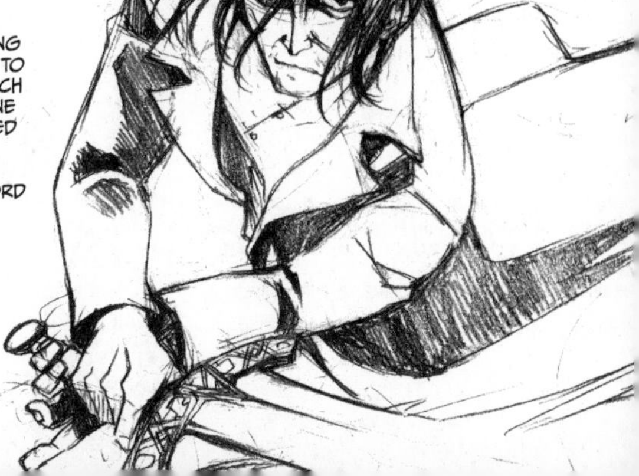

AT FIRST, I WAS THINKING ABOUT MAKING HIM MUCH TOUGHER-LOOKING LIKE RAMBO, BUT ONCE I DECIDED TO MAKE HIM A PRIEST, HE BECAME MUCH THINNER, ESPECIALLY FOR SOMEONE WHO WAS THE LEADER OF AN ARMED GANG.

I UNIFIED THE DESIGN OF THE SWORD IN THE BOOK VERSION, AND THERE WAS NO CHANGE TO THE DESIGN OF THE CROSS.
HOWEVER, THIS PRESENTED ME WITH A BIG PROBLEM LATER ON, WHICH I WILL TALK ABOUT BELOW.

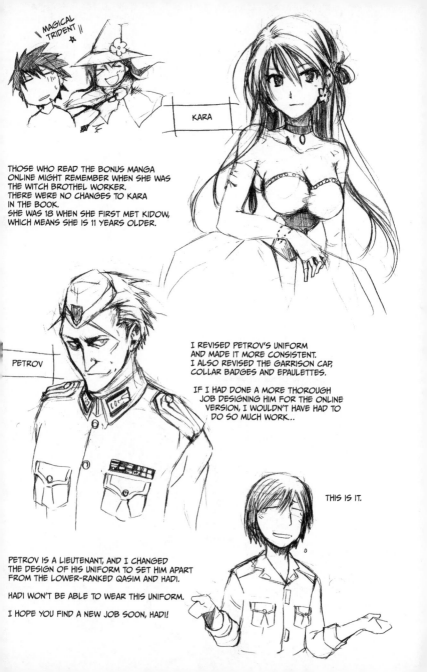

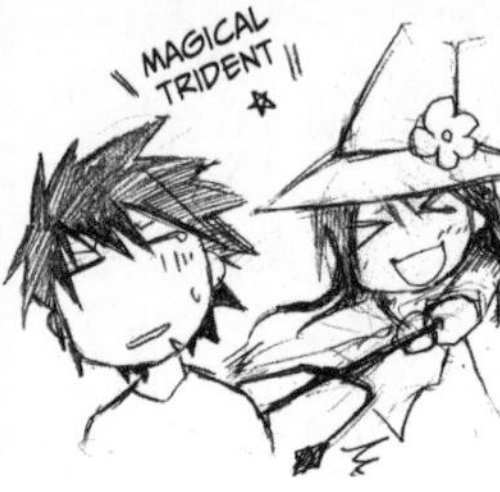
MAGICAL TRIDENT

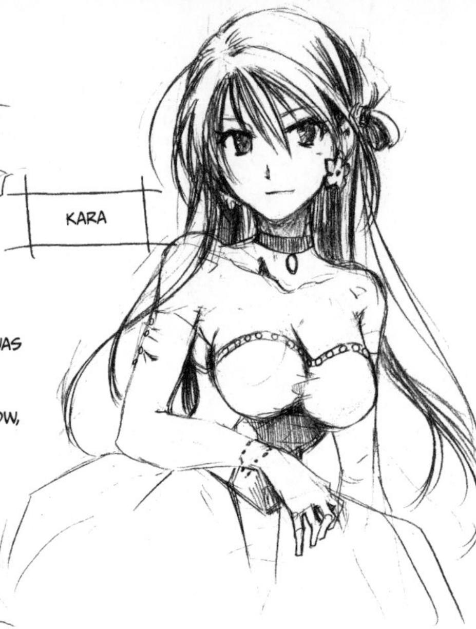
KARA

THOSE WHO READ THE BONUS MANGA ONLINE MIGHT REMEMBER WHEN SHE WAS THE WITCH BROTHEL WORKER.
THERE WERE NO CHANGES TO KARA IN THE BOOK.
SHE WAS 18 WHEN SHE FIRST MET KIDOW, WHICH MEANS SHE IS 11 YEARS OLDER.

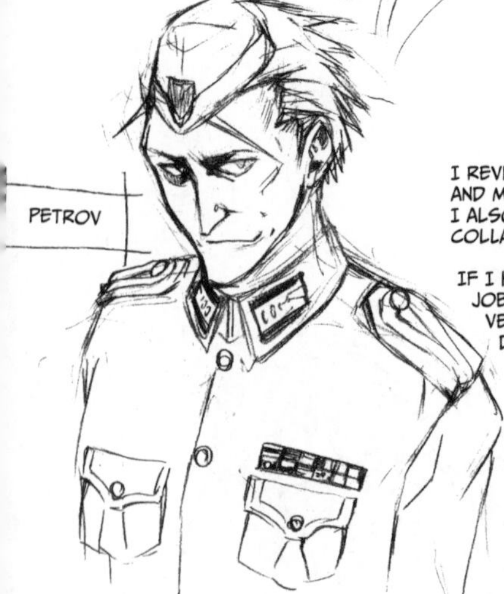
PETROV

I REVISED PETROV'S UNIFORM AND MADE IT MORE CONSISTENT.
I ALSO REVISED THE GARRISON CAP, COLLAR BADGES AND EPAULETTES.

IF I HAD DONE A MORE THOROUGH JOB DESIGNING HIM FOR THE ONLINE VERSION, I WOULDN'T HAVE HAD TO DO SO MUCH WORK...

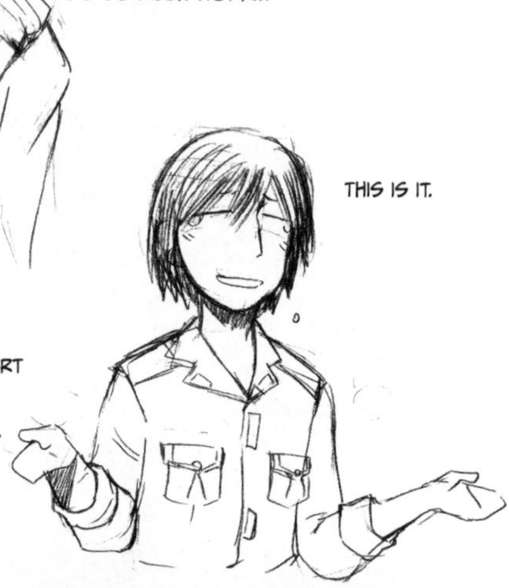

THIS IS IT.

PETROV IS A LIEUTENANT, AND I CHANGED THE DESIGN OF HIS UNIFORM TO SET HIM APART FROM THE LOWER-RANKED QASIM AND HADI.

HADI WON'T BE ABLE TO WEAR THIS UNIFORM.

I HOPE YOU FIND A NEW JOB SOON, HADI!

CUT SCENES

THERE WERE VERY FEW REVISIONS THIS TIME, SO I THOUGHT I WOULD ADD THE CHARACTER STUDIES AS A BONUS. WHAT DO YOU THINK OF THEM?

IF YOU LIKE THEM, I'LL TRY TO PUT SOME IN LATER VOLUMES AS WELL.

THERE HAVEN'T BEEN MANY ESSAYS OR POSTSCRIPTS UP UNTIL THIS POINT, SO I DUG UP SOME CUT SCENES AS AN ADDED BONUS. ENJOY!

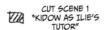

CUT SCENE 1 "KIDOW AS ILIE'S TUTOR"

ILIE TRIES TO SAVE KIDOW FROM THE EXTERMINATOR KILLER AT THE END OF CHAPTER 6.

KIDOW WANTS TO DO SOMETHING TO PAY HER BACK, SO SHE CASUALLY ASKED HIM TO "TEACH ME HOW TO STUDY".

SHE DREAMS THIS WILL LEAD TO THEM SPENDING MORE TIME TOGETHER, BUT THOSE DREAMS ARE SHATTERED WHEN HE APPROACHES THE TASK FAR TOO SERIOUSLY.

IN THE BOOK VERSION, THEY GET TO GO ON A MINI-DATE IN 01. AREN'T YOU GLAD YOU DIDN'T CHOOSE THE STUDYING THIS TIME, ILIE?

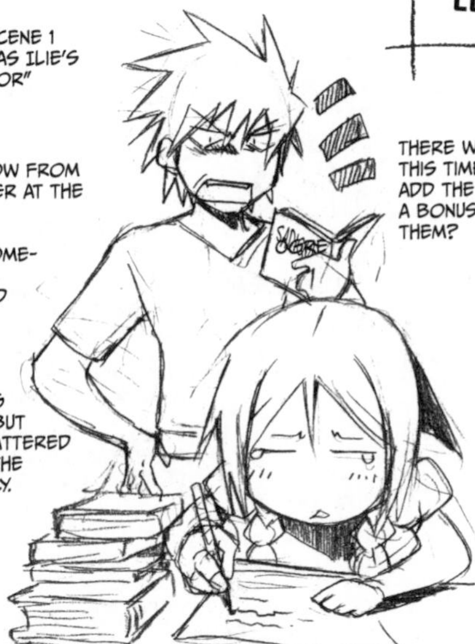

CUT SCENE 2

JOINT OPERATION WITH HADI AND THE OTHERS TO INVESTIGATE THE SALE OF A BUG BODY ON THE BLACK MARKET. THEY INFILTRATE AN AUCTION TO CAPTURE THE SUSPECTS IN THE ACT.

I THOUGHT ABOUT PUTTING THIS IN AT THE VERY BEGINNING TO SET UP THE WORLD VIEW, BUT I DECIDED TO KEEP IT OUT DUE TO THE INADEQUATE WORK PUT INTO IT, AND THE FACT THAT IT WOULDN'T BE MISSED IF IT WASN'T THERE.

THIS FORMS THE BASIS OF THE "ADVENTURES OF PRINCESS BUTTERFLY" SPIN-OFF, SO IT WILL NOT GO AWAY FOREVER.

PERHAPS I JUST WANTED TO DRAW KIDOW AND JIN IN SUITS.

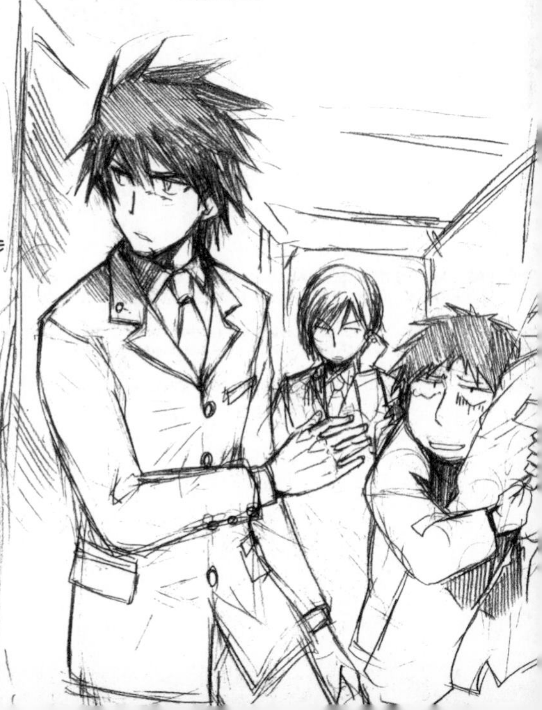

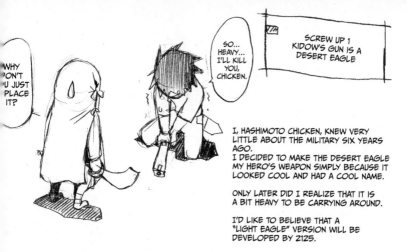

SCREW UP 1
KIDOW'S GUN IS A DESERT EAGLE

SO... HEAVY... I'LL KILL YOU, CHICKEN.
WHY ON'T U JUST PLACE IT?

I, HASHIMOTO CHICKEN, KNEW VERY LITTLE ABOUT THE MILITARY SIX YEARS AGO.
I DECIDED TO MAKE THE DESERT EAGLE MY HERO'S WEAPON SIMPLY BECAUSE IT LOOKED COOL AND HAD A COOL NAME.

ONLY LATER DID I REALIZE THAT IT IS A BIT HEAVY TO BE CARRYING AROUND.

I'D LIKE TO BELIEVE THAT A "LIGHT EAGLE" VERSION WILL BE DEVELOPED BY 2125.

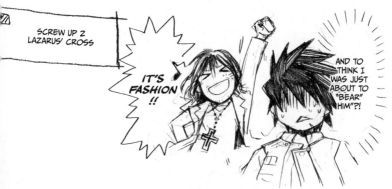

SCREW UP 2
LAZARUS' CROSS

AND TO THINK I WAS JUST ABOUT TO "BEAR" HIM"?!
IT'S FASHION !!

THE "FAR EAST" IS THE REGION CURRENTLY CALLED TURKMENISTAN.
THE MAIN RELIGIONS IN THIS REGION ARE ISLAM AND ORTHODOX CHRISTIANITY.

HOWEVER, IN THE ORTHODOX CHURCH, I GUESS THEY DON'T USE THE CROSS AS IMAGERY, AND THEY USE A ROSARY WHEN PRAYING.

LAZARUS... ARE YOU JUST USING THE CROSS TO BE STYLISH?

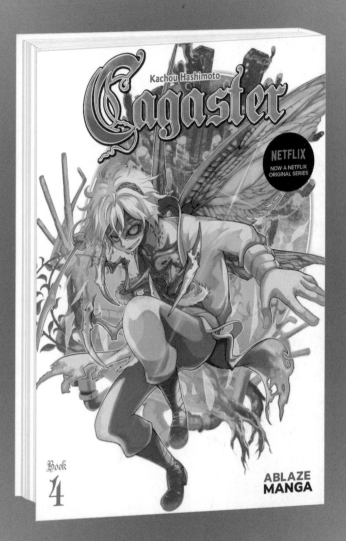

Kachou Hashimoto

Cagaster

NETFLIX
NOW A NETFLIX
ORIGINAL SERIES

Book
4

ABLAZE
MANGA

Cagaster

Book
4

Coming soon!

Complete series in 6 volumes

**ABLAZE
MANGA**

CAGASTER
by Kachou Hashimoto

Translation: Matthew Johnson
Lettering: Studio Makma
Editor: Rich Young
Designer: Rodolfo Muraguchi

CAGASTER, VOLUME 3. First printing. Published by Ablaze Publishing, 11222 SE Main St. #22906 Portland, OR 97269. CAGASTER © Editions Glénat 2014-2016 – ALL RIGHTS RESERVED. Ablaze and its logo TM & © 2020 Ablaze, LLC. All Rights Reserved. All names, characters, events, and locales in this publication are entirely fictional. Any resemblance to actual persons (living or dead), events or places, without satiric intent is coincidental. No portion of this book may be reproduced by any means (digital or print) without the written permission of Ablaze Publishing except for review purposes. Printed in China.

For advertising and licensing email: info@ablazepublishing.com

Publisher's Cataloging-in-Publication Data
Names: Hashimoto, Kachou, author.
Title: Cagaster, Volume 3 / Kachou Hashimoto.
Series: Cagaster
Description: Portland, OR: Ablaze Publishing, 2020.
Identifiers: ISBN 978-1-950912-09-4
LCSH Mutation (Biology)–Fiction. | Cannibalism–Fiction. | Dystopias. | Fantasy fiction. | Science fiction. | Adventure and adventurers–Fiction. | Graphic novels. | BISAC COMICS & GRAPHIC NOVELS / Manga / Dystopian | COMICS & GRAPHIC NOVELS / Manga / Fantasy | COMICS & GRAPHIC NOVELS / Manga / Science Fiction
Classification: LCC PN6790.J33 .H372 v. 3 2020 | DDC 741.5–dc23

/ablazepub   @AblazePub   @AblazePub
ablazepublishing.com

To find a comics shop in your area go to:
www.comicshoplocator.com

STOP!

THIS IS THE BACK OF THE BOOK!

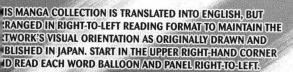

THIS MANGA COLLECTION IS TRANSLATED INTO ENGLISH, BUT ARRANGED IN RIGHT-TO-LEFT READING FORMAT TO MAINTAIN THE ARTWORK'S VISUAL ORIENTATION AS ORIGINALLY DRAWN AND PUBLISHED IN JAPAN. START IN THE UPPER RIGHT-HAND CORNER AND READ EACH WORD BALLOON AND PANEL RIGHT-TO-LEFT.